WHILE YOU'RE HERE, DOCTOR . . .

WHILE YOU'RE HERE, DOCTOR...

by

Robert Russell

AE 05713

SOUVENIR PRESS

First published 1985 by Souvenir Press Ltd,
43 Great Russell Street, London WC1B 3PA
and simultaneously in Canada

ISBN 0 285 62711 2

Photoset and printed in Great Britain by
Photobooks (Bristol) Ltd.

To my mother and father

1

He looked at me with his one good eye.

"Tea bags?" I asked. He nodded and touched his other eye gingerly with the back of his hand.

"That's right. Tea bags."

"Mr Groves, who on earth advised you to put tea bags on that eye? I haven't heard that one since . . ."

"Your wife. I rang last night, but you weren't in. It was your good lady who advised me. Change them every four hours, she said."

"Oh, I see."

In the silence that followed I wrote out a prescription for Chloromycetin eye ointment. "Tea bags used to be advised for this sort of trouble at one time," I mumbled, "but there's, er, more up-to-date treatment now."

He took the prescription and went away, only to return two days later. His inflamed eye was now grotesquely swollen – a shiny pink mass of closed lids which had engulfed his eyelashes. He was allergic to the ointment.

He glared at me. His anger and resentment, channelled through his good eye, seemed to intensify like a laser-beam which threatened to burn my face off.

"My God," I said.

"What do you mean – my God?" he snapped. "Calling on the Almighty won't rectify the problem, believe you me, doctor."

"That's an allergic reaction . . ."

"I am well aware of what it is, and what's caused it, too." He flicked the tiny tube of ointment onto the desk like a croupier dealing a bad card. "You can have your ointment back, doctor. There is still sufficient left, I would have thought, to cause discomfort and misery to another dozen of your patients. I'll stick to tea bags."

He turned and made for the door, catching the book-case on

7

his blind side and knocking a small pile of journals onto the floor as he did so. He left without turning round or saying another word.

The allergy thing was sheer chance, of course, but Alfred Groves would not see it that way, being the kind of person he was. One way or another, he saw me as the agent of his various medical misfortunes. Two years ago, when I had diagnosed his inactive thyroid, and when my treatment had transformed him from a pale, dry, reptilian torpor back to his normal slim, intolerable self, he had commented bitterly that what I had achieved was to condemn him to a lifetime of taking thyroid tablets. In a relationship like this, triumph was short-lived and empathy still-born.

I had completely forgotten about all this until I received a telephone call on a warm, limp afternoon in August, about two weeks later. The caller was Alfred Groves' wife, Edith.

"Doctor? Can you come right away? It's Alfred – his legs have gone."

The shrill resonance of the earpiece faithfully transmitted the vibrations of fear in her voice and I was alerted by its unfamiliar sound. Edith Groves was a plump, pleasant woman who laughed a lot when she wasn't with her husband, always giving me the impression that a good knees-up round the pub piano, clutching a Mackeson, would give her more pleasure than the brittle formality of those endless Ladies' Evenings at the local Masonic Lodge where Alfred was the Worshipful Master. But now, her words cracked like glass in her dry throat.

"He was walking home from the station and had just got to the garden gate when they suddenly went numb and he went down just in front of the privets. A neighbour helped me to get him indoors. He can't feel his legs, doctor, and they're so *cold*, all the way down."

I had never seen a saddle thrombus before, but I was sure that this was what it was. I wrote down the address on the desk blotter, picturing the blood clot straddling his aortic bifurcation – a lethal blob of blackcurrant jelly cutting off the blood supply to his legs. I would need to hurry if he was not to lose his legs – or his life.

I left the surgery and wove my way through the early rush-hour traffic, taking barely ten minutes to reach the crisply painted house with its obsessionally neat front garden surrounded by a rococo privet hedge. The door was open and before I got inside I caught a fleeting glimpse of Edith Groves as she darted from her anxious vigil behind the net curtains of the living room to greet me in the hallway, nearly knocking me over as I went in. She ushered me breathlessly to her husband who was on the sofa by the window. Beneath the tartan blanket which reached to his chin, he lay gloomy and still, while Edith Groves hovered round the room jerkily folding a piece of paper over and over until it became a very small, multi-layered wad. Mr Groves answered my questions irritably, as if he regarded me as an irrelevance, making me feel like an insurance investigator making notes amidst an inferno.

I pulled back the blanket to find that his trousers, shoes and socks had been removed, revealing a pair of white, hairless legs and very ugly feet. The legs were cold and pulseless and seemed to confirm my diagnosis. There was no time to waste, so I explained the situation quickly to them both.

"Can't say I like the sound of this," he said, folding his arms on his chest.

"You've always had poor circulation, though, Alfred," said Edith Groves nervously. "Look what happened last week when you came in late after that dinner at the Round Table. Climbed into bed with feet like blocks of ice and nearly made me jump clean out onto the landing."

"One thing, doctor," he said, glancing coldly at his wife, "is there any possibility of them sorting my feet out at the same time as I'm having this other business attended to? I've had these bunions for long enough."

I looked up from the note I was scribbling to the hospital. "I wouldn't have thought so, Mr Groves," I replied. "They will probably view 'this other business', as you put it, as a major priority. Your feet are the least of your problems at the moment."

He grunted. "You may be right. All the same, I'd be obliged if you would mention my feet in your letter. If I am to be incarcerated for any length of time I might as well have everything else taken care of as well."

Two weeks later I was back at the house. The surgeons had removed the clot from the main descending artery, saving his life. He was fortunate to have been in the hands of such a dexterous, dedicated team – although his eyes reflected none of this as he stared at me over the top of his *Financial Times*.

"Can't say I'm impressed by the system," he said.

I stood at the foot of the bed, thinking that, had he woken up in heaven instead of his hospital bed, he would have got used to it in about ten minutes. He folded his paper into a neat rectangle and placed it on the bedside table.

"While I was in there, both before and after I went on the operating table, I made a point of mentioning my feet. In fact I made quite an issue of it. They said that I would have to be referred by yourself to another department of the hospital." He sniffed and stared at the ceiling. "Now *that*, doctor, is bad organisation, if you ask me. "You simply can't run a business like that, you know. Red tape, bureaucracy – call it what you will. Smacks of inefficiency, to my mind."

I gazed across at him, suppressing the professional pack instinct that urged me to defend the surgeons who had failed to give his bunions a quick trim at the same time as they had removed the life-threatening rubbish from his circulatory system. I could feel my skin prickle with anger but I said nothing. I watched him delicately pick up a glass of Lucozade from the bedside table and take a small sip through barely parted lips.

"Your silence is significant, doctor. Do I take that as meaning your tacit acceptance of the system, of your colleagues? Being in business, I am bound to say that a free enterprise system would not tolerate that sort of unnecessary humbug."

"If your health *did* depend on a free enterprise system, Mr Groves," I said tersely, "your recent operation would have wiped out your entire savings – and if you'd had your feet done as well, you'd have needed to take out a second mortgage."

"On the other side of the coin – if I may say so – if you fellows were in the free market, a lot of you wouldn't last a fortnight. Oh yes, *granted*, a few of you would get rich, but a lot of you . . . well . . . quite a few of you would go to the wall." He buried his chin in his chest and belched languidly. "After all, the system feeds *you*, but you also feed the *system*, so to speak."

"I don't quite follow, Mr Groves."

"Well, it's true isn't it, that quite a bit of illness is actually caused by medical treatment? I mean – look at Israel a few years ago. The medical profession chose to go on strike, and what happened to the death rate? I'll tell you what happened, doctor – the death rate went down by seventeen per cent, that's what happened."

I opened my mouth to reply, looking like a fish starved of oxygen. Groves waved his arms about. "Oh, I know what you're going to say, doctor – don't think for a minute that I'm not happy to have again received the gift of life and so forth –"

"Except that you don't care for the wrapping paper," I snapped.

"Oh come now, doctor. That's not . . ."

He was interrupted by Mrs Groves who came bustling through the bedroom door carrying another bottle of Lucozade.

"Did Alfred mention his bowels, by the way?" she beamed.

"Not exactly, Mrs Groves," I replied. "Mind you, he has been talking a lot of . . . no, I don't think you did get round to mentioning your bowels, did you, Mr Groves? Constipation, is it? Of course, all that Lucozade will fill you full of gas, you know," I added cheerfully. He scowled.

"As a matter of fact I am . . . somewhat stubborn at the moment. Which is hardly surprising after that appalling food in the infirmary."

I opened my bag and wrote out a prescription for some particularly effective suppositories. They usually acted explosively within half an hour of insertion. Just the job.

"And there's another thing, doctor," said Mrs Groves. "Alfred's brother is coming this evening to take him to Southport for a few days for a bit of convalescence – door to door, in his car. Will it be all right for him to go?"

"Very good idea. Change of air will do him good."

I turned and went out of the door, wishing them both well as I went down the stairs.

I worked through the evening surgery like a dervish that day, trying to erase the memory of the miserable episode at the house of Alfred Groves. I finished early, and as I drove home the front of the car seemed to suck up the road like a vacuum cleaner, taking with it some of the guilt and anger which I still felt. I slowed down at the narrow bridge crossing the river Dane and caught sight of my senior partner, Ian McDonald. He was leaning on the stone parapet, gazing into the dark, oily water below. I stopped the car and walked over to join him. He turned his head and smiled.

"Hullo, Steven. All finished?"

11

"Yes. How about you? You must have got a move on this evening."

"Not especially. This warm sunshine caused a lot of cancellations. People decided to sit in their gardens instead of coming to see me. Can't blame them. More therapeutic, for one thing." He peered down at the river again. "Just take a look at this water. My God, it makes you despair for the human race – a million generations of wildlife wiped out by one hundred years of industry."

"It's hardly the river Tay," I replied. "You can count the oxygen molecules in that lot with the fingers of one hand." I leaned over the parapet and let my eyes follow the river as it snaked and curled back on itself into the distance, like a glistening black ribbon which had been casually thrown along the floor of this lush, shallow valley.

"D'you fancy a wee stroll down the way?" asked Ian, nodding his head towards the footpath which wound down from the bridge. "Or maybe you're in a rush to get home to Tanya and the bairns."

"No, that's a good idea," I replied. "I just hope the gnats have already eaten."

We followed the path down to the river bank and walked slowly along a line of trees which cut the haze of the mellow evening sun into slanting bars of light and shade, mottling the path ahead of us.

"How did it go today?" asked Ian. "Manage to cure anyone, by any chance?"

Behind his casual question lay genuine concern for the patients as well as for Molly Kirkham and myself, his junior partners. Thirty years as a GP in Overton made him now the Elder Statesman of the practice. He drew on his rich experience in order to stimulate thought, but he did not lean on this experience to stifle new ideas: he had authority without being authoritarian.

"Whatever good I may have done was wiped out by one particular episode," I said. I told him about Alfred Groves, feeling my scalp prickle as I did so.

"You still sound a bit put out, even now," Ian said.

"I know – but he's such an ungrateful bugger." I ducked under the low bough of a willow in front of me. Ian stopped, half turned, and looked thoughtfully across the valley.

"Ungrateful, eh?" he murmured. "To the way the world has treated him in general, or to the way you have treated him in particular, I wonder."

"Both, I suppose."

"But mostly the latter, I suspect." He laughed quietly. "Is that what makes you angry now?"

"Well, it's nice to feel that your efforts are appreciated –"

"Ah." He looked straight at me with a quizzical expression on his face. His moustache twitched as his lips formed into a smile. "And you find it difficult to be a doctor to this sort of patient, is that it?"

"It isn't easy."

"No, it isn't. But a patient is free to pee on your pedestal if he so chooses, even if he does splash your ego at the same time. After all, gratitude doesn't necessarily form part of the contract between you both."

"True. It's a nice bonus, though, now and then," I said.

"Just so long as you don't look for it every time," said Ian. We turned and walked slowly back the way we had come, silent for a while. I chewed over what he had said, and knew at the same time that this was what he intended me to do, for he was a great user of silence. Eventually he spoke again, reflectively, almost as if to himself.

"There was a time . . . it seems a hell of a long time ago now . . . when I seemed to be surrounded by fawning and grateful patients who regarded me as omnipotent. I probably thought I was omnipotent at that time. But we've all grown up since then, thank God." He sniffed in a great lungful of air noisily. "Things are different now. There are times now when knowing that your diagnosis and treatment has been spot on is the only gratification you'll get . . . the only thing that nourishes your motivation as a doctor. Make the most of it, even though it is a solitary pleasure."

"That's heavy stuff, Ian. I'm not sure I go along —"

"Fair enough. Let me put it another way. I have a feeling it's learning to live with uncertainty and disappointment that causes most of the anger and stress within us as doctors."

"How come?"

"Think of all the undefinable problems our patients have . . . not nice and neat, like in your hospital. And think of all the problems they have that we can do damn all about because they're to do with rotten housing, rotten jobs, rotten marriages and so forth."

"Which we are not equipped —"

"Precisely so. We have been taught to cure, when we need to learn to care. We are thrashing around in a sea of insoluble problems most of the time and we simply have to come to terms with the fact. So when you make a nice diagnosis and maybe save a life once in a while, of course it feels good. But if the patient seems ungrateful and doesn't give you a pat on the back – so be it. That shouldn't be your problem. Your problem only begins if you *expect* a pat on the back. The child seeking the approval of the parent, if you like."

I smiled. "I think I'm beginning to get your drift. It sounds as if you're describing the adolescent stage of a general practitioner."

"Adolescent? I've always associated that with rebellion rather than approval," Ian said. "Either way, many of us remain at this stage for a lifetime." He began to laugh and his eyebrows danced on his broad forehead. "Hell, I don't think you should take it too seriously, Steven. After all, Alfred Groves has *always* been an ungrateful bugger."

We climbed the path back to the bridge and, as we reached the clearing where we had parked our cars, a small white Fiat pulled up sharply, disgorging the generous form of one of the district nurses, Pat Grimsey. She waved and trotted across to us.

"I always thought you doctors were overworked," she panted. "What's this – an out-of-hours medical conference?"

Her huge breasts heaved beneath her blue uniform and when she folded her arms she looked as if she was hugging a sack of potatoes which, if she relaxed her hold, would surely crush her feet. Her bare forearms were pink and massive like ham shanks, tapering sharply to hands whose slightly dry skin betrayed the effect of a lifetime of meticulous scrubbing and exposure to surgical spirit. How fortunate we were that her physical dimensions were matched by the generosity of spirit and kindness which she showed to all our patients.

"I'm glad I've seen you, Doctor Rushton," she said, smiling. "It's about Alfred Groves."

I glanced at Ian. He coughed and fiddled with his car keys.

14

"I called in earlier to do a routine post-op visit," she continued. "Apparently his brother took him to Southport this afternoon, according to Mrs Groves."

"That's right," I said. "I thought it was a good idea. Why? What's the problem?"

"Those suppositories. Mrs Groves said you had insisted that he use them as soon as he got the prescription . . . which was about ten minutes before he left for Southport in his brother's car."

"You don't mean to tell me he —"

"I most certainly do, doctor," she said brightly. "The whole thing was supervised by his wife. She said she wouldn't have dreamed of letting him set off without your treatment." She saw my expression and laughed. "That's just what I thought. Anyway, I thought you'd like to know in case someone contacts you tomorrow. 'Bye for now."

She waved cheerfully and went back to her car. I was thinking how far along the East Lancashire road they would get before the suppositories acted with their characteristic element of surprise, and I squirmed at the thought. Ian turned slowly and looked me straight in the eye.

"One thing's for sure," he said gravely, "you'll not get a pat on the back from Alfred Groves for that particular therapeutic gem. Nor from his brother, come to think of it." He opened the car door and sat down with one hand on the driving wheel, looking thoughtfully out of the window. "It's almost perverse, really," he murmured. "When one thing goes wrong between ourselves and a patient it somehow triggers off another set of events which inevitably makes the original difficulty a damn sight worse."

"You're not kidding," I said. "I cannot imagine how Edith Groves got that idea about the suppositories. I didn't say anything of the sort."

Ian smiled. "No . . . I'm sure you're right. Maybe it was the way you acted. Either way you look at it, it's almost as if she . . . she became the agent of your revenge, in a way. And yet somehow I can't help thinking that it was a fitting end to the whole episode – if you see what I mean."

He started his car and drove off slowly up the winding hill to Breadburn, glancing in his rear-view mirror and waving as he disappeared round the first bend in the road. I followed a few

15

minutes later, controlling the car with one half of my central nervous system while the other half performed the infinitely more difficult task of steering my thoughts away from Alfred Groves.

2

I sat on a grassy slope under a Constable sky. It was mid-day, in late September. As the bright-edged cumuli moved across the sun, patterns of light and shade seemed to make the landscape below me move like the swell of the ocean. The leaves were drier than they had been when I had sat here a month ago, and the sound of the wind amongst them now had a thin, tense quality which reflected my own anticipation of change.

I looked across the ox-bow Dane valley to the road which twisted lazily up the hill into Breadburn on the other side. A stream of cars followed slowly behind a tractor pulling a trailer full of hay. Even from this distance I could see the tanned, weathered face of the driver as he bounced up and down on his rigidly sprung seat, occasionally twisting round to check his load and to see that none of the vehicles following would be foolish enough to overtake on this narrow, winding stretch of road.

I lay back in the coarse grass and felt the warm sun against my closed eyelids. The warmth, the distant throb of the traffic across the valley, and the hypnotic hum of the summer's last geriatric wasps and flies close by, was still not enough to calm the restlessness which I now felt. I sat up again and screwed my eyes up to gaze at the hills on the skyline. Something wasn't right. Here I was in a good practice, in partnership with people I liked, looking after patients with whom – apart from the odd exception – I got on well. And yet it did not seem enough, somehow. Of course, the surgery problem might have something to do with it. I hadn't minded too much at first, but then, as the months had gone by, the effect of such an inadequate place began to represent something that was wrong: we were no longer in control of the way we wanted to do things. Having agreed to go into the health centre we seemed at the mercy of innumerable groups of people, all of whom had disparate aims and who all seemed to be pulling in different directions – the net result of which was that the progress on the building was so painfully slow and the consultative meetings so hide-bound with ritual that it made me apprehensive about our independence and effectiveness once we got in and started to work there. There had been so many disappointments along the way that we had been powerless to influence, and I had started to have serious doubts about whether or not I wanted to go in at all. The rigid hierarchy in the hospital service was one of the reasons I had left for general practice, but now we appeared threatened by an even more insidious bureaucratic machine whose shape and form was more difficult to define and whose ground rules were juggled around by those who had most political clout.

I slowly drew from my coat pocket a tightly rolled-up copy of the *British Medical Journal*, straightened it out on the grass and glanced down the list of contents on the pale blue cover. It read like a recipe for a primaeval soup. I flicked automatically past the tersely-written papers on the greatest advances in medicine since last month's offerings, until I reached the jobs vacant (overseas) section. I had no idea why I was doing this, but I took a pen and a scrap of paper from my pocket as I read through the long, juicy columns. A practice in Seal River, Manitoba, was looking for a young, go-ahead physician who liked to be independent, practise *real* medicine without the shackles of administration; colossal earnings, good schools, wonderful opportunities in pollution-free environment, and so on. Apply Doctors Heisenberg, Weisacker, Meittner and Frisch. The names sounded more like a roll-call for a Panzer division than a medical partnership, but I found myself writing down the address before I returned to the surgery to see if there were any more visits.

*   *   *

That evening, after surgery, I drove home slowly. The wind had dropped and it was warm and clear. I had a clear image of myself clomping around the frozen wastes of northern Manitoba in snow shoes, relieving the suffering of wild-eyed trappers who showed their eternal gratitude by heaping upon me armloads of fresh fish and beaver pelts. For some reason, the idea had a certain appeal. I would think about it. Maybe.

18

When I arrived home, our three boys were sitting at the table eating their tea. As I came through the door they blurted a noisy chorus of greeting through mouthfuls of cold salad. I responded by waving and doing clownish things with my feet which led to an exchange of face-pulling and raspberry blowing. It was the sort of nonsense that, although we had done it so many times in the past, was now obligatory at these times, and it never failed to draw the same enthusiasm and enjoyment.

Tanya appeared at the dining room door carrying a trifle, just in time to spot my purposeful move to the drinks cabinet. I poured myself a large gin with clinical precision as she laid down the trifle, took one hand and led me to the table.

"Hard day at the office, dear?" she said brightly, Hollywood style. "Come on, let's eat. And go easy on the gin – you're on call tonight, aren't you?"

I grunted and swallowed an eye-watering mouthful. Tanya smiled and arched an eyebrow. "If it's been that sort of day, then you can be sure that you'll get a call tonight. It's always the same. The hand of fate, Sod's Law, or whatever . . ." Her voice trailed off as she reached forward unsuccessfully to save the peppermill which was being taken apart by Carl, our middle son, aged five. There was a brief flurry of wrist action before a shower of black peppercorns bounced over the surface of the table, amid shrieks of approval from our youngest child, Conrad. In the time it took to gather up the component bits of the peppermill, reassemble it and gather up the majority of the black peppercorns, I had finished my drink. I began to tell Tanya about the difficulty of getting one of my elderly patients into hospital, but in the giddy, chaotic atmosphere that now prevailed around the table, my account was rendered a rambling, inconsequential affair.

"I just hope there are no big problems following what happened this afternoon. I could do without —"

"Ooh, look!"

I was interrupted by the urgent cry from Conrad who had picked up a black peppercorn on the end of a wet index finger. He flexed and straightened the finger in front of his face and squinted at it intently. I turned to Tanya again.

"I mean, what gets me is —"

"Bogey."

"What . . . ?"

"Big bogey," said Conrad gravely. The other two watched him gleefully over their spoons as he plunged his finger into the trifle, withdrawing it almost immediately with a broad grin.

"Bogey gone!" he cried triumphantly.

I found myself joining in the laughter of the others, enjoying the simple innocence of this infantile cabaret which seemed to wash away the last, cloying fragments of the day's mess.

After we had eaten and the children had finally gone to bed, Tanya and I sat outside in the still evening and talked for a while. From somewhere far off, a transistor radio scratched the air with its insistent, sibilant gibberish and I began to feel that I was sitting on a thistle.

"Bloody transistors," I growled. "Like having your ears syringed with crushed ice. You get goose-pimples on your cerebral cortex."

"Touchy, touchy," murmured Tanya.

"I can only think of one thing worse, and that's coming across nuts in trifles. Highly neurotic, of course —"

"Which reminds me," Tanya said, "have you been to see how they're getting on with the health centre lately?"

"Ah . . . ! Do I detect an almost imperceptible change of subject?"

She smiled sweetly, then laughed. "No. Just thought you'd like to talk about all your other hang-ups while you were about it."

I sat back in the chair and for a while stared through the tops of the trees at the pink mackerel sky. "No. I haven't been to see it. I was leaving it until Molly comes back from her holiday next week. I hear they've nearly completed the roof."

"How long do you think it will be before you move in?"

"God knows," I sighed. "How long is it now since we got chucked out of the old surgery and moved into our purpose-built shoe-box – our present temporary hell? I'll tell you. It's one year, six months and twenty-two days. Time off for good behaviour, I should think we'll be there for at least another year before we move into the health centre."

"Mary Street surgery isn't as bad as that," said Tanya. "I've seen lots worse."

"I know – and that's a sobering thought. But eight hundred

and sixty square feet, with a list of nine thousand patients! We must have been demented to agree to move in there – even temporarily."

"You didn't have much choice, as I recall."

"True. And we were mesmerised by the architect's cute little sketches, with all that cross-hatching and those dotted lines." I burst out laughing. "Christ, were we naive! To open any of the doors you first have to warn everyone inside the building, in case anyone gets trapped or crushed. One of the girls opened a filing cabinet drawer yesterday and accidentally pushed five patients into the street."

Tanya shook her head. "OK, OK. I get the general idea. There is one consolation, though."

"Really? What's that?"

"You only have to work in it. Think of all those poor patients who have to be ill in it. Tea or coffee?"

Without waiting for a reply she went indoors and I heard the rattle of cups. I put my head back again and, probably because of the meal and the gin, fell asleep. Almost immediately I began to dream vividly of salmon flashing beneath the surface of a bright cold stream. The Canadian spruce, so green by the water's edge, became bluer on the distant slopes where the water tumbled from its icy origin, and the air was so clear that, if I clapped my hands, the sky would shatter like a wine-glass. It was straight out of *National Geographic*. I was wakened briefly by the grunting sound of my own soft palate sagging down onto my tongue, then I turned my head to one side and fell asleep again. I began to dream once more, but this time it was not the same. I dreamed that I was stitching up a perineum after a perfectly normal delivery. The midwife was discussing the virtues of catgut as opposed to silk and nylon, when quite abruptly the mother's insides began to fall out. Coils of small intestine cascaded onto the bed, slithering onto the floor like squids out of water. As I frantically tried to shove them back, the midwife began to scream and charge blindly around the room, knocking over the dressing trolley. Then the patient began to scream. When the liver and spleen slithered out and bounced all over the floor, I began to scream as well.

I woke up, sweating. Tanya was shaking me gently with one hand, holding a mug of tea with the other. I took the tea and began to tell her about the dream. She nodded her head solemnly from side to side.

"I've got bad news for you, Steven. That wasn't a dream at all. You really *are* in the delivery room grappling with that woman's insides. *This* is actually the dream." She spread out her hands and looked round the garden, then back at me. We both began to laugh at this old joke.

It seemed like only a few minutes after getting into bed and falling deeply asleep that the telephone rang. I switched on the light, picked up the receiver and checked the time on my wristwatch. One-thirty a.m. A well-spoken but clipped, almost military voice sounded through the earpiece.

"Hullooo? Hullooo . . . Is that Dr Rushton?"

"It is. Who —?"

"Ah, good. Can never tell these days. Thought I might be speaking to one of those emergency service nig-nogs, d'you follow?"

My brain cleared and I sat up, the sudden movement waking Tanya.

"What . . .? Is this a social call, or are you doing some sort of market research on behalf of the National Front?" I said through my teeth. I was wide awake now. Tanya groaned and dug me in the ribs.

"No, no, no, no," I heard the voice say at the other end of the line. "Peel here. Neville Peel. Got a bit of a panic on here, I'm afraid. Half a tick – I'll put my wife on the 'phone. She'll put you in the picture, d'you follow?"

I lay back on the pillow and looked sideways at Tanya. She screwed her eyes up against the light. "Told you so," she mumbled sleepily. "Ten to one it's another delivery." She closed her eyes and turned over. I stared at the ceiling. With the earpiece wedged between the pillow and my ear, I could hear the muffled conversation on the line as a hand was placed over the mouthpiece. It was a woman's voice, angry and agitated.

"What was that supposed to be about? Honestly, Neville . . . and will you *please* put some clothes on and have a word with Gaynor." The hand was taken away from the mouthpiece and the tone of the voice changed. It was polite and apologetic, but the carefully intoned vowels wobbled precariously as moans of anguish in the background distracted the caller.

22

"Dr Rushton? I'm most *awfully* sorry to bother you. It's Gaynor Peel's mother here. Will you come right away, please?"

"Gaynor . . . ?"

"Yes. You remember – we used to live at The Grange, Bowden Lane, until Neville retired . . ." A horrendous groan drowned her words for a moment and her hand covered the mouthpiece again. Her voice changed to its previous exasperated, aggressive tone. "For Christ's sake, Neville – give the girl a brandy. Don't just stand there – do something. And *will* you get dressed!"

I closed my eyes and had began to drift into sleep when Mrs Peel spoke again.

"The fact is that Gaynor came to see us tonight. She's home for the weekend from college and she began with *excruciating* abdominal pain. She really does look *appalling* – rolling about and so on. Please come and see her . . . Hello? Hello?"

"Mmm," I mumbled.

"What's that? Are you still there?" A wail of pain sounded again in the background.

"Pain. Tonight. College. Home." I spoke the words as if I were in a hypnotic trance, for I could feel that this was going to be a call, whatever I did or said.

"Yes . . . Now you won't know our new address," Mrs Peel continued. "It's called High View and it's on Peak Lane. We're set back a bit, about half-way along. There's no number on the house, so you'll have to watch carefully on the right as you go in the Hiley direction from the Joel Cross end of Peak Lane. Got it?"

As she spoke I could feel my abdominal muscles tighten up: no number on the house, just a name – and Peak Lane was quite long, with no lights, of course. If it was anything like their last house I would need a torch, compass, ordnance survey map and God knew what else to find the place. It would take half the night.

"OK, I've got it. I'll find it somehow." I replaced the receiver and rolled out of bed. I knew I dared not put my head back on the pillow, for if I did so I would fall asleep again and dream convincingly that I was driving to the house. I would arrive, diagnose and treat the patient and then return home again – all in this dream – to be wakened and momentarily perplexed by a second telephone call from the same household asking me where I was. It had happened before.

Malper, on the border of Derbyshire and Cheshire, was about four miles from Hiley. Separating the two towns were the steep slopes of Loweth Heights, part of the Pennine chain. It was peculiarly satisfying to drive fast up the snaking narrow road on the Malper side of the Heights, especially in the dead of night, first winding lazily round the outskirts of Royley golf course, then shooting up a one-in-four incline straight to the summit. I drove up this last stretch and, in the light of the main beams, could only see a small area of asphalt in front of me. When I reached the top, the car dipped abruptly, causing that familiar sinking feeling in the pit of my stomach. For a fraction of a second there was a breathtaking sensation of taking off into space: suddenly, in front and below, were the countless street lights of Greater Manchester as far as the eye could see, merging without a horizon into the clear night sky with its blanket of stars.

I swung right, along the top road for a short distance, then down the other side towards Hiley. On the right was a dark, narrow road, lined on either side with beech and poplar which partially obscured the occasional house set far back from the road – too far back to identify by name or number.

Peak Lane. I knew as I turned into it that it was going to be a matter of luck and guesswork to find the Peel house. There was no moon and in the dim starlight I could only make out the light paintwork of eaves and window frames against hunched black rectangles, as still as death behind the gently moving trees.

I stopped after driving past a row of stone cottages on my left. I got out and walked slowly back. I heard a movement behind the door of the last one and, as I passed, the door opened, throwing a thin corridor of orange light on the path outside.

"Are you lost, young man?"

I turned round. The creaking, high-pitched voice came from an old woman stooping in the doorway. She had wiry white hair pulled back into a bun, a very lined face with deep-set, beady eyes glinting in the poor light and a lipless, concave mouth spreading into a questioning smile which revealed one or two stumpy teeth. Around her neck she clutched a woollen

24

shawl whose ragged ends hung over a dirty black skirt, and from her legs a pair of wrinkled grey stockings sagged down into her slippers. She had walked on the inside edge of the slippers for a long time, deforming them until the heels stuck out at right angles from the sides of her feet. I stared back at her, but she showed no apprehension at all, grabbing the edge of the door with one arthritic hand and leaning right out towards me. She smelled of gravy.

"Not lost, are you?" she repeated, cocking her head to one side and screwing her eyes up.

"No – I'm looking for a house up here. I'm the doctor."

"The doctor? Well I never! Best come in, then." She turned and shuffled jerkily into the small untidy living room, her head bobbing up and down like an old parrot.

"I'm looking for the Peel house. It's called High View."

"What? Can't hear you proper," she wheezed, making her way further into the room. I hesitated, then followed her in. I could hear the unfriendly growl of a dog coming from somewhere and then I saw the snout and bared teeth of what looked like a border collie sticking out from under the table cloth. The old woman picked up a cane walking stick which lay on the table and whacked the dog sharply on the nose. It withdrew with a startled yelp.

"Go on – go to sleep, y'owd bugger," she muttered. She turned round, put both hands on the top of the stick and looked me up and down.

"Doctor, eh? You dunna look like one," she cackled. "Any road, 'appen I shouldn't say, with it being twenty year sin' I seen one. Who did you say you were looking for?"

"High View. Peel."

"Eh?"

"Where the Peels live," I said, a lot louder. "It's called High View." The dog growled again, and I glanced apprehensively at the cracked lino near the table. The old woman swung the cane over and rattled it amongst the chair legs, and the growling stopped.

"Peel? Oh aye . . . Peel." Her voice dropped in pitch as she said it, as if it was something she didn't like to talk about. "New people. Just up the road, first house on t'other side. You can't miss it."

"Well – thanks." I turned to go.

25

"Hang on a minute, young man. Being as you're a doctor, whilst you're here will you have a look at this." She bent down and started to unravel one of her stockings. It was tangled on a piece of elastic which had been knotted above the knee. She tugged at it impatiently until it snapped, handing me the frayed remnants without looking up. "Just hang on to that. It won't take me a minute."

The mention of time made me sweat slightly. "Well you know, I think I ought to get moving —"

"Oh give over! That's the trouble these days. Nobody's got time for owt. Always rushing about, can't even pass the time of day, some road. Now then – what d'you mek of that?"

She rolled down the stocking, exposing the grey, translucent skin of her leg. It was heavily mottled with a brown stain over the skin from years of sitting in front of an open fire on winter nights.

"What – these brown marks?" I said. I smiled with relief at the thought that she might conceivably have wanted to show me her prolapsing piles or strangulated hernia if she had got them.

"Aye, what are they?" She straightened up and looked at me with her old eyes.

"Oh, that's nothing serious. They're just due to poor circulation. Your age. Nothing to worry about. Well, I must be off . . ."

"Aye, all right, doctor. Any road, it's a relief to know it's nowt serious. I've been wondering about it for a year or two now."

I put the elastic on the table and turned to go through the door. Outside, I caught my foot on an uneven flagstone and, as I stumbled forward, I heard a scuffling noise behind me, then felt a sharp pain in my right calf muscle. I shouted out and spun round to see a medium-sized black dog shoot into the house and back under the table. The old woman leaned forward and cracked it hard on the head with her stick and the dog yelped with pain, moving quickly to a safer place out of her reach.

"You bad-tempered devil! Just wait, that's all." She turned and smiled apologetically. "She's a bit too quick for me sometimes. Has she done owt?"

I pulled up my trouser leg. There was a bunch of teeth marks

26

on the back of my calf, one or two of which had punctured the skin and were bleeding. The rest were swelling nicely. She peered out of the doorway and could just see the damage in the light from the room behind.

"My word, doctor – she got a fair good grip of you there, didn't she? D'you want to come back in, I've some boracic lint somewhere. And comfrey."

"No, no it's all right. It'll be OK in a while. I'll sort it out when I get back." It was hurting like hell.

"Sloan's Liniment – now I've some of that – or 'appen a bit of Germolene . . ." She began to babble like a demented Kleen-Eze salesman, but I knew she was just trying to be helpful. I thanked her profusely through gritted teeth and limped back up the road. I heard her piping voice for a minute before she closed the door and then there was silence, apart from the light rustle of leaves in the trees, stirred by the gentle night breeze.

I found the Peel house further up on the other side. It was a large, nineteen-twenties detached with big bay windows on either side of the front door. From the road a loose gravel driveway ran straight to a single-storey double garage at the side of the house, and a narrow off-shoot of the path led to the main entrance, dividing the front lawn into two roughly equal triangles. In the driveway, parked outside the closed doors of the garage, stood a tatty white Triumph Spitfire which I assumed belonged to Gaynor Peel.

I stood at the door and rattled the knocker, which was a large brass ring attached to the flaring nostrils of a lion's head. I trapped my knuckles painfully between the ring and the gaping lower jaw of the lion and cursed its designer who had managed to combine such vulgarity with utter uselessness.

I did not hear anyone come down the hallway, and when the door opened I was still cursing under my breath and blowing on a superficial tear on the skin of my middle finger. The smarting it produced took my mind off the dog bite on my leg, which had now settled down to an unpleasant, dull throb.

"Doctor Rushton?" It was Mr Peel. There was no light on in the hall and at first I could not see him very clearly. He beckoned me in, closed the door, then put a light on. When he saw my grazed knuckles he began to smile broadly.

"Caught yourself with the old lion, I see. Well, shouldn't worry – nearly everyone does that!" He laughed heartily and I immediately regretted the fact that the oozing was insufficient to drop onto the green, virgin acres of the Axminster carpet in the hallway.

"Neville, what on earth —"

I heard Mrs Peel's exasperated tones coming from a room off the hallway, and a split-second later she appeared.

"I don't . . . oh – it's you, doctor. Thank God for that." She glared briefly at Mr Peel who was adjusting the belt on his silk dressing-gown. "Neville, you look a *sight*," she said sharply. He carelessly brushed his hands through his thick white hair and snorted.

"Can't say you look like an oil painting y'self, Doris, at this moment."

I couldn't help thinking that he was quite right, for as I edged up the hallway to where the action was, I caught a powerful whiff of cold cream. Mrs Peel's face was pale and shiny with the stuff, applied in front of a mirror a few hours before. It was a sad, unsuccessful rearguard action against the cruel army of creases which had slowly but inexorably forged their way across her attractive features. This was not simply the effect of chronological ageing: it was partly a result of stress. She was the only daughter of the notorious Billy Bevan, a hard-drinking greengrocer who, until recently, had been Lord Mayor of Overton. He was a man whose coarseness and insensitivity had cast a shadow over her early life, so that over the years she felt driven to pay particular attention to her own speech, manner and dress in order somehow to neutralise the image that her father projected. Now and again she over-compensated and tonight was fairly typical, for she was wearing a beautifully-cut trouser suit with matching patent-leather shoes, and had a cluster of expensive-looking rings on both hands. All this seemed wildly inappropriate at that time of night when most people, having just jumped out of bed in an emergency, would have simply put on a sweater or a dressing-gown. The top two buttons of her jacket were undone, revealing a twisted bra-strap. The harassed expression on her pale, oily face, together with her hair which was sticking out in all directions from hastily pulled out pins, made her look as if she had been attending a fashion parade which had suffered a direct hit in an air-raid.

The biggest contributory factor to her wear and tear,

28

however, was Neville Peel. Twenty years older than his wife, he was now retired from his highly successful electronics business. In the past he had invented several microscopic marvels of solid state circuitry which had been used extensively in the communications industry, and the royalties were still rolling in. Since he had retired from the total absorption of his work, his precise, intolerant brain had limped to a standstill and he had withdrawn into the sycophantic rituals of the local Conservative Association and the local Masonic Lodge. His declining energy coincided with his wife's growing reputation as leader of numerous voluntary organisations in the district, so that he had become increasingly irritated by her involvement in (as he put it) 'those hopeless cases and idle layabouts'. It never occurred to him that the reason she immersed herself in these activities was simply to escape from the dreary presence of his own rigid personality.

Neville Peel was in his late forties when Gaynor was born, and only when she reached her mid-teens did he really notice that she was there. He would often refer to her as a 'damned attractive girl' (which she was), but he seemed incapable of communicating the normal feelings of warmth and affection: he thought of her more as a rather precious ornament. When she went off to drama college he fretted endlessly at the thought of her being exposed to a life style of which he thoroughly disapproved, often muttering darkly about her "mixing with those unwashed bloody trotskyites and degenerates".

I went into the lounge to find Gaynor lying on her side on an olive-green chesterfield. She did not look well. Her face was flushed and her forehead was wet with fine beads of sweat. Wisps of her long auburn hair adhered to her forehead and the rest of it fell untidily over the shoulders of a large borrowed dressing gown, the top of which was open, revealing a faded denim shirt. She was puffy round the eyes and had put on some weight since I had last seen her over a year ago.

She looked straight past me at her parents who followed me through the open door.

"Mummy – can you and daddy please wait in the study. I want to see the doctor alone, if you don't mind." Her voice was tense and weary. Doris Peel glanced at her husband, then at me. Neville Peel cleared his throat.

"Er . . . d'you think that's wise, my dear . . . ?"

Gaynor winced and gave a low moan, clutched her abdomen then rolled onto her side, retching into a small bowl on the floor. Mrs Peel moved forward but Gaynor waved her away.

"No, please . . ."

"Well, if that's what you want us to —"

"I do . . . please. Ooooh . . ." Gaynor's face became contorted with pain and she rolled against the back of the chesterfield, her eyes screwed tight shut. Mrs Peel took a deep breath and turned towards the door.

"Very well, Gaynor. Come along, Neville." Her face was full of 'you-work-your-fingers-to-the-bone-for-your-children-and-they-treat-you-like-dogs' martyrdom. When they had shut the door behind them, Gaynor put both hands up to her face and moaned quietly for a moment before stopping abruptly as if she had thrown a switch. She wiped her eyes and blew her nose.

"I'm sorry about this, doctor. My God, what a shambles."

"What exactly —?"

"I'm pregnant."

"Ah . . ."

"But it's not that . . . well, it is really of course . . ." She began to speak quickly as if there wasn't much time, and I was beginning to sense impending disaster. "I planned to have the baby away, near college —"

"You mean they don't know?"

"No. They haven't a clue. Well – what do you expect?" she snapped. She sounded annoyed at my question. "I mean – mummy always at the WVS and daddy with his bloody Conservative meetings. I am not due for three or four weeks, but tonight I had to get up with this pain and when I went to the lavatory I lost some blood. The pains have got worse since then."

Oh Christ, I thought – she's in the second stage of labour already. My mouth went dry. I hadn't brought my obstetric bag – just my ordinary bag. It was no use for this.

"All right, let's have a quick look at your tummy," I said, kneeling down at the side of the chesterfield. She undid her dressing gown and pulled up the shirt. She was wearing nothing underneath. As I laid my hand on her abdomen she had a massive contraction and cried out in pain. I glanced down and noticed a small trickle of bloodstained liquor and mucus run onto the dressing gown from the vagina.

"How often are the pains?" I asked, trying to sound casual.

"About . . . about every five minutes," she gasped, squeezing the words from the back of her throat.

I listened to the foetal heart when the pain had eased off. One hundred and thirty, steady. Right . . .

"I'm getting you into hospital right away. There's still time," I said. She nodded and closed her eyes. I picked up the telephone and rang the ambulance station. It was only a mile away and it would take five minutes. Meanwhile I gave her one hundred and fifty milligrams of pethidine and asked her what she wanted me to say to her parents, which really was a stupid question.

"I'll tell them," she said. "I must. Although it's a bit late." Her half-smile stretched into a grimace and then she gave a strangled cry as she got another pain. I opened the door and called her parents in. I was just about to put them in the picture when Gaynor spoke. She was panting a bit, and I prayed silently for the ambulance to arrive.

"Mummy, daddy, better sit down. I – I've something to tell you."

Doris Peel clutched her throat, Neville grabbed her arm and I felt as if I were taking part in a very bad play. A nightmare theatre in the round.

"I'm having a baby," Gaynor said firmly. A taut, muted little sound came from Mrs Peel's throat and she sat down. Neville's eyes stuck out like organ stops and his jaw dropped open.

"What, dear? What did you say?" Mrs Peel's voice was a hoarse whisper. Her eyes closed, her nostrils flared and the corners of her mouth twitched involuntarily. "I don't think I . . . I can't grasp it . . . it's too . . . I . . . I can't think . . ."

"Mummy, there's not time to think. Can't you see?" said Gaynor in exasperation. Mrs Peel's eyes opened wide and she looked at her daughter in horror.

"What . . . what do you mean?"

Gaynor clenched her fists, screwed her eyes tight shut and pointed her face to the ceiling, yelling at the top of her voice until her neck veins stood out like ropes.

"When I said I'm having a baby I meant I'm having the bloody thing RIGHT NOW!"

Mrs Peel gave a low moan and pitched forward in a dead

faint, knocking over the vomit bowl by the side of the chesterfield. Gaynor convulsed with another powerful uterine contraction and Neville Peel, after a moment's hesitation, stumbled forward to his wife's aid, his hands flopping helplessly and his lower jaw wobbling as he fought for the words that his stunned brain could not let him articulate.

"Something's coming! . . . oo . . . ah . . ." panted Gaynor through her teeth. I went over and lifted up her shirt to have a look at what was going on.

There was a foot sticking out of the vagina.

I shut my eyes for a moment, hoping that when I opened them again I would see Tanya standing there in the garden handing me a cup of tea. I opened my eyes again and . . .

There was a foot sticking out of the vagina.

Here was the reality. An undiagnosed breech with a presenting foot; no midwife, no obstetric equipment, no ambulance, the patient's father beside himself with uselessness and the patient's mother sprawled unconscious in a pool of vomit.

"I want to push!" cried Gaynor.

"No you don't. Not yet," I replied tersely. I grabbed my stethoscope. Foetal heart still OK. That was something. A thunderous knock on the front door heralded the arrival of the ambulance, thank God. Neville jumped up, stumbled down the hall, opened the door, then returned breathlessly to kneel by his wife. She moaned and rolled her eyes, while Gaynor lay back quietly on the chesterfield, staring at the ceiling and taking deep breaths.

Two ambulance attendants walked crabwise through the open lounge door. There was plenty of room for them to walk normally, but I supposed that they spent such a lot of their working day walking sideways and squeezing themselves between stretchers and the walls of narrow institutional corridors that their eccentric mode of walking was now sheer habit.

They had brought with them what looked like a heavy duty folding picnic chair in canvas and tubular steel, a ludicrously inappropriate device on which to bundle a sick individual. They swiftly unfolded it and made straight for Doris Peel who was still lying on the floor amid the vomit, with Neville kneeling by her side anxiously massaging her wrists. They put the chair down and nudged him out of the way.

"Hey up, squire!" said one of them cheerfully.

"Do you mind?" said Neville weakly, waving his arm towards Gaynor, "I think you —"

"It's quite all right, sir," said the other one soothingly, winking reassuringly at him. "We're used to this. Just leave it to us. Our job, see? Right, Norman – you get her feet . . ."

They started to bundle Mrs Peel onto the folding chair and would have carried her out had I not intervened.

"Put her down, for God's sake. The patient is the one on the couch – that's her mother who just happens to have fainted."

They looked at each other, then both grinned at me.

"Oh hello, doc. Didn't see you there."

"Thanks very much. Now come on – there's not much time. This baby's on the way out and it's a breech."

They picked up the chair, moved it nearer the chesterfield, and hauled Gaynor onto it. As they did so, her shirt lifted and they caught sight of the tiny blue foot of the baby.

"See what you mean, doc," said one of them. The other turned to Gaynor.

"OK, love, just relax – we'll have you in hospital in a jiffy. You'll be all right."

They covered her with a coarse grey blanket and began to manoeuvre backwards out of the room, picking their way through the furniture and stepping over Doris and Neville Peel.

"Neville, what are the police doing here . . . ?"

"Mind that vase, Norman."

"They're not the police, Doris . . ."

"Swing round the other way, Norman."

". . . They're ambulance men . . ."

"Further round. Right. You go through first – excuse me, squire. This way. There you go."

"Ooooh – I want to push again!"

"Right, get her into that ambulance – fast."

"Is this really happening, Neville?"

I ran with them to the ambulance and clambered up the little metal steps to the interior. They slid the stretcher into position. The driver went to the cab to start the engine while the other attendant folded up the steps and began to close the rear door. Gaynor suddenly gave a cry of pain and I saw both legs of the baby appear, followed by the buttocks, then the shoulders. The tiny right arm was folded in front of the chest and I quickly hooked it back out of the way, at the same time yelling to the driver not to move. Delivery of the head was imminent, and I did not fancy doing that tricky procedure while bouncing down Peak Lane.

I checked the cord. It was pulsating satisfactorily and not wrapped round the baby's head. The baby, as the night air cooled its body, gave a few convulsive respiratory movements even though its head was still inside the vagina. When the nape of the neck became visible I lifted the tiny feet and swung them upwards, sticking the fingers of my other hand in its mouth. I tugged gently. To my relief the head popped out easily and, while the baby coughed and spluttered, I found a pair of Spencer-Wells forceps in my bag to clamp the cord. One of the ambulance men took him from me, wrapping him in another coarse grey blanket.

"Hey – it's a boy, love," grinned the ambulance attendant. Gaynor smiled weakly, looking cross-eyed at her baby. She licked her lips and shook her head, trying to clear away the numbing effect of the pethidine which was only now starting to work.

"T'rific, S'really f'ntassic," she mumbled. She put her head back and closed her eyes. I shouted to the driver to get going as I prepared to check her blood pressure. The other attendant slammed the doors shut and the vehicle set off.

The placenta was still attached to the uterus and I prayed that it would stay that way until we reached Wishton General. If it did separate I hoped that it would do so cleanly. Without any ergometrine to contract the uterine muscle down on the placental site there was a risk of a post-partum haemorrhage.

The baby snorted and whimpered quietly while Gaynor dozed, unconcerned. Not until we had got onto the main road to Wishton did I realise that Mr and Mrs Peel had been left behind at the house in Peak Lane. Gaynor opened her eyes after a few minutes, then looked up as I checked her blood pressure again. She was pretty stoned with pethidine. I shook my head and began to laugh, partly with relief that at least the baby had arrived safely.

"S'madder you?" she said thickly.

"How you managed to get this far with your pregnancy without your parents noticing anything is quite beyond me."

She laughed softly. "S'quite simple, really. I awllz wear

34

sloppy clothes, ponchos, men's shirts 'nd all that sort've thing." She suddenly sat up unsteadily as if she had remembered something, looking round with glazed eyes. "By th'way – where are Mummy and Daddy? They aren't here."

"They're probably following in their car." I looked out of the tinted rear windows of the ambulance and could see a small white car approaching slowly. It looked vaguely familiar.

"I don't see how, Daddy's car's away being serviced, or something," she mumbled. "God, I feel dizzy. Is the baby all right?"

She lay back again and I quickly checked. It was sleeping quietly and I nodded to her. No sign of any movement of the placenta yet. I looked out of the window again and the car was close behind. From this short distance I could see that it was Gaynor's Spitfire. Neville was driving and his wife was in the passenger seat, hunched forward against the windscreen and holding a handkerchief to her face.

"It looks as though they've taken your car. They're following right behind," I said. Gaynor sat up again and started to shake with laughter.

"Oh no, that's the end. That will kill daddy."

She lay back, giggling hysterically. I stared hard at the car behind and then it dawned on me what she meant. I had not noticed it at first, but now I could clearly see that on the bonnet of the car was a large poster on which was printed in large black letters, "FORWARD WITH LABOUR." Gaynor had unintentionally delivered the last twist of the knife to her parents, for Neville Peel was an arch anti-socialist. In view of the fact that a local by-election was imminent, he must have been beside himself at the irony of these words. Gaynor suddenly stopped giggling and winced. I had a quick look down below and saw that her laughter had helped separate the placenta; for a few seconds there was an alarming gush of blood. I massaged the abdomen and delivered the placenta as quickly as I could, giving her the baby to nurse in the hope that a quick spurt of hormones released in the blood stream would cause the uterus to contract and stem the flow of blood. To my great relief, it seemed to work. I checked her blood pressure once again, just as we drove into Wishton General and stopped at reception. The rear door flew open and Norman cheerfully jumped in.

"All right, love?"

Gaynor smiled and nodded. I got out and was nearly knocked over by Neville Peel and his wife as they dashed up to the ambulance.

"Is – is everything all right?" Neville blurted. His breath smelled of brandy. Doris was sniffing and chewing her handkerchief.

"Yes, everything's OK," I replied, stepping to one side. "It's a boy. They're both in good order."

Norman and the other attendant wheeled a trolley over and put Gaynor onto it. Norman took the baby as they wheeled Gaynor through the brightly lit reception area. Neville and Doris Peel trotted by the side of the trolley, their words bouncing off the shiny walls and ceiling.

"Gaynor, dear, if only you'd said something."

"Oh mummy . . ."

"I'd like to know who the father is . . ."

"Daddy —"

"Not that fellow we met at —?"

"No, you don't know him —"

"This has been quite a shock. At least you might tell us who the father is —"

"He's big and black and a socialist!"

"Gaynor, that's not very funny! Your father and I . . ."

Gaynor burst out laughing again as the whole bunch of them jostled for position at the top of the reception area to turn into the main corridor. Mrs Peel took the baby off the ambulance attendant and they disappeared without a backward glance to the lifts and the labour ward.

I picked up an internal telephone in reception and rang to inform the labour ward that the patient was on the way up, and to ask the ambulance people to pick me up in casualty on the way back so that I could get a lift back to my car.

I put the receiver down and turned round to find that one of the reception porters had appeared from nowhere and was standing in front of the door of his tiny office holding a clip board in one hand and stuffing a folded-up copy of the *Daily Mirror* into his coat pocket with the other hand. His face had a grey, waxen appearance in common with most of the porters in this hospital and his whole countenance sagged, from his drooping eyelids down to his pendulous lower lip which was very thick and made up for the fact that he had almost no chin. His neck, with its shrivelled, tremulous vertical lines of flesh, began just below his lower lip and disappeared inside a frayed, bent collar that was three sizes too large. His narrow, steeply sloping shoulders were only just able to prevent his brown coat slipping off completely and falling round his ankles. The coat itself hung as if it had lead weights in the pockets and hems, and although it reached below the knee, it was very short in the sleeves so that it revealed at least two-thirds of his thin, white forearms. He looked as if he consisted of candle-wax which was in the process of melting. I stared in wonder at the thought of this man being responsible for the security of this entrance to the building. He cleared his throat and blinked slowly like an iguana, pulling a ball-point pen from behind his ear and fiddling with his clip-board.

"Did I hear a patient come through here a few moments ago, doctor?"

I nodded. He dropped his hands to his sides and tutted in exasperation, causing minute shock waves to ripple down the front of his neck and into his collar.

"That's put me in a fix, that has. I'm supposed to get their particulars before they go up to the ward. They aren't supposed to be admitted without these admission slips being made out." He prodded the multicoloured slips on his clip-board. I yawned. "A real quandary, that," he continued in a peevish voice. "I'm not supposed to leave this office, but someone will have to go after them to get these filled out. I'm supposed to be stationed here all night long. It's not on my job-sheet to go chasing up there, not my job at all. It puts me in a very funny position, that does." He shook his head and tutted again, looking at his clip-board as if there might be a message on it.

"Life," I sighed, "is full of decisions, isn't it? Quite overwhelming at times, the responsibility and so forth. I just don't know how you cope with it."

"That's not the point, doctor. You can't just have patients coming in right left and centre without proper admission slips being made out. I should have been consulted . . ."

I groaned with exasperation and fatigue. This man personified so many of the things which were wrong with the health service: limitless inertia and an obsession for ritual which had nothing to do with the needs of the patients.

"Next time I send a patient in who's having a baby in the ambulance, I'll make quite sure I phone you personally to let you know we're on the way. How will that do? How we've managed tonight without you and your admission slips I'll never know."

I turned and walked slowly over to casualty to get some coffee. A stiff breeze rolled down from the Pennines, turning my sweat-soaked shirt icy cold, and as I made my way down the sloping path by the side of the haematology lab I became aware of the dull, aching throb in my leg where I had been bitten. The events of the last hour had chased it from my mind until now. I was thankful that it was only a superficial wound which would heal quickly. I wondered vaguely how Mr and Mrs Peel would eventually respond to the more lasting trauma they had just received to their orderly lives. I doubted whether things in that house would ever be the same again.

When I arrived home I made more coffee to quell the hunger I always felt whenever I had been out on a night call. In the stillness of the night, the house ticked and creaked as it cooled, like an old ship becalmed at sea, its massive walls amplifying the soft, vulnerable sound of one of the children as he turned over and mumbled in his sleep.

As if in some sort of trance, I searched out some writing-paper and an envelope. I stared at the paper a long time before I began to write: "Dear Doctors Heisenberg, Weisacker, Meittner and Frisch. In reply to your advertisement in this week's copy of the *British Medical Journal* . . ."

3

The next morning I drove into Overton, and it was only when several vehicles had overtaken me with honking horns and impatient gear-changes that I became aware of the fact that I was driving slower and slower as I approached Mary Street, where the surgery now was. I suppose that this reflected an unconscious desire to prolong my journey and delay my arrival as long as possible, and the more I considered this the more gloomy I felt. It was not simply lack of sleep last night which filled my head with cotton-wool and made me feel as if I had breakfasted on three of sand and one of cement – it was the prospect of another day grappling with difficult problems with such pitifully inadequate facilities. A couple of years ago, before the old surgery was demolished to make way for a supermarket, I used to look forward to the challenge of new problems which welled up from the local community and flowed into the consulting rooms each day. But there was something about this temporary surgery, this cold, neon-lit rabbit hutch, that dampened the spirit. It had a make-shift meanness which I couldn't help feeling somehow diminished our self-respect, but worse still, was an insult to our patients. We had thought at first that it was only going to be for about six months – until our new health centre was ready – but one and a half years later we were still here, with no immediate prospects of moving. The idea of making the best of it was (for me at least) wearing a bit thin.

Ann and Christine were in the tiny reception area pulling out the record cards for the first few patients of the day, doing their best not to damage their elbows, hips and knees on the closely-stacked filing cabinets which surrounded them like an ambush. I admired their devotion and good humour under conditions which would have caused the members of the Health and Safety Executive to have a collective stroke. I exchanged a few pleasantries with them before going into my consulting room to read the mail.

We had two consulting rooms, and because there were three of us in the practice, it meant that we consulted in shifts, the partner not occupying a room usually busying himself or herself with house calls or administrative matters. It seemed to work quite well, once the patients had got used to the uncertainty of turning up on the doorstep without first finding out whether the doctor they wanted to see was in or not.

I enjoyed going through the mail, even though there seemed to be more of it each day. Without doubt, the biggest increase was the requests for reports on patients' health from insurance companies and the like, but it also seemed that, over the last few years, an increasing number of individuals and organisations wanted a note from the doctor to verify, clarify or sanctify something or other: a note for the sick, the factory, the chiropodist, to confirm pregnancy, for contraception advice, to get a new council house, to get priority for a telephone installation, or to the coal merchant to ensure an adequate supply of coal over the winter period. There were other strange letters, too. One or two from the Royal Infirmary showed that the brain and the typewriter were not always in complete harmony. From one department I read: "Mr Clayton had his appendectomy on the 14th of August and I am pleased to say that he had no post-operative recovery whatsoever." From another department was a letter which made me smile. "Dear Dr Rushton," it read, "I saw your patient, Richard Atkinson, today and, as you say, she is indeed a remarkable young woman." Mr Atkinson, a six foot, sixteen stone bricklayer, would have been amused to read that particular piece of absent-mindedness.

The one which took first prize for audacity and insensitivity that day was a request from an obscure local life assurance company. A female patient and her husband had applied for a joint mortgage. What, asked the company, were my observations on the chances of her becoming pregnant in the next two years, since a pregnancy would adversely affect their application. I took pen and paper and, after some deliberation, replied with a combination of honesty, good taste and indignation, that I felt that the company had addressed their letter to the wrong person since my medical education did not encompass a true working knowledge of the use of a crystal ball.

I was riffling through the remainder of the letters and

40

hospital reports when Christine came into the consulting room, stooping apologetically.

"Mr Norton's here," she said, handing me his record cards. "He wants to see you before you start surgery. Says it's very important."

"Did he say what it was about?"

"He said it was about the dose of some tablets you prescribed the other day. Shall I ask . . . ?"

"Tell him to come in. It'll probably only take a few seconds."

She nodded and went out, and a moment later the massive frame of Jack Norton filled the doorway, reducing considerably what available natural light there was in the room.

"Morning, doctor," he mumbled, whipping off his cap and lurching clumsily towards the desk. "Sorry to bother you before you start, like, only can you tell us what it says on this here bottle of pills?"

He wrestled with the side pocket of his jacket to take out the bottle – a task made more difficult because the size of the pocket only allowed him to admit thumb and index finger of his huge rough hands. He pulled out the bottle, handed it to me then sat down by the desk, breathing heavily.

I looked at the label and recognised the writing of Harold Dunlop, a pharmacist long past retiring age who had a shop on the outskirts of Overton. His shop window was quite unlike any other chemist's in the district, for he despised the commercial diversity practised by his colleagues and seemed only to make a living from his dispensing fees. Not for him the glittering display of deodorants, after-shave and thermos-flasks – his window contained only a few shapely winchesters of coloured fluid, a tin or two of Slippery Elm – and a couple of hernia supports straddling a display of corn-plasters. The dispensary at the rear was a dusty tip of a place with a large, centrally placed oak table on which, among the coffee-stains and overflowing ash-trays, he lovingly mixed his various creams, pastes and lotions and counted his tablets one by one like a bank cashier counting coins. Ready made-up commercial preparations, electronic tablet counters and the like were to him a sign of professional decadence, as were pre-formed 5ml plastic teaspoons and smooth metric screw-top bottles from which you could not pour out a damn thing without it dribbling down the side of the bottle, your arm or your shirt

41

front. In fact his pride and joy was a large stock of pre-metric bottles and corks which he maintained in pristine condition in a sealed cupboard, as if waiting for a renaissance – a return to a time more suited to his obsessional, quirky skills. Many years ago his handwriting had reflected his personality, but his ageing arteries were having a subtle effect on his co-ordination, so that his once ornate copper-plate was slowly deteriorating into a spiky, eccentric scrawl which could now only be read with difficulty.

I looked at the label. "It says – take two on retiring, Mr Norton." I had to smile. Only Harold Dunlop would have written "on retiring".

Jack Norton took the bottle, looking perplexed. He stared at the label a moment, then looked up. "Well, I can't see how that's going to do me much good at the moment," he said. "How do you know they'll keep that long?"

"What do you mean, Mr Norton?"

"Well, what I'm thinking is – I'm only sixty-one. It'll be four years before I retire, tha knows."

He laughed in a friendly, self-effacing way when I explained that it was Harold Dunlop's quaint way of instructing him to take the tablets at bed-time.

"Anyway, I don't think I'll need them much longer. It's only since I got out of hospital —"

"Oh yes, I'd forgotten about that," I said, glancing quickly at his notes. He had had a hernia repair nearly four weeks ago. I reached for a sick note.

"You'll need this for a couple of weeks longer with your job. All that lifting," I muttered as I wrote out his note. He sighed.

"Aye, that's another thing I want to ask, doctor, if you don't mind."

"Hm. What's that?"

"Well, you know I was supposed to be under Mr Littleton for me operation? Mind you I never clapped eyes on him the whole of the time I was in. Probably too busy buttering up his private patients to bother with the likes of me. Any road, when I was being discharged, there was a doctor Dindiraji or something who had me a bit puzzled by what he said." He hesitated and looked embarrassed.

"Go on."

"Well – don't get me wrong, doctor, because he was a clever

young bloke – everybody spoke highly of him. It's just that we couldn't tell what he said half the time. But I did hear him say I'd have to be off work sixty-eight weeks after my operation. Sixty-eight weeks! That can't be right, surely?"

"Six *to* eight weeks, Mr Norton," I said. "Six *to* eight weeks."

"Ah, I thought there were something not right."

He slapped his knee and threw back his head, letting rip a shout of laughter which, within the confines of the small room, was like a grenade exploding in my ears. Within seconds the laughter disintegrated into a rasping, crackling spasm of coughing, convulsing his whole body and turning his face bright red. It was a characteristic sequence of events which, in this bronchitic part of the country, made a well-filled concert hall or theatre sound more like a sanatorium than an auditorium.

I looked at him with alarm as he suddenly let out a cry of pain. He grabbed his lower abdomen and slid off the chair onto his knees, gasping and coughing and catching his breath with pain each time he coughed.

"Oh, Christ!" he whimpered. "That's . . . done it."

He slumped forward onto his left arm. I jumped up from my chair, catching my right ear on the book shelf. The stinging pain involuntarily brought tears to my eyes and as I bent down to help him I felt a warm trickle of blood run across my temple and into my right eye. Half blinded, I tried to help him up but he winced and groaned with pain.

"Me stitches . . . have . . . burst!"

He squeezed the words out from the back of his throat and rolled over onto his side, shaking with pain and apprehension and clutching the clothing over his groin as if he had trapped a live ferret down his trousers.

"That's impossible," I said. I quickly wiped the blood from my eye and tried to pick him up, but realised right away that it would need a block and tackle to move him. I began to sweat with panic when my efforts to get him on his feet produced more cries of anguish and I stumbled over him to the door to get help, just as Christine opened it. The edge of the door hit me just above my right eye. I reeled back, clutching a blood-smeared hand to my blood-streaked face and she fainted silently and abruptly in the doorway. I watched her with a

43

detached fascination as her body and limbs crumpled like a marionette whose strings had been severed, realising that this shambles was quite beyond the control of mortal beings. In spite of my discomfort I began to shake with silent laughter, before pulling myself together and getting the help of a couple of patients, together with Ann, our other receptionist, to lay her out in the corridor. When she showed signs of rapid recovery I signalled to Ann that I would explain later. I went back and tried to inspect Jack Norton. After a brief struggle I managed to separate sufficient clothing from his rigor mortis-like grasp to see the extent of the problem. Beneath his well-healed skin scar was a hard, painful lump the size of a golf-ball. I attempted to manipulate it but it was hopeless. Not only had his hernia recurred – it was also irreducible.

"I'm sorry, Jack," I said. "You're absolutely right. You've not only got your hernia back but it's stuck fast as well."

"What's that mean?" he groaned. "Not another operation, I hope."

"Afraid so. I'll have to get you in right away." My sympathy mingled with growing consternation at the thought of having him lie there waiting for the ambulance while the waiting room silently filled to bursting point. There was not much I could do: he couldn't move, I couldn't move him and there wasn't a spare room in the place in which to put him.

I rang the hospital to arrange his admission, rang the ambulance station to arrange his transport. After a few futile attempts to persuade him to climb onto the examination couch, I sat down, gingerly exploring my right ear for the first time. There appeared to be a small laceration somewhere in the region of where the top end joined my head. The blood had dried leaving a tacky, matted mess at the hair line.

"I'm sorry about this, doctor," the patient groaned, looking up at me.

"Not your fault, Jack," I mumbled, swabbing off the dried blood from the corner of my eye. "Just one of those things," I added automatically. I couldn't make up my mind which hurt most – my eye, my ear or my leg which had started to throb from the dog bite I had sustained last night.

Minutes later the ambulance drew up outside the surgery and the two-man crew, with hardly a word but with a chilling, casual efficiency, bundled him unceremoniously into the waiting vehicle. I quickly checked to see that Christine had fully recovered and found her to be more or less back to normal, if a little subdued and embarrassed by what had happened earlier.

The first patient I saw, once I had started my surgery, took one look at my bruised eye and swollen ear and laughed. "You should go and see a doctor," he said, without a hint of malice. The next three patients said the same thing and by the time the fourth came in the joke was wearing pretty thin – so much so that I had a fleeting urge to hit him over the head with my sphygmomanometer at the mention of it, stopping myself at the thought of Hippocrates swivelling his eyes up to Heaven and spinning in his grave somewhere. Plus the fact that several ounces of mercury from the sphygmomanometer, blobbing and scattering their way into every inaccessible corner of the room, would have caused havoc and prevented me from taking anyone's blood pressure for days until I got a replacement. I wasn't sure what it was that made patients react in this way, but they always did so whenever one of us crawled into the surgery with a bad cold, a limp or the occasional hangover. Some patients cracked the joke in a tentative, exploratory manner, as if uncertain how we would react to being thought of as members of the same species as themselves, susceptible to the same hazards. Others clearly drew enormous comfort and reassurance from such a situation, seeing in it something intrinsically, inexplicably funny: it buffered their own sense of vulnerability in the face of the uncertainties of day-to-day existence. Either way, the joke was no more inane than the way we doctors often mumbled, "Just one of those things," or, "there's a lot of it about," because we could not or would not explain a problem that a patient had presented to us. Both sides were, I suppose, unconsciously taking refuge behind comfortable clichés, avoiding the possibility of exploring the minefield of feelings which lay between.

Nearly two hours later I came to the last record card on the desk: Nasir Patel. Mr Patel was a new patient and, as far as I could gather, had not been in this country long. He had been to see me last week and again yesterday with what sounded like indigestion, but his English was so rudimentary that eliciting his symptoms had been almost impossible. He came in and now stood by the desk, a small thin man wearing a heavy dark overcoat two sizes too big and wide flannel trousers which

45

flapped three or four inches above his ankle-joint. Tucked tightly under one arm was a brown paper parcel. With his free arm he gesticulated nervously, rubbing his abdomen and shaking his head from side to side.

"Badjeet," he said earnestly. "Redjeet, too much redjeet. All day redjeet, badjeet."

It was exactly the same story as yesterday and the week before. I wondered what these words meant. Urdu for wind, pain or what? I nodded and spoke to the patient slowly in a very loud voice as though the man were deaf. It was an automatic response when confronted with patients with a language problem, an idiotic and futile pantomime.

"Is the medicine not helping?"

Mr Patel frowned and shrugged but said nothing.

"The medicine. Isn't it helping?" I said, twice as loud.

"Medicine, please." The patient pointed to a prescription pad on the desk.

"I gave you medicine yesterday."

"Medicine, yes. No good – more redjeet, too much redjeet, badjeet."

I was just as baffled as before. I stood up with the intention of giving him another examination, hoping vainly that by doing so I might gather a clue to what was going on, but I was interrupted by a knock on the door. In walked a dapper-looking Asian with twinkling, humorous eyes and a thick, neatly-trimmed moustache. He smiled, clasped his hands together and cocked his head apologetically to one side.

"I am sorry for coming in late – it was my intention to accompany Mr Patel from the beginning but I was asked to move my car since it was causing an obstruction," he said with immaculate diction. He nodded to the patient. "I have come with my good friend Mr Patel in order to help him."

"I think we both need help," I replied, smiling with relief.

"Quite so. The thing is . . . I believe he has something to show you that I think you will find of great interest." He nodded to Mr Patel and rattled off a few words at him, presumably in Urdu. Mr Patel, who was looking grey and drawn, took the parcel from under his arm and began to unwrap it. He took out a catering-size tin of Nescafé and prised open the lid.

"Redjeet! Badjeet! All time too much redjeet!" he said in an

46

anxious voice, pointing inside the tin. He pushed it in front of my face. When I looked inside I recoiled so fast that I nearly fell over the back of my chair, for the tin was more than half-full of heavily blood-stained faeces. Redjeet, badjeet – of course. The penny had finally dropped.

Feeling rather sheepish, I examined Mr Patel again. The unfortunate man was obviously quite ill by now. He looked anaemic and his pulse was over one hundred per minute. He must have lost an awful lot of blood – presumably from a duodenal ulcer – during the time that he had been trying to tell me what was wrong. I arranged his admission to hospital immediately and while I wrote out the letter Mr Patel gloomily muttered a few phrases to his friend who nodded gravely. I didn't dare ask for a translation. I thought it would probably be something like: "God Almighty, these bloody British doctors are all the same. Thick. Don't understand simple English. They talk in a loud slow voice as if you're stupid and even then you can't understand a word they're saying. You've got to be half-dead before they realise that there's something wrong with you!"

I escorted them both out to a waiting car more out of guilt than out of courtesy. As Mr Patel got into the back seat his friend smiled and shook my hand.

"Thank you, doctor. There is absolutely no need to feel guilty, for I can assure you that I fully understand how difficult it is with these patients who don't speak English. I have a brother who is a doctor in the UK. He is a casualty officer at the Halifax Royal Infirmary and he is having a very bad time. Before that, he was in Glasgow and, oh dear, I do not think he understood a single word any of his patients said for the whole six months he was there. Now, for you, your foot is in the other shoe, isn't it?"

I stuck my hands in my pockets. "That's about it, yes. Now I should get him to the hospital right away and he'll be OK – no thanks to me," I said. "I bet he's not feeling too friendly towards me after this. I can't say I blame him."

Patel's friend roared with laughter and climbed into the car. "Well," he said, "he just told me in there that it's always the same with these bloody foreign doctors! Nothing personal of course." He laughed again and drove off slowly. Mr Patel turned round and fixed his dark watery eyes on me with a cold glare until the car turned the corner at the end of the street. The accusing after-image of the little man's face, framed by the rear window of the car, remained as I stared down the empty street for a few minutes, reflecting on what a close call that had been.

I don't know how long I had been standing there before I became aware that someone was standing beside me.

"He has, hasn't he?" I heard a voice say. I turned and looked at a small middle-aged woman whom I recognised immediately as Jack Norton's wife Alice. She had an empty shopping bag slung over her arm and clutched a purse as thick as a family Bible.

"I'm sorry, I was just —"

"Jack. He's been in this morning? He was supposed to have come to see you first thing this morning to sort out a prescription."

The skin prickled on my scalp as I realised that I had forgotten to contact her to tell her what had happened to Jack.

"He was supposed to meet me to do the shopping when he'd got that sorted out. I've been stood outside the post-office for above an hour," she said.

"Come inside, Mrs Norton. I'll explain what's happened."

She looked at me quizzically but said nothing more as I took her to my room and sat her down.

"I'm sorry, Mrs Norton. I meant to get in touch —"

"What have you done to him? There's something not right. I can tell —"

"Hang on a minute, Mrs Norton. Jack came in about his tablets as he said he was going to do, only . . . while we were talking he had a bad bout of coughing and burst his stitches —"

"Oh my God!" she put her hand over her mouth and went quite pale.

"He's all right, though. His hernia came out again and got stuck so I had to send him in again. They'll be able to put it right soon enough."

I had little doubt that these words were more reassuring to me than they were to the patient's wife. She rested her elbow on the desk and put her hand over her eyes.

"I wish you could have let me know. That's the last thing we need. Why didn't you —"

"I'm sorry, Mrs Norton. It all happened so fast and I had a surgery full of —"

"Oh I know all that," she said with a mixture of irritation and apology. "It's just . . . the last thing I needed. The final straw." She sniffed and turned her head away.

"The final straw?" I asked. She took a small crumpled paper tissue out of her coat pocket and wiped her nose.

"It's everything at the moment. When I think of this summer and all the plans we had . . ."

She began to cry silently and turned herself further in the chair as if she did not want to share her difficulties with anyone. I remained silent for a few seconds. She blew her nose and turned towards me again.

"I bet you think I'm a fool. We've got Peter coming home next month for Christmas leave – he's been out in Saudi for the past eighteen months and he's saved his leave for spending with us this Christmas and we'd planned to give him a right good do, like."

"Why not?"

"I'll tell you why not. I've just been made redundant, for a start. And at Jack's place it's become very difficult. They were very funny with him when he went into hospital in the first place, with what he's got, his hernia and that. He's got a very heavy job, you know."

"Hasn't he applied for a —"

"Oh I know what you're going to say – has he asked for a lighter job? No chance. Everyone wants one of those and they're as rare as hen's teeth, where he works. I just know what's going to happen now." Her eyes filled again.

"What's that, Mrs Norton?"

"You don't know what they're like at Johnson's. Any excuse they can find to make you redundant. Makes no difference how long you've worked there – soon as there's any trouble with your health you're down the road as far as they're concerned."

"Mm. If that's true, what will that mean for you both?"

She blew her nose again. "We'll be in queer street. That's what it'll mean. We're having the house decorated from top to bottom and buying new furniture for when Peter comes home. Went without a holiday this year to pay for that and if there's no proper money coming in I don't know what we'll do. Won't be much of a Christmas now, I shouldn't think." She stood up slowly. "I'm sorry to take your time up telling you all this, doctor. I hope I haven't delayed you."

49

"That's OK. By the way, I'd better let you know which ward he's on." I scribbled the ward number on a piece of paper and gave it to her. "Let me know when he gets home and I'll come and see you. Things may not be as bad as they seem."

"Happen not. We'll see."

Mrs Norton thanked me and went out, leaving me with the sinking feeling that she was probably right about Jack losing his job. In Overton, where many new industries had sprung up all over the place in the past couple of years, some of the more traditional establishments – especially heavy engineering – had slumbered obliviously on and were now waking up too late to the fact that they were still doggedly making things which no one seemed to want. Jack Norton looked like joining the growing number of men who wandered in and out of the pubs or the betting shop during the day, or who awkwardly clutched shopping lists and string bags as they walked slowly through the town centre, staring at their shoes and knowing that they shrank a little with each step.

4

The sound of a telephone ringing two feet away from your head at three o'clock in the morning is not an amusing experience. The shock was even worse because I was not on call. I buried my head in the pillow and blindly fumbled for the receiver, feeling the sound producing shock waves through my brain like a knife plunging into aspic.

"Dr Rushton? Dr Steven Rushton?"

I became instantly wide awake. The voice had a clear, North American accent. So clear, in fact, that for a moment I thought it might be a colleague playing a practical joke in poor taste. But the hum and ping of thousands of miles of telephone cable told me that it was not a joke.

"Harry Heisenberg, Seal River. We got your letter this morning."

"Seal River, Manitoba?" I asked, and nearly burst out laughing at my own dim response.

"There's only one Seal River, my friend. Now, we got your letter . . ."

Tanya was awake, too, by now. She rolled against me and grunted quizzically. I reached out, attempting to put my finger on her lips, but managed to stick my thumb in her eye and in the process lost track of the voice from Seal River.

". . . coupla things we wanted to clarify from what you said in your letter." He asked a lot of questions about my entire curriculum vitae and I attempted to answer them as accurately and concisely as I could. My mouth was on automatic pilot.

"That's good. That's fine. Very interesting . . ." He seemed to have all the time in the world. The call must have cost a fortune. "Now you say that you have done some surgery and accident and emergency work – is that right?"

"A couple of years ago . . ."

"Fine. You any good at stitching knife-wounds?"

51

"Knife-wounds? I can't say it was a particular speciality of mine but I have done plenty of stitching. Why?"

There was a barking laugh at the other end. "Well, why, in Seal River we have a big mining community, mostly Indians, come down from the hills weekends with their pockets full of money, get a few beers inside them and we have plenty of arguments, knifings – that kinda thing. Think you could handle that, doctor?"

"Uh-huh. I was going to ask —"

"Right, sure. You want to know something about us. Okay . . . well now – let me share with you some of the things we have to offer in our practice and our little community . . ."

My heart sank. People who started off sentences like this were invariably the harbingers of doom.

"Our office is in the town where we have about four thousand patients, but then of course we have another office fifty miles down the road in Lead Hills. Here, why, the catchment is maybe some eight thousand more patients, miners and timber men, over an area of approximately a thousand square miles or so."

"Did you say a thousand?"

"That's right. Hell, Canada is a big country, doctor. But we have good highways and fast cars. Our post-graduate centre and main hospital is three hundred miles or so down the main highway in Winnipeg, and of course there are two flights a week, so we're not exactly isolated when the weather's right."

"The weather? What about the weather?"

He laughed. "You like snow, doctor? We have snow maybe three or four months during the winter period. Now I know what you're going to say, but don't worry. Even though it's thirty below you don't feel it, believe me."

"You don't feel it? At thirty below?"

"No, sir. What you have to appreciate is that you're used to high humidity and all that stuff. We don't have that over here. And all our homes and vehicles are properly equipped, so you don't really notice the mercury level. You got kids, you said."

"Three. Boys."

"Aw, hell, they'll love it here. It's a great outdoor way of life even in the winter months."

"Three or four months is a long winter."

52

"Oh sure, but there is plenty to do. Curling and ice fishing, for example."

"Curling and ice fishing," I said in a dazed voice. I began to wonder whether I was dreaming again.

"Why, that's right. One sport we get from the Scots and the other I guess we get from the Eskimos. Well—what do you think? Think you may be interested? Let me tell you that you sound to us like the kind of guy we're looking for."

There was something in his voice which reminded me of a dentist's confident assurance before applying the drill. My body tensed up with the realisation that I was being drawn into making a momentous decision, and the extent of the commitment began to send the blood pounding in my ears.

"From what you have said so far, er, it's given me something to think about. I think I need —"

"More information, right? Sure, I appreciate that. Tell you what I'll do. I'll send a letter giving you a complete profile of the job, the environment and so on. And my wife will write, too, to give her side of things. Your wife will find this helpful, I'm sure."

"That's very kind of you —"

"Hell, no. Not at all, doctor. You'll hear from us soon, I assure you. Keep in touch."

I replaced the receiver and rolled over onto my back.

"What was all that about?" Tanya asked. I stared straight ahead and the darkness between my head and the ceiling pressed gently down onto my eyes.

"Someone wanting me to join their practice in Canada," I said. It struck me then that since I had written the letter over a week ago I had not seriously expected a response and I had not mentioned it before. I felt guilty and foolish.

"Oh. Is that all?" Tanya said. She laughed. "Thank goodness it was nothing important."

"I'm sorry. I meant to tell you. I wrote to this place over a week ago – just on the spur of the moment, as a matter of fact."

"That's a hell of a thing to do on the spur of the moment. Who were you speaking to?"

"Doctor Harry Heisenberg, from Seal River, Manitoba."

Saying it out loud in the darkness made it sound more unreal than it sounded over the transatlantic cable a few minutes ago.

I began to outline the conversation. Tanya propped herself up on one elbow.

"What was all that about curling and ice fishing?"

When I told her she fell back, laughing. I got a fleeting mental image of someone huddled over a small hole on an endless frozen lake and I began to laugh as well.

"And while you're doing all this, just think of me having the time of my life salting legs of moose or drying out beaver pelts over the stove. Oh, Christ!" She burst into a peal of laughter which shook the whole bed and it was several minutes before either of us could get our breath back.

"It sounded very different from what I imagined it would be," I said. Tanya turned towards me and, when she spoke, the laughter had gone from her voice.

"Are you going to tell me what it really *is* about? You don't write letters applying to a practice thousands of miles away for no reason," she said. "Aren't you happy in Overton?"

"Yes . . . most of the time, anyway. I mean, it's not the patients – and of course Ian and Molly are great to work with. I don't know, really. It's difficult to put my finger on it. It's . . . it's something to do with not being able to get things done the way they should be done. I mean – take this old duck I saw today, for example. She'd got a bit of heart failure, a bit of bronchitis. That's what had taken her off her feet. Medically simple. What she needed was rest in bed and the right medication and she'd be OK in a few days. She lives on her own in that new estate, her only relative is a sister a hundred miles away, neighbours out at work all day long. In other words, no one to see to her basic needs. So the result is that I have to send her into hospital to have the same simple care. The only problem is that now she's surrounded by all that unnecessary expertise and high technology which is costing a fortune a minute, being looked after by strangers."

"So what's the answer?" murmured Tanya.

"If we had the facilities of a GP hospital with a few nurses and minimum equipment, we could look after her ourselves at a fraction of the cost. It *is* within our capability, you know."

"Why don't you campaign for a GP hospital, then?"

"Oh, God, that's the trouble. You know what it's been like getting the health centre built. What chance have we of bringing about a major policy upheaval like getting a

54

community hospital? The other thing is that a lot of the knowledge and skill – such as it is – which seemed to take decades to learn, is simply not being used. It's rotting amid a pile of administrative clap-trap."

Tanya grunted. "Forget some old skills, learn some new ones."

"Maybe. But I'm supposed to be a doctor, not an administrator or a politician. I just thought that Canada might be an opportunity to practise real medicine, whatever that means."

"It sounds to me," said Tanya softly, "like an infatuation with an idea. The promise of greener grass. And it's a long way from home . . . for all of us."

I turned to look at her. A thin slit of orange light sliced across her face from a small gap in the curtains. As she blinked, I could see a shimmering reservoir of moisture at the rim of her lower lids. She closed her eyes. I put my arm round her and buried my face against hers, feeling a warm tear which rolled down her cheek into the ravine of skin between us.

5

Gaynor Peel came home from Wishton the following week and I went to see her. Neither she nor the baby appeared to have suffered the slightest ill-effect from the premature delivery in the ambulance – in fact she was so happily immersed in her role as mother of a newborn baby that the question of her continuing her course at drama college did not arise. I gathered that the father of the child was a freelance journalist who at that moment was in Poland doing a story on the economic decline of the Eastern bloc. She seemed completely unperturbed by the fact that she had no idea when he would be back, but was going ahead with her plans to return to their Bayswater flat in the next week or so. Doris Peel's silent anguish indicated that the matter had been thoroughly discussed and that Gaynor was going to do what she pleased, whatever she or Neville said. Even so, it was clear that in spite of her obvious disappointment and apprehension, she had been busying herself in all sorts of practical ways to help her daughter since the baby had arrived, partly no doubt to take her mind off the visible deterioration in Neville Peel's physical and mental state, which had taken place as a result of the shock. In the half-hour or so that I was at the house he never uttered a word, but simply wandered around tapping his chin with a small screwdriver, his eyes staring straight ahead and his mouth half-open with his tongue resting against the back of his lower lip. His brain had slipped into neutral. He looked as if he was searching for something but somehow couldn't quite remember what it was.

Molly arrived back from her holidays that week, looking tanned and healthy. After giving us all a memorable account of the hazards and side effects of eating and travelling in North Africa, she launched into her work with enthusiasm and a ferocious energy which, by comparison, made Ian and me appear physically disabled. Her return coincided with a sudden increase in the workload caused by an outburst of measles in

56

the district, and I was glad that this extra work could be shared amongst the three of us, now that she was back. At the same time that the measles epidemic broke – as if this wasn't enough to contend with – there were a number of children of school age who presented with mysterious blemishes which were definitely not measles but whose precise diagnosis remained a mystery. Spots and rashes appeared all over the place. The saving grace was that they all got better with no treatment at all. Our negative reassurance that these particular cases were not measles, whatever else they might be, for some unaccountable reason gave parents more comfort than if we had actually put a name to it. Which was just as well, because we really hadn't got the faintest idea what was going on: we just had to be doubly careful, doubly watchful with them, simply because they did not fit into one of the familiar categories. Once we had seen the natural history of the first few cases take a benign course from start to finish, we could then relax a little as we were able to predict with more accuracy and confidence the subsequent course of the later ones that we saw. A famous scientist once said that biologists worked amongst uncertainty and bewilderment, and that life was complex, messy and richly variable. He might well have been talking about doctors and their diagnoses.

At the end of that hectic week, we decided that we would see how the health centre was progressing. After morning surgery on the Friday, Ian and I set off walking to the site which was barely half a mile away. Molly was out visiting patients that morning and we had arranged to meet her there.

For a few minutes we walked in silence. The mixture of old and new exteriors of the banks and shops which lined the four roads intersecting the busy town centre, were reduced to a dreary monochrome in the grey, damp drizzle. I wasn't sure why we had decided to make this visit; over the past four months it seemed to have become a ritual, like a visit to Mecca, but no doubt with far less purpose. Even so, every four or five weeks we would wander over to get mud on our shoes and cement dust up our noses, to come away more despondent than the time before at the apparent lack of progress towards completion.

Ian wrinkled his nose and sniffed. "Why are we walking there I wonder?" he muttered.

"I've no idea, Ian. I seem to remember that you suggested it. Good for the circulation, I think you said."

"Hmm, yes, I think you're right. Good for the circulation but bad for the bones in this weather. But you've no need to worry about either of those problems at your age. God, I'd give my eye teeth to be at your stage again."

"Chronologically or medically?" I said. I stepped sideways to avoid a mud-filled puddle in the uneven pavement and almost collided with a woman pushing a large pram.

"Chronologically, of course," said Ian when I had caught up with him again. "I mean . . . ideally it would be nice to know what I know now but have the youth and energy to go with it. That's why in a way I envy you and Molly."

"Really?"

He didn't answer right away, but stopped when we reached the traffic lights at the town centre. He put his hands in his pockets and gazed for some time down Hiley Road, wincing at the rumble of heavy traffic which trundled incessantly across the junction of the four major roads.

"When I came here nearly forty years ago things were a hell of a sight different."

"Less traffic for one thing," I said, raising my voice above the bellow of a heavy truck which drew away from the lights in low gear.

"Aye, that's right enough. Less people, too."

We crossed over and walked down Hiley Road, threading our way through mid-day shoppers until we had walked beyond the main commercial centre. Ian pointed his finger across my line of vision. "Of course, you realise that not all the changes have been bad, especially when you look at that lot over there," he said grimly. I looked over the slate roofs of the houses and shops and saw the dark, still outlines of the immense factories, mills and warehouses which now stood for the most part cold and silent, their windows grey and opaque like a corpse's stare, only transmitting the cavernous emptiness which lay within the upper floors. Above everything else towered the slim, tall chimney stacks with soot-stained tops and white capitals each ten feet high which spelled vertically their names: Trojan, Ajax, Chief.

"Half the working population in this town seemed to be employed at these places at one time, which no doubt was the major contribution to the prosperity of the whole area. No problem about unemployment in those days."

"At a price," I said.

"Maybe. But that was a long time ago. The town is pretty clean now – you wouldn't know what it was like before —"

"Hang on a bit, Ian – it was only in the fifties that the industrial revolution ground to a halt round here. That's about the time when all three factories stopped spewing all their muck and filth into the lungs of the local populace – and what's more I've had my fair share of it. There were times, going to school in winter, when you needed a white stick to find out where you were going, and you could take a knife and fork to the air you were intended to breathe."

I glanced to my right, down a narrow asphalt path. The memory of it came rushing back. At the end of the path a group of pollarded Manchester poplars partially obscured the decaying brickwork of the Victor Ruskin primary school which I had attended thirty years before. I could taste the sulphurous, acrid air in my throat again and smell the burning wool fibre and rubber as if it had never gone away. I remembered the morning assemblies: in winter the strains of 'Gentle Jesus, meek and mild' were drowned by an endless chorus of harsh coughing from infant lungs, in spite of the fortissimo playing of Miss Gertrude Frindell who hunched over the piano-keys like a vulture, her thin frame as dry and dusty as the piano itself.

"Yes, of course. I'd forgotten that you were brought up here," said Ian. "Anyway, there have been a lot of changes, as you'll know – and many of them are good ones, too. Come to think of it, I suppose that we were too busy looking after individuals to notice that everyone around was getting healthier through none of our doing, really. Better food, better housing, cleaner air and so forth. I feel, in a way, that we didn't involve ourselves too much about that sort of thing, then. That's why I think that you'll benefit a great deal from working in a proper purpose-built place like this health centre."

"What d'you mean, 'you'? Don't you mean 'we'?"

"Well, I'm not going to carry on for much longer once we've moved in. You and Molly are going to be the ones to take this business by the scruff of the neck and practise medicine in a place which will give you room to move and think. I'm sure

59

you'll be wanting to use all the latest innovations. Computers, maybe."

I laughed. "I'll be glad to move into a place where I'm not in danger of fracturing my skull every time I stand up. Or go for a pee without having to fight my way through the waiting room."

"Hmm. I know what you mean. Still, there's light at the end of the tunnel, as they say. And you've got a lot of travelling to do once we're out of it. I have the feeling that it'll be an interesting journey if you use the opportunity. Come away, we can cross here."

He turned abruptly, and strode ahead across the main road. It was a clear signal that he didn't want to talk any more. He loved what he did and his patients loved him for it, and I had learned to detect in his Highland accent a brusquer, more severe tone when he wanted to push away from himself an unpalatable truth. On this occasion it was the thought of his retirement, of giving up the work that he loved, knowing that he would lose something but not knowing how lost he might become.

We walked across some wasteland then onto an open, grassed area on which the health centre was being built. The few clusters of slender silver birch which had once stood here had been sawn down, although they had in no way interfered with the limits of the building and its planned car park. This, together with the windowless building and the timber skeleton of its roof, the scattered assortment of vehicles axle-deep in mud, mounds of earth and debris all over the place, reminded me of one of those photographs taken in Northern France shortly after D-Day. As we approached, I could hear the syncopated patter of a generator motor coming from the other side of the building, and from within came the sound of hammering and whistling, interrupted by an occasional cadenza of obscenities. Molly suddenly appeared in the main entrance. A small gust of wind disturbed cement dust round her feet and blew her long hair across her face.

"Hello there! I thought you weren't coming," she said cheerfully, disentangling a few strands of hair from the hinge of her glasses. "What d'you think?"

We stepped inside and wandered aimlessly about. "What do I think?" I said. I took a deep breath. "Much the same as

60

before. I can't see much change since the last time we were here. Looks as if it'll take years to complete."

Ian sneezed. "Damn! It's the lime in the cement," he said, blowing his nose. "It's amazing, really, how long it seems to take to build a place like this, when you consider that Matco built their supermarket from scratch and had it operating within nine months."

Before any of us could think of anything to say a voice boomed out of the gloom of a doorway somewhere behind us.

"How do. You the doctors as were here a few weeks ago?"

We turned and saw a squat figure in what looked like a fluorescent life-jacket which clutched his short neck and was buttoned tightly down to his wellington boots. "You weren't thinking of buying this place, were you?" he said cheerfully.

"No. We're only leasing part of the —"

"Thank Christ for that. Made a wise move there. What do you think of the floor, by the way?" He jumped up and down a few times. Ian waved his toe from side to side in the dust and all three of us stared at the floor as if it might reveal a hidden message.

"Seems solid enough to me," Ian said thoughtfully.

The man laughed. "Solid! Bloody right there, squire. Under that composition is eight bloody inches of concrete." He sniffed and lit a cigarette. "Pity half of it's got to come up tomorrow. Load more cable to go under that lot which we weren't told about. Architects? Wouldn't pay 'em in brass washers. Eric!" He spat noisily into the dust, then turned his head back through the passageway behind him. "Eric – are you there?"

"Hallooo . . . !"

"Have you seen the time? You'd best get your skates on if you want to put one on for the two-thirty at Doncaster. It'll be dinner time in half an hour. Don't want to be doing that in your own time, do you?"

"Right-o, Clem."

Ian cleared his throat. "I don't suppose you have any idea when the building will be ready? We were hoping to move in after this Christmas."

"*This* Christmas? You must be joking, squire. Somebody's been pulling your leg. *Next* Christmas'll be more like it."

He turned and walked away, singing 'O Sole Mio' in the

grossly exaggerated sobbing style beloved of pub entertainers everywhere.

The three of us exchanged a few desultory comments as we left the building. It was all part of the gloomy ritual, so that when the rain came down harder and we climbed into Molly's car, there was nothing else to say. As we drove back, the silence was broken only by the nyoing-nyoing of the windscreen wipers and the drumming of the rain on the car roof.

After doing a couple of home visits I decided to go to Wishton to see how Jack Norton and Nasir Patel were progressing. I enjoyed the occasional hospital visit to see one of my own patients – not only from the point of view of the clinical interest but mainly because the patients appeared to get a kick out of seeing a familiar face in such unfamiliar surroundings. The pleasure and gratitude they showed often seemed out of all proportion to my own efforts, but I guessed that this was partly because patients underwent a profound change of status when hospitalised: in the community they were (for the most part) vertical, ambulant and assertive, whereas in hospital they were horizontal, immobile and submissive. A visit to the bedside by the hospital medical staff, who had taken over the patient's insides, was the result of the patient being *where* he was; a visit by a doctor from outside the hospital – his own GP – was the result of the patient being *who* he was, and for those few minutes his individuality was returned to him. At the same time, I needed to do something constructive in the next hour or two to wipe out the feeling of frustration and foreboding which I always felt after one of our periodic visits to the health centre. It wasn't that I did not look forward to moving in – it was the nagging thought that the price of escaping from our present unsatisfactory building into first-class accommodation might turn out too high in terms of our own independence and individuality; it seemed to me that in our new surroundings we would have to become a different breed of doctor, to learn unfamiliar skills, in order to come to terms with the fact that our effectiveness as doctors might be at the mercy of an itinerant plumber, or thwarted by a committee from the various authorities whose main function was to apply a soothing poultice to our throbbing impatience.

Wishton was about seven miles north of Overton, lying at the foot of the Pennines which separated it from South

62

Yorkshire. The Romans had at one time trundled peat and stone down these hills, now obscured by the rain, into the basin which today was filled by the sprawling conurbation of Greater Manchester. I wondered what they would have thought of it now. As I drove near to the town centre, a huge sign on my right announced the opening of a new trading estate on the other side of the town, with prefabricated industrial units ready for instant occupation: it was like a smile to hide the tears, for behind the hoarding lay a desolate waste-land of disused cotton-mills and warehouses, overgrown railway sidings and sagging sheds, round which flowed the brown filth of the river Dane, as blind and indifferent as a worm.

Like the towns which it served, Wishton General Hospital was a cramped, messy hotch-potch of structures in varying stages of decay and regeneration. It was like some primitive life-form: when one part had been amputated, it grew another part somewhere else, with a brainless facility which had more to do with survival than either purpose or function. But it was something more than that – and this only struck me for the first time as I squeezed my car near to the main entrance: the whole untidy collection of buildings, while reflecting the social and economic history of the region, also demonstrated the enormous change in medical care over the same period of time. At the far side was the sombre black stone of the original work-house, built in the early part of the nineteenth century, which now, by a quirk of fate, housed the department of geriatrics; the main building, built of Accrington brick at the turn of the century, housed the main medical block; the grey monolith adjacent was the high-rise of the midwifery block which had sprung up fifteen years too late in response to the post-war baby boom, but which now stood with its half-empty wards – a monument to contraception; and finally, the vast scatter of newly-built, rectangular blocks housing the resident medical staff, the laboratories, diagnostic equipment and, of course, the administrative staff. The changes which had occurred in the ten years since I first began as a houseman here were truly breathtaking, but it was an odd thing that, while the place was now bristling with personnel and high technology, the number of patients that the hospital had in its beds remained precisely the same as it had been ten years before. Which made me wonder whose needs were being satisfied by all this growth.

63

The male surgical ward was up on the top corridor of the main building, and before going in to see my two patients I had a quick look through the case notes in the ward-sister's office. Mr Patel had required four pints of blood to get him into shape for surgery – a fact which made me feel uncomfortable; had I continued to be so slow-witted in gathering what he was actually complaining of, he would have been fit for nothing. Jack Norton had had further surgery on his hernia and would be discharged in a few days.

Nasir Patel lay in his bed, his dark eyes morosely following the shuffling movements of the stooping post-operative patients as they aimlessly made their way backwards and forwards across the polished floor. When he saw me approach his bed, his eyes widened with apprehension rather than surprise, and he quickly pulled the sheets up under his nose. I made some encouraging noises about how well he was doing, but his only response was to swivel his eyes pleadingly towards the office, as if he wanted to be rescued. Under the circumstances this was hardly surprising. I decided that further attempts at cementing the doctor-patient relationship would be cosmetic rather than reparative, so I gave up.

At the far end of the ward I saw Jack Norton lying on top of his bed in a faded tartan dressing-gown, reading the daily paper which he held above his head with outstretched arms. When he saw me approach, he folded up his paper and gingerly rolled sideways until he had manoeuvred himself into a sitting position on the edge of the bed. We shook hands.

"Don't go cracking any of yer jokes, doctor, for Christ's sake. I couldn't go through all that again. Any road, this is a nice surprise. Didn't expect to see you up here."

"Uh-huh. How are you doing?"

"Oh . . . healing up a treat. No problem that way at all." He lowered his eyes and stared down at his huge feet.

"No problem . . . that way?" I said.

He glanced up at me quickly and smiled, but the muscles of his round, generous face twitched with the effort. "Well, you know how it is, these days," he muttered.

"The job?"

"Aye. Up the Swanee. Would you like a grape, doctor?" He reached forward and took a large plastic dish off the top of his locker. I shook my head.

64

"No thanks. How —?"

"Can't say I care for 'em myself, either. Pips get behind my dentures. Besides, I'd probably choke on this particular lot, being as they were my golden handshake." He snorted with disgust and put the dish back.

"You're joking . . ."

"Wish I were. Mind you – I suppose you have to bloody laugh to keep you sane. I don't mean *you*, I mean *me*. Works Manager and someone called Jaritts from personnel trooped up from nowhere yesterday. How are you, Mr Norton? So sorry to see you laid up again, thought you should be the first to know, rationalisation and so forth, no consolation but there will be others going too, no other suitable jobs available, decision out of our hands, hope you enjoy the grapes we brought along."

"I don't know what I can say, Mr Norton. I didn't think they could —"

"Oh they can, doctor. It's like I say – that's how it is these days."

"What about severance pay?"

He shook his head. "Haven't been there long enough. And it's a case of last in – first out. What gets me is that they're closing the most profitable part of the factory. Moving production to their main factory in Nottingham where they haven't made a profit in years. That's bloody stockholders and accountants for you. They'll let the rest of the works here run down of its own accord, say they can't afford to keep it open, then sell off the site to speculators and such like. If that's what higher education does for you, I'm glad I had none of it."

"And where does that leave you?"

"Well I shan't get a fresh job at my age. It's a funny thing – I've been around scrap-heaps all my life. Never thought I'd get chucked on one." He sighed deeply and stared at his feet again.

"Maybe when you get home and on your feet again things will look different," I said. In the face of this man's feelings my comment was complete gibberish and I regretted opening my mouth. He grunted and shook his head.

"Bloody won't. Alice has been made redundant as well, which will mean a right merry Christmas for us with the lad coming home. She told you that, didn't she? So you can see, doctor, that the operation has been a success but the patient is in a right mess. That's about the size of it, to my way of thinking."

I glanced at my watch while pretending to adjust the sleeve of my overcoat. "I . . . I really will have to go, Mr Norton. I'd like to have another talk with you when you get home."

"Aye, OK, doctor." He smiled and held out his hand. "Thanks for coming to see me, any road. Time's always against you in your job."

We shook hands again and I left, thinking that time was the one escape route we often used when faced with an uncomfortable truth or an insurmountable problem for which there was no answer. The discomfort I felt now, as I walked down the highly polished corridor towards the post-graduate library, arose from something I could not quite put my finger on. I had the feeling it was to do with the fact that I had been educated to solve problems but hadn't the skill yet to help others to come to terms with their own problems, and somehow these two things were related to each other; I had been brought up in hospital to be a sort of medical Mr Fixit, but now the problems presented were outside my sphere of experience, even though the urge to supply the answer remained stronger than ever. The option seemed to lie between changing my whole approach and redefining my role as a doctor, or else growing some pretty thick skin and rejecting any problem that presented which was not primarily a medical one. It was a disturbing reminder of what had actually been going on in my head for the last couple of years and I felt sure that the contents of the post-graduate library would shed no light on the matter.

I leafed through a few shelves in a half-hearted manner, marvelling at the explosion of new journals which seemed to have burst onto every available surface over the past few years, many of the articles in them representing the stony steps of someone's career, where advancing the status was more important than advancing the state of the art; where procuring the next rung of the ladder was more important than curing the next patient. The whole place was a Sargasso of soporific, unread manuscripts which had the smell, but not the substance, of scientific endeavour.

Like iron filings to a magnet, I was drawn to the new issue of the *British Medical Journal*. I leafed through its thin pages which would have been easier to eat than to read, stopping at the sight of a familiar face in the obituary column. The photograph had been taken years ago, when his hair was dark and he was wearing those severe, round, dark-framed spectacles from the 1940s, but it was Alec Duncan, all right. I read the column with a growing sadness which was at odds with the many happy memories that flashed through my head. I recalled the days after school when I had peered down his microscope into a new world illuminated by the light which slanted through the windows of his dusty study, or the wet days when I had gazed in wonder at his old books. He would sometimes come in and nod in his stern Scottish way, smiling imperceptibly as if he approved of me looking into the heartless mirror of his cold, hungry days as a medical student in Edinburgh. I thought, too, of the picnics on Southport sands and getting ill on crab-apples in their endless garden with Bill Duncan, with whom I had spent most of my school days. I hadn't seen them for almost four years, even though their home was only sixteen miles away. I wondered why I had not heard anything from Bill. I knew that he had been in South Africa these last few years, but he must have come over for the funeral. It was a sad reflection on both of us, I thought, that we had become so obsessed with our respective careers that we had not kept in touch – as if we had distanced ourselves from our roots with an increasing acceleration as time went on.

I told Tanya as soon as I got home that night and I could see that she felt the same as I did, for although she had not known the family for as long as I, she had grown especially fond of Bet Duncan whose warmth and laughter was a sharp contrast to Alec's quiet seriousness.

I couldn't eat until I had telephoned the house. The ringing tone sounded for a long time before the familiar sing-song, almost girlish voice of Bet Duncan came through the earpiece. She had a voice which seemed never to have heard bad news, and even now it was only slightly less cheerful than usual.

"Hal-lo. Stonebridge two four seven. Mrs Duncan speaking."

"Hello, Mrs Duncan. It's Steven . . . Rushton. How are you?"

"Ah, Steven! How nice to hear you. It's been so long since we've seen you."

"I know. Time flies. We've . . . been busy with one thing and another. I'm sorry to hear about Doctor Duncan . . . we only heard today. I don't know what to say."

Her voice dropped in pitch a little and she sighed. "Yes, I know. It was all very sudden, really. He'd had some chest pains on and off for a few days but he wouldn't ease up or cancel any of his surgeries. It was a coronary, of course. I'm so sorry you didn't know."

"We only found out today —"

"We did ring you a couple of times but there was no answer. And then the funeral was in Kirk Bantock. I stayed there with Alec's family for a while – as a matter of fact I've only been back a few days."

"Did Bill . . . ?"

"Oh yes, Bill was here. He was so sorry not to have seen you. He had to dash back almost as soon as the funeral was over, so he didn't get a chance to speak to you. He's coming back just as soon as he's completed some important building project he was working on. I know he'll want to get together then."

"Yes. That would be nice. Maybe . . . we would like to come over to see you this weekend. Would that put you out?"

"I'd like that, but I'm going away for a few days. Why not the weekend after? It would be so good to see you. Will you all come?"

"If that's OK with you. There are five of us now, you know."

"My God, of course. I haven't seen your youngest one yet. I'm looking forward to seeing them all again. How is Tanya?"

"She's well. She sends her love."

"Give her mine. And to all of you. See you the weekend after next."

I ate my tea slowly and rather automatically, my mind on other things. Alec Duncan would be greatly missed by the people of Stonebridge, especially since he was one of a dwindling number of single-handed practitioners left in these parts. I pushed my plate slowly away and gazed through the dining-room window, but I didn't see the darkening sky or the drizzle through the restless beech trees in the garden. All I could see was the vast expanse of Ainsdale beach with its glistening, finely corrugated sand which was as unyielding as cobbles on bare feet.

I heard Tanya's voice from a long way off and turned round.

"I was just wondering what happens in a case like this," she said. She was carefully pouring out two whiskies. As she looked down, a length of her long auburn hair fell in front of her eyes. She brushed it back with her hand. "I mean – who is looking after all Doctor Duncan's patients now?"

I reached across the table for one of the whiskies and took a sip so small that it had almost evaporated before it got beyond my lips.

"I don't know, really. I expect Ron Leaford will put his finger in the dyke, temporarily. They had an arrangement, you know, for holidays and so forth. Can't imagine why because they were so very different. Do you remember Ron?"

"Of course I do." She smiled. "A big untidy fellow. A likeable rogue. But surely he can't be expected to hold the fort for long?"

I took another sip of whisky, this time big enough to feel the drink burn its way past my tonsils and down to my stomach. "No. They'll have to get a locum in until such time as it takes the Family Practice Committee to advertise and appoint a successor, I expect. God knows how long that will take."

I finished the whisky off in one gulp and, without saying anything more, I wandered into the garden and looked over the faint outline of the hills to the north-east, beyond which lay the town of Stonebridge where Alec Duncan had had his practice. I stood for a while in the rain and gathering dusk until Tanya appeared at the door of the house.

"You going to stand there all night? You're getting soaked."

I turned and went indoors. She shook her head.

"I sometimes wonder about you. Staring into the distance in the pouring rain."

"Staring into the distance?" I said, brushing the rain from my sleeve. "No . . . no – I think it was more like staring into the past."

"Is that what it was? Well, come and take a glimpse into the future. An optional one, anyway."

"Eh?"

"This arrived today, after you'd left. The post was late."

She flipped a pale blue airmail envelope across the table. It was postmarked Manitoba. I sat down and pulled the flimsy pages from the envelope, glancing up at her. She turned away.

The letter was addressed to us both, written by Mrs Jonie May Heisenberg. She described the lifestyle of the partners and their wives with an effusive cheerfulness that I found profoundly depressing, for it confirmed my worst fears. Between the lines I could detect the enormous adaptive behaviour required to overcome such a bleak physical environment. Her last sentence, asking us if we would care to share their way of life in the Seal River backroads, was like someone enquiring about the health of a close relative, unaware that they had just died.

"Sounds like a thousand and one ways to enjoy your stay on Mars," I said, pushing the letter away.

"That's not very friendly," Tanya said. She sat down at the other side of the table and stared at me. I met her eyes but said nothing, knowing that what she was going to say would be uncomfortable. "Who are you putting down?"

"I'm not with you."

"Oh, come off it, Steven. The way I read it, it was a spirited reply to your enquiry about the job. *You* wrote to *them* in the first place, as I recall. She is naturally painting the best possible picture, which is what —"

"God forbid," I muttered. She ignored my interruption.

"I was going to say that I would have written a similar letter myself if I was in the same situation. The fact that it doesn't match up to your vision of life in the Canadian wilderness is another matter altogether. If that's the thing that chokes you off, then maybe it's because you hadn't thought the thing out carefully enough in the first place."

She spread her hands out on the surface of the table, but her eyes never moved from mine.

"I thought . . . the last year or so . . ." I struggled for the words which came only with difficulty. "In the practice we've done little else but stand still and react to things which we know are basically wrong but which we don't feel we are in much of a position to influence, one way or another. The health centre, I mean. We're like Pavlov's dogs, really. If the future is shaped by what we're doing *now*, then it promises to be a bit dismal. That's the way it feels. I suppose I was trying to invent a different future."

"Invent a different future?" said Tanya, smiling. "Tell me, Steven – what's the difference between doing *that* and simply playing out your fantasies?"

"Not much," I grunted. "Except that one requires a lot of thought and preparation —"

"And the other is nothing more than a daft impulse."

"Hmm. I don't need to ask into which category you put this lot," I murmured. "It . . . seemed like a good idea at the time."

"Exactly. I rest my case. Except that you also now know why you reacted that way to the letter."

I laughed. "Yes. Between my fantasy and the reality lie a thousand square miles of frozen wasteland and moose-droppings. I'm going to write back immediately and kick this correspondence into touch. Oh boy . . ."

I found some writing paper and a pen and sat down at the table again, thinking about nothing else. I had to do this right away: it was like an act of exorcism to rid myself of the guilt and anger I felt at making such a hopelessly ill-considered move. I was hardly aware that Tanya had got up and walked round to my side of the table, until I felt her arms round my neck and her warm breath against my right ear.

"Maybe you were rattling the wrong door," she breathed. I pointed my pen at the writing paper, but I could only feel the cold eyepiece of Alec Duncan's microscope against my eye, and smell the pages of his beautiful old books. Past, present, future.

"Maybe," I said.

6

I didn't need a calendar to know that October had arrived. As September whimpered to an end, everyone in the town seemed to walk a little faster, their heads bent a little lower, against the incessant, slanting rain which over the past couple of weeks had sallowed their modest summer flush. Each day during September, groups of young mothers watched their infants file into school for their first term, but by the end of the month the gathering had become smaller and the quick, reassuring smiles which they exchanged had become less anxious as they peered through the school gate or over the railings of the playground. Some of the infants skipped through the entrance door in anticipation of a day more interesting than it would have been at home; others scowled and scuffed the toes of their shoes, resenting their removal from the warm familiarity of the living room into the bright echo of the classroom where the teacher seemed nine feet tall and spoke so clearly and crisply.

The end of September brought the first requests for "the jabs for colds and 'flu" in which many patients seemed to have great faith but which probably had little effect against the apparently haphazard mutation of nature's rich variety of micro-organisms. October brought the start of the autumn term at universities and colleges, and with it came an upsurge of requests for the pill, so that by this time two sections of the population had more or less protected themselves against invasions of entirely different sorts – for the next few months, at least. It was as predictable as the leaves turning brown and falling from the trees.

I paid a visit, as promised, to Jack Norton to see how he was getting on after his operation. It turned out to be a strangely depressing call. Jack and his wife were bravely trying to decorate the spare bedroom in readiness for their son's visit. Since they could no longer afford to get anyone else to do it, they were struggling to do it themselves. It was a rough, proud effort and the adverse change in their circumstances had, at first glance, dampened their spirit less than I thought it would. Only after talking to them for a while did I detect the bitterness and apprehension which lay just below the surface of their wry banter. While his wife carefully measured the walls and moved unnecessarily round the room, I stared at Jack who stood awkwardly holding a roll of wallpaper in his huge hands. I was struck by the passive resignation in his posture which seemed to make him physically smaller. He wasn't like a man looking forward to getting better after his operation; it was almost as if he was anticipating his inevitable decline, physically and mentally.

Evening surgery that day began quietly enough, and it made a pleasant change not to feel rushed, to have time to talk to patients and even, in a few cases, to find out the real reason why they had come. I had got half way through the pile of notes on my desk, when I saw that my next patient was Harry Pankhurst. I knew that from this point the whole nature of the surgery would change: it would be a long and exhausting consultation which would make me late, the rest of the session with the remainder of the patients being compressed into a hurried superficial and unsatisfactory affair if I was to get home before nightfall.

If Harry Pankhurst had been an unhappy man, his affliction would have been a tragedy. As it was he was a cheerful, gregarious individual who, when he wasn't working, liked to spend a few bob on the horses and go down to the pub with his friends to swap jokes and sink as many pints as possible in an evening. Sometimes he would drag his long-suffering wife along, sit her behind a table in the corner of the vault and supply her with glass after glass of milk stout, ignoring her completely while he got on with the serious business of drinking and playing darts. Mrs Pankhurst's smooth round face contrasted sharply with her legs which, after the stresses and strains of her five pregnancies, years of chronic constipation and of standing over the ovens at the local bakery, had produced a cluster of varicose veins which bulged like great, malevolent grapes round her generous calves and behind her broad knees. She had led a joyless existence for most of her hard working life, taken for granted by her husband and treated like a dog by her five ungrateful (now grown-up) children. In spite of this she never complained much. It was only her "bad legs" which gave her the excuse she needed in order to stay at home and avoid some of Mr Pankhurst's more boozy excesses.

The fact that he seemed to be happy and reasonably well-adjusted was to me a shining example of triumph over adversity, for Harry Pankhurst was afflicted with the worst stammer imaginable. It was not just a routine halting and faltering between syllables: it was a truly spectacular affair – a convulsive dyskinesia with flailing arms and legs, facial grimacing and spasmodic movements of chest and abdomen which, at the height of his efforts, usually dislodged his lower set of false teeth.

As he came through the consulting room door I knew at once that he had come on behalf of his wife, not himself, for in his hand was a mangled scrap of paper on which was written a message in his own beautifully neat handwriting. He sat down beside the heavy oak desk and I began to write out a prescription for a pair of elastic stockings, full length, two-way stretch, lightweight. I knew what Mrs Pankhurst had requested without seeing the note. It was always the same. But out of the corner of my eye I could see that Harry was going to speak, and I braced myself.

"C-c-c-c-can I 'ave a ton-on-on-oo-oo-non-non-non-non-ic as well?"

As he blurted his way through the word he gripped the corner of the desk with his right hand, his left elbow flapped like a chicken shaking off ticks and his left knee jerked rhythmically up and down to within a few inches of his fearfully screwed-up face. His bottom set of teeth shot out and skidded across the desk like a flat stone which had been skilfully thrown across the surface of a pool. He calmly replaced them, wiping the end of the desk with the sleeve of his other arm. He cocked his head slightly to one side and raised his eyebrows in expectation. Mercifully, he had decided not to add 'please' or anything else. By now, his features had returned to their normal contours and I couldn't help feeling that nature had dealt the man a cruel blow in the form of such a paralysing stammer which belied his true intelligence.

My pen hovered over the prescription pad. I knew that my response at this stage would profoundly influence what happened next: if I agreed to his request he would be going through the door within fifteen seconds, clutching a prescription for a bottle of vitamins which would do him no good whatsoever but would bump up the share value of some multinational in Basle. On the other hand, if I questioned him I would release from him an unco-ordinated avalanche of words, unfathomable in content and painful in execution. And perhaps even then I would be none the wiser.

"What makes you think you need a tonic, Mr Pankhurst?" I heard myself saying. His teeth fell down the inside of his raincoat as he replied explosively that he had had a bad chest and was losing weight.

"I'm sh-shush-shush-sh-sh —"

"Short of breath?"

"N-no. I'm sh-sh-sure all I need is a ton-on-ic. Tonic." He sat back and smiled, his whole body relaxing again. I pursued my line of enquiry relentlessly, my palms beginning to sweat as I sensed the time slipping by during his long, laboured answers. When I heard Molly close the front door and start up her car I realised, even without looking at my watch, how late it was. I visualised my evening meal drying up like beached kelp in the mid-day sun.

I gave him a hurried examination, found nothing, and sat down again.

"Anyone else in your family had any chest trouble?" I asked.

"My sis-sis-ister had to-t-t-to —"

"Your sister had to have some tests?"

"N-no. She had to-to-to —"

"To go into hospital?"

"Mm,mm. Because sh-sh-she had to-to-to —"

"Tuberculosis?"

"N-n-no. Sh-sh-she had-ad two broken leg-leg-leg-legs. Two broken legs."

I slumped, exhausted, into the back of the chair. "Two broken legs. I see," I said. I reached limply forward and wrote out a prescription for a tonic. His eyes lit up as he took the prescription and he thanked me profusely. I asked him to come back in a couple of days so that I could arrange a chest X-ray, but he nodded and waved as if he hadn't the slightest intention of taking up my offer.

I told Ann and Christine to go home, that I would call the

remaining patients myself. I worked through the rest of the surgery with a subdued, mechanical efficiency which was harmless and undemanding both for myself and the patients. When the last patient walked in and sat down, I looked up and felt myself blanch. It was Alfred Groves.

"Mr Groves . . ." I said faintly.

"Dr Rushton." He folded his arms and paused. "Well now. I'm glad we have established who we are." His mouth moved quite independently from the rest of his stony features, rather like a lizard chewing its prey.

"I, er, didn't expect to see you in the surgery for a bit," I said.

He pursed his lips. "I can assure you, doctor, I wouldn't have taken the trouble except that you omitted to give me a sick note when you came to see me. So if you could oblige I'd be grateful." He looked at his watch. "I was brought by car. My appointment was actually for five-fifty. It is now six forty-eight. Which doesn't say much for your so-called appointment system, if I may say so."

"Yes well, when you get difficult problems you can't always tell . . . I mean – I don't work with a stop-watch you know, Mr Groves."

"Hm. I should have thought you would make allowances for that sort of situation," he grunted. I ignored him and wrote out a sick note.

"Have a nice trip to Southport?" I said brightly. "Everything went all right, I trust?" I felt a brief flush of guilt as I thought about the untimely suppositories.

"Very well, doctor."

"Fine. Good journey?"

"As a matter of fact, it didn't take much longer than it's taken waiting to see you this evening, doctor."

"Ah. No difficulty getting a road through, then?"

"Getting a road through . . .?" He paused and stared at me for a moment.

"To Southport, I mean," I said hurriedly.

"Getting to Southport, doctor, is hardly like travelling through the Serengeti. As a matter of fact," he added icily, "we did have the odd unscheduled stop but I would prefer not to talk about it."

The truth, whatever it was, lay out of reach behind his impenetrable gaze. He stood up and took the sick note from the desk with finger and thumb, holding it out in front of him as if it was contagious.

"I'll take this now, if you don't mind. I've waited long enough for it and, God knows, I've more important things to do. May I suggest that before long you might inject some organisation and efficiency into your system in order to prevent this interminable waiting. Good night, doctor."

I stared after him as he went out. I hadn't got the energy to feel angry or rise to the bait. Thank God it was Friday night.

The next day was one of those miraculously perfect autumn days whose yellow sunlight was like a mellow wine which you hoped came from an endless bottle. After an early lunch we drove slowly over to Stonebridge. Tanya and I spoke little on the journey and our silence was interrupted only by the occasional squabbling and scuffling of Carl and Stacey in the seat behind. Conrad slept throughout the whole journey, frowning and twitching his eyes involuntarily in the sunlight which, shining through the window, was fleetingly broken as we passed trees and houses close to the road's edge. It was only as we approached the outskirts of the town that he woke, his body detecting a change in the character of the vehicle's motion just as surely as if an alarm had sounded.

Stonebridge lay in a shallow basin surrounded by the rounded Derbyshire hills, whose strong, coarse grass was kept short by grazing sheep and the cold winds which blew from the north-east. The road could have run straight and steep into the town, but years ago the town planners in their wisdom had decided to zig-zag the route down the hills into a series of gentler gradients with hairpin bends which were presumably less hazardous for the heavy trucks which took granite, limestone and coal from the quarries on the other side of the town. The flint-hard stone was everywhere: not only was most of the town built from it, but the surrounding grassland was divided into undulating rectangles by dry-stone walls as far as the eye could see, replacing the low hedgerows of neighbouring Cheshire. The alkaline soil here was no use for growing crops and, because great areas of grass were needed for grazing, what woodland there had once been was now confined to occasional small groups which creaked and roared with the wind in their dark branches. And always, on the rim of the hills, were the thin lines of stunted, stooping willow and hawthorn which, from a distance, looked like camel trains against the sky. It was a harsh, uncompromising landscape, but such a different harshness from that in Overton's part of Lancashire, where so much of the town and countryside had been shaped and scarred by two hundred years of industry. It was difficult to escape the conclusion, when you saw the clean-scrubbed austerity of this corner of Derbyshire, that Overton had paid heavily for its industrial prosperity. "No blight – no bite" used to be an old saying in Overton, which was a variation on "where there's muck there's brass", I suppose. It was funny how the muck and grime had become engrained in Overton's social rituals – how often I had seen men pick up a freshly-drawn pint of beer and hold it up to the light before taking their first drink, as if expecting to find iron filings in the bottom of the glass. There was no such grim suspicion in Stonebridge. The people here respected the fact that the ground they stood on yielded nothing easily, whether it was the soil on the surface, or the minerals beneath the surface. And in doing so they, in return, gained self-respect.

It was not a small town. About fifty thousand people lived here, mostly within its compact centre, although in recent years the edges of the outlying farms were being nibbled away by newer property whose design and external materials of brick and stucco were like abrasions on the hillsides. The neat, rectangular gardens of the new houses were bursting with a lush display of young weeping willow and conifer which seemed to accentuate the disharmony rather than create the sense of permanence so sought after by their owners.

We crossed the centre of the town which was graced by a large square, chequered by slabs of light and shade from the banks and public buildings lining the four sides. In the centre was a stone monument topped by a bronze sculpture of a ram. Now green with age, it scowled down with its blank bulging eyes and scornful, flaring nostrils at the shoppers nattering and wandering about below. Across the town, down beneath the railway viaduct and past the pretty cemetery with its prim chapel of rest, we eventually turned into an unmade road leading to Alec Duncan's house. It was partially obscured from this approach by its high wall, behind which was the stable now used for garaging the cars.

We drew into the large flagged courtyard at the rear. The

78

stone surfaces of the house and the courtyard walls amplified each sound, even the gentle rustling of the surrounding trees, and we automatically lowered our voices as we got out of the car and walked to the wooden entrance porch.

The door opened and Bet Duncan stood before us, her face lighting up and her arms flinging themselves wide in a characteristic gesture of pleasure and welcome. For a few moments there was a shuffling mêlée at the door as she hugged each one of us in turn and fussed over the children before leading us along the oak-floored hallway into the lounge at the front of the house. Carl and Stacey ran, yelling and laughing, through the open french windows into the vast garden, disappearing among the bushes and trees as if they knew every inch of the ground intimately. Bet opened the top of a roll-top desk and out fell an assortment of toys which she placed on the floor for Conrad who squatted amidst this new treasure, beaming with delight.

We talked for some time. She eagerly asked all about the children and what we had been doing over the four years or so since we had last been, and had it really been four years since we had last sat here like this? I watched her as she talked, and wondered with discomfort how we had managed to become so involved with what we were doing in Overton that we had come adrift from people we knew and liked so much. Since I had last seen her she seemed to have changed little: now in her late fifties, she was still good-looking, which hardly surprised me since I had seen an old photograph of her when she had been on the stage. In those days she had been strikingly beautiful. She still had one or two theatrical mannerisms in the way she emphasised her words with her hands, sometimes making slow and graceful movements with them as if she were carefully unwrapping a parcel; at other times she would raise her face as she smiled with her broad mouth, shaking her grey curly hair like a young girl. At first she sparkled as we talked, but I noticed that after the momentum of the initial tumble of conversation, her shoulders seemed to sag a little, the life going out of her eyes as if someone had turned down a dimmer-switch. She looked out into the garden and sighed. To surface above her sadness took a tremendous effort that she could only sustain in short bursts.

"I love this garden," she said, half to herself. "Goodness

knows how I'm going to look after it, now. Alec did such a lot
. . . of course Joe Radcliffe still comes about three times a week
– do you remember how you and Bill used to pull some awful
tricks on that nice old man? You used to drive him mad. I think
he only carried on coming here because he was Alec's patient."

I smiled and followed her gaze out across the lawn. I could
hear Carl and Stacey crashing about in the undergrowth but I
couldn't see them. At the other side of the trees part of a small
low building was visible, the rest being hidden by huge
rhododendron bushes.

"What's happened to the summer house?" I asked. "All I
can see is —"

"Of course! I forgot to tell you," she exclaimed, brightening
suddenly. "We had to take the summer house down – the wood
was rotten and it was becoming unsafe. So what you can see
now is Alec's pride and joy. He decided two years ago to build a
surgery for himself at the far end of the garden near the road.
He said he'd had enough of patients coming in and out of the
side of the house so we had that part converted into a work-
room and library. Why don't you go and have a look at it? I've
got a spare key somewhere . . . Ron Leaford has got one, and
the other is here . . ."

She got up and opened the roll-top desk, taking out a newly-
cut Yale key from a small compartment. "Go and have a
browse round. Alec would have loved you to see it. He kept
saying he was going to ring you to tell you about it, but
somehow . . . somehow he never got round to it." She smiled
with moist eyes as she handed me the key. "I don't know what
state it's in at the moment. We've had a stream of different
locums using it lately, as you can imagine, and they never seem
to take the same amount of care when it isn't their own. Ron's
been marvellous, though. He'll be sorry to have missed you."

"It must be six years since . . . how is he?"

Bet Duncan shook her head and laughed. "Oh, Ron is fine!
He's just the same as he always was. Busy with one of his
business deals, rushing around in four places at once, as usual.
But for all that, he's the kindest man I know, next to Alec."

She took Tanya's arm and squeezed it gently. "Come along,
love. Help me bring the lunch out into the garden while Steven
has a look round. You can cheer up an old lady by telling her
what you've been doing all this time since we last saw you."

I walked through to the rear of the house again instead of going through the french windows; outside, in the courtyard, there was something I wanted to see. I wandered into one of the stables which Alec had previously used as a work-shop. The marks on the stone floor still faintly showed where the work-bench had been. I turned and looked at the brittle whitewash of the wall near the window and reached up with one hand, brushing away the cobwebs and the translucent empty carcases of flying insects which had been trapped and long since sucked dry. It was still there: a grey stain which streaked right up to the ceiling. That was from the day Bill and I had compressed one of Alec's golf balls as hard as we could in the vice on the work-bench; then we had chiselled into its outer layers to see what it was made of. The interior – a grey, tacky rubber solution, had exploded in all directions, and it had taken a week to get it out of our hair. Alec had looked at us both with grey despair over his half-moon spectacles, murmuring gravely, "Can you not see that this is a high price to pay for a scientific discovery which some would say was of questionable importance? I trust that you will both apply the same dedication to your studies when the time comes for you to do so." Then he gave us both the *look* – the look which was the question and at the same time the answer to the question. And the smile. The barely perceptible smile which, as he turned away, signalled that this was a foolishness which he understood, had experienced himself; the smile of the teacher who had seen it all before in different times and who knew that the question was more important than the answer.

I walked by the side of the house, between the old surgery annexe and the crab-apple trees, feeling disorientated by the easy recall of that memory which still shone through the stupefying detail of medical science that I had since committed to the same area of my brain. I passed the sundial on the lawn and still felt the effect of that dizzying vortex of time as I remembered how we had moved the plinth on its foundations, trying to convince Joe Radcliffe that he had arrived to prune the roses at three a.m.

Alec Duncan's surgery was a neat, small, L-shaped building surrounded by an asphalted area from which extended a short driveway between the overhanging trees down to the road. I struggled to get the newly-cut key in the main entrance door

81

and heard Carl and Stacey run out from the bushes behind me.

"Is this another house? A little one?" asked Carl.

I turned and shook my head. "No. This is Doctor Duncan's surgery. I'm just going to have a quick look round inside."

"Does he have those special little bottles and things like you bring home?"

"I expect he does," I said. They both beamed with anticipation.

"Can we see them, too?"

I shook my head. "Not just now. I want to have a look round on my own for a minute. I won't be long."

Their disappointment was only fleeting, for they turned and ran through the trees back to the house when I told them that there was some lemonade waiting for them.

The main entrance door led into a small open area which was bathed in sunlight from the skylights in the flat roof. A well-planned reception area where the records were kept overlooked a plant-festooned waiting room containing a dozen brightly coloured pre-formed chairs. Down a short corridor was a well-equipped treatment room and examination room and, next to that, Alec Duncan's consulting room. I reeled in admiration at this carefully thought out, attractive design. I went into his consulting room, tiptoeing around and hardly daring to draw my breath, as if I had arrived late for a church service.

At one end was his magnificent oak desk with leather top and ornate brass-handled drawers down either side, the familiar swivel-chair pushed against the back wall. On the wall were the framed scrolls of his degrees and diplomas and an assortment of family photographs in black and white. Along one of the adjacent walls was a new examination couch and against another were the glass cases I had years ago explored a hundred times, picking up one by one the dozens of stainless steel instruments from the shelves and hearing them clatter so satisfying when I replaced them. On the sink work-top was the Dolland microscope, miraculously still in pristine condition and still in use, for on its stage was a glass slide. I looked down the eye piece and adjusted the focus. Skin scrapings, probably a fungal infection. I picked up the slide and realised that it was covered with a month's deposit of dust. Someone had clearly decided that it was not to be disturbed since it was last in use, so I carefully, almost reverently, replaced it. I moved to the book-case and opened the delicate mahogany-framed glass doors, knowing exactly what I was looking for and still feeling almost the same anticipation and pleasure I had experienced when they were first shown to me: a thin, flat walnut box, inside which were three trays divided into twenty-four compartments; each compartment contained a beautifully prepared microscopic section on a glass slide, the cover-slip being glued with canada balsam, ringed and sealed with lacquer, labelled with faded grey ink. Transverse section cat's tongue; pollen-sac of bee; proboscis of house-fly; brain, liver, nerve and blood vessel. Each one was a work of art as well as a document of anatomy, made by Alec Duncan when he was a medical student in Edinburgh.

I carefully replaced them and took down two books: Dunlop's *Textbook of Medical Treatment*, and Gray's *Anatomy*. I opened Dunlop's book and glanced through the index which made no mention of penicillin or the word antibiotic or tranquilliser, for this was the 1943 edition. I smiled and wondered what the author thought of today's therapeutic plethora. Putting the books to one side and sitting down on the corner of the desk, I opened the cover of Gray's. In the same grey ink was written, "Alec Duncan, University of Edinburgh, December 1922." I gazed in admiration at the astonishing pen drawings which had so much depth and clarity, you felt you could walk right round them to the other side, plucking at the nerves and blood-vessels as you went. The pallid wash of the up-to-date versions couldn't hold a candle to this masterpiece.

I heard a noise at the door and looked up. Tanya was standing in the doorway holding Conrad in her arms. He was rubbing his eyes and she was smiling patiently across the room, the sun through the window stagelighting her long auburn hair and summer skin.

"Didn't you hear us come in? You must have been miles away," she murmured.

"About two decades away," I said, laughing softly. I slid the books back and closed the doors of the book-case. "Nice, isn't it? The surgery, I mean."

"Mm. Very. He must have been a very meticulous man. You can see that. Everything seems to have been designed with a definite purpose, without any sign of being obsessional."

"Not like our place, you mean?" I said. "The health centre,

not Mary Street. Oh, Christ, yes. This *has* something . . . not designed by a committee. I suppose this is purpose-built in the true sense – not built to hold the occupants into grey uniformity but built as an extension of what the occupant wants to achieve as an individual." I burst out laughing. "That, Tanya my love, didn't come out quite right, but somewhere amongst all that crap is a nugget of truth."

"Maybe," she said. "Anyway, while you've been milking your childhood memories we've been having lunch. Come on, everyone else has nearly finished."

We had a pleasant meal and talked while the children played, then said our goodbyes late in the afternoon. On the way back home the boys dozed in the back seat, exhausted with their non-stop activity in the fresh air. For a long time we didn't speak. I glanced at Tanya and found her looking at me, smiling a Mona Lisa smile which was neither sad nor happy.

"I didn't quite hear you," I said.

"I didn't say anything," she murmured.

"The enigmatic smile. Tell me what it means."

She settled back in her seat and gazed out of the window at the empty road in front of us. "Oh . . . I was just thinking about the look on your face when you were in Doctor Duncan's surgery."

"Really? What look was that?" The skin of my face pricked like a small boy who had been caught red-handed smoking behind the bike shed.

"You know damn well what I'm talking about," Tanya said. "You really liked it, didn't you? Come on, you will be telling me next that it never crossed your mind —"

"Crossed my mind?" I put out my left hand and squeezed her knee, but continued to look straight ahead. "You bet it crossed my mind. The thought of applying for Alec Duncan's practice has trampled backwards and forwards across my mind so many times this afternoon that it's a wonder I haven't . . ."

The rest of my sentence was interrupted by a moan and a spasm of coughing from behind. I glanced back quickly in time to see Stacey throw up three helpings of peaches and ice-cream over Conrad and Carl who woke up screaming with startled indignation. I stopped the car and we lifted the boys out of the back seat to clean them up. They stood on the roadside with their faces screwed up and their arms stuck out from their sides like napalmed refugees, but a few soothing words and armfuls of kleenex soon brought order and calm. We resumed our journey, with the windows open, fifteen minutes later. For some reason that I could not explain, the interruption released the tension and excitement which had begun the moment I had stepped into Alec's surgery, and the tentative possibilities I had felt earlier were suddenly converted into an absolute certainty about what I was going to do.

Tanya turned and checked that all was well on the rear seat, then she reached out and tickled the hair on the nape of my neck.

"So what's it to be now? Plan B?" she said. I glanced at her and saw that she was smiling, searching my face for confirmation of what she already knew.

"I'm afraid so." I thought about what I had just said and laughed. "That doesn't sound too positive, considering it's the most positive thought I've had for a while," I said. "What I meant was . . . it's not something I can do in isolation. It involves us all. We'll have to move house for one thing, and schools . . ."

Tanya sighed. "I know. The thought of packing and unpacking years of accumulated rubbish and leaving . . . of course this is assuming that you would get the practice in the first place. We are sitting here talking as if it's a foregone conclusion."

"Single-handed practice. FPC appointment – applications in triplicate, selection committees – I know all that," I said, irritated at the thought of these necessary obstacles. I changed into third gear, letting the clutch in too quickly. The car jerked round a sharp bend in the road. "That's just the mechanics, the process. What d'you think of the idea?"

"What would you gain?"

"Freedom," I said firmly. "Freedom from outside inter-ference, for one thing. There would only be one finger on the pulse, and that would be mine. You saw the set-up. No one from the health authorities stomping up and down telling you what you can do and what you can't do and where. That's a very attractive thought at the moment, even if it does mean leaving a good practice with Ian and Molly. I would miss that. And on the other hand, of course, single-handed practice ties you down more, even if you do have a relief rota."

Tanya was silent for a few moments. "It's what you want to do, I can tell. It's written all over you," she said. "Anyway, you know the score. You have to make sure that you're not substituting one lot of problems for a different set of problems."

"You don't think I'm mad? I mean, you don't mind?"

I looked across at her, scanning her face for signs of doubt. She met my eyes and her lips spread into a smile. I felt my hands relax their grip on the wheel and I looked ahead again.

"At least it's not a million miles away," I said. "And another thing . . ."

"What's that?"

"No stewed moose."

She grinned. "And no curling or ice fishing."

I nodded. "That's right. No ice fishing. Especially no ice fishing."

7

During the following week, I sent off to Derby my application for Alec Duncan's practice: a potted history in triplicate of my education and achievements so far, all in the correct manner. It was a meagre chronological list which seemed to be a wafer-thin slice of what I had actually gone through as an individual, and of the ups and downs that Tanya and I had experienced bringing up a family while on the move to different parts of the country in search of peace and fulfilment. I got a curt acknowledgement from the FPC in Derby, although, to their credit, there was an added note to the effect that they would respect the confidentiality of my application – for obvious reasons. It was like walking on cheese crackers.

Towards the end of the week I caught up with my mail and was sifting through the pile which had uncharacteristically remained unattended from the day before. On the desk was a large, carelessly wrapped parcel accompanied by a note in a buff envelope. It had my name on it and was marked 'personal' – doubly underlined. I unwrapped the parcel and found a packet of biscuits of which only two of the original contents remained intact. The rest of the packet contained a powdered, fragmented mess which made me wonder whether it had been thrown directly from the supermarket where it had been purchased to my desk where it now lay. I opened the envelope. Inside was a note written by Harry Pankhurst.

There is a belief in this part of the world that cheap, rubber-soled shoes 'draw your feet'. In other words, they make your feet swell, ache and throb, and ultimately drain the energy from the rest of your body down into the ground. Harry's letters had precisely the same effect on my eyes. They were always completely devoid of punctuation and, as they progressed, the speed and momentum that they gathered gave them a careering, out-of-control quality which I found both mesmerising and exhausting all at the same time. By his normal standards, this letter was quite short.

"Dear Doctor," it read. "Please accept this small gift in appreciation of that tonic you gave me it has done me very well appetite as good as ever put on weight and my chest is as right as rain which has put her mind at rest as she was worried but you know what she's like which is why I hope you weren't put out me not turning up for tests and so forth being as that means hospital and might mean being away from home which wouldn't suit as you know or rather don't know that we have a paying lodger now who is always eyeing up the wife which she doesn't care for I can't say I do either but the extra money is handy as you can appreciate and if I went away you can see what that would mean specially as how she is not too quick on her feet these days so if you could let me have another bottle of the same and oblige. H. Pankhurst."

I picked up my coffee after I had finished the surgery and took the note into Ian's consulting room. He had his spectacles pushed down onto the end of his nose and was peering over the top of them to look at the list of home visits. He greeted me without shifting his gaze.

"Good morning, Steven. Not often we can afford the luxury of a coffee and a wee chat before we go racing around healing the sick, eh? The last time we had a quiet morning like this was when there was a strike at Bailey's bakery. Shops bereft of bread, queues at the supermarket, first things first and all that."

"Folk too busy to be ill, you mean?"

"Precisely, quite so. Still, one has to be thankful for small mercies. God knows, the work seems to get heavier."

"Ah ha. Showing your age, by the sound of it," I said.

"Maybe. It's a funny thing – not working full-time any more makes it more and more difficult to get up a head of steam to do what bit I have to do. When you're working full-time, flat out, you seem to generate a sort of mental momentum which carries you through to the end of the day."

I smiled and handed him the note from Harry Pankhurst. "Talking about gathering momentum – read this. It was on my desk this morning."

He read it and laughed. "Let's hope he doesn't drive a car like he writes letters. Still – the thought was there, as they say.

What was it – a case of another patient riding roughshod over your scientific methodology?"

"In a way. I was wanting to do a few tests and all he wanted was a tonic."

"Hmmm. Difficult, sometimes."

"What is?"

"Well, you know . . . knowing when to interfere, and when to shut up and do nothing."

"Ah yes. Especially when there's always the uncertainty of whether or not something is seriously wrong."

Ian smiled and leaned back in his chair. He took off his spectacles, folding them carefully into their case. "The uncertainty, Steven, is always there. Never goes away. The only thing is that as you get older you learn to live with it." He stared at the backs of his hands on the desk. "By the way . . ." he said hesitantly, "I was giving one or two things a bit of thought last night . . . I was hoping Molly would have arrived by now. Maybe we should talk about it later sometime."

"Talk about what?"

"Well, the way this health centre is going it looks as though I shall have retired before we get in."

"God forbid. Unless you . . ."

He shrugged. "I was only thinking that next year or the year after is about right . . . I mean for me to start thinking about it, at least. I wonder whether this is the time to start looking around for a replacement."

"Replacement?"

"Oh I know you and Molly are on top of things, but the list size seems to be growing all the time."

"I've never given it a thought," I said. "Although I know that we seem to have been taking on a lot of new patients recently."

"That's what I mean," he replied. "It's such a gradual process. You don't notice, when you've got your head down, that the work is getting heavier. And it is, you know. Don't be fooled by a day like today. I've noticed it. I don't think it's a good idea taking on a new surgery with all the problems unless you are really sure of keeping on top of the work. As I recall, when we got thrown out of our last surgery we hardly had time to look after the patients for a while – simply because we were too damn busy getting this place sorted out. And, by God, this is a tiny wee place compared with the size and complexity of the health centre. So maybe this is the time to start looking round for a likely new partner."

I turned away and looked out of the open door of his room at the single small opaque window in the corridor, watching the condensation run down the ribbed glass and gather on the window ledge below. I noticed for the first time that the frame hadn't been put in straight, so that when sufficient drops had collected at one end of the sill, they abruptly coalesced every few seconds into a single mass which wobbled hesitantly along to the other end and fell onto the floor. My brainless preoccupation with this had nothing to do with a love of fluid dynamics – I felt guilty about my application for Alec's practice and was wondering how to steer the conversation in another direction. Fixing my gaze on something other than a blank wall made me less painfully aware that I was avoiding Ian's eyes.

"You may be right about this being the time to choose another partner," I said, trying to sound matter-of-fact, "although I can't think who would be attracted to working in this place. I didn't mind it at first but —"

"Oh I know how you feel," Ian said, "but it's not going to be forever – even if at times it does seem like it. Anyway – think about it. Good partners don't grow on trees."

I felt sick with shame from the deception which had to be continued for the time being. I got up and began to walk through the door.

"Yes . . . yes. We must give it some thought," I mumbled. "I'll, er, discuss it with Molly when she's got a minute. Then we'll talk again. I'll have to get going on my visits, Ian, so maybe you'll . . ."

I waved my hand woodenly in the air. He looked at me and raised his bushy brows.

"You all right?"

"Me? Oh yes. I've a few things to do, that's all. What you were talking about . . . it's best left to when we're all three here and there's time to, er, discuss it more."

He grunted and got up. "Yes. You said that a moment ago. Nothing on your mind, Steven?" He looked straight at me with kind but penetrating eyes. I tried to laugh but all I managed to produce was a harsh, ugly sound which hurt the back of my throat.

"No. Apart from a big overdraft and a goldfish with a defective swim-bladder."

He said nothing as we walked together to the front door. He opened it and stood in the doorway looking up at the sky as if expecting rain.

"Heard some sad news on the golf course yesterday," he said, without shifting his gaze.

"What was that?"

"About Alec Duncan. He had a coronary last month. I haven't seen him in years. We used to see a lot of each other at the Manchester Medical Society a long time ago. Nice fellow. You knew him, didn't you?"

I looked at him but could see nothing in his face apart from polite enquiry.

"Yes, I did. I went to school with his son. I read it in the BMJ. As a matter of fact we . . . went to see Mrs Duncan last weekend. Just a visit. I spent a lot of time there once." I took out a bunch of keys and made a big issue out of selecting the ignition key of my car which must have looked faintly ridiculous since there were only three keys on the ring.

"Last of a dying breed, Alec Duncan," Ian said. He was still in the doorway and I was dying to edge past him and stand in the street to take a few deep breaths. "Single-handed practice is a hard life, no let-up at all. He'll be a hard act to follow. Whoever takes over will have his work cut out, and he'll have to know what he's taking on. Don't you think so, Steven?"

I looked directly at him. "I'm sure you're right. I . . . he . . . would have to give it very serious thought and have to be convinced in his own mind that it was the right thing to do," I said without emphasis or emotion.

Ian nodded. "Quite so," he said gruffly. "I hope I haven't delayed you on your visits. See you later, no doubt."

He turned and went back to his room. I got into my car, started the engine but didn't move away immediately. My hands were shaking and I stared through the windscreen. He *knew*. He had been around a long time and was nobody's fool, and I had no idea how he knew but he did. I was sure of it. And if that was so, it was going to make the next few uncertain weeks even more uncomfortable.

91

8

Tanya adjusted my tie for the third time and stood back.

"Hm. You look surprisingly presentable, really."

"Thanks. It all helps. I'd better get moving."

I put my arms round her and she whispered good luck in my ear.

It took about an hour to get to Derby. The notification that I had been short-listed for interview for Alec's practice had arrived a week ago. I stopped on the ring road and studied the photostat of the street map which they had thoughtfully enclosed, although I had looked at it so many times in the last few days I knew it by heart. Half-way along King Street, which was desolate with swirling litter, stood the Area Health Authority Building, a perpendicular slab of glass on which was reflected the mean grey insurance offices across the road.

I went in through the double-glazed doors and was met in the foyer by an administrative clerk with tinted glasses and a drooping moustache. He looked like a night-club bouncer. He ticked my name off a list on his clip-board and politely showed me up a flight of stairs.

"Along the corridor, turn right at the end, then first right again," he said when we got to the top. "Room T fourteen. You're a little early. There are some other interviewees waiting because the members of the selection committee aren't all here yet, I'm afraid. You'll find some tea and coffee on the table."

I entered T fourteen, nodding to two Asian doctors who were sitting in the far corner. One of them was a tall, slim Sikh. He sat like a woman with his knees together and his hands clasped on his lap, listening inattentively to a small, grey-haired Indian whose dark eyes darted about nervously under the hooded upper lids as he talked rapidly and gesticulated with his hands. They smiled briefly and raised their eyebrows in a sort of greeting as I helped myself to the coffee and sat down.

I looked round. The Swedish carpet-tiles, the smoked-glass and stainless steel coffee table were straight out of Habitat, as were the expensive lounge chairs which lined all four sides of the room. No wonder there was never any money for walking-sticks and bed-pans for our elderly patients. On the hessian walls were posters with grim warnings about the hazards of smoking, alongside bulletins from NALGO which warned grimly about the hazards of not employing enough administrators in the health service. I got up and walked over to the window which looked out onto a building site at the back. A workman had just completed urinating against a half-built wall. He turned round and looked up, grinning and waving cheerfully before he vigorously jerked two fingers up in the air at me. As I went back to my seat the door opened. A suavely-dressed individual breezed in and introduced himself. His fresh face and flaxen wavy hair made him look about twenty-five, but he was probably older.

"Morning. This must be the mortuary, I assume? Drayton – Richard Drayton. Hello, hello, hello. Are we running late or are they going to take us in all at once?"

The two Asians grinned uneasily. Drayton glanced round the room, his eyes lighting up when he saw the coffee. He rubbed his hands together.

"Ah, coffee. Just the job. Sustained a fair bit of brain damage on the train up last night with some friends. They were on the way to a charity ball they happened to be organising up in Leeds or somewhere. I'm afraid we drank the raffle prizes. God Almighty!" He poured himself a black coffee and sat on the edge of the chair next to mine. "Stayed at this frightful bloody place last night. The Royal George. Breakfast equivalent to a lifetime's intake of cholesterol, I shouldn't wonder. I'm amazed I can still walk after attempting that little lot." He shook his head and rolled a mouthful of coffee round his teeth.

"Your accent," I said, "You're not from these parts, I take it."

He pulled the corners of his mouth down. "God no. Esher, actually. You?"

"Manchester – actually. I did spend a little time in your area once – in Dorking. Doing a bit of surgery."

"Dorking? Oh well, coming from Manchester that must have been an awfully nice change for you." He nodded and

93

smiled sympathetically, as if I had told him I suffered from a mild but embarrassing congenital disorder. "Manchester graduate, then?"

I shook my head. "Edinburgh."

"Ah, yes. Porridge and Presbyterianism. I'm a Bart's man, myself."

"You make it sound like a consumer durable," I laughed. "What brings a St Bartholomew's graduate so far away from his usual stamping ground?"

He leaned back casually in the chair, putting one arm over the back and brushing non-existent fluff off his lapels with his other hand.

"A touch of independence for a while, old son," he said with a lopsided grin. "I'm in practice with my father, two uncles and a brother-in-law. Dad's on the part-time staff at Bart's, and has opened a very nice private nursing home in Reigate. Naturally, he wants me to run it eventually, but we thought it would be a good idea for me to cut away from the old dynasty for a short spell, just to see how the other half lives, so to speak. He's pretty thick with the Medical Practices Committee, actually, so I expect he'll wield a fair bit of influence on the selection. You're a local chap by the sound of it – got any inside griff about the practice?"

I remembered my phone call to Bet Duncan a few days ago. I had told her for the first time that I had applied for Alec's practice and had been short-listed. She had cried and laughed and cried again. She knew some of the selection people, and whatever I did or said she was going to put in a good word, I knew that. Any reservations I had at the time about her attempting to influence the selection were rapidly disappearing in the face of Drayton's patronising patter.

"I just thought, you know . . ." His voice trailed off momentarily as he caught sight of the look I gave him.

"No I don't," I muttered. "I don't have any . . . griff . . . about the practice."

"Pity. Actually I came up a couple of weeks ago to get to know the score. Quite a nice little set-up, really, although I reckon the old boy was a trifle eccentric – the microscope and centrifuge and all that, I mean. Probably thought he was a latter-day Louis Pasteur, I shouldn't wonder. Which is a bit of a joke when you consider most of the folk round here probably

94

only want a cough bottle or a sick note, no questions asked. Tell you one thing, though . . ."

"Oh? What's that?" I asked. The tone of my voice was a complete shut-off but he ignored it.

"The house is a dead snip at the price. I think the old girl wants to unload it as soon as possible to get somewhere smaller. My God, I'd have to pay half as much again in Esher for a house like that. I suppose that's one of the few advantages . . ."

He was interrupted by one of the administrative assistants who came through the door armed with a thick folder and disposable ball-point pen. The fact that the ball-point had his own name taped on with adhesive plaster for some reason made me feel profoundly depressed.

"Sorry to keep you waiting, gentlemen," he said. "The Committee members are all here now, so I wonder if we can . . . Doctor Drayton will be first as he's got a train to catch, followed by Doctor Rushton, then Doctor Singh and finally Doctor Subriman."

"Soubramani," corrected the little grey-haired man, smiling politely.

The Administrator licked his fingers and flicked through the file. "I beg your pardon. Doctor Soubramani. Now, Doctor Drayton, would you care to come this way, please?"

Drayton got up and went out of the room with the clerk. We fidgeted in silence for about fifteen minutes, the three of us collectively sympathising with the one first through the hoop. When Drayton returned to collect his briefcase after his interview he was red-faced and sweating. As he bent down to put his expenses form on top of an immaculate silk shirt, his temporal blood-vessels stood out like ropes.

"Rough time?" I asked. He snorted, straightened up and lit a small cigar.

"Bunch of bloody peasants in there," he said through his teeth. "More than a touch of local ambience, I regret to say. One old duffer asked me what 'getting a road through' meant, for God's sake. I mean – what sort of bloody inscrutable question is that? I should think they're looking for a sort of Albert Schweitzer with clogs on, old son." He laughed and turned to the door. "And watch out for the mutton on the far left. Her breath could stop a rhino in its tracks at fifty paces. She's either in a diabetic pre-coma or else her cerebral cortex is in an advanced stage of decomposition. See you on the ice!"

He went through the door and a moment later the same clerk with the personalised ball-point came through. He ticked my name off the list and accompanied me to a room further along the corridor. I stepped inside and was shown to a chair behind a small formica table. I quickly looked round at the interviewing panel who were seated behind a semi-circle of similar tables like cavalry taking refuge behind upturned wagons. I thought I vaguely recognised two of them but couldn't place them. A tall, bookish-looking figure at the centre of the gathering stood and introduced himself as Vincent Lloyd, chairman of the FPC. He introduced the others in turn, but I didn't hear him because I suddenly recognised Jim Ashton, a general practitioner whom I had met years ago at Alec Duncan's house. He grinned and nodded a recognition across the desk in a manner which made me feel more at ease. Lloyd began by asking routine questions about my qualifications and so forth, clarifying a few things about my previous experience. This all took a few minutes, during which I answered rather automatically since I was distracted by the other familiar face on the panel. I racked my brains, trying to remember where I had met him before. Wherever it was, I had the unpleasant feeling that he knew something about me that was definitely not going to be in my favour.

"Well now, doctor," Lloyd was saying, "I think we've established your basic . . . er . . . so to speak. I'd like to ask the other members of the panel if they've any, er, Councillor Pavey . . . ? Would you care to . . . ?" Lloyd was a master of the unfinished, suspended sentence – obviously experienced in committee work. I suspected that his apparent vagueness was an affectation which belied an astute and authoritarian personality: he could get people to do things he wanted them to do without them realising that they were having their arms twisted.

"Horace Pavey, doctor."

I looked at the owner of the gravelly voice and the familiar face suddenly slotted into place. Horace Pavey, Superintendent of Parks and Recreation in Stonebridge in the year Bill Duncan and myself, one summer holiday from university, had worked in a memorably unskilled capacity at the cemetery. His wiry hair was thinner – freshly washed, it now looked like

96

tumbleweed – and there were a few more lines in his face. But the executioner's smile hadn't changed.

"You were under my employ, as I recall. Quite some time ago, of course. Funny how time seems to move in circles, somehow," said Pavey slowly. He leaned forward on his elbows and peered intently at a silver-plated propelling pencil he was twirling between his fingers. "You and Doctor Duncan's son . . . you perhaps understandably don't recall it too well. I certainly do, though."

So did I. I began to perspire at the memory and at the bad luck to have met him again under these circumstances. I glanced at the others who – apart from Jim Ashton – were staring at Pavey. Ashton was cleaning out his pipe and smiling to himself as if his mind was on something else.

"You'll be pleased to know that Stonebridge Memorial Park has been restored to its former glory since you were last there," said Pavey. I swallowed as I remembered that day Bill Duncan and I had been given the task of spraying the weeds around the asphalt paths of the memorial park prior to a visit by a minor member of royalty. We were using an extremely potent systemic preparation not available for domestic use and had not allowed for the strong breeze. The stuff was blown half-way across the park and it wasn't until two days later that we saw the devastation we had brought upon the beds and herbaceous borders of the whole of the north side of the park. The local press had described it as a 'horticultural Hiroshima' and there had been a demand for a public enquiry. Pavey had elected to take early retirement shortly afterwards.

My mouth twitched into a semblance of a smile and I nodded imperceptibly, hoping that my muted response would encourage him to get on with the business of the day rather than ramble on about an episode which, although funny at the time, would right now do little to clinch my selection as one of Stonebridge's pillars of society.

"Tell me, doctor – what sort of new ideas would you be wishing to introduce if you did take over this practice?" Pavey asked. I couldn't tell from his voice whether he would view the idea of innovation with approval or apprehension.

"Very few . . ." I began.

"Really?" he growled, frowning. "That's a surprising statement from a younger man in your situation."

"I was about to say very few – in the first place," I replied, pulling myself together. "Apart from a few minor administrative changes, that is. I'm sure it would take a little while to let the dust settle, let the patients get used to a new doctor. From what I have seen and what I know of the way Doctor Duncan practised medicine, I shouldn't have thought that major changes were necessary." I said it with conviction because I believed it to be true. Pavey grunted and some of the other members nodded with approval.

"Quite so, quite so. I wonder if I could ask the doctor . . ." piped a female voice from the far end.

I turned towards her. She was in her late forties, with fiercely permed hair and the most ornate pair of spectacles I have ever seen – a truly baroque piece of facial furniture with jewelled rims which flared from the side of her head. As she spoke, her brightly made-up lips writhed vainly about in an attempt to hide her bad teeth. This had the effect of moving the rest of the facial muscles which caused her spectacles to jerk up and down like a tropical flying insect about to alight on the bridge of her nose.

"Nancy Aspinall, Doctor Rushton," she said, cocking her head apologetically towards Pavey, who folded his arms and scowled at the desk in front of him. "I wonder if I may take up the point that I'm sure Councillor Pavey was going to develop. I'd like to know what you think about the special needs of women in view of their changing role in society?"

Her question was straight out of the *Guardian*. I had read the same article a week ago. Jim Ashton groaned quietly and turned to look out of the window. Lloyd took off his half-moon spectacles and cleaned them languidly with a large white handkerchief. I interpreted this as a non-verbal sign that he felt he was in the presence of a tedious burden. I sensed that she was irritating the rest of the committee and I decided to capitalise on it.

"Special needs?" I said. "I shouldn't have thought that their needs were any more special than the other special groups – the young, the old, the chronic sick, the disabled —"

"Doctor Rushton, I don't wish to appear . . . I speak as a member of a group of women who feel strongly that, as a body, we —"

"All I'm saying is that I wouldn't have used the word

98

'special'," I said firmly. "Different, maybe. And to be aware of their different needs is a prerequisite for being more effective. It's all a question of priorities. Don't you agree?"

"Quite so, doctor. Oh, I *quite* agree" she said sourly, showing her irritation at my pre-emptive strike by screwing up her eyes and tucking her elbows into her sides as if a lump of ice-cream had found a sensitive tooth. Lloyd put on his spectacles and cleared his throat.

"Thank you, Mrs Aspinall. It's an intriguing topic which perhaps we should . . . er . . . I wonder whether before we do, though, we should ask Doctor Ashton, who I'm sure . . . Perhaps we could come back to . . . ah . . . Doctor Ashton, have you any . . . ah . . . ?" His charming smile and his gentle interruption floated like gossamer in the air, effectively neutralising Mrs Aspinall. She gave a tight little smile and moved her chair back slightly to signal that she had relinquished the baton.

"Just a couple of quickies, Mr Chairman," said Ashton. He turned towards me and grinned as if he didn't intend to cause any trouble. "Doctor Rushton – you'll be leaving a group practice which, as I understand it, is just about to move into a brand new health centre. And you're opting now to fly solo. That's a big change, what with everybody changing their roles and so forth. How come?"

Although I had expected someone to ask this, I was no more equipped to answer it than when I had first thought about it. If I had been in the position of disliking my present partners or of having no respect for them, either as friends or as practising doctors, then it would have been easy to rationalise a glib answer. Since this was far from the case, the apparently benign question made me hesitate and shift in my seat. How could I explain something that seemed to fly in the face of logic – a deeply held personal belief that it was the right thing to do, even if I wasn't sure why? Whatever I said was sure to sound contrived or even faintly ridiculous.

"I've given this a lot of thought . . ." I began hesitantly. He correctly interpreted this to mean that I hadn't the faintest idea how to answer his question and he came to the rescue.

"A bit apprehensive at the thought of a medical Marks & Spencer's?" he said, smiling.

"Something like that," I replied. "A big expensive building

is not necessarily synonymous with a good standard of medical care."

"Depends on the people in it, surely?" said Ashton.

"Of course. But the administrative constraints and complexity, given that the place is leased by the doctors from the health authority, might . . . get in the way, if you see what I mean."

"You mean it might be less personal, between doctor and patient?"

"It needn't be. But I can see that it would be more difficult to maintain personal, er . . . I suppose that if you feel you are part of a big organisation, it's easier to shelve your responsibility."

To my relief he nodded in agreement.

"Size and efficiency has a price. I know what you mean. You don't go to ICI if you want a tin of baking soda." He picked up the file of papers on his desk and tapped the edges on the desk, looking round at the others. "Right. That's all I want to ask, Mr Chairman."

The rest of the interview was routine. A pharmacist and a jumpy, ageing community physician reamed off a series of mechanical questions from their pencilled list in front of them, but neither seemed to listen to the answers. At the end of it, Lloyd stood up. He put the fingers of both hands on his chin and stooped, with his long thin neck stuck forward like a preying mantis.

"Well now, I think that concludes the, ah . . . You will of course be notified in due course, doctor. These things take . . . and we have others to . . . Thank you for coming, doctor . . . er . . . Mr . . . ah . . . when you go out . . . will see to your expenses and that kind of thing. Good day. Nice meeting you. So if you would, er . . ." He gestured towards the door. I was met by the same clerk and made my way downstairs while he explained the procedure about notification of the results of the interview. I didn't hear a word. I just couldn't get out of that pastel-grey catacombe quickly enough.

Once I had got away from the town centre and onto the ring road I began to relax a little. I had taken two days' holiday from the practice and I was in no hurry. By the time I got home the adrenalin had tapered off and the endless play-back of the interview had stopped looping round inside my head.

I parked the car in the drive and Tanya came out of the house to meet me, followed by Conrad who trotted unsteadily towards me holding out a half-eaten apple in his hands, insisting that I share it with him.

"How did it go?" asked Tanya.

"Mm-mm," I mumbled through a mouthful of apple, pointing to my mouth and then to the door. I took her hand and we went inside.

"I've made you some lunch. We've eaten already . . ."

"That's the story of my life," I said, laughing. "I'll have it in a little while. Not hungry yet."

I helped myself to a small scotch and we sat down at the large, oval kitchen table. I put Conrad on my knee.

"Well? And what have you been up to while daddy has been toiling away all morning?" I said to him.

"Playing," he replied. He stroked his hair with the apple core and smiled. "Going playing again, now. You come". He slid off my knee and tugged at my jacket.

"I'll come in a minute. I promise," I said. He looked up with his solemn brown eyes.

"You said that . . . before."

"Before? When was that?"

"Don't know. Before . . ." He turned away and went out. Through the open door I could see him slowly and carefully climbing the stairs. I looked across at Tanya and sighed.

"Another brief but meaningful exchange between father and son," I said.

"Heavy with messages," she replied. "Do you think his brown eyes are trying to tell you something?" She cupped her hands under her chin and rested her elbows on the table, arching her eyebrows and smiling with a question that she had asked before but from which she knew she would never get a straight answer.

"Of course, yes, I know." I said quickly. I grimaced and closed one eye like a mad pirate. "His eyes, me beauty, be the dark pools of my guilt – Ha har! And now, afore I deal with the boy, you'll be wanting to know about the inquisition?"

She closed her eyes and put her hand on mine.

"When you've finished the pantomime," she murmured. "Sorry. I know you're still charged up about it. It's just that I've been with him all morning and . . . children see the truth so clearly – unfettered by the excuses and rationalisations of grown-ups. Tell me about the interview first."

I went through it again, and this time it didn't seem so bad. Talking about it was like going through exam questions after the event, the re-telling of it seeming to smooth off the rough edges of ignorance and giving the answers a patina of credibility. I stood up, finished off the whisky, then restlessly paced around the room.

"So you don't think it went too badly?" said Tanya.

I shrugged. "Who can tell? God knows what they wanted – or even what they were thinking half the time. It's in the lap of the gods, as they say."

"How long will it be before you know?" she asked.

"Two, maybe three weeks. The decision goes to the Medical Practices Committee in London for rubber stamping. Then we'll know."

"It will seem like a long wait."

"You bet. But the worst comes after, when I have to tell Ian and Molly."

"Hm. How do you think they'll react?"

"I've no idea. Shouldn't think they would be over the moon, what with the disturbance it would cause. I don't want to think about it at the moment." I looked down at the floor. "I'm just going to see what Conrad is up to."

"Don't you want . . .?" She ran her hand through her hair and shook her head. "Never mind. Go and see what Conrad wants. He's been asking all morning for you to do something for him, knowing that you weren't in the surgery. Maybe you should sort out whatever it is before the other two arrive home from school and take over."

I went upstairs and into his room. He was squatting on the floor amid an assortment of his favourite toys. He looked up and beamed as if the sun had risen behind his eyes. Without looking away he reached out and held up a stuffed dog with three legs.

"Want a doctor. Fix his leg off," he said earnestly.

"Fix his leg *on*," I said, taking the offering. "His leg's *off*".

He nodded solemnly and reached out among the oddments strewn around him, picking up an isolated fabric limb which trailed cotton wadding from one end.

"This is to fix," he said. "Doctors do that. If you don't make it better, dog will die."

I looked at the pieces I now held in both hands.

102

"That's right," I said, smiling at his logic which saw cause and effect so clearly. "Wait until I get my special things from downstairs to mend it. It's a mess."

He nodded thoughtfully. "Mess," he said nodding his head in approval of the word. I went and got some suturing equipment from my emergency bag and sat down on the bedroom floor. As I sorted out a gleaming curved needle and stainless steel needle holder, together with a length of black silk, he stared in awe and said nothing, wiggling his shoulders in anticipation. I threaded the needle and bent over the tatty fragments of fabric as if they were the most important thing in the world at that moment. Which they were.

9

Most days the mail arrived in a thick bundle with an elastic band around it, presumably to make it easier for the postman to shove through the letter box; increasingly it consisted of medical journals and unsolicited marketing bulletins from a host of pharmaceutical organisations, which arrived with a relentless regularity. The use of an elastic band, besides being a technological breakthrough by the Post Office, meant that most of this slippery polythene-wrapped nonsense no longer scattered itself down the hallway like confetti but could be picked up in one movement, to be sorted out at leisure over the nearest wastebin. Most of the promotional literature, easily recognisable by the banal hyperbole showing through the long white envelopes – "Megagesic is Magic for Migraine" – went straight in the bin, thus speeding up the ecological sequence of events which began with the felling of great trees and ended up in the re-pulping machines. The only satisfaction I got was that, by throwing the stuff away unopened and unread, I had to some extent neutralised the effect that this mind-litter was supposed to have on my prescribing habits.

It was nearly three weeks after the interview in Derby. I was late that morning, and I snatched up the bundle of mail from behind the door, throwing it on the passenger seat of the car before driving off. As I drove I glanced down and quickly fingered the collection of circulars. I could see the edges of one or two long, thick manilla envelopes which looked interesting and I drove impatiently to the surgery. Hardly noticing the gathered patients, I mumbled briefly to Ann and Christine before sitting down at my desk and ripping off the rubber band which held the bundle together. The letters and magazines scattered onto the surface of the desk, nearly knocking over a cup of tea which the girls had placed on the large blotter in front of me. One of the envelopes was postmarked Derby. I ripped it open and drew out a wad of typed sheets, on top of

104

which was a letter from the FPC. I only needed to read the first sentence to know that I was home and dry.

"Dear Doctor Rushton," it read, "we are pleased to inform you . . ."

The rest, I knew, was sheer formality. I scanned the page, then stuffed the sheets back in the envelope with shaking hands, gathering up the rest of the mail with an unco-ordinated carelessness and, in doing so, knocking over the tea into my lap. It wasn't very hot but it made a huge, embarrassingly situated patch on my trousers. I jumped up and stood as close as I could to the single-bar electric fire on the wall, hoping that the heat would dry it off. My mind was a turmoil of emotions, and I didn't know what to do next. I picked up the letter, read it through again and began to pace up and down the room, taking deep breaths in an effort to calm down. Eventually I sat down and put my head in my hands and closed my eyes until my pulse rate had returned to a reasonable level. When I opened them again a minute later, I stared down between my fingers and saw the pile of record-cards belonging to the patients who were waiting outside. I put the envelope away in my pocket and took another deep breath, knowing that the only way of switching my mind off the letter of acceptance was to draw on all my powers of concentration and get on with the surgery. I glanced down and saw to my dismay that the wet patch was no less noticeable, so I pulled the chair as close as I could to the desk and edged forward slightly, praying that, for the next hour or so, it would not be necessary for me to move from this position before I had dried out.

The surgery began quietly enough – the first few patients requiring either a repeat prescription or a sick note – but as we progressed through the usual gamut of problems it became an increasingly difficult test of inventiveness on my part in order to avoid moving. Several patients posed a serious threat to my dignity when they mentioned their bad chests, each one starting to unfasten a few shirt buttons with the implied request for me to clap the stethoscope on – a feat which would have been impossible without getting up and walking round the desk. To each one, at the first sign of a button being undone or a jacket being taken off, I was forced to respond in much the same way by smiling grimly, and exclaiming: "Good grief, you were absolutely right about your chest – why, I can hear it from where I'm sitting!"

I hated this dishonesty, necessary though it seemed to be, and felt sure that I couldn't keep it up, even if it did stop me from thinking about Alec Duncan's practice.

When Paul Frayter came into my consulting room my ingenuity was tested to its limit, for he was probably the tallest nineteen year-old I had ever set eyes on. He wanted me to look into his ears. They were full of wax, he told me.

I instinctively reached for my auriscope. He stood quite still at the other side of the desk, waiting for me to come over; I remained in my chair trying to think of a good excuse to avoid standing up. There was an awkward silence and the whole scene had a frozen quality about it like a medieval wood-cut. The patient looked at me expectantly with his head craned forward and with one ear inclined towards me. I released my hold on the auriscope and grasped the arms of my chair, staring at his ear, and for a few seconds we remained immobile, like two naturalists in the wilderness listening for the mating call of some rare species of wildlife. It was only when I heard the rumble and clatter of the window cleaner's ladder against the outside wall that an idea occurred to me. I persuaded him to come over by the window. The surrounding bookshelves in that cramped corner meant that he could only position himself a foot or so away from my chair. I kept up a stream of drivel about the light having to be critical in direction and intensity to look in his ears, but he was much too tall to be examined from the sitting position. Eventually, after much bobbing up and down, he was more or less forced to crouch on his hands and knees for me to get the auriscope in his ear without falling out of my chair. As I squinted down the instrument, he let out a shout of anguish, followed by a string of obscenities. I recoiled in surprise.

"My God – was that so painful?" I asked.

"No no," he panted, red in the face with discomfort. "Sorry about the language, doc. It's not my ear – I got my bleedin' foot jammed underneath your chair. It's . . . oh . . . that's OK now."

He got up and stamped about the room, shaking one leg about as if trying to dislodge something from the inside of his trousers.

"Sorry about that, Paul," I said. "We're a bit cramped in here, as you can see."

I wrote out a prescription for some ear drops and asked him to come back in a few days so that I could syringe his ears out. He threw back his head and laughed.

"Better leave it for about a week, doc – I need a little more practice at standing on my head. Or perhaps I could bring a trampoline – you could try syringing me ears while we're bouncing up and down on that, doctor, seeing as how you like to do things the hard way. That'd be a bit of a challenge, wouldn't it?" He grinned broadly and waved as he went out.

Mrs Christine Parr came in next with her four year-old son, Christopher. Mrs Parr unravelled a long, involved tale of her other son's mysterious fever from which he was now suffering while staying with his grandparents in Peterborough. She wanted to bring him all the way back for me to see and treat, which did not seem to be a good idea at all. She kept saying what a sensitive little child Justin was and how I seemed to understand him. Justin was sensitive, right enough, I recalled. About as sensitive as a boa-constrictor. In the last year or two, during our countless consultations, he had dismantled every movable object in the consulting room, and if he hadn't been able to move it, he had chewed it. I imagined that when the lad grew up he would be in a circus bending steel bars with his teeth, and that by then he would probably have jaws the size of a coal scuttle.

My attention to Mrs Parr's monologue began to waver, especially when Christopher wandered round to my side of the desk to look at its contents. As he did so, he caught sight of my soaking trousers. I attempted to distract the child's attention by flashing a pocket torch in his eyes, but he was transfixed. I slid myself further down the chair until I was almost horizontal, practically disappearing under the desk while still nodding and smiling inanely at Mrs Parr. To my relief, she called the child over. The little boy looked across at me, tapping his mother on the knee. She ignored him.

"Mummy, that —"

"Shush, dear. Mummy's talking to the doctor."

"But that —"

"Shush, Christopher."

"That master's done a —"

"Christopher! It's rude to interrupt mummy when she's talking."

Christopher stared sulkily at me. Mrs Parr got up, having made up her mind what to do about her other son. I wasn't sure whether this was the right decision or not, because I had completely forgotten the original question. As they went out Christopher turned and gave me a wide-eyed look of fascination, and in the corridor I heard the child's deep penetrating voice.

"Mummy . . ."

"Yes, dear?"

"That master's done a big wee in his pants, just like our Justin does!"

"Now hush! That's very rude, Christopher."

"But he has, he has! I saw it."

"Christopher! Now that's enough."

"Big wet patch. I *did* see it. I *did* . . ."

He was still insisting on my incontinence as they went out. Once she had closed the outside door, Mrs Parr smacked his bare legs and dragged him, howling, down the street.

Ann brought in a few more notes and I sat for a while, fiddling with the telephone. I wanted to tell Tanya about the letter, but decided to save it until I got home at lunch-time when there would be more time to talk. Besides, it seemed to me that although the telephone was adequate for communicating hard facts, it was no use at all for this sort of thing.

I finished off the surgery as briskly as possible and, having by now thoroughly dried out, went to the visit book. To my surprise, there were only two home visits, and Molly had signed them both. She came breezily out of her room, carrying her medical bag in one hand and a shopping bag over her other arm. She nodded at the book.

"Lucky for some," she said.

"Amazing. Would you like me to see one of . . . ?"

She shook her head. "No. I've been seeing both these people. I know them. You can get an early bath."

She grinned and went out. I turned to go back into my room, thinking sadly that one of the things I would surely miss was the cheerful energy of Molly, who never once cribbed at the work load or the way it was shared out. When I thought about the many medical partnerships I had seen, where crabbiness and petty animosity were the normal way of life, it suddenly struck me what a rare and valuable thing I would be giving up by moving to Stonebridge.

Before I had got through the door of my room, the outside door burst open. A tall, gangling figure stooped and gasped on the step. I recognised him immediately and groaned, for it was the relentless James McNair.

"Ah, doctor," he grated, "can ye see us ferra wee minute? It's ma stomach again, y'ken." He clutched his abdomen and staggered forward into the passageway towards me. Without saying a word I waved him into my room, smiling reassuringly at an old lady who was standing by the reception desk, clutching the repeat prescription which she had come to collect. She stepped forward, grabbing Jimmy's arm.

"Come on, love" she said in a kindly voice. "You've come to the right place if you're not feeling too good of yerself. I don't know what we'd do without doctors." She looked at me, puckering up her face with ancient sympathy and understanding. "Always somebody worse than yersel', what I always say," she said, stuffing her prescription into her coat pocket with her free hand. "Are y'all right, love?"

McNair grimaced and jerked his chin down onto his chest.

"Oh aye – dinna fret, hen. Ah'll manage, even if it kills me."

He palmed her off gently. As she hobbled out, he went into my room and gingerly lowered himself into a chair, breathing heavily. I sat down at my desk, detecting a faint smell of beer, even though it was only eleven o'clock in the morning.

Jimmy McNair was a native of Glasgow who had come to Overton some years before. He was a plasterer in the building trade, and always explained his prodigious alcohol intake as a necessary antidote to the lime he swallowed during his working hours. His sunken eyes, hollow cheeks and unshaven face were a source of embarrassment to his wife who looked after him as best she could, for his outward appearance was one of dishevelled self-neglect. He even threw on his clothes as if his mind was on something else.

He was well known to the three of us as one of our patients whose every organ had been subjected to most of the tests known to medical science. He had presented himself with strokes, coronaries, ulcers, ruptured spleens, malaria, tropical sprue and brain tumours, to name but a few, and had seen every specialist in the area over the last few years – yet his notes were stuffed with one negative investigation after another. When he came in with one of his complaints, he invariably arrived at the busiest times, forging a pathway through the rest of the patients who recoiled in alarm at his hunted expression and by the sheer energy of his histrionic behaviour. What amused and puzzled me most of all was the fact that, when offered a sick note at the end of one of these consultations, he would shake his head and gasp: "No thanks, doctor, I'll struggle on. The family's got tae eat, y'ken." He would then rise painfully, holding on to the wall or the furniture, and stagger out while dragging one leg or clutching his abdomen. Sometimes he did both at the same time. Within a few hours he would effect an amazing recovery and, later in the day, I would often see him running for a bus or else darting into one of the local pubs as if prohibition was going to be declared within the hour. I could never work out why he behaved the way he did, but in spite of it all I liked him, and in tolerating his barmy behaviour as much as I did, I earned an enormous amount of respect from the rest of the family who presumably recognised that we were all sharing the same cross.

One of Jimmy's more frequent complaints was severe abdominal pain. During one of these episodes I could guarantee being plagued to death every single day for days on end, and I had learned to grit my teeth and ride it out. He had had three barium meals and various other tests which were normal, and the experts had unanimously concluded that his symptoms were entirely psychogenic. To be truthful, when this complaint was viewed alongside the rest of his incredible ailments, their conclusion was inevitable. And dangerous.

I got him to climb onto the examination couch. He thrashed about so much he nearly fell off and it was difficult to examine him properly. I felt a fleeting impatience as I thought about the letter from Derby and how much I wanted to get home to show it to Tanya. With an effort of will, I shut this out of my mind and concentrated my thoughts on Jimmy McNair's white, skinny abdomen. It was as hard as a board, and when I touched it he threw his head back and shouted in pain through his clenched teeth. This was nothing new: he behaved like this every time his abdomen was examined.

"Jesus Christ – yer killin' me right enough, y'are!" he yelled.

"Oh come on, Jimmy," I said, "we've been through all this

110

before, a dozen times. It's no different than it always is."

"It's no' the same, ah'm tellin' ye," he groaned. "Ah'm bladdy deein', man. Can ye no' see tha'?"

The tortured Glaswegian vowels mangled their way past his vocal cords and down his nose. It was a sound that could not have been improved on in its ability to convey suffering. Unfortunately the degree of discomfort he was now experiencing was impossible to assess with certainty, since Jimmy's everyday conversational voice had an irritable whining quality, as if he had stones in his shoes.

"Right, Jimmy," I said, "if it's as bad as you say it is – then it's definitely the chop this time." I was hoping that this would make him pull himself together. It usually worked.

"Ah, but yerra hard bastard, that's a fact. No disrespect of course, doctor," he said, swinging himself into a sitting position. He slumped forward on the edge of the examination couch. "But if that's the way it's got tae be, ah can take it."

I looked at him with surprise. Normally he would have been staggering out by now, but this time he made no attempt to move.

"You know what that means, don't you?" I said. "They'll probably have to make an incision from your Adam's apple down to your testicles to find out what's wrong with your insides. I mean – let's face it – you've been in and out of hospital like a yo-yo in the past year or two, and they've never yet found anything wrong with you. You're giving me no choice, carrying on like this."

I felt a growing exasperation that was only partly a response to Jimmy's behaviour. I wanted to get home, for one thing, and the last thing I needed was this sort of pantomime. On the other hand, I knew I couldn't win: you simply could not be one hundred per cent sure about a man like Jimmy McNair. One of these days he would cry wolf too often. After a moment's hesitation, I picked up the phone.

"Wishton General? RSO, please. Yes, I'll wait."

I looked at him as he sat hunched on the couch, breathing noisily and wincing every now and again. His abdomen *had* been a bit rigid when I examined him. There was just a remote chance – a very remote one – that he had got a perforated duodenal ulcer. Or maybe I was just trying to rationalise my own actions, now. It would be the ultimate irony if Jimmy really did have something life-threatening after his string of imaginary ailments. I conjured up a picture of his ghost floating over Overton cemetery, wailing in his harsh Glaswegian voice which could be heard twenty miles away: "Away, ya bastards! Ah told ye ah wuz a sick man! A pox on yer bladdy stethoscopes!"

"Hullo, hullo, RSO here. What have you got?"

"Steven Rushton here. It's Jimmy McNair. He's, er, complaining of severe abdominal pain."

There was a loud groan on the other end, and I pressed the receiver hard against my ear so that Jimmy would not hear it.

"When the bloody hell doesn't he complain of abdominal pain?" said the dismayed voice.

"I realise that —"

"Can't you send him somewhere else? Give us all a break – send him to the Royal."

"I've tried everywhere else," I lied. "See if you can find him a bed. He's rolling about in agony here."

The RSO sighed, then told me to hang on. There was a brief, muffled conversation at the other end. "OK. I suppose you'd better send him to male surgical, although I hope you realise that I'll get bollocked by my consultant for agreeing to take him."

"Thanks. I owe you a pint," I said.

"Bloody right, you do. And I'll lay you ten to one that there's nothing wrong with him. We'll keep him in overnight and I'll kick him out tomorrow before my chief does his rounds, or else it'll be another nail in the coffin of my career. Cheerio."

I arranged for the ambulance to pick Jimmy up from the surgery. He cursed and groaned as the doors closed and the vehicle took him away. Feeling no satisfaction or sense of achievement whatsoever, I got into my car and drove home.

I found Tanya on her hands and knees on the kitchen floor, sorting out a pile of medical journals, some of which were still in their cellophane wrappers. She looked up and smiled.

"Hello. You're early." She picked up an armful of journals and started to get up. "How many of these things haven't you read yet? They're beginning to block out the light . . ."

"Come here," I said, taking the pile of magazines she was holding. I dropped them to one side where they scattered over

112

the quarry-tiled floor like a new pack of cards. I pulled her towards me, holding her so tightly that she gasped.

"I felt the warmth of her eager body next to mine," I murmured in her ear, "and I inhaled deeply as I caught the intoxicating fragrance of her hair in my flaring nostrils . . ."

We both burst out laughing and she dug me in the ribs.

"And I thought that you wanted me for my mind, you swine!" She drew her head back and grinned. "What's all this about?"

"Alec's practice. I've been accepted."

She sighed and put her head on my shoulder. "I'm so glad. At least now we know."

"The letter came this morning. Hang on . . ."

I disentangled myself, took the manilla envelope from my pocket and gave it to her. She took out the letter without taking her eyes off me, then, after reading it quickly, she flung her arms round me and we kissed each other so enthusiastically that we both nearly fell over. After a few minutes I took her hand and we went into the lounge where the pale sunlight slanted through the gothic windows, lighting up the centre of the room like a stage.

"It's a pity we're going to have to move," I said. "I love this house."

"There are a few things we'll miss if we ever get time to think about it," Tanya murmured. I looked at her and smiled.

"We probably won't get time. There's a hell of a lot to sort out."

"When will you tell Ian and Molly?"

"I don't know," I said. I got a peculiar feeling somewhere underneath my diaphragm at the thought of it. "I suppose the sooner the better really. Tomorrow after surgery, maybe."

She reached across and gave my hand a squeeze.

"Don't put it off," she said quietly. "That's going to be one of the more difficult things you have to do. The rest . . . moving and settling in somewhere else, we'll be doing together. We've done it all before, more than once."

I grunted, remembering the icy tenement in Edinburgh. We had hauled all our possessions up five flights of stone stairs to the top flat where the draught from the rattling sash windows made the ceiling lights swing about like lanterns on a storm-bound ship. That was when I was making my first – and last –

unsuccessful attempt at a surgical career. It seemed a million years ago now.

"It'll be a lot different from the last time we . . ."

The telephone rang. I reached out and picked up the receiver, not taking my eyes off Tanya's face. I could still smell the damp dust of those one hundred and four stone steps, and for a moment I was not aware of the voice on the other end of the telephone.

"Steven? Is that you?" It was Molly.

"Sorry. I was miles away," I said.

"Oh. I thought I'd been cut off. You haven't forgotten, have you?"

"Forgotten what?"

"Oh, God, of course you have, I can tell," she said. "The meeting. The three of us have got a meeting this afternoon at the surgery."

"Yes, I remember. Ian wanted to talk about . . . About what time?"

"An hour."

I looked at my watch, "OK. I'll have some lunch and see you in an hour."

She rang off and I took a deep breath.

"We've got a meeting at the surgery in an hour," I said. Tanya twitched her eyebrows.

"So I gather."

"What did Henry the Fifth say before Agincourt? Something about setting the nostrils wide and taking on the action of a tiger. Damned if I can remember . . . Anyway, it looks as if I'm going to have to break the news this afternoon."

I left a half-eaten meal and paced round the garden going over and over what I was going to say to Molly and Ian, trying to imagine what their responses would be. It didn't help, and after a while I gave up.

Driving back to the surgery seemed to take no time at all and I spent a lot of time parking my car and performing a laborious ritual of locking the doors and fiddling about to delay going into the surgery. When I went in, I could hear Molly and Ian talking in the other consulting room. Christine was standing behind the reception counter waving the telephone receiver around like a flag.

"RSO at Wishton for you."

114

Out of the corner of my eye I saw Molly poke her head round the door and I grabbed the receiver, turning away from her. The feel of the telephone against my ear and the sound of the voice at the other end gave me an agreeable sense of isolation. I took my time.

"Doctor Rushton here. What's the problem?"

"Hello. RSO here. About James McNair. I've just this minute come out of theatre."

"That was quick. What . . . ?"

"I owe you ten pints, professor. He hit the jackpot this time, believe me. We had a short list this morning. Took one look at him and stuck him in at the end."

"You opened him up?"

"Not half. Did a laparotomy and found a perforation you could drive a truck through. Half his breakfast floating around on top of two pints of brown ale in his peritoneal cavity. Bloody mess, I can tell you."

"Is he all right?" I asked anxiously.

"Oh, yes. He'll be a bit shot up for a couple of days, but he'll be OK. Bloody good job you sent him in, though."

I thanked him and replaced the receiver. A duodenal ulcer. My God. My relief at sending him in lay uneasily because I still felt that the action I had taken was based more on expediency than sixth sense. I knew that it had been a case of getting him out of my hair and that the dividing line between triumph and disaster had been, in this case, paper-thin.

I turned and went in to join Ian and Molly. I closed the door firmly behind me and braced myself.

"Before we start, there is . . . something else which I have to tell you both."

As I heard the words coming out of my parched mouth I knew that there was no going back now.

115

10

The Ram's Head, just off the main square in Stonebridge, was no longer the quiet, relaxing place that I remembered a few years ago. At that time, apart from the low, continuous mutter from a few sheep farmers and market traders, the only other sound was the whine of the beer pumps. Now, even allowing for the fact that Christmas was barely a week away and the place was almost full from end to end, I still couldn't get over the ugly transformation which had taken place since I had last been there.

I edged my way to the brightly-lit bar, trying not to brush against the plates of quiche and chips which occupied every inch of space on the small round formica-topped tables. While the lads round the tables guffawed at their own accounts of how legless they had been the Christmas before, the girls flashed glances round the room and held their cigarettes over their food, each one selfconsciously blowing the smoke vertically over her lips as if she were trying to blow fluff off the end of her nose. Through the clatter and laughter threaded the brainless tinkle of piped music, punctuated by the sound of the gaming machine which spat out coins with the ferocity of a Gatling gun. These were surely the sounds of hell.

I bought a pint of beer and found an empty space at the other end of the room, nearly sitting on the lap of an old lady who was drinking a milk stout and smiling at her hearing aid which she had disconnected and which was lying in the ash tray in front of her. She nodded at me and poured the contents of her glass into her dark concave mouth, wiping her chin with a tremulous, arthritic hand.

"Nice to see young folk enjoying umselves," she bellowed above the din. "Speshly being as it's this time of year."

I opened my mouth to reply, but she put her fingers to her lips, picked up the hearing aid and slipped it into her handbag. I took a mouthful of beer and leaned back into a cloud of

116

tobacco smoke which seemed to come from all directions.

"Well, well, well – if it isn't the young Doctor Rushton," a voice boomed. I turned round. It was Ron Leaford, looking more bulky and red-faced than when I had last seen him. He was about sixty, and wore a heavy tweed suit whose cavernous pockets bulged with so much medical paraphernalia that I wondered why he bothered to carry a medical bag at all. With his ruddy complexion and his large rough hands, he looked as if he would be more at home baling hay than looking down the delicate ears of infants.

"Hello, Ron. Nice to see you again." I looked round the room and shrugged apologetically. "When I suggested we meet here I didn't realise . . ."

He grinned and started to walk towards the far door by the bar, signalling to one of the girls behind the bar and waving me to follow him. We went through two doors into an empty private room with dark oak tables and bench seats. The walls were panelled with the same wood and covered with prints of horses and old maps.

"Now then, here we are. There's still one room the brewery hasn't buggered up," he said. We sat down and he lit his pipe. "You'll never believe this, but I used to run a surgery in here when I first came. Before I got fixed up with somewhere a bit more suitable, that is. Patients used to wait in the main bar, I used to sit in here and, when I wanted a patient in, I used to have to ring a bell that was so big it needed two hands to pick up."

A woman in her forties entered the room carrying two pints of beer. Ron beamed.

"Ah, Elsie from yonder bedlam. How are you, my love? Still getting the hot flushes, I see."

"It's not hot flushes today, Doctor Leaford," she said, wiping her face with her apron. "It's serving behind that bar that's done it. My God, if anybody needs any legal work done at Dakin and Platt's they can forget it for today, the way their staff have been shifting them Bacardi and cokes. Will you want anything to eat?"

"Two soups, Elsie, if you will." He turned and looked at me with his humorous blue eyes. "Try the soup first. It's very substantial, to say the least, so you may not want anything else. It's up to you, of course."

117

She went away and returned a moment later with an entire wholemeal loaf cut into slices the size of doorsteps, and two huge earthenware bowls of soup which looked as if they had half the countryside in them.

"So when do you start?"

"February."

"Not long, then. Can't say I'll be sorry. Been a bit untidy with locums, sharing the patients and so forth. How's all the preparation going?"

"Very smoothly. We've sold the house and, as you know, we negotiated Bet Duncan's house along with the surgery and all the contents."

"Yes. She told me. Nice big house. Just right for your family. She's moving across the town to a small place, you know. Hmm . . . so you'll have met the formidable Mrs Addy while you've been coming over these last few weeks?"

I smiled. Beatrice Addy had been Alec's receptionist for many years. I had met her again a couple of weeks ago and found that she had not changed one bit. She had been a qualified nurse many years ago but had quit the profession to look after her husband who had died in his late twenties after a long illness. She neither re-married nor did she return to nursing, but instead devoted herself to Alec's practice and, like most people who have witnessed prolonged suffering, she now maintained a tight rein on her sympathy in the knowledge that there was only so much rope to pay out. Behind her prim austerity, however, she showed occasional flashes of warmth and humour which had made the polite neutrality of our recent meeting rather less depressing than it had first appeared. It would take a long time to establish an easy working relationship in the place of Alec Duncan, but I had the feeling that, once it was established, her loyalty would be unshakeable.

"Yes, I met her again recently," I said.

"She'll miss Alec. As we all will, I expect. Poor old Alec. He'd been getting angina for months but still kept running after his patients as if tomorrow had been cancelled. Ran himself into an early grave."

We finished our soup in silence. Ron leaned back and stared at the soapy froth in the rim of his glass.

"How d'you think you'll like single-handed practice?" he said. I took a deep breath and shrugged.

"I can see that it's going to be different from what I've been used to," I said.

"You're in one of these group practices at the moment, aren't you?"

"Three of us."

"Oh yes. With Ian McDonald, of course. There's a nice bloke. Bloody good doctor, too. Oh well . . . three's not too bad, I suppose. It's these very big groups I don't like. Couldn't put up with it. Have to hold a conference before you can order a fresh bar of soap. Farcical. Anyway, I hope you know what you've let yourself in for. Single-handed practice is a young man's game."

"You don't look too bad on it," I said. "How long is it now?"

"I've been at it thirty-five years." He sighed and finished his beer. "Thirty-five years . . . that's longer than you've been on this earth, I bet. It's had its moments, I can tell you. I remember doing some running around years ago. I didn't mind it, then – making two or three visits a day for someone with pneumonia, or sticking a knife into a big, throbbing abscess and so forth. And not much in the way of antibiotics like you've got now. It's a wonder we didn't kill more people in those days. Damn sight different now. Folk only need to fart before they pick up the 'phone and want a visit or else want to go to hospital for tests. Most of the stuff I see these days seems to be either social or marital, and I don't have any prescription for that sort of carry on. Come on, Steven, drink up and I'll get another."

I finished my beer and handed him the glass. He went through to the bar and returned a minute later with two full glasses. As he sat down, something heavy in his pocket banged against the table-top. He cursed, put down his pipe and took an ophthalmoscope from his jacket pocket. He flicked the switch unsuccessfully a few times, shook it, then put it back in his pocket.

"That's buggered. Bulb's gone. Don't last five minutes, these days. Well, one thing's for sure – I won't be buying many more of them."

"How's that?"

"Oh well. I've had enough. I think I'll do another couple of years and then pack up. This business with Alec finally switched me off, you know."

119

Behind his matter-of-fact exterior, Ron Leaford had a keen brain and was not half as hard on his patients as he pretended to be. When I saw his face visibly sag I knew that it was a measure of his feelings, since he had always made a virtue out of being apparently unmoved about the misfortune of others. I looked down at my beer and said nothing.

"Of course, you wouldn't know, would you?" He smiled grimly. "I'm up before a Service Committee in a couple of weeks. Formal complaints procedure and all that."

"I'm sorry. I . . ."

"Hang on. D'you know what happened? A patient of mine whom I've known for years had a coronary one Tuesday afternoon – and it happened to be the afternoon they held the local church service for Alec. Not the funeral – Bet had him taken to Scotland, as you know. So anyway, there's no one at home, naturally, and there's no one at the surgery either, because my receptionist finishes at lunch-time. Patient's thrashing around with chest pain, his wife's ringing round trying to contact me and going crackers in the process, not surprisingly. First I hear of it is when they ring from hospital. His wife eventually dialled three nines. Ambulance took him to casualty where he popped his clogs, poor sod. Imagine how I felt. And then some bright bugger up there tells the wife that had he been seen earlier he could have been saved, which helped everybody no end, of course. As a result of that, the family get together and file a complaint which has been upheld by the family practitioner committee. Have you ever attended one of these hearings?"

"Er . . . no, I haven't."

"They're not very amusing. Like a court martial, only more polite. And very uncomfortable, with everyone saying their piece in the same room."

"How do you think it will go?"

He shrugged and a bitter edge crept into his normally avuncular voice. "I expect I'll be hung, drawn and quartered one way or another. Being at a colleague's funeral is no excuse when it comes to the deadly Paragraph Thirteen of our terms of service, old son. Failure to make proper arrangements for care of the patients while not available, et cetera."

"Seems a bit harsh," I said. "I mean, under the circumstances —"

"Harsh? Just bad luck, that's all," he said. "If I'd been

120

flagrantly dishonest and said I was out visiting another case, it might have been different. Who knows?" He grunted in disgust. "Two hours! That's the thing that really wears you down mentally and physically, you see. Total responsibility for your patients all round the clock, three hundred and sixty-five days a year. It starts to get to you after a while. I spend two bloody hours at Alec's church service and look what happens." He put his empty glass on the table and stretched his arms above his head.

"So what are you going to do with your spare time when you retire?" I asked him. I was relieved to see him brighten up immediately. He winked.

"Oh, don't worry about me. I've got my fingers in a few pies. I've bought a part-share in a new private nursing home in Dilshaw, over the hill. I might even avail myself of a few sessions just to keep my hand in. We've a beautifully equipped operating room, you know. The private sector's a growing industry and it'll keep on growing while these NHS waiting lists get longer and longer."

I couldn't help smiling.

"Somehow I can't visualise you, of all people, prancing discreetly round a private nursing home."

"You mean all this?" he laughed, rattling the pockets of his voluminous jacket. "Cheeky young sod. Private medicine isn't all pin-stripes and professional flannel, you know. Those who pay the piper are more interested in the tune he plays than the state of his pipe, if you see what I mean."

"I shouldn't have thought that private medicine had much effect on the waiting lists round here," I said. "More of a drop in the ocean, surely."

"Maybe you're right," he said, "only it depends who's gathering up the drops. Have you never fancied doing a bit of private work?"

I shook my head. "I'm not sure it's my —"

"Oh, come off it, Steven," he said. "Don't tell me you're going to stay in Stonebridge for the rest of your life. Staring down the same throats and throwing valium at the same people."

"I haven't even started in Stonebridge yet."

"I know, I know. Don't take any notice of me. I'm just being . . . have you ever thought of going abroad?"

121

I got my mental picture of ice fishing again and laughed softly to myself.

"Some time ago . . . I did think of going to Canada."

Ron put his head back and roared with laughter. "Canada? Oh, bloody hell. Used to be very good for British doctors years ago. Brain drain and so forth. They've got all the doctors they want now, except for the remote areas. And when I say remote areas – I mean something you just can't imagine. Hundreds of miles from anywhere, tundra and permafrost as far as the eye can see; two men and a clapped-out moose every hundred square miles. And the climate! I was in Saskatchewan years ago and I'm telling you – you have to be made of stainless steel and your blood vessels need to be filled with mercury to survive that bloody lot."

He looked at his watch and pushed his chair back.

"Shall we move? I thought I would take you round and introduce you to a couple of colleagues in the town. You can leave your car here and pick it up on the way back. We'll take my vehicle and I can tell you the sort of working arrangement we had before Alec died. See how it suits you."

We paid the bill for the food and made our way outside. I stood and shivered in the car park while Ron cleared the front seat of his Land Rover of a mass of record cards, note pads and medical magazines. He stuffed them unceremoniously behind the driver's seat.

"Not very elegant, these things," he yelled above the chatter of the diesel engine and the rattle of a dozen loose body panels, as we drove off. "More like a bloody tool-box on wheels. Very handy when we have snow, though. I've got quite a few patients up in the hills who would never get a visit in the middle of winter if I hadn't got it. Totally inappropriate ninety-nine per cent of the time, mind you. I once went to a big shindig at the Midland after a spell of bad weather. Kathleen and I were dressed to the nines and the vehicle was covered in shit from end to end. Needless to say, I was treated like a pariah, a *persona non grata*, an unmentionable disease, by the flunkey at the door. As it turned out, he happened to be a patient whose life I had saved a few years previously. Refused the keys and told me to park the vehicle myself as far out of sight as possible. Mind you – and this is where your faith in human nature is restored – he must have gone a bit soggy at the knees with

122

remorse, because the head waiter gave me one of those funny looks and told us that the drinks for the evening had been taken care of by a grateful patient. Now then . . ."

He grappled with the gearstick and turned into a busy main road, trundling the clumsy vehicle amongst the traffic with a confidence born of habit rather than innate skill.

"What you have to remember," he continued, "is that being so far away from the metropolis, we don't have a commercial deputising service. Whatever the rights and wrongs of it, we've managed without one all these years, so we've never missed it, although at times I wonder if it wouldn't be a good thing. Anyway, Alec and I used to cover each other's nights off tit for tat, and then we recently got into a rota with the two fellows we're going to see now. We used to involve Jim Ashton, too, whom you met at your interview. He lives on the outskirts, so he found it better to tie up with a group in Dilshaw, after a while. Here we go."

We parked outside a large Georgian house set back from the main road. The downstairs windows were fitted with venetian blinds, and by the side of the main door was a large brass plaque which was the only outward sign that this was a place of business rather than a private house.

"Gerald Crawley and Rami Prakash," Ron said, noisily zipping up the handbrake. "Don't call him Gerry, by the way. His wife hates it. She's a very bright lady, a haematologist at the Royal. With their combined income it allows him to have a small list and he does a lot of research – writing papers and so on. You can't open a journal without seeing an article by Gerald. He's a bit of an egghead but basically all right, and of course Rami Prakash does all the work. Rami looks like a guided missile about to detonate, but I find him OK and he speaks the lingo very well, which is a godsend. We don't really have all that much contact except for the odd night when we're covering for each other, which suits me."

Gerald Crawley met us as soon as we walked through the front door. His half-moon glasses and his carelessly combed white hair gave him an unmistakably academic appearance which was accentuated by his stooping posture and thin, humourless smile. He seemed faintly embarrassed by the mechanics of greeting and almost immediately distanced himself by attempting to show us the progress he was making in

123

his latest research project. We wandered among exasperated secretaries funded by the University research department who scurried from one desk to another, sifting and sorting colour-coded cards like termites repairing a storm-damaged colony. Prakash, a tall, slim Indian with burning eyes, had retreated into the far corner. Writing out a stack of repeat prescriptions while answering one telephone call after another, he was at the same time attempting to find somewhere to sit without disturbing piles of data-sheets which seemed to spill over every available surface. Clearly he was a man pushing out the frontiers of what it is possible to achieve with one pair of arms and one pair of legs.

As we threaded our way towards Crawley's consulting room, I was struck by the fact that it was impossible to walk anywhere in this surgery without disturbing something highly significant, which perhaps was why Crawley had adopted a curious, toe-to-heel gait as if he were traversing a precarious rope bridge. I later found out, to my great amusement, that he walked like this all the time, which had given rise to him being called Creepy Crawley by his inventive but bewildered patients.

Over coffee in his chaotic consulting room we were given a long dissertation about the disease profile of the local population, which was interrupted from time to time by Rami Prakash who zoomed in every few minutes, only to be summoned out again a few seconds later by another telephone call. By the time we were ready to leave, Prakash's eyes were popping out as if he was about to have a stroke.

When we got back to the car park at the Ram's Head, Ron got out of his vehicle and we walked together to where I had parked my car.

"So there you are, then," he said, smiling. "Pretty varied bunch, aren't we? It must seem a bit haphazard, the arrangement we've got, but it seems to work out quite well. And the beauty of single-handed practice is that you're not in each other's laps all the time. The amount of contact you have with any of us depends only on the amount of contact you yourself think is necessary. Having second thoughts?"

I looked at him and grinned. "Second thoughts? It's a bit late for that, Ron. No, I don't . . . as a matter of fact, since I met my replacement in Overton the other day I've felt I was in no-man's land. I'm really looking forward to starting here."

"That's good," he said, nodding his head. "I'm glad about that. You've no idea how pleased Bet Duncan is that you're taking over from Alec. She thinks of you as one of the family."

"I know that."

He held out his huge hand and shook mine.

"Good to have you with us. Look forward to seeing something of you in February. If you're half as good as Alec you'll do all right."

"Thanks. I . . . I hope all goes well at the service committee hearing."

"Oh, that," he said gruffly, shrugging his broad shoulders. "Well, I've become a cynical old bugger in my old age and I've developed a thick skin over the years. I'll survive."

He turned and shambled across the gravel car park to his Land Rover like a great friendly bear, his coat flapping in the cold wind.

11

I did not enjoy the next couple of weeks. I knew that the inevitable awkwardness between us was of my own making, for neither partner had shown anger or resentment at the news of my resignation. Molly had reacted with incredulity at first: moving from a reasonably well-organised group into the more vulnerable position of a single-handed general practitioner, she thought, signified a temporary madness that I would soon get over. Ian responded with sadness and disappointment, but there was a lack of surprise which, although he said very little, gave me the impression that he had known what was going on and that he understood why I wanted to do it. An air of unreality pervaded the place as Ann and Christine fussed around with a subdued cheerfulness, like nurses in a hospital for the incurable; but, as it slowly dawned on everyone that my decision was irreversible, the silences became longer and the exchanges between us became briefer and more gloomy.

There was nothing else to be done or said about it, and during the hours of surgery I busied myself in the patients' problems to such a degree that by the end of each day I felt physically and mentally drained. The work temporarily became a drug which dulled my capacity for feeling sorrow or remorse at leaving, but at the same time I hardly had the energy to talk with Tanya about all the things which we needed to discuss. Her considerable patience and understanding were stretched to their limits.

Towards the end of the second week I got a message that Jimmy McNair had come home from hospital. Whatever misgivings I had about the manner in which I sent him in were now diminished by the thought that at least the end had justified the means. As I drove up to his house, with its oppressive wilderness of a front garden, I even began to think that my judgement had outweighed good fortune in his case.

126

When I saw the face of Mrs McNair darting from behind the front room curtains to reappear in the doorway with a welcoming smile, I knew in a flash that my immodest self-deception had been wholly out of place. In her broad honest face, the skin deeply lined from the stress and strain of thirty years of marriage to Jimmy, there was still enough generosity of spirit to light up half the Third World. I walked through the gate opening, noticing with some amusement that the gate lay almost engulfed by grass and dead rose-bay willow-herb. It had fallen off nearly two years ago when I had come to see Jimmy's father. As I remembered it, Jimmy had been unsuccessfully trying to get his father to eat a hearty breakfast, not realising that the old man had been dead for hours.

Mrs McNair waved me inside. Jimmy was sitting by the fire with a beer in his hand and the racing pages of the daily paper spread all over the place. He got up and shook my hand vigorously.

"Halloo, doctor. It's guid tae see yer, right enough it is," he said. "Youza bladdy genius – isn't that right, hen?"

He grinned broadly, nudging his wife in the ribs.

"Oh ay, we're verra pleased, right enough," she replied, nodding approvingly.

"Hey, get the man a wee drop, eh, hen," Jimmy croaked, waving his glass around. "D'ye fancy an Export? Or maybe you'll have a wee taste of somethin' *speyshul*?"

He winked and grinned maniacally with his small, caved-in mouth. His wife opened the door of an appalling cocktail cabinet which stood in the corner of the room. It was designed like a saloon bar, complete with beer pumps and brasses. She pulled out a bottle of malt whisky. I took the glass and drank the first small mouthful, watching Jimmy's eyes which lit up as if he was drinking it himself. He prodded me in the chest with his glass and in doing so, spilled a small quantity of beer on my shirt.

"Ya *knew*, ya bugger!" he cried. "Ya bladdy knew all tha time!"

"Knew what?" I said uneasily.

"Aw, c'mon, man. Dinnae gi'me aw tha' shite! Ya knew ah wasnae playin' about when ah came to yoor place."

"Oh – I see. *Then*, you mean. Yes, I remember."

He cackled and sat down. "Shudda seen the boy, hen. He

127

takes one look at me, ken, picks up the 'phone and orders me straight intae hospital. Christ, what a guy, eh? Just speaks to the wee boy at the other end, no shite, and in a flash ah'm being sewed up good as new. Fill his glass, hen – a wee gnat couldae pee'd more'n that."

Before I could move a muscle Mrs McNair obliged. I took another mouthful of the pale malt whisky which brought tears to my eyes and made me cough.

"Now look, Jimmy . . . the fact was that I only sent you into hospital because I couldn't stand the thought of you pestering the living daylights out of me for the next fortnight, as you usually do." I glanced apprehensively at the liquid in the glass as if it was the font of my reckless honesty. To my amazement he slapped his knee and roared with laughter.

"How aboot the boy, hen?" he gasped. "Saves ma bladdy life and then gives us aw' tha' shite aboot he didnae ken!"

He jumped up unsteadily to shake my hand and in doing so nearly fell into the fire.

"Well, we've got a wee prezzy for ye for wha' ye did," he said. He signalled to his wife who took an untidily wrapped bottle from the sideboard. I could see through the loose fold of the brown paper that it was an expensive whisky and I began to feel ashamed. I finished off the drink in my hand in one gulp.

"Oh . . . really, I don't deserve this, you know . . ."

"Away with ye!" growled Jimmy. "Jesus, ah feel like a new man already. Ah've got a lot tae thank ye for. Will ye have another wee drop?"

"Oh no, Jimmy," said Mrs McNair, taking my glass, "the doctor's got a lot to do, I'm sure. He cannae stop here all day drinkin' with you."

I made my way out of the house to a chorus of "cheerio", and drove off feeling like a charlatan, thankful that Jimmy had recovered so well, thankful for the bottle of scotch, and thankful that so many of our patients had an uncritical generosity which made our own shortcomings that much easier to live with.

12

There was a time, when I was very small, when I used to watch the smoke from my grandfather's briar curl and twist from the bowl of his pipe up to the high ceiling where it paled and flattened, then diffused into the still air of the room. The more my eye followed the movement from its source, the more impossible it became to distinguish from the haze which betrayed itself in the sloping grey rectangle of light from an old sash window.

So it seemed with our last Christmas in the house. From its warm, excited beginning it drifted into a dreary January where the debris and the boxes of the children's presents mixed with the packing cases and tea chests which now seemed to occupy every room. There was hardly a usable space on the floor, and while the children salvaged their broken, long-forgotten toys, Tanya methodically filled the containers with the bits and pieces which families gather over the years.

In the middle of that month I said my farewell to the practice. Before taking two weeks' holiday, during which we would be moving, I tidied up the loose ends at the surgery. Molly and Ian opened a bottle of Glen Grant and we sat for an hour or two reflecting quietly on our future. There was no rancour, only regret and sadness – certainly on my part. It was a new phase, we said. The fact that we had worked so well together, and had remained good friends, curiously enough made the dissolution easier. Everyone else reacted differently. Ann and Christine were tearful and bewildered, while some of the patients I saw were brimming with ambivalence at my departure. As they pulled out gifts from carrier bags their main concern was about who was coming next – to whom was I going to pass on the baton of their endless problems? One or two viewed the prospect with dismay, conveying gloomily that I understood their gastric stomach or dropped kidney, and that a successor would only plunge their mysterious symptoms back into the wilderness of polite, smiling rejection which would be the overture to yet another prescription for valium. Bleak though this observation was, it was no less so than my own at that time: that I would probably miss most of my patients in Overton more than they would miss me.

A couple of days before I finished, I called on Jack Norton and his wife. The house seemed to be full of people. Jack's son and daughter-in-law, with their two children, were bumping into each other in that small terraced house, but their proximity and make-shift sleeping arrangements provided the temporary chaos which now buffered Jack and his wife from the prospect of their empty years ahead, with little money and no chance of finding work again.

Peter Norton was nothing like his mother. A graduate in chemical engineering, he was thin and tall, with a quiet, self-assured manner and a voice that was both friendly and direct. His wife, Jean, was short and dark with widely set eyes and small, strong limbs that moved with a surprising grace as she picked up a trail of children's toys from the floor. She introduced herself.

"Pete's dad told me a lot about you, doctor," she said in a light, gentle North Wales accent. "You done a lot for him and his mam and dad across the back, I gather."

"Oh, I don't know," I said. "They've all had their ups and downs, but I'm not sure I've done all that much."

"That's not the same as what we heard," she said. She flashed a perfect set of teeth as she turned to smile at Jack Norton who shuffled awkwardly and put his hands in his pockets.

"Aye, well, I'm sorry to hear you're leaving us, doctor," he said. "We had a letter from the health people the other day, telling us, like. D'you fancy a cup of tea? There's one in the pot."

There was a good deal of side-stepping and clearing of chairs before we all managed to sit down. Alice Norton returned from the kitchen with a large mug of tea, which she handed to me with an apologetic smile.

"Hope you don't mind it in that, doctor. We seem to have run out of cups." She sat down and put the youngest grandchild on her knee. "What do you think of our family?" she said. "This is Philip. He's not two yet, and that's Sarah over there. She's four. You won't have seen them before, of course, with our Peter going all round the world for the past few years."

Sarah looked up briefly from a jigsaw she was completing and gave a shy smile. The younger child pushed his head back against his grandmother, stuck his thumb in his mouth and frowned at me.

"I didn't realise you would be all still here," I said, looking at Peter Norton. His sallow complexion, I noticed for the first time, was in complete contrast to the evenly tanned, olive skin of the rest of his family. Maybe he had spent most of his time working indoors while they were in the Middle East, I thought.

"We wouldn't have been, in the ordinary way," he said. "But something cropped up not very far from here, so we decided to stay put for a while. Supervising some work on oil extraction from coal, that sort of thing."

"Where's that?"

"Just outside Stonebridge. Dilshaw."

"I'll bet he'll find it a damn sight different from some of the places he's been to," laughed Jack. "It's a right one-horse town, that is. Plug your electric razor in and the street lights go dim, so they say. D'you know it, doctor?"

"Oh yes. As a matter of fact that's where I'm going. To Stonebridge."

"Give over!" he exclaimed, slapping his knee. "Bugger me, now there's a right coincidence. Well there's one thing, Peter – you'll be all right for a doctor while you're over there. I'm only sorry that we won't be able to carry on being patients ourselves – me and the missus, like."

"I should think doctor's seen enough of us to last him quite a while," said Mrs Norton.

"What's the idea?" asked Jack. "Like a promotion, sort of thing?"

I put my empty mug of tea down on the table and stood up.

"No. It's nothing like that," I said. "It's just . . . something that I wanted to do, that's all. I'll be on my own, single-handed. It sounds a bit old-fashioned I suppose . . ."

"There nowt wrong with that," said Jack, shaking his head from side to side, "and if it's what you want to do, then bloody good luck to you, doctor. There's too many medical places these days that are like, well . . . supermarkets. You don't know who you'll see from day to day. Very efficient, I'll grant you – but a bit impersonal, if you ask me. Give me the old way any time. You might have had to wait bloody hours to see the doctor, sitting on uncomfortable chairs and with nowt but broken lino on the floor, but at least you knew who you were going to see. Any road – it's been nice seeing you, doctor. Nice of you to call before you left. Are you sure you don't want any more tea?"

I shook my head.

"No thanks. I only called in for a few minutes to say cheerio – and I was just going to call across the back to see how your folks were getting on, Mr Norton. Last time I called I had a hell of a job getting in because they can't hear you when you come to the front door. I thought, maybe if you had a key, you'd like to slip across with me."

Alice Norton laughed.

"I believe you had to shin over the back yard wall last time you called," she said. "Jack's dad happened to be looking through the kitchen window and it gave him a nasty turn. I think he must have took you for an intruder. Hang on – I've got the key in here, where we always keep it."

She got up and put her hand inside a vase on the mantelpiece, pulling out a Yale key on a grubby piece of string. She gave it to her husband.

"Tell them I'll be across shortly with some dinner will you, Jack?" She turned to me and sighed. "I never realised what a terrible thing old age can be, when you think what it can do. They can't do much for themselves now. Like little children again. It's perhaps as well I'm not working these days, because it's a full time job looking after them, with all the washing and running around I have to do. It seems hard, after bringing up our own three children . . . we've no sooner got them off our hands, so we can start looking to our own lives, when we've got another helpless pair to look after. It just seems to go on and on. Sometimes I feel like a donkey on a treadmill."

"I know," I said. "I don't have any answers, either. We've tried to get them sheltered accommodation but they don't want to move from where they've been all their lives . . ."

"Oh, we know you've done what you can," Jack said. "It's one of these things we've got to put up with. Come on – we'd best get across there, then you can be getting on your way. You must have a load of things to do, apart from nattering to us."

We all shook hands. The others stayed in the house while Jack and I walked to the gate. We walked along the street in silence, turning down a narrow, weed-strewn passageway between the terraced rows, across a piece of waste-ground, where broken bricks and rubble from recent demolition spilled against the crumbling back yards of a facing row of houses, whose fraying edges represented years of neglect. The neat plans in the foyer of the town hall which forecast the future for this urban mess gave no hint of the hiatus of misery that lay between the concept and the realisation.

As we trudged over the uneven ground, he repeatedly threw sidelong glances in my direction as if he wanted me to say something. I turned and looked at his huge, craggy face.

"Hectic Christmas with the family?" I said.

He dropped his eyes and scratched his hairy forearms.

"Oh aye. Mind you, it was good for us both. Alice and me, with us both at a loose end, with no work for the first time in our lives . . . we'd been getting on each other's nerves a bit. Happen it's her change of life – I don't know. You'll know more about these things than I do. Any road, it's not been easy, I can tell you – especially with my mam and dad being the way they are. I feel right upset you're leaving us, you know, though we weren't great ones for doctorin' and that – I mean we only come when we had to. Not like some buggers who're never off your doorstep. Anyway, I'm pleased you're getting ahead and taking opportunities. You've a lot to look forward to. Not like me and the wife."

"You've got your family close by, now. That's something," I said.

"Aye, I suppose you're right," he said grudgingly. "Only . . . it's a funny thing, doctor – after we'd all been together for a couple of days, Peter and me . . . we had a job finding something to say to each other. It's never happened before when they've been home. He seemed embarrassed, some road, me being out of work . . . but I can't help feeling it were my fault, partly. Him being embarrassed like that, I mean. You know what I think it were?"

An icy wind stung my face and whipped the collar of my coat against my cheek. Jack Norton stood there in his shirt sleeves,

133

oblivious to the cold as he struggled to find the words to express a totally unfamiliar experience.

"I'm not a scholar, and I know my words come out funny sometimes," he said slowly and carefully, "and I've never even spoken to Alice about it, but it's true what they say about losing your self-respect. I mean – I've had my head down and worked in some bloody hard, dirty jobs since I left school and in those days they didn't have factory inspectors and all your bloody 'health and safety' like they do now. I've come home many a time covered from head to foot in industrial shit as took all night to lather off. But I've always done my whack, whoever I worked for, and seen to it that the family's been looked after from what I managed to earn, I've never let them down that way. And now, all I seem fit for is brewin' tea and puttin' the cat out. Not like a man any more, some road. Like growing old from the inside, if you see what I mean. And that's all our Peter can see now."

"I doubt it, Jack," I said. "I think he see a lot more than that. He probably feels angry about what's happened to you, that's all. Maybe it's anger you're seeing, not embarrassment."

"Happen you're right," he grunted as he stuck his finger into a back yard door and lifted the latch, "although I can't see as what you say makes much difference, whichever way you look at it."

He coughed noisily and pushed open the door – an act which, for the time being, shut off any further thoughts that he had on the matter. We stepped across the short, flagged yard without saying another word. He pulled out his key and opened the kitchen door, calling out a greeting as he went in. I followed him, inhaling the smell of unwashed pots and incontinence.

Jack's parents were now in their early eighties. In the past few years that I had known them, old Stanley Norton had suffered from increasingly severe arteriosclerosis. Slowly but remorselessly, as a result of the poor blood supply to his brain, he had developed Parkinson's disease, whose poverty of movement gave him a shuffling, stooping gait and a rigid, expressionless face, with a dribbling mouth and eyes which were perpetually moist with tears of frustration. His weepy tantrums had become much less frequent of late which I had mistakenly interpreted as a response to the treatment that he was taking, but I soon realised that it was due to nothing of the sort: it was simply that he was becoming increasingly demented, unaware of anything around him for quite long periods. During these episodes he dozed, babbled under his breath and woke from time to time with a startled grunt, lighting up yet another cigarette whose ash fell from his shaking fingers, burning small holes in his trousers, the upholstery and the surrounding carpet.

Mrs Norton had suffered her first stroke four years ago, which had left her partially paralysed down her right side. Her speech was almost unintelligible, although she knew what she wanted to say and understood what others said to her. The books called this expressive dysphasia, but the term could not express the exasperation she felt inside her head. With the help of an aluminium walking aid she was able to make her way round the ground floor of the house, and because her bed was downstairs in the lounge she managed surprisingly well. In spite of all their appalling disabilities they had obstinately refused to move from their own home into institutionalised care, and it was only through the tireless efforts of the rest of the family that they had maintained their fragile independence.

I asked them both how they were, and they struggled to reply as best they could. Old Mr Norton reached down under his chair and grasped a small cardboard box with trembling hands, handing it to me. Jack turned away with tears in his eyes, bending down and busying himself with the thermostat on the gas fire.

"Family snaps," he growled hoarsely. "Take you all day to look at that lot."

I lifted the flaps of the box and pulled out a handful of grainy sepia prints, brittle and ragged with age. The regiment in barracks; Gallipoli; a handsome Stanley Norton with subaltern's hat under one arm and strikingly attractive wife in wedding dress on the other; walking in the Yorkshire Dales, 1921; Blackpool with the family, 1927; foreman at Ajax Mill, 1929. And so on. It was all there – a pictorial chronicle whose faded little rectangles were like frozen sections on a microscope slide, thin slices of time across a long hard life lived by uncomplaining people.

When I had looked through them all I thanked him and put the box on the table. I told him how much I hd enjoyed looking

135

at them and he seemed pleased, even though he cried. After I had made a few minor adjustments to their treatment I said goodbye and went out with Jack Norton. He closed the back yard door and we retraced our steps back to his house.

"Quite a character, my father," Jack said as we stopped outside the gate to his tiny front garden. "In his time, like. So was the old lady, for that matter."

"So I could see from the family snaps," I said.

He took a deep breath and sighed.

"Aye, well. That's how as I like to remember them. Not like they are now. It's bloody pitiful, really, to see what old age has done to them. All that cleaning up . . . I hope I never live that long. It's a funny thing, though . . ." He scratched the top of his large grizzled head and gave a deep throaty chuckle. "I know I shouldn't laugh, but the other day I was cleaning him up . . . he was a right mess. Seemed like he was covered from head to foot, because some days he doesn't seem to have any control at all. Anyway, there I was, cleaning all this up and cursing under my breath, and then he turns his head round and clear as a bell says: 'I don't know what you're complaining about – if I'd have had as many hot dinners as the number of times I've wiped your arse, I'd be twice as big as you, Jack!'"

I burst out laughing and he dissolved into one of his head-bursting, gargling coughs.

"But the funny thing is –" he said as soon as his breathing had returned to normal, "and it's difficult to put into words as you'd understand, being a professional man and that – but we think the world of them, in spite of the state they're in. I mean – they brought us up, they're still my parents. D'you know what I mean? And they always saw us turned out proper, even when times were hard. So I suppose that's why I feel . . . well . . . *resentful* some road – that they should end up like this. There's neither dignity nor any justice in it, to my way of thinking."

I stared at him. His face had sagged again and he looked down at the pavement.

"Are you still talking about your parents, Jack?" I asked.

He looked up sharply.

"I'm not sure what you're on about, doctor."

"It seems to me that you could have been talking about yourself, in a round-about way. And Peter."

"That's a bit deep for me. How d'you make that out?"

"Well . . . maybe he feels angry, too, or resentful. About you being chucked out of work. I don't know, of course. It's just a thought."

"Hm. I never really looked at it that road," he said. "Well, I might have done in my own way – but I didn't see the connection until you mentioned it . . ."

"Sounds very similar to me," I said, groping in my pocket for my keys. "I'm sure your family feel the same way about you, if you'd bother to ask. You're still their dad, whether you're stoking a furnace or putting out the cat. Once you've stopped convincing yourself that you're worthless, you'll be a great help to them, now they're settling nearby."

"Aye. You've put your finger on it, I think," he said, nodding thoughtfully. "I suppose I have been feeling a bit sorry for meself of late. Anyway – you don't want to be spending your time listening to me . . . thanks, doctor." He stuck out his arm and engulfed my hand in a bone-crushing handshake. "Thanks for listening. And all the very best to you in your new place. We might see something of you when we come up to visit the family, eh?"

"Of course. Look after yourself."

As I drove the car slowly down the narrow street, I glanced in the mirror in time to see his broad shoulders and back framed in the doorway as he stepped back into the house. It was probably my imagination, but I could have sworn that the gap between the top of the door and his head was less than it had been when he left the house earlier.

13

When we first moved into the house at Stonebridge, its twelve cavernous rooms echoed with the yells and clattering of our three children as they dashed from end to end, like pups exploring every dark corner of their new home. Eventually they found a corner of the cellar which served as their own private hide-out, furnishing it with old boxes and planks; here they took biscuits and milk to sustain themselves between their endless games of invention that they played during the long hours when Tanya and I were preoccupied arranging our possessions. Stimulated and excited by their strange new surroundings, their imagination fed on itself, and for the first few days we only saw them at meal-times and at bedtime.

Bet Duncan had kept away while we were settling in, but in her usual thoughtful way had left in the porch a beautiful porcelain bowl brimming with fruit and goodies for the children, with a message of welcome and good luck. Throughout the house she had left other amusing notes, about the idiosyncracies of the plumbing or the best way to open a sticking door, which seemed to soften the shock of moving from the familiar warmth of our previous house to the stark emptiness of this one. Our new home at first was like an old, aching tooth needing to be filled before it became comfortable once again.

It seemed as though I had hardly drawn breath before I found myself wandering down the garden to start my very first surgery on a cold February morning. I had been in the day before, making one or two minor adjustments and moving the furniture around – more to allay my anxiety than to effect any functional improvement. Beatrice Addy had come down to talk about a few matters of organisation and to fill me in on certain items which had been left in the air by the last locum, and which needed clearing up fairly soon. A quick glance through a small, neat pile of notes on Mrs Addy's desk showed that he had been a man whose faith in high technology medicine had apparently warped his sense of proportion, for he had promised to order a whole batch of tests on patients for what appeared to be inappropriate reasons. Then I realised that some of my own decisions about my patients in Overton had also borne little relationship to what had been scribbled on my notes. I was simply going to have to start from scratch and avoid making premature judgements, either about my new patients or about the doctors who had been looking after them prior to my arrival.

To my surprise, there was only a couple of patients waiting to be seen when I began the morning surgery. Because Alec Duncan had never run an appointment system, I had had no idea how many would be waiting. Both patients were friendly and politely inquisitive, and both simply required a renewal of their long-standing treatment. Even so, it took some time to go through their past medical history and so forth, which I felt I had to do. They responded to my enquiries with great patience, showing none of the usual irritability which many feel when called in to discuss their treatment. I had found that, while some patients often interpreted this necessary enquiry as "the doctor showing a degree of interest", others reacted in a hostile manner, as if the comfortable status quo by which they received their endlessly repeated prescriptions was about to be threatened. It was almost as if they had accepted the role the doctor had designated for them, which neither party dared alter thereafter, for fear of breaking the collusion of anonymity between doctor and patient – to the unbearable discomfort of both.

Beatrice Addy entered the consulting room with a cup of coffee. Her starched white coat crackled like wrapping paper as she bustled around, making unnecessary adjustments to the window catch and obsessionally rearranging the soap and scrubbing brush so that they lay with their long axis parallel to the draining-board.

"This quietness makes me nervous," I said. She smiled and wiped out the sink with an efficient swirling movement which betrayed her nursing origins.

"I shouldn't fret, if I were you," she said. "Since the doctor died we've had so many different locums in here, the patients don't know where they're up to. Once things settle down I'm sure you'll find we're just as busy as everyone else."

"Doctor Duncan never had an appointment system, did he?"

"He most certainly did not, doctor," she said with a hint of distaste. "Oh, he did think about it, you know. He went around to see how some of his colleagues were coping with it."

"And what did he think?"

She leaned against the sink. The light from the window brightly outlined her prematurely grey hair and, in the demarcation between light and shade on her face and neck, the tiny creases of encroaching middle age were thrown into sharp relief.

"Doctor Duncan thought that a lot of hot air was talked about appointments. He thought that when doctors talked about appointments making it easier to plan the day's work and more civilised for the patients, what they were really talking about was a system to control the amount of work they themselves had to do."

"Hm. There *are* only so many hours in a day, though."

"Precisely doctor. And Doctor Duncan used to say that whatever else he could do, he had never gained the ability to be in more than two places at once."

"I don't see that that's —"

"Think of the antipathy that results from a patient who turns up here and sees two people waiting to be seen, and I tell him that he can't see the doctor that day because he's fully booked. He doesn't know – can't see – that you may have patients to attend to for the next two hours or so. All he can see is a nearly empty waiting room. It must all appear very unconvincing to him. If, on the other hand, the patient calls in and sees that the waiting room is full, he'll go away and come another day if it isn't urgent. If it is urgent enough to be seen that day, he will stay and wait. At least he is aware that the doctor is busy. So, without all the nonsense of extra staff and telephones ringing every two minutes, the patients come round to regulating themselves. Which is why we don't have too much aggravation."

"It must be a well informed population we've got here," I said.

She smiled and walked to the door, pausing thoughtfully after she had pulled it open.

"Possibly," she said quietly. "I think you'll find, in time, that

140

the patients' attitudes only reflect those of their doctor. What I mean to say is . . ."

She was interrupted by the telephone on her desk, and I had little doubt that I was being deprived of another nugget of insight from this remarkably perceptive lady. I made a mental note to check her salary. I had no intention of allowing such a valuable asset to be seized by a private nursing home or a local typing pool.

She disappeared into the reception area to answer the telephone, and returned a few moments later with a set of record cards. She placed them on my desk.

"You're wanted down at the cemetery, doctor. Right away," she said. I could tell by the tone in her voice that this was an important test of my reaction to the bizarre uncertainties of general practice, but I was prepared for it. I burst out laughing.

"Right away, Mrs Addy? I always understood that the cemetery was the *result* of emergencies – not the *cause* of them."

"There's someone . . . in the bottom of one of the graves," she said, without showing a flicker of emotion.

"Oh, I see. Hmm . . ." I leaned forward and fiddled with my pen in what I imagined to be a thoughtful way. "That's probably quite common down at the, er . . . cemetery, I should have thought, Mrs Addy. I don't think you're telling me the whole story."

An imperceptible movement at the corner of her mouth told me that I had passed the test with flying colours.

"No, of course I'm not, doctor," she said. "The foreman grave-digger has had some sort of accident. Apparently he's done something to his shoulder and can't get out of the grave. They tell me it's a new grave, so you'll know what the problems are, I expect. Being as I recall you dug one or two in years gone by . . . I'll tell anyone who comes in that you've been called out and will be back directly, if that's all right, doctor."

I nodded and collected a few things together.

"Don't tell them where I am, for God's sake. I've only been here half an hour and now I'm called to the cemetery to pull someone out of a grave. That might go down rather badly if its misunderstood. Shades of Burke and Hare, don't you agree?"

"Absolutely, doctor. I wouldn't dream of giving them any idea . . ."

I had complete confidence that if the surgery filled to the brim in the next hour while I was away, she would have the doting crowd singing or knitting blankets for Oxfam, if she so wished. The inability to be in more than one place at once was easier to live with by having people around like Beatrice Addy.

Stonebridge Cemetery was small and very pretty, surrounded by trees on three sides but now open on one side to a new housing estate which acted like a funnel for the wind blowing across the surrounding hills, bending the grass and rustling the odd clump of dead weeds against a few unkempt gravestones and against the small brick hut housing the grass-cutting equipment.

I had dug a few graves here as a medical student in my long summer vacations, working to the limit of my physical strength and endurance. New graves were dug twelve feet deep into the solid clay which lay beneath the thin layer of turf and soil, and we were allowed a day and a half to complete the task. When a member of a family wanted to join another already buried there, it was a blessed relief to know that we only had to dig down nine feet, for which we were allowed one whole day. But there was a grisly price to pay: you knew that you had reached the required depth in these 're-digs' when you suddenly found yourself standing in bones and rotten wood, looking up at the black silhouette of the spade as you threw it up against the bright rectangle of sky above and wishing that you were somewhere else.

I drove between the massive stone pillars supporting the wrought-iron entrance gates, crunching onto a loose gravel path which led to the chapel of rest. From behind one of the workmen's huts sauntered a familiar-looking figure in over-sized wellington boots and a donkey jacket. He stepped in front of my car, holding a yard brush against the windscreen like a bayoneted rifle. I pulled up sharply and wound down the window, immediately recognising the wild eyes and protruding lower jaw of Sid Dean, chief mechanic in charge of all grass-cutting, hedge-trimming and tree-felling equipment, parks and cemeteries.

"By 'eck – look who it is!" he exclaimed through a nicotine-stained lower set of teeth.

"Hello, Sid. Nice to see you again. Must be ten years . . ."

I grabbed my bag and got out of the car. He shuffled back a few paces and grinned.

"Must be. You've come on a pace or two sin' you were last here. Couldn't hold a shovel proper when you worked for us, and now you've probably got letters behind your name as long as this 'ere brush handle."

"And I'm not sure what particular skills are going to be best for the job in hand," I said. "It sounded to me as if you needed the fire brigade rather than a doctor. Where is he?"

"Over yon side."

He jerked his head in the direction of the far end of the cemetery where the land sloped steeply away to a line of poplars; in the distance I could only see the heads and shoulders of a bunch of workmen as they stood behind mounds of clay from a newly dug grave. He started to walk down towards them and I followed him.

"We thought about the fire brigade," he said, "But he was in such a state we didn't like to move him until you'd seen him. I was right glad when I heard thursizere and saw it were you."

"Thursizere?"

"Aye. You know – thursizere. Sound of wheels on t'gravel. Nobody can drive in here without makin' that noise. If there's a funeral due and we're havin' five minutes in the hut, one of us'll keep his ears open and, as soon as he hears that sound, he'll shout 'Th'earse is 'ere! Th'earse is 'ere!' – and then we'll all jump up wavin' our shovels about and generally lookin' busy for when they come down here. He's a bugger, our boss. Can't abide the thought of you takin' a break. Always likes to see us rushin' about, which is why this lot happened this mornin'."

We came off the main path and made our way between neatly kept plots with headstones of all shapes and sizes. As we passed from the older part of the cemetery to where the sloping new plots were, it struck me how the inscriptions had changed over the years. In place of the older, more brutal record that Aunt Clara had 'died' was now, on the newer headstones, a profusion of ornate euphemisms which presumably meant the same thing. I wondered vaguely whether this reflected the fact that an increasing number of our aged relatives do not die at home, surrounded by their families, but in hospitals and institutions which, by their very nature, screen us from the concept of dying as an inevitable, empty finality.

143

"What happened exactly?" I asked Sid.

He grunted and lowered his voice so that we wouldn't be overheard as we approached the group of workmen by the graveside.

"Rush job, see? Some cock-up by the vicar. Only told us late on yesterday that they wanted this new one finished by eleven o'clock. That's when t'funeral's been arranged for. I mean they'll be putting him *down* at eleven. So Cliff re-starts this mornin' and when he's near done he shouts to Eric to throw him a shoring plank. Well, Eric's tryin' to do three things at once as usual and actually throws a ten-by-two which catches Cliff on the shoulder. Now he can't get out on his own and we didn't like to pull him out without you seein' him, on account of causin' him more damage."

"Eric?" I said.

"Aye – Eric Thwaites. He were 'ere when you was last with us."

"I thought he got sacked."

"He did. Just as you left to go back to college, as I recall. Any road, after he got his cards, he used to turn up at cemetery gates on time, every mornin' for weeks, and dead on break-time he'd get out his flask and sandwiches, still standing at th'entrance. Then at five o'clock he'd go back home."

"What —?"

"Well, he didn't dare tell his mam he'd got sacked, see? It was t'first job he'd ever had after leavin' school. For some reason, t'boss took pity on him and reinstated him, but I don't know – he'll never be any different. Give him more than one job at a time and he doesn't know what to do fer t'best. Like a fart in a colander that doesn't know which 'ole to rush out of first, is Eric. He were proper upset this mornin' after it had happened, so I told him to take a couple of bags of lime to the park and make himself scarce for a bit."

"Good idea. I can only cope with one disaster at a time between breakfast and lunch."

The bunch of men at the graveside stepped back as we approached and eyed me with benign interest. I cleared my throat.

"Good morning," I said briskly. "Nice to see such a hive of feverish activity. Anybody phoned for an ambulance yet?"

144

The four of them looked at each other and put their cigarettes out guiltily.

"Clem said he was —"

"No, I thought you —"

"One of you go and do that," I said, taking off my overcoat. "And the rest of you hold these ropes while I go down and take a look at Cliff."

"Funeral'll be here in twenty minutes," said one of the workmen gloomily.

"Then we'd better not stand about, had we? Otherwise they'll be lowering the coffin on top of Cliff, and that would upset quite a few people."

There was a ripple of nervous laughter as they scrambled over the sheets of artificial turf draped over part of the clay mound surrounding the grave. I stepped to the edge and looked down. Clifford Tansley was sitting at the bottom, slumped against the yellow clay wall and clutching his right arm against his chest. He looked up and gave a weak smile.

"Hello, Clifford," I said. "Hang on – we'll have you above ground in no time." I tried to get a picture in my mind of all those films that I had seen on mountain rescue operations, where an injured climber was being lowered down a vertical rock face swathed in a bewildering arrangement of ropes. I lowered myself into the grave and my shoes immediately stuck in the sticky mud at the bottom. Sid saw my predicament and, without a word, took off his wellington boots, dropping them down at my side.

"We can't keep on meeting like this, Cliff," I said, taking my feet out of my shoes and putting on the huge boots. His eyes opened wide.

"Bloody hell, it's you! They said you were coming back but it never twigged . . . How are you, professor?"

"Better than you at the moment. Let's take a look at you."

He winced as I pushed my hand under his shirt and felt around to assess the damage.

"One broken collar bone and a dislocated shoulder," I muttered. "I'll have to rig these ropes up so we can pull you out."

I pulled the ropes down and knotted them round his body in a crude harness. It was a long, difficult job in that confined space and I silently prayed that it wouldn't slip or give way.

After checking all the knots, I gently tucked his injured arm inside his shirt.

"Bet you never thought you'd ever be back here again, down one of these things," Cliff said. "Any road, you'll be more at home at what you're doing now than when you were last here. You and that mad bugger Bill Duncan. I'll never forget . . ."

"Save it until later, Cliff," I said, grinning. "If we don't get you out soon there'll be a traffic jam of bodies over this grave – you'll be going up while the other one's coming down."

"Aye, you're right, professor. Like a ski lift in t'bloody Swiss Alps. Oh, Christ!"

He winced with pain as I signalled to the others to start pulling the ropes up.

"Grab the rope with your good arm and don't let go, otherwise you'll spin over and come out feet first," I urged him. I steadied him as far as I could reach, but half-way up he fainted with pain and let go of the rope, with precisely the result I had feared. They hauled up his sagging body, grabbed his feet and pulled him over the top, bundling him out of sight. From where I stood I could hear muffled sounds of consternation. Sid Dean poked his head over the side.

"Ambulance has arrived, doc. Cliff's out cold – is he all right?"

"Fainted, that's all."

"Oh. Right. We'll just help take him —"

"Hold on a minute. Sling those ropes back. This clay's too slippery to get out of here on my own."

I climbed out in time to see a frail old lady fifty yards away slump down in a dead faint, scattering a small bunch of flowers over a loved one's grave, no doubt overcome by the sight of Cliff's limp body being hauled feet first out of this nearby grave. As they bundled him into the ambulance, I went across and saw that she had caught her head on the headstone, giving herself a nasty gash on her scalp. While she was coming round, I picked up the flowers and put them into a pot by the side of the tiny memorial stone. I helped her up and walked her gingerly to the ambulance, gently explaining to her what had happened.

"Can you fit another patient in there?" I asked the ambulance attendants. Without asking any questions they nodded sympathetically, taking her arm and leading her up the three small steps at the rear of the ambulance. She stopped at the top and looked round with dazed eyes at the grave where she had just been, mumbling and shaking her head. I had begun to reassure her when I heard the crunch of wheels on gravel and saw the black cortège turn through the entrance gates and roll sedately in our direction. After quickly checking that Cliff had come round, I signalled the driver to get on his way, making myself scarce with the rest of the workmen behind a memorial monument which belonged to a prominent local family. Apart from the chapel of rest, it was the biggest stone edifice in the cemetery.

While they smoked and talked quietly amongst themselves, I watched the huddled black procession of mourners approach the graveside, some with shoulders hunched and heads bent into small handkerchiefs, others staring ahead and propping up the older members of the bereaved family who were now more frail with grief. The vicar, with both his hands clasped on his Bible, walked with long, slow strides, his eyes never leaving the ground as the cold wind blew his cassock around his ankles and carried across the grass the broken sound of sobbing.

"Best get over and rope him down," said Sid Dean to the others. They stubbed out their cigarettes and walked across to the graveside. "Can I have my wellies back, doctor?" he asked. I looked down. Sid Dean was standing in a pair of coarse woollen socks. I began to laugh, taking off the boots which I was still wearing.

"I'm sorry, Sid. I'd forgotten about that."

I straightened up and stared across for a few moments to see the coffin being lowered into the grave. I watched the ropes slacken as it came to rest at the bottom of the twelve-foot hole, the men then retrieving the ropes with nonchalant expertise before they turned and walked slowly back towards us, already rooting in their pockets for their cigarettes and matches.

"First day, innit, doc?" asked one of them as he sidestepped round the massive stone monument. He stuck a cigarette in his mouth and lit it, cradling the flickering match in his massive, grimy hands. "Not much of a start, having to go down a grave, eh?"

"No" I said, grinning. "Although it's better than ice-fishing."

"Eh?"

"I'll tell you about it sometime. I must get back to the surgery . . . Anyone seen my shoes, by the way?"

I looked round over the surrounding grass, trying to remember where I had put them.

"Hey up – they're off," said Sid, crushing the end of his cigarette with his horny fingers and putting it under his hat. I looked up to see the mourners settle back into the black Daimlers. The procession moved slowly off over the gravel. "Fastest bloody vicar we've had here in years," added Sid with grudging admiration.

Clem nodded vigorously.

"You're right there, Sid. Boss was sayin' he'd got another one up in Dilshaw at eleven forty-five, back here for that one at t'far end at twelve-fifteen, home for a quick snack with the missus, then out again flat out 'til tea-time. It's all go, you know. I've watched him a time or two. It's no sooner your ashes to ashes and he's slammin' the book shut and stridin' like the clappers towards th'earse before we've got the ropes out. Mind you – I'd sooner have him than the barmy bugger we had afore at St Martin's. Lost all the maps of the plots. Didn't know which plot belonged to whoever. Half the time, we'd be shoulder-deep in a dig and he'd come up wringin' his bloody hands and telling us it was the wrong plot, could we fill it in and re-dig the one next to it."

I wasn't listening. I was staring across at the newly dug grave, only half aware of the cold penetrating my stockinged feet.

"How difficult is it to bring up a coffin again before the grave's been filled in?" I asked. "The one you've just put down, for instance."

Clem frowned and sucked his teeth.

"Wouldn't like to say. Oak cask, very heavy – and big. Only just enough clearance all round for t'ropes, that one. Be bloody awkward. Why?"

I took a deep breath.

"I've just remembered where I left my shoes," I said.

In the distance, among the black, brittle fingers of the elm and sycamore, a handful of rooks hunched their shoulders and clattered their wings, startled by the sound of the raucous laughter that echoed across this normally peaceful place.

14

With a heavy overcoat slung over my mud-stained suit, and a pair of cement-impregnated boots borrowed from the cemetery workshop, I shuffled from my car to the rear of the house, looking like a prisoner of war from the Eastern Front. Tanya looked in disbelief as I explained what had happened.

I changed quickly and made my way across the garden to finish off the surgery which I had abandoned earlier. None of the remaining patients expressed the slightest irritation or impatience from waiting so long – or if they felt it, they did not show it. They seemed grateful that I had come back to attend to them. Being called out so urgently, they said, made them feel that their own complaints were of little importance. I realised, of course, that Beatrice Addy had laid the groundwork for this response, but it raised my spirits, nevertheless.

The two home visits I had that first day were strange, contrasting affairs. The first visit took me to a neatly-kept private housing development on the other side of the town, off the Dilshaw road. It was the kind of estate where lawns were mowed on Saturdays, cars were cleaned on Sundays and at eleven p.m. each night the cat and the empty milk bottles were put outside the front porch – the final muted sounds at the end of an orderly day.

I soon found the house. It was a large neo-Georgian detached with an immaculately kept garden in front. The door was opened by a sad-looking woman in her early forties who was wearing a silk scarf tied loosely round her neck, the ends hanging casually over the top of her cashmere sweater. Her well-brushed hair and carefully applied make-up suggested that she could afford to take her time when she got up in the mornings. She smiled briefly when I introduced myself, and as she led me down the short hallway I glanced quickly at the notes I was holding to check the surname again. Horrocks.

The lounge, which was as clean and neat as an illustration

from a furnishing catalogue, had a sterile, frozen quality which seemed to me to be incompatible with the presence of even one child – if my own experience was anything to go by – but six-year-old Stephanie Horrocks was no ordinary child, it seemed. She sat primly on the edge of the couch reading a book, a flaxen-haired little girl with grown-up eyes and skin as pale and translucent as bone china. She put the book on one side and clasped her hands in her lap, gazing without curiosity at her mother as she described the child's symptoms. Mrs Horrocks told me that she had thought Stephanie was "starting to come down with something" last week, so she had kept her off school because of her delicate nature. Even though Stephanie now appeared to have recovered from whatever it was, she had thought it advisable that I check the child over before she was sent back to school. Mrs Horrocks spoke of the school as if it was a bacterial breeding-ground which threatened to keep Stephanie at home far more in the future.

The child was silently co-operative while I examined her thoroughly. She was completely normal and healthy in every respect.

More puzzled than irritated by what seemed to be an unnecessary visit, I sat down in an arm-chair and sucked the end of my pen. Mrs Horrocks brought a cup of coffee which I took to be a clear signal that I had not heard everything and, as I drank it slowly, staring over the rim at her increasingly restless movements, she began again to tell me about Stephanie's delicacy and how she understood the significance of this, as she herself had been of a similar disposition when she was a child. I listened with fascination for the next fifteen minutes or so as she drifted into an account of her own problems: husband a company accountant, always away; her feelings of loneliness and inadequacy; her desire to do something useful with her life, which she was unable to do because Stephanie was so illness-prone and needed her at home . . .

The more I listened the more I realised that Stephanie Horrocks was not the real patient at all, but was a presenting symptom of her mother's unhappiness. The penny, working its way through the coarse sieve of my rudimentary knowledge of psychology, finally dropped: Mrs Horrocks was using the child as an apparently rational explanation of her own inadequacy. Or so it seemed.

I was struggling to take this on board when Mrs Horrocks squatted on a stool, hunched herself up and wept quietly. Stephanie slid off the end of the couch and went over to her; but when she tried to grasp her mother's sleeve, Mrs Horrocks recoiled, flashing the little girl a look of alarm. It was almost as if the child was a mirror of her own over-protected childhood; in that reflection she saw the source of her own present sense of deprivation.

This was not totally unexpected but was becoming too complicated for me. I stood up and mumbled some comforting clichés, realising as soon as I spoke that I was talking to myself. After a moment's silence, during which she dried her tears, I suggested that she come down to the surgery in the next day or so and talk a bit more about her own feelings, although at the time I had no clear idea how I was going to handle this. To my surprise, she agreed.

Feeling somewhat shell-shocked by the way such an apparently simple visit had turned out, I drove thoughtfully to my next call.

When I arrived at Crag Moor Farm, which lay in the hills overlooking the south side of the town, there was no doubt at all who was the patient among the robust gathering which came out of the stone porch of the main house to greet me.

Len Garlick, according to his thin medical records, was ninety-four years old – but the tall, bronzed figure walking towards me with a dipping gait did not look a day over seventy. His strong bony hand squeezed mine with the confidence of a man determined to live a lot longer.

"How do. Doctor Rushton, isn't it?"

"Yes. Mr Garlick? I expected . . ."

"Aye, I know what you're going to say – that I don't look my age. That's through hard work and keeping out of the way of doctors."

He grinned, displaying a fair number of his own teeth, although they now tapered precariously into the retracted old gums.

"Alec Duncan never saw me above twice while he were here, God rest his soul. Now come on – the lads'll show you indoors."

The "lads" were in fact four of his sons, all in their early seventies and all displaying the same youthful vigour of Len Garlick. They introduced themselves and showed me through to a large living room illuminated by the mellow light from two small, leaded windows set in the thick, stone walls. The furniture was clean and simple, and in the middle of the room was a large, scrubbed pine table. Down the stone-flagged hallway, I could hear the sounds of a meal being prepared, and from the kitchen somewhere came the mouth-watering smell of freshly baked bread.

The four sons folded their arms and said nothing. They looked at me with a polite curiosity which made me feel that I was being put to some sort of test.

"Now then," said Len Garlick, hobbling into the middle of the room, "I'll tell you what it is. Two weeks ago, I slipped and fell cleaning out one of the sheds —"

"You were cleaning —"

"Oh aye. Still do a day's work, you know. Oh, granted, I don't do the heavy stuff I used to – lads see to that —"

The four of them nodded at me in confirmation.

"Like I said, I fell awkward, like, and hurt my leg. Couldn't get up right away – then I had this pain in my knee which wouldn't go away. Which was a bit of a puzzle because it weren't swollen, you know – and I was able to move it all right. Any road, this 'ere pain wouldn't go away and it made me limp, so after a few days, Tommy here took me down to Jessop's for an X-ray, although it weren't my idea, I can tell you."

He scowled at his sons and they shifted their feet uneasily.

"A right waste of time that was. They waggled me knee about a bit, poked and prodded and all that. Then they sent me for an X-ray and there was nowt wrong with that. Waited about three hours, we did, with all that carry-on. Want to have a look?"

Without waiting for me to answer, he slipped his braces off his shoulders and took his pants off in the middle of the room without ceremony or embarrassment. I walked slowly round him as if I was inspecting a second-hand car, his four sons watching every move I made.

"Mr Garlick – would you mind walking round the room a bit?" I asked. He obliged without a word, hobbling around in the curious dipping walk that I had noticed before. It rang a bell somewhere: one leg was shorter than the other.

152

"One leg's shorter than the other," I murmured to myself. He grunted scornfully, giving his sons a look which seemed to convey that he would have preferred to contact the vet. I got him to climb onto the pine table and looked at his knee. There was nothing wrong with it.

"Have you got a tape measure?" I asked. One of the sons produced one from the sideboard. The tape was frayed and barely readable, but with some difficulty I managed to measure his legs from his umbilicus to his ankle bone. The left one was shorter by an inch. I said nothing but turned my attention to his left hip, gently flexing and rotating it. With some excitement and disbelief I felt the grating sensation which could only mean a fracture at the neck of the hip joint. Because he had chosen to walk about on it after his fall the two fractured surfaces had been driven together and had shortened his leg.

I straightened up. "It's not your knee, Mr Garlick. It's your hip."

He sat up and fumbled for his trousers, scowling at me beneath his heavy brows.

"Me hip, eh?" he growled. "Well look, doctor, I don't want to sound disrespectful – you being a professional man and all that – but it's *me* whose got the pain and it's not in me hip. It's in me knee. I should know the difference between me hip and me knee – they've been holding me up for the last ninety-four years and I know where I've got the pain."

"I appreciate that," I said patiently, trying not to let the situation get out of control in the face of my precarious credibility, "but sometimes when you damage your hip you can get pain in your knee. It's because of a nerve —"

"A nerve?" he said, screwing up his eyes. "The only nerve here is the one you've got, telling me a story like that. They must teach you some funny bloody things in medical school these days. Not half."

He slid off the table and fastened his trousers, eyeing his four sons with despair. They looked at me in embarrassed silence, although I couldn't tell whether it was because of the way Len Garlick had rejected my diagnosis or whether it was because they didn't know what to say next. One of them cleared his throat and smiled uncertainly.

"You'll have to excuse dad, only he . . . we thought it would be best for you to have a look at him. It does seem a funny do, though . . . if what you say is right. Can't you give him summat to rub on his knee?"

I took a deep breath, pulled a ten-pound note out of my pocket and slapped it on the table.

"I'll tell you what I *will* do," I said, "I'll give you a letter to take him back to Jessop Memorial, and if your father's hip *isn't* broken I won't come back to collect this note. If he doesn't get it seen to he won't be able to walk at all in a few months."

Without knowing them and how they might react, it was a cheap, offensive and extremely risky thing to do. There was a stunned silence during which I prayed that I would not get thrown out. Len Garlick stared hard at me.

"Right. Now I'm not a betting man myself," he said slowly, "but I appreciate a man who has the courage of his convictions – even if they do sound a bit fanciful." He limped forward and picked up the note, stuffing it in my top pocket. He put a hand on my shoulder and looked me in the eye. I held my breath. I saw in his eyes nine decades of hard experience which seemed unclouded by a brain years past its peak.

"Now I'll tell you what I'll do," he said quietly. "I'll go down to Jessop's, like you say – and I'll have my X-ray. And if you're right, I'll show my thanks in my own way. If you're wrong – well, no harm done, I suppose. Although you'll be able to chalk it up to experience, seeing as you're so sure about it."

"Fair enough," I said. I sat down and wrote a letter to the hospital, looking up briefly as I sealed the envelope. He was leaning on his stick by one of the little windows, smiling slightly.

"I was just thinking," he said, scratching his chin, "you're a bit like Doctor Duncan in some ways. I remember him when he first came here. He'd be about the same age as you then and, as I recall, he were just as sure of himself, too." He laughed. "He said a funny thing a few years after I first met him, though. Can't recall the exact words but it were something to do with the fact that the older he got the less sure he became of anything when it came to sickness."

"I know the feeling," I muttered.

"Then he said something else," the old man went on. "He said – when it comes to doctoring and that – 'the young feller sees what he knows, whereas the old feller knows what he sees'."

154

"Providing that he profits from his experience, Mr Garlick," I said. He dipped his chin into his chest and laughed out loud. It was a good-natured laugh which eased the tension between us.

"That's just what I said to Alec Duncan! Go on with yer – bugger off and get your dinner afore it's cold on the table, and I'll go and get this 'ere X-ray, like you say."

He waved his stick at the wall-clock and I got up to go. One of his sons saw me to the door.

"Don't tek too hard on dad, doctor," he said apologetically as we walked to the car. "He's always been a strong man, in more ways than one. Can't stand the thought of being carried about, I suppose."

"I can see that. That's probably why I stuck my neck out in there. Believe me, it wasn't for the good of my health, you know."

"Hm," he grunted. "Either way, I hope you're wrong. I can hardly believe —"

"Can't you?" I said calmly. "Well – try to think of it this way: if I'm right, we'll have done your dad a good turn. And if I'm wrong, you'll have wasted an afternoon at the hospital but it's me who'll have the egg on my face for some time to come."

He smiled and turned to go back indoors.

"I don't envy you fellers your job. I don't, honest."

"Oh, now don't start getting soft on me," I said, laughing. "I've got a thicker skin than I used to have. Give me a ring later today and let me know the verdict."

He nodded once and went inside the house as I started the car and drove slowly out onto the main road, back down the hill into the town.

15

The tension and anticipation of my first day at my new surgery, together with the morning's activities, had sent the adrenalin round my circulation. But human physiology has a remarkable capacity for maintaining its dynamic equilibrium, which meant that after lunch a drain-hole opened up somewhere inside me, causing all that adrenalin to disappear without trace, leaving me feeling like an oily rag. I fell asleep for the next two hours. When Tanya woke me with some strong coffee, she did not ask me about the earlier part of the day. She knew that I would talk about it eventually, but probably only after the day was over and when I could see more clearly what, if anything, I had managed to achieve. And being a good listener, she would wait until she felt I wanted to talk about it, for she knew how important this first day was.

I began to wind down a little after the enforced caution with which I had approached the evening surgery. The patients had shown a touching mixture of curiosity, shyness and genuine concern that, after the long years of Alec Duncan, followed by the uneasy interim period of makeshift care, they should now have a doctor of their own who would remain to share their good times and their bad times. Especially their bad times. It was an awesome responsibility, made more so by the fact that, being single-handed, my own shortcomings would not be buffered or masked by the presence of competent professional partners like Ian and Molly.

When I stepped into the porch I nearly fell over a large parcel. I unravelled it and inside found the pair of shoes which I had left at the bottom of the grave earlier that day, very muddy and squashed very flat. There was a neatly written note pushed into one shoe which read: 'Tomb it may concern. These shoes have truly trod the path of righteousness. Resurrected by yours truly, Clem Bowlacre.'

Laughing, I went into the kitchen, clutching the shoes at

arms' length. Tanya was putting out the evening meal, but stopped what she was doing when I showed her the note, enjoying the joke as much as I had done.

When we had finished eating and the children had disappeared to watch television, she smiled across at me from behind her coffee cup.

"We had an invitation to dinner tomorrow night," she said.

"Had? Sounds like the invitation's dead and buried," I replied. "Who from?"

She sighed.

"Marjorie Crawley. You met Doctor Crawley when . . ."

"Oh yes. Gerald Crawley. Research freak. Nice bloke, when he stands still."

"His wife sounds very nice."

"Hm. Why the past tense? Has it been cancelled?"

"Steven, you may have noticed that we have three children. At this short notice, how are we going to find someone to look after them?"

"Sorry. Tomorrow night . . . Tuesday's a funny night for one of these things, though. What did you say?"

"I'd let them know as soon as I could. What else could I say?"

"Not much," I grunted. "Well, we'll just see what turns up. I suppose we could . . ."

The door bell rang. When I went to see who it was, I found myself face to face with one of Leonard Garlick's sons, smiling apologetically over the top of a large cardboard box which he was clutching to his chest.

"Begging your pardon, doctor, calling at your private residence at this time."

"That's OK," I said. "It's, er . . ."

"Tom. Tom Garlick."

"Won't you come in, Tom?"

"No, I don't want to intrude on your privacy. Thanks all the same, doctor."

He heaved the box in my direction. I took it and put it down in the hallway. I could see that it contained several bottles of pale yellow fluid and I looked at him quizzically.

"A present from dad," he grinned.

"What's this for?"

"You were right. He's broke his hip. They've kept him in

157

Jessop's on account of that and they say he's for an operation in the next day or so to have something done to it. A pathetic hip joint or something, they said."

"Prosthetic, Tom. It's like a metal bit to replace his broken hip. I'm sorry to hear that. Still – they'll have him up and about in no time and he'll be nearly as good as new, I should think."

"We're very grateful to you. He . . . we . . . were a bit surprised, I must say. He said I'd to pass the message on to you that you must know what you see." He began to laugh. "Talking about seeing things – I wouldn't drink that home-made wine too quick if I were you, doctor."

I glanced at the box on the floor. "Is that what's in the bottles?" I asked.

"Aye. Some of his best that he's had put down a few years back. Go easy on it, though, doctor. Makes you fall over, that stuff. He's well known for his wine, is our dad."

"That's very generous of you, Tom. Although from what you say, it sounds as though I'll get legless even if I clean my teeth with the stuff."

He grinned and touched his frayed cap as he turned to go.

"Good night to you, doctor – and thanks again for what you did today."

"Good night, Tom. Thanks."

I stood in the doorway as he shambled across the courtyard and along the road to his battered grey Land Rover. I closed the door and the clattering roar of the diesel faded quickly as he turned into the main road.

When the children had gone to sleep, I opened a bottle of Garlick vintage and poured out a glass for both Tanya and myself.

"Let's celebrate my first day with one of its by-products," I said as we sat in the kitchen, still warm from the cooking of our evening meal.

"Something to celebrate?" asked Tanya gently.

"Only the end of my first day. Well . . . let's put it this way: starting in a new practice I suppose is rather like jumping on to a moving carousel – you're bound to graze a limb or two. At least I didn't fall on my face, even if some of the movements were a bit unsteady."

I thought uneasily for a moment about Mrs Horrocks. Maybe I had left it hanging in the air a bit, but we both needed

158

time to think about what to do next. I took a sip at the wine. It had an unfamiliar, strangely pleasant earthy taste and was mercifully without the vague aftertaste of industrial solvent with which most home-made wines are afflicted. After two or three mouthfuls I felt a pleasant glow under my diaphragm. I stretched back in the chair and outlined the day's events. Tanya said very little, but listened with her eyes, which had a greater effect than the wine in that I found myself talking almost without pause for the next hour. After a couple more refills of wine she pushed her empty glass to the middle of the table and smiled sleepily.

"Come on, Steven," she murmured. "It's been a long day for both of us. Why don't we go to bed?"

As she spoke, the doorbell rang and I got up from the table, glancing at my watch. Tanya groaned.

"It's OK," I said. "Whoever it is – I'll deal with it. You carry on. I'll join you later, as they say."

She yawned and went up the stairs as I went to open the back door. In the dim light of the porch I could make out the bulky figure of Ron Leaford.

"Hello, Ron."

"How do, Steven. I hope I'm not . . ."

"No – come in. We were just having a glass of wine. Tanya has only just . . . I'll give her a shout."

He grabbed my arm as I went inside and shook his head, following me into the kitchen.

"Don't bother, Steven. Much as I'd like to see her and so forth, I was just passing. I only called in to see how your first day went. Bit chaotic, was it?"

"Not too bad. Have some wine. A present from a patient."

He grinned and took a glassful.

"My word. Getting gifts from patients on your first day! That's an impressive start." He sniffed at it then swallowed a mouthful.

"I know who you've been buttering up. That's some of Len Garlick's nectar. Am I right?"

"Correct."

"Rum bugger, Len. I only know him because he calls in my local now and then. Is he not well?"

I told him the story. He sat down at the table and laughed, topping up both our glasses at the same time.

"Well, if it's this stuff that makes him so bloody healthy at his age, we'd better get some down us. Bad luck about his hip, though. Cheers."

We emptied our glasses and I opened another bottle. Ron leaned forward and put his elbows on the table, jangling the contents of the side pockets of his heavy jacket as he did so.

"Did I tell you what happened at the Service Committee Hearing?" he grunted. I shook my head.

"No, I forgot. I haven't seen you since that time a few weeks ago," he said. "I got the verdict last week . . . last week."

He said it twice as if he couldn't believe it.

"What happened?"

"Complaint upheld. I was admonished."

"Admonished?"

"Bollocked, my son."

He drained his glass and I followed suit, mesmerised by his change of mood. I poured out some more wine and we drank in silence for a few minutes.

"I'm sorry," I said eventually. He grunted and stared at his glass.

"It's a bit of a bugger when you think about it," he growled. "You nip off to pay your respects to a colleague who's been breaking his neck for the community over the years, and you end up being on the receiving end of an inquisition like that."

"What happens now?"

"Oh . . . not much. Just told I had to adhere more closely to my terms of service in future. Polite way of saying I was a slob."

"And that's the end of it, now?"

His eyes hardened and he gave a mirthless laugh.

"The end of it, as you say, is rather like getting hanged. The hanging takes a few seconds and there's very little to it. It's the trouser-filling waiting before the hanging which is the real punishment, take it from me. Anyway, I don't need sympathy, Steven. When you're single-handed you have to take proper care of these things. I slipped up and that's all there is to say."

"Even if you'd got to the patient, it didn't sound as if it would have altered the outcome in his case, from what you said."

I spoke slowly and carefully, vaguely aware that my tongue felt as if it had got thicker and heavier in the last half-hour. Ron shook his head.

"Makes no difference – that's one thing you'll learn if you don't know it already. People will always forgive us if we can't cure, even if it *is* because we're a bit dim sometimes. But if we don't seem to care – no matter what the circumstances – then they'll never forgive that."

He stood up and pushed his chair back.

"Anyway, enough of that," he said, grinning broadly. "What I wanted to mention was that I believe you're going to Gerry Crawley's tomorrow night. I saw him today in the town."

I stood up a little unsteadily, glancing guiltily at the two empty bottles of wine on the table.

"Well . . . we might have some trouble seeing to the children," I mumbled.

"Not to worry about that," he said, waving his massive hands about. "He asked me to go but I made an excuse. Oh, he's all right once in a while, but I didn't feel like going. So we'll come round and look after them for you, if you like. Kathleen's good at it, you know. We've three grandchildren of our own now. I know what it's like when you're stuck with young 'uns."

"That's very nice of you . . ."

"That's OK. Think nothing of it. Might even see some more of Len Garlick's wine off for you." He laughed and manoeuvred himself awkwardly to the door. "You know they call that stuff Sneaky Feet, don't you?"

"Well no, I didn't —"

"Well, watch out. You won't feel it for a bit, but it'll get to you shortly, you'll see. We'll come round at seven-thirty, OK?"

"Right. Thanks, Ron. Seven-thirty."

He waved and, as I watched him disappear into the darkness, I became aware of a buzzing inside my head and the sound of my own breathing. It was like the first stage of general anaesthesia. I stumbled back into the kitchen, banging my shins on all the chairs, suddenly realising how many we seemed to have acquired. When the telephone rang again I was grateful for its shrill intervention, for it was the sensory input I needed in order to concentrate my mind, giving me something to aim for without falling sideways.

"Hello? Is that Doctor Rushton?"

I breathed heavily down my nostrils into the mouthpiece for a moment before answering.

"Yes, it is I," I said slowly and deliberately. I sounded like Valentine Dyall introducing 'Horrors of the Black Museum'.

"Eh?"

"Doctor Rushton speaking." I took a deep breath and pulled myself together again, trying my best to ignore the fact that my brain cells were keeling over in droves, awash with Len Garlick's home-made wine.

"Sorry to bother you, doctor. It's the police station here. What it is, is this – we've got a gentleman at the station who's been driving with an excess of alcohol . . ."

My heart sank. The first thing I thought was that they had picked up Ron Leaford on his way home. If he was anything like I was beginning to feel, he'd be well over the limit.

"What's his name?" I asked anxiously.

"Name? well, I'm not . . . hang on a tick, doc."

There was silence for a moment. I could hear some paper being shuffled about amid other familiar sounds in the background, which were the same in every police station I'd ever been in – the adenoidal squawk of a two-way radio, the laborious clack of a typewriter and, always, someone whistling brainlessly in a dimly-lit corridor somewhere.

"Hello doctor? Still there?"

"Mm".

"I didn't realise who he was – I've only started my shift this minute. He's called Spiky Wills, doctor. One of our regulars. D'you know him?"

I sighed with relief.

"No, that's . . . How did you get my number?"

"Ah, well . . . our regular doctor isn't available just now and your name happens to be on our list. I believe you were the police surgeon over in Overton for a time."

"Yes" I said. "I resigned a couple of years ago. I thought I'd seen the last of the insides of draughty police stations in the dead of night."

"I know how you feel, doctor. I'm sorry we've had to call you out like this, only it's very rare we have to get anybody else in apart from our regular Doctor Hansford. D'you know Doctor Hansford?"

"No, not really," I mumbled. I vaguely recalled him contacting me about the occasional relief duty for the police but I had since put it out of my mind. I screwed my eyes up and shook my head to clear the dancing images of the patterned Italian tiles over the sink, cursing my luck at having been called out on this particular night.

"Right. I'll, er, be straight down there," I said wearily.

"Smashin'! Thanks, doc. You know where we are? You're at Doctor Duncan's old place, I believe. Two miles down the main road towards the town centre from where you are. See you, doc. Cheerio."

I put the phone down. After throwing some cold water over my face I crept upstairs to see if Tanya was still awake. The light was on in the bedroom and she lay, fully clothed, on top of the bed, sleeping peacefully. I trod on a plastic toy which one of the children had left lying about and it shattered with the sound of a pistol shot, which woke her up suddenly. She looked round, bewildered, and I began to giggle like an idiot.

"Oh, no. I must have dropped off. I felt so tired. Must have been that wine you brought," she murmured, shivering.

"I know. Sneaky Feet."

"What?"

"Ron Leaford called."

"Mm, I thought I heard someone." She took off her sweater and looked at me through long strands of hair which had fallen over her eyes. "You look ashen, Steven."

"Do I? I must admit I feel a bit . . . Ron and I had some more of that wine. I've been called out, too."

"A patient?"

"Police station." I hiccoughed, wrenching my diaphragm painfully.

"Oh, God," Tanya groaned. "They'll probably keep you there, looking like that. Are you sure you're fit to turn out?"

"Don't worry about me," I said, grinning. "I'll open all the windows while I drive down. That'll clear my head. I'll be OK. See you later."

I realised my confidence was misplaced when I went outside and felt the cold air on my face. As I fumbled to get the keys in the car door I dropped them, and nearly pitched forward in the dark when I went to pick them up.

The street lights seemed to be swaying about like Blackpool illuminations in a high breeze as I drove slowly to the old stone police station. I walked round the car park, taking deep breaths for a few minutes, before going in. The duty officer greeted me in the short, neon-lit passageway.

"Before we start, I wouldn't mind just freshening up a bit, if there's time," I said. He looked at his watch and yawned like a hippo.

"Aye, that's all right, doctor. You look as if you've had a hard day, one way and another. Down the corridor, last door on your right."

The washroom had the gloomy ambience of a lift-shaft. It was small, dark and rectangular, and from the high swivel windows dangled several lengths of frayed, knotted cords down to the level of the gritty washbasin which stood in one corner.

I filled the basin with water and stuck my head in it, holding my breath for as long as I could and repeating the procedure several times, in the vain hope that this would overcome the disabling effects of the wine. I heard a weary shout from up the corridor.

"We're ready any time you are, doctor."

I took this to be a polite enquiry as to whether I had actually passed out. Stepping sideways towards the grimy roller towel, I slipped on a piece of soap, falling forwards. As I fell, my flailing hands caught one of the window cords and for a moment I was suspended forty-five degrees from the horizontal until something gave way above me. I hit the floor and there was a tremendous crash of breaking glass. I looked up and saw to my dismay that I had pulled an entire window out of its casing. There was broken glass everywhere. Nearby, there was a soft, familiar laugh.

"Well now, doctor. The question, at this moment in time, is who is more bloody pissed? Is it Spiky falling about in there, or is it you falling about in here? I ask myself."

I looked up through the open door of the washroom and saw the tall figure of Jim Early, Inspector in CID when I had been the police surgeon in Overton. I hadn't seen him for a couple of years and I wasn't sure I could see him now. I screwed up my eyes to sharpen his fuzzy image, but when he leaned back slightly and stuck his pipe in his mouth, his eyebrows dancing with private amusement, I knew it was him. Among his fellow officers, like a diamond among a heap of coal, he was a shining allotrope of the same element, a man of intelligence and

164

humour who instinctively sensed the shortcomings of his own contemporaries and the limitations of experts in other professions.

I got up and picked a few slivers of glass from my hair.

"Sorry about that," I mumbled, looking round at the debris scattered all over the floor.

"Not to worry, doctor," he said, grinning round the stem of his pipe. "That's covered by depreciation; average wear and tear, that is – even though you've managed to accelerate the process to a certain degree. Pity you didn't manage to demolish the sink while you were at it – God knows we need a new one. Would you like some coffee?"

"Thanks. I wouldn't mind. What about . . . ?"

"Shouldn't worry about Spiky. He'll still be legless even if we keep him here until next week. Come and have a brew before you start and tell me what's brought you to these parts."

"I was going to ask you the same thing," I said. I brushed myself down and stepped gingerly through the doorway. As we walked past the main office at the far end, Early stuck his head round the open door. The station sergeant was warming his ample backside by a two-bar electric fire, vacantly picking his teeth with a match-stick. He took the match out of his mouth slowly and threw it languidly into a waste-paper basket.

"You can relax now, Tom," Early said, smiling benignly. "It wasn't the revolution starting. Just in case you were wondering what all the noise was."

"Was it breaking glass I heard?"

"It was, Tom. The doctor here had some difficulty opening a window. Can you get one of your lads down there with a brush?"

"Aye, OK, sir. It did cross my mind that it were breaking glass . . ."

Early ushered me into his office, shutting the door and chuckling to himself.

"You've got to laugh, really. Tom saying it crossed his mind, I mean. Wouldn't take too long to do that if distance was the only criterion. If we got a four-minute warning of a thermo-nuclear holocaust, Tom would require it in writing, so he could judge the degree of urgency. Motivated by the thoughts of

165

retirement and his homing pigeons, that's his trouble. Nice bloke, though. Talking about motivation – what brings you to this particular part of hell?"

He fiddled with a small coffee machine in the corner – a technological marvel amidst a heap of Dickensian office chaos. He eventually produced two plastic cups of black coffee which tasted like Bovril.

I could still hear the sound of my own breathing, as if I were using an aqua-lung, and the objects in the room seemed to have a disconcerting tendency to slip down in front of my vision, like a TV set which needed adjustment to the vertical hold. I managed to disguise my basic inability to stay on the chair without slipping off it, or stand upright without swaying, by concentrating my mind on a series of restless, purposeless movements, such as pacing about and checking the contents of my pockets as I talked to him.

"And what about you?" I asked as I poured out a fourth cup of coffee from the machine. It was a sure sign that my condition was improving, albeit temporarily, by the fact that this time I managed to fill the cup without spilling any on my shoes. Early smiled and shrugged his shoulders.

"I had a touch of heart trouble over a year ago. Nothing too bad, so your people tell me. But it looked like early retirement or else being put out to quieter pastures, so I chose the lesser of the two evils. I'm not complaining, though. It gives one time to stand and stare a bit."

I looked at my watch.

"Which reminds me – I have a job to do," I said. He laughed quietly and scooped out a heap of ash from his pipe, throwing it carelessly into a waste bucket.

"Oh aye, I almost forgot. You won't have met Spiky Wills, will you, doctor? He's one of our more relentless clients; been banned from every licensed premises in the district. When he's had his fill he's like the kiss of death to any respectable public house in this town. Tonight he was kicked out of the Rose and Crown for carrying on, effing and blinding and singing at the top of his voice, while they were holding a domino champion-ship. So when he gets outside he pinches someone's motor bike – how he managed to sit on it, never mind ride the bloody thing, baffles me. Anyway he gets this machine going and zooms straight through the front door and ploughs through all the tables, dominoes and crisps flying all over the place like shrapnel."

"My God, that could have been disastrous," I said, moving towards the door.

"Oh it was, doctor. They had to abandon the match. So, while everybody's diving for cover, Spiky roars out straight into a car that's parked across the other side of the road. That's when one of our lot picked him up – literally." Early began to chuckle again, and stopped me by the door. "The thing that tickles me is, when they get him to the station he suddenly starts screaming he's been mortally injured on account of the fact he sees all this blood and God knows what else down the front of his shirt. Put the wind up our lads for a minute, until they found he'd got two dead crows pushed down the inside of his jacket. They must have got knocked about a bit when he hit the other vehicle."

"Two dead crows?"

"Aye. Shot them this afternoon. Now don't ask me why, because you have to remember he's as daft as a brush. The ragged edge of life's rich tapestry, so to speak, is Spiky."

I left Early filling his pipe and went through into what they called the medical room.

The arresting officer stood in the doorway of the small neon-lit room which contained an examination couch, a small washbasin at the far end and a chair in the middle on which sat the accused, Spiky Wills. The officer droned out the relevant bit of the Road Traffic Act while Spiky grinned at me gormlessly. It was difficult to tell his exact age, but I guessed that he was about fifty. He had matted fair hair and his round, plethoric face seemed to rise straight from his chest. His trousers were tied round his middle by thick rope, the ends of which he had tucked into his pockets. He appeared friendly enough – in fact he seemed to be viewing the whole thing philosophically.

"How do, doctor. Sorry to drag you out of bed on my account, although I supposed you're used to it. We've all got us jobs to do, eh? I'll hold my hand up straight away – I've supped some bloody ale tonight. Still, if it's over the top, that's all there is to it. Can't do owt about it, really. I'm only sorry they got so uppity at Rose and Crown, otherwise I wouldn't have lost me rag, way I did."

He grinned sheepishly and his eyes moved independently of each other as he looked up at me. I turned to the basin to wash my hands and looked down to see that it contained two dead crows. The officer coughed apologetically.

"Sorry about that, doctor," he said. "Our fridge was full. There was nowhere else to put them."

"Got them down near the cemetery this afternoon, doctor," said Spiky, "You can tek 'em if you like – they'll make a right good pie."

I looked at the tick-infested, partly crushed birds and made a mental note not to go too near his clothing. After I had fiddled about with the syringe and needle for a few minutes, he rolled up his sleeve and revealed a fat plexus of veins on his brawny arm. As I leaned forward to stick the needle in, I got another disconcerting attack of dizziness and double vision which heralded a counter-attack by Len Garlick's wine against the caffeine now swilling round my system. I closed one eye and instinctively placed the needle in the right place, grateful for the many months I had spent as a house physician in Wishton General when I had done this so many times before, my brain half asleep from round-the-clock duty rotas. I could now complete this procedure from memory.

When I had finished I walked out into the corridor and took a few deep breaths before being confronted by Jim Early again.

"You've picked a bad night, I'm afraid, doctor," he said apologetically. "I know you're dying to get your head down but I've got this young lady I want you to have a look at. One of my lads from CID has just brought her in. It's nothing bad, d'you follow, but I'd like you to have a quick look, just for the record. Incidentally, I'm going to ask her to tell you the story herself. It's so bloody bizarre you won't believe it. Anyway, I'll leave it to you. You've got a good imagination, so if you can conjure up the picture you're in for a treat, take it from me."

I was too tired to argue. I followed him upstairs into one of the CID interview rooms where he introduced me to a short, overweight woman in her late thirties with very dark hair back-combed into a brittle heap on top of her head. She was talking to a policewoman who was thinking about tomorrow's shopping list.

"Pauline – this is the doctor," said Early. "Pauline Stopes, doctor. Pauline's going to tell you what happened earlier tonight aren't you, Pauline, love?" He stood back against the wall, filling his pipe.

"What – again?" she asked irritably, sitting up in the chair. The policewoman crossed her legs and looked at her own reflection in the window, shifting her head from side to side and touching the hair on the nape of her neck.

"Yes please, Pauline," said Early patiently, putting his unlit pipe into his mouth. She glared at him and he held up his hands in silent apology.

"Just you don't start laughing again, that's all – it wasn't so bloody funny for me, you know," she said. She turned towards me, hitching forward in the chair. A note of enthusiasm crept into her voice as she started to recount the incident. "It was like this, see. I was asleep – I'd gone to bed early on account of Jeff being on nights. And I woke up all of a sudden and realised summat were wrong – you know how you do, like. Well – with Jeff not being there and that. So when I looked up I nearly died, because I could see a man kneelin' over me with a dirty great knife in his hand." She swallowed and took a deep breath.

"Bread knife," said Early softly, almost to himself. She looked across and jabbed a finger at him.

"S'all right you sayin' 'bread-knife' like that. Oh it's all right sayin' it like that after it happened, I mean. You weren't bloody *there*. I'm tellin' you, it looked more like a bleedin' sword – wavin' it around in front of my face, he was."

By this time she had really got warmed up, throwing her arms about and glaring wide-eyed at us as she relived the whole thing.

"Go on, Pauline," Early murmured.

"Well," she said, "by this time my eyes were getting used to the dark – you know how they do – and I could see that he had a nylon stockin' over his head. Well, actually it were a pair of tights, because I could see the two stockin' legs and feet danglin' down in front of his face and he kept flickin' his head back to get them out of the way. The other thing was – he had this streamin' cold and kept sniffin', like, and all the time, flick flick, sniff sniff, flick, sniff – just like that, he was. So I says to him, 'What the 'ell's this about?' – and he says, 'Let's see what you've got under there," and I says, 'Under where?' and he points to the blankets and starts mauling me about. Then he said, 'I want to get me hands on your valuables,' so I mean, I burst out

169

laughing and says 'You'll be bloody lucky – we haven't got two brass farthings to rub together.' Well, he sniffs and flicks these two stockings from in front of his face, then he sneezes and falls off the bed and bangs his head on the dressing table, so I says, 'you've got a rotten cold – I've got some Anadin somewhere' – and he just gives out a right mouthful and runs like the clappers downstairs and out of the house. That were it, really."

As she finished she sat back in the chair and lit a cigarette. I heard a muted choking sound and looked across at Early. He was standing against the wall with his eyes closed, gripping his pipe with his clenched teeth, the upper half of his body gently shaking with silent laughter. It was too much for me and I burst out laughing. I couldn't help myself. She jumped up out of the chair and rolled up her sleeves.

"I might have known you'd laugh your professional bleedin' head off," she snarled. "You're all the same, you doctors. Just you take a look at this . . ."

She pointed to a bunch of fresh red marks on her arm, where presumably she had been grabbed.

"I'm sorry, Mrs Stopes," I said. "I didn't mean to seem, er . . . but it is a pretty unusual account – are you sure you didn't dream this? I've seen it happen before."

"Did I 'ellers dream it. What do you think these are? Fragments of me imagination?" she cried indignantly. I coughed and tried to look more serious, desperately fighting off an intense, gut-trembling desire to burst out laughing again.

"Well no – these look like fresh bruises, all right." I took a close look and made a mental note of their size and distribution. "Are there any other injuries?"

She shook her head and pushed her sleeves down again. I looked at Early.

"Is that it? Not a lot for me to do, is there?"

He pushed himself off the wall with his elbows and shook his head.

"No. That's about it, really. Would you like to come through and write a note or two for the record, doctor? Right." He patted Mrs Stopes on the shoulder and smiled. "Thanks, Pauline, love. Sorry you had to go through all that again. It'll have been worth it, believe me."

"That's all right," she muttered. "So long as you catch the bleeder, that's the main thing."

170

"I'll have a word with you about that in a minute," he said, winking at her.

We went down into his office. He brought out a couple of claim forms and placed them on the desk in front of me.

"There you go, doctor. Makes the whole thing worth while, filling those in."

"What did you make of that?"

"Ah, well now . . ." Early smiled and sat down, cramming the bowl of his pipe with fresh tobacco. "Granted, her story does have a touch of the ridiculous, but we happen to think it's true in every detail."

"Are you kidding?" I said, laughing.

"No I'm not, doctor, believe you me. Someone – a neighbour – saw this man dashing out of the front door of this lady's house a while ago, and what's more, we have picked up a gentleman who incidentally lives in the next street. A search of his premises revealed a pair of stockings – sorry, tights – and the bread knife in question. Now, he lives on his own and naturally the presence of the tights was a bit suspicious and, what's more, he's got a very nasty cold as well as a bump on his head the size of a lemon. He's denied it, of course, but with the evidence we've got, identification of the knife and clothing et cetera, I should think he'll get a couple of years. Breaking and entering, assault with a deadly weapon. Truth stranger than fiction, eh? He'd have been better having an early night in his own bed with a couple of Anadin. It just goes to show."

"Goes to show what?" I said.

"Well," said Early, lighting his pipe again, "you shouldn't take things at face value. I mean, look at the way you reacted, doctor. Laughed like a bloody drain, you did."

"I know I did, mainly because it did sound —"

"Preposterous? A complete fabrication? Early laughed softly. "No . . . anybody round here who comes out with a daft tale like that must be telling the truth. When that's read out in court the jury'll be falling about in the aisles, that's for sure. It's right when they say there's nowt so queer as folk. This good lady probably screams blue murder if she finds a spider in the bath – then a feller threatens her with a knife in the dead of night and she offers him Anadin for his cold. Bloody hell!"

He gave a short burst of laughter with his pipe in his mouth, causing a shower of sparks and ash to spew out of the bowl

171

onto the surface of the desk. I got up slowly, aware of a dull, throbbing ache inside my head and a taste in my mouth which was enough to put me off alcohol for life.

"I can't say that this evening has been any less strange than the rest of today," I said. "I'll drop you in a written report about Mrs Stopes sometime tomorrow. I don't feel like doing it right now."

"Fine, doctor. As you wish. It was nice to see you again after the last time. It's not often I get the chance to share part of life's piss-poor panorama with someone who appreciates its breath-taking perspective. Well, you'll be wanting to climb into that lovely warm bed, I've no doubt, now the day's work is done."

There was something in the way that he said that which reminded me of something he had told me a couple of years ago, when we had attended a particularly grisly suicide case. His wife had left him years ago and his domestic life had been pretty bleak ever since.

"How about you these days?" I said, before I could stop myself. "Still, er, the Chinese carry-outs in front of the TV?"

He grunted and tapped the electric fire with his foot, causing its ancient circuitry to fizzle as if it was going to retaliate in some mysterious way.

"Something like that," he said. "It's the condensation which is the worst bit, though."

"The condensation?"

"Mm . . . when you get in and the place has been cold and empty for twelve hours . . . you put the gas fire on and you get this bloody awful condensation everywhere. Dampens the spirit, that does. Quite apart from the wallpaper. Funny how different things affect people that way."

"I'm sorry it's like that . . ."

"Oh, hey up, doctor," he said, looking up sharply, "I don't need bloody sympathy. This is beginning to sound like a consultation – which neither of us needs at this time of night."

"Right," I said, feeling foolish at putting my foot on a sore spot. "See you again, no doubt."

"Very likely."

He swept ash off the table with the sleeve of his jacket, then looked up and burst out laughing.

"You'd best get off home, doctor. You really do look bloody dreadful. And mind how you go because some of the lads are as keen as mustard with the breathalyser."

I took a different route back to the house, but soon wished I hadn't. After five minutes I found myself driving up a wide street lined on both sides with clay and rubble. I had no idea where I was. I passed a large hoarding at the side of the road which said something about buses, and I slowed instinctively as I caught a fleeting glimpse of the orange stripe of a stationary police car poking out behind it. A uniformed police officer suddenly appeared in the glare of my headlights, causing me to pull up sharply. I wound down my window as he walked slowly towards me, banging his leather-gloved hands together. I took a few deep breaths and the cold air stung the inside of my nose.

"Good evening, sir." He leaned with one arm on the roof, bending his head near the open window. "Going anywhere in particular?"

"Home," I said.

"I see. You've got two problems, then."

"How's that?"

"Well, it's like this. First, this is a one way street and you're travelling the wrong way. And second, it's buses only . . . and, correct me if I'm wrong, sir, but you're not a bus."

"I'm sorry – I didn't know that," I said.

"Didn't know? We haven't been having a few too many drinks tonight have we, sir?"

"Good Lord, no. Why?" I looked down at the instrument panel in order not to show him the whites of my eyes.

"I just wondered how you hadn't seen that notice back there," he said, jerking his thumb back in the direction I had come. "It's a very big notice, sir. Thirty feet by twenty – that's about six hundred square feet, according to my calculations. No expense spared round here when it comes to communicating to the general public. Now . . . I suppose you could argue that it's *possible*, and I'll grant you that it's *conceivable*, that we could have put up an even bigger one, so as people could read it. But I would argue that you'd really have to be either blind or pissed – or both – not to have seen that notice, sir."

"Look – I'm really sorry about this," I said. "The fact is, I've actually been on official police business."

He sniffed. "Really, sir? In what particular capacity, may I ask?"

"Police surgeon. I've just been to Stonebridge to do a Section Six – and an assault."

"Well, well. We *have* been busy tonight, haven't we, sir? Who was the officer in charge?"

"Inspector Early. Jim Early."

"*Jim.* Hmm . . . got friends in high places, have we?" He rubbed his chin. "I'll just check, if you don't mind. Full name, please, sir."

I told him. He walked back to his vehicle. I stared at the dashboard in dismay, visualising the headlines in tomorrow's local papers; "DOCTOR FOUND DRUNK IN CHARGE AFTER EXAMINING A DRUNK IN CHARGE."

He returned a minute later with a stony expression on his face.

"I've just had a word with Inspector Early, sir. He says he's never bloody heard of you."

"Never . . ."

"But he has given me very specific instructions, sir, on what we should do. Now then . . ."

He reached into his pocket and pulled out a small black notebook.

"Let's play a little game, shall we, sir? I'm throwing down the gauntlet, so to speak. You start your engine, select the appropriate gear – they're all there by your left hand – and see if you can reverse this vehicle of yours and get back to the end of the road before I can write down your registration number in my little book here."

I didn't need to have it spelled out again. With the engine howling in reverse and my neck nearly breaking as I looked over my shoulder, I somehow found myself back on the main road to home.

My head was still buzzing when I crawled into bed. I put my arm across Tanya's warm back and she stirred with a soft moan.

"You're cold," she murmured. "What time is it? You've been ages."

"I know," I said. "It wasn't exactly straightforward. It never is."

She turned towards me and we put our arms round each other.

174

'Well. The end of your first day," she whispered. "How do you feel?"

I ran my tongue over my front teeth and groaned.

"Chewed up and spat out by the grape."

"Serves you right."

"I know, I know."

I held her closely and buried my mouth in her neck.

"Mmmm . . . this is better than Chinese carry-outs in front of the TV," I mumbled. "No condensation, either."

Tanya drew back her head slightly. I knew that her eyes were open with a question, for I could hear the occasional soft sound of her eyelashes brushing against the pillow as she blinked. I smiled sleepily and moved against the warm, gently pulsating skin of her neck.

"I'll tell you about it tomorrow," I said, and fell asleep.

16

The next day was mercifully unspectacular. Beatrice Addy impressed me even further as a highly effective buffer between my limited availability and the threat of a potentially limitless demand, so that between us we managed to satisfy the most urgent needs of the day. I went to see Clifford Tansley. We exchanged a few light-hearted words of encouragement as he sat in a forlorn heap watching the racing from Newmarket, waving a bottle of beer around in his usable hand. In the afternoon I made my way to Jessop Memorial to see how Len Garlick was coming to terms with his enforced immobility. I needn't have worried. In that glistening, pastel-painted ward he was enjoying every minute of attention from a bunch of Jamaican auxiliaries who leaned back, their hands on their wide hips, laughing uproariously at his teasing banter.

By the time Kathleen and Ron Leaford had arrived that evening, the children were asleep. Although they were both as familiar with the house as we were, we showed them where everything was before setting off, in the knowledge that their relaxed, easy-going manner made it unlikely that our three boys would present them with any difficulty.

I drove across the town, glancing occasionally in admiration at Tanya's auburn hair, whose highlights danced briefly in the orange glare of each streetlight we passed.

"You look terrific," I said.

She smiled. "It must be the thought of going out for the evening. We haven't been out for ages. I hope you're not going to talk about medicine all night long."

"Hell, no," I said, laughing. "I don't usually do that, do I?"

"Sometimes," she said. "You know what you're like when you get going, and I'll probably be the only non-medical person there tonight."

"In that case, the responsibility for maintaining an intelligent conversation will fall on your shoulders," I said. "And it won't be easy, from what I've seen of Gerald Crawley. He seems to think of nothing else apart from medicine. Very cerebral, is Gerald. His idea of physical recreation is snipping articles out of the *British Medical Journal*, I shouldn't wonder."

The approach to the house was along a tree-lined drive which ended in the shadows of a vast, early Victorian edifice whose gothic arched windows, in the darkness, suggested that it might have been a church at one time. As we climbed out of the car a light came on over the front door. Gerald Crawley appeared, welcomed us in, and for a few moments we shuffled awkwardly round the hall as we all introduced ourselves. Marjorie Crawley, cool and assured, with greying, swept-back hair, smiled and apologised before disappearing briefly back into the kitchen, while Simon Crawley, Gerald's youngest son, collected our coats. An embarrassed, intelligent-looking sixteen-year-old, he had the fresh awkwardness of his age, in that he took to his task with enthusiasm while clearly wishing that he was somewhere else. He disappeared down the hall, grateful that by taking the coats, he could also take his gangling frame to a part of the house that the rest of us were not likely to occupy.

As we entered the lounge, a large Dalmatian sniffed our legs indifferently, then retired languidly into a corner, merging tastefully with the rest of the soft furnishings. Marjorie Crawley came in from the kitchen holding a glass of wine.

"Just making one or two small adjustments . . . Gerald, have you asked these good people what they are going to have to drink?"

Gerald did a lot of ritual hand-rubbing and bobbing about in front of the booze, like a magician in front of his table full of tricks, which culminated in Tanya receiving the smallest scotch I have ever set eyes on. With last night's episode still fresh in my memory I settled for a tonic water, although it did cross my mind that, in the presence of Gerald Crawley, an evening of total abstinence might be more than I could bear.

"Ah yes," he said, "I meant to mention . . . I've asked my trainee and his wife to come along this evening. You didn't meet Peter Lowe when you came round to see us, did you? Peter started last August. Stays with us until the summer, then hopes to find a partnership of his own. As his trainer I have to see to it that he learns something about general practice before

177

we let him loose on his own, so to speak." He smiled apologetically and shrugged his shoulders. "Of course, that's putting it very crudely, you understand. Did you do a trainee-ship before you became a principal?"

"No," I said. I was going to leave it at that, but he craned his head forward slightly, clearly expecting more. "I . . . er, jumped in at the deep end and simply got stuck in, I suppose," I added lamely.

"Hmmm . . ." Gerald nodded slowly and pursed his lips. I wasn't sure whether this was meant to convey understanding or disapproval.

"Oh, I realise that jumping in at the deep end must have its drawbacks," I said. "You swallow a lot of water, for one thing, but learning from your mistakes —"

"Ah!" exclaimed Gerald, sticking his finger in the air and tip-toeing across to the fireplace. He spun round and beamed maniacally. "Providing . . . *providing* that one is *aware* that one is making mistakes. For if one is *not* aware of one's shortcomings, how is one able to discover what one has to learn? Hm?"

He wrapped his arms round his middle and rocked backwards and forwards in front of the fireplace, thrilled to bits with himself for delivering this shaft of insight into the gathering gloom of my own thoughts. I looked down into my tonic water.

"Well, Gerald," I said, "I've never had any difficulty spotting my shortcomings or mistakes –they always appear to be so painfully apparent."

Gerald gave me a patronising smile.

"Oh come now, Steven. You're being far too modest, I'm sure . . . Have you never thought of doing some teaching or academic work?"

"Teaching? Good God, Gerald – I'm too busy learning."

"Aren't we all? And, you know – in one sense anyway – teaching *is* learning, Steven. By teaching, we begin to explore our reasons for doing things . . . question our beliefs . . ."

"Confirm our prejudices," I said, without thinking. "Who said that? Somebody did. I read it somewhere. Sorry, Gerald. Go on."

"I can see that you are not convinced," he said, frowning. "Of course, I realise that at the moment you'll have a lot on your plate with Alec's practice to reorganise. What a wonderful challenge. I wonder, though, when you feel on top of things, whether you might consider participation in a bit of research. I'm starting to launch a project on comparative morbidity in the indigenous population . . ."

"Who falls ill and how often, you mean?"

"Yes . . . if you like to put it that way," he said. "What I *thought* . . ." He put one foot on the chair next to me and leaned forward with an evangelistic glint in his eye. "What I thought was that it would be interesting to compare morbidity rates in two different practices. Yours and ours. Might be quite illuminating, you know. And of course we could always write it up. As a matter of fact, I'm writing a paper at the moment on the incidence of undescended testicles in the local schoolboys. It's quite fascinating, really, what I've found."

"I bet," I said. "Tell me, Gerald – how do you find the time to do all this and look after the patients on your list?"

He stood straight up again and waved his arms about airily. "Being organised I suppose. Of course, you're right when you imply that it's time-consuming. I have to take a weekday off to collate data and take it to the University for processing, and then I have another half-day where I do most of my planning and writing."

"Who sees the patients when you're doing all this?" asked Tanya. I caught her eye and winked encouragingly.

"Very simple," said Gerald, helping himself to a tomato juice. "They have to see someone else. Whenever I'm not available – which is quite a bit – they usually see the trainee. Peter has been marvellous, really. And then there's Rami Prakash. Extremely conscientious. Works like a . . . er . . . so the patients are shared round, really. They don't seem to mind, I must say."

"Don't they find it a bit disruptive, seeing different people each time they come? I should have thought . . ."

"Disruptive?" Gerald replied patiently. "No . . . I don't think so. I don't see it that way at all, er . . . Tanya. I think if patients want us to be better doctors, want us to improve our level of competence, raise our aspirations, then they have to accept that there is a price to pay for all this."

"I think I know what Tanya means, though, Gerald," I said. "It's the irony of the situation."

"Irony? What irony?"

"Well . . . here you are, rushing around raising your aspirations and striving to improve the standards of general practice, and meanwhile the thing which seems to be central to general practice is sliding by the wayside in the process."

"Oh? And what might that be?"

"Personal care," I said. "Continuity. One doctor for one patient – wherever possible. I mean – I know we all have to delegate, but . . . it's like a jockey jumping from horse to horse during a race. Ten to one, he'll end up flat on his back and not finish the race. The patient, I mean."

Gerald roared with laughter.

"Steven my dear chap, what an appalling metaphor – and how anachronistic. Unless, of course, you see us as carrying the patients on our backs from start to finish. How fascinating. We really must discuss this later." He looked at his watch. "Peter and Moira said they would be a bit late. Been unavoidably delayed, apparently. We thought it would be nice to have them along, since they're about the same age as yourselves. I haven't met Peter's wife as yet."

Marjorie Crawley glanced anxiously towards the kitchen, probably thinking about the cauliflower *au gratin* dying the death in the oven, when the doorbell rang. The dog grunted and padded out, followed by Gerald. Marjorie excused herself to rescue the meal and Gerald returned to introduce Peter and Moira Lowe.

Peter Lowe was small and bearded and, although he was smiling an awful lot, I noticed that he was perspiring and that he had a warm, clammy handshake. He stepped to one side to introduce his wife who swayed uncertainly in the doorway. Moira Lowe was attractive in a gaunt sort of way. She had deep blue eyes, high cheek bones and raven-black hair which spilled onto the top of her crimson dress. She began to speak, holding her lips as if she was playing the flute and as if her tongue was out of control. I became transfixed. I couldn't understand a word that she was saying. The vowel sounds had a sort of piping Home Counties quality mixed with a trace of something I couldn't quite identify, but, for all I knew, she might well have been speaking fluent Martian. What came out was an incomprehensible babble, as if she was recovering from a general anaesthetic. Peter stepped in front of her and waved his arms about, his face glistening in the light of the room.

"Er . . . sorry we're a bit late," he said, "we put some money on a horse this afternoon at Doncaster and it won, so we . . . well, Moira mostly, er, we've been celebrating a bit. You know how it is."

He coughed and avoided Gerald's look of abject disappointment, taking Moira's hand and leading her towards the sofa where she flopped down and gazed at the drinks cabinet.

"Well, I mean, that's jolly good, isn't it?" said Gerald uncertainly. "Fine, good. Yes, that's . . . fine."

His hand moved hesitantly over the array of bottles and cut-glass goblets. "Well now, before we . . . what will you two people have?"

"Gin!" called Moira immediately. "Gin right over here."

She shot her left arm up in the air, then let it drop back on the arm of the sofa, like a hemiplegic limb. Gerald turned and smiled urbanely and reassuringly to Tanya and me. Marjorie walked into the centre of the room and smiled reassuringly to us as well. Peter sweated and grinned at everyone, including the dog.

"Right!" Gerald said briskly. "Gin. Right. I think we have time for just a small one before we, er . . . Peter? Gin for you, is it?"

"Mm, please. Moira – are you sure . . . ?"

"Oh, God, yes," she drawled. "Jayzus, 'twas ages since we finished dat bottle of gin dis afternoon. I wouldn't mind another just now, at all."

It was only then that the penny dropped. The Home Counties accent had slipped and a strong Irish accent smeared itself over her dysarthric mumbling. I looked at her eyes as she slumped on the sofa. They were moving quite independently of each other, which was a sure sign that her central nervous system was reeling from the effect of an alcoholic blitzkrieg earlier that day. There was no doubt about the diagnosis: she was stoned out of her mind. Realising this, my spirits rose immediately, for it was obvious that our hosts were pretending not to notice. This meant that within this haven of good taste, the evening was poised on the brink of becoming, unexpectedly, a complete farce.

Moira took the glass, emptied it in a couple of swift gulps, then jumped up unsteadily, beaming at Marjorie Crawley.

181

"Well now, that's better, so it is," she piped through her flute embouchure. "Jayzus, but the gin makes me hungry." She slapped her abdomen to emphasise her point.

During the meal Moira was such a breathtaking distraction that most of the time I didn't know what I was eating. She was really incredible. During the soup course she drank a nicely chilled hock which caused a noticeable deterioration in her condition – as if the fresh onslaught had reactivated the gin of that afternoon. On a couple of occasions I thought she was going to slump face-down into her bowl of steaming minestrone. As she related some rambling anecdote about life and death at the Royal Infirmary where she worked, her head bobbed up and down, causing her long hair to plunge into the bowl, picking up the parmesan cheese like iron filings on a magnet. The more outrageous she became, the greater were the efforts of the others round the table not to notice, giving her performance a surrealist quality which made me want to laugh out loud. I was relieved when the meal came to an end, however, because her worsening co-ordination was ruining the only decent suit I possessed. Every time she put her elbows on the table they slipped off again, jerking the upper half of her body violently forward and ejecting food off her fork or wine from her glass onto my lap. I had not seen anyone so cork-legged for years.

After the meal we went back into the lounge. Moira kicked off her shoes, lay on the couch and within seconds went off into a deep, snoring sleep. Every now and again, as the rest of us droned on about the problems of the health service, she sat up suddenly and smacked her lips noisily for a moment before sinking into oblivion again. While Peter smiled, his sweat glands in overdrive, Marjorie chatted with a carefully controlled charm, although from time to time her eyes fleetingly betrayed genuine fear. She was obviously wondering whether Moira would throw up on the carpet – or alternatively, become doubly incontinent where she lay. When Marjorie brought in some coffee the rattle of cups brought Moira round and she sat up, gazing shakily round the room.

"Moira, I wondered if you would care for a drink of coffee?" Marjorie said hopefully, as if she was offering Complan to a debilitated grandmother. Moira brightened up immediately.

"No thanks, Mrs Crawley – but I'd love a beer."

Majories eyes widened but she managed a weak smile.

"A beer?" she said faintly.

"Mm, a beer," beamed Moira. "Clears out the system it does, to be sure."

"Well . . . I, er, thought that we might have some coffee."

"Oh, God no, I can't drink coffee at all. For one t'ing it upsets me stomach and, another t'ing, the caffeine in it is not good for the heart, gives me palpitations and keeps me awake. Mainly, though, it makes me fart."

Gerald winced almost imperceptibly. He tried to smile but his facial muscles seemed to go into a painful spasm.

"Really?" he said in a strangled voice. "How very . . . odd. Well, if that's what you would . . ."

He poured her a brown ale and she drank it in three seconds flat. Simon Crawley, who had appeared in the doorway a moment earlier, stood in open-mouthed admiration as she drained the glass. He cleared his throat politely.

"Er, the dog isn't here, is he, Dad?"

"No, he . . . he went out earlier, I think," Gerald replied without taking his eyes off Moira.

"It's just that I heard a dog barking at the chickens in the paddock, that's all," said Simon. "I'd better go and see."

Moira threw back her head and burst into a peal of high-pitched laughter. Simon stepped back quickly into the hallway, aghast, as she suddenly lurched forward through the doorway and grabbed his arm.

"Come on!" she yelled, "let's go and look for the poor dumb animal before there's shit and feathers everywhere!"

Simon was jerked violently sideways as she pulled him down the hall, his protests being completely drowned by Moira's shrieks of laughter as they went through the rear of the house. Gerald helped himself to a large scotch.

"I think I'll have one as well," said Marjorie quietly.

"Yes, quite," Gerald replied, flinching at the sound of another maniacal scream of laughter from somewhere outside.

Peter stood up and spread out his hands in a helpless gesture.

"Sorry about this, folks," he said cheerfully. "I'm afraid Moira's a bit over the top tonight."

"Peter, do you think that it's wise . . . ?" mumbled Gerald. "I mean . . . I wonder if they're all right out there . . ."

"Oh yes, she'll be OK," Peter replied. "Moira can take care of herself."

"Yes, I'm sure she can," Gerald said thoughtfully. "I wasn't really thinking of Moira."

"I shouldn't worry Gerald. She's just very exuberant when she's had a drink. She's got more energy that all of us put together. Could keep this up for hours."

"Really? Hm, I was afraid of that."

Gerald glanced at Marjorie. She swallowed hard and looked at her watch.

"Is it really that time?" she said. "Good Lord, I had no idea . . ."

The phone rang and she dashed out into the hall to answer it, grateful for the distraction it provided. I suddenly remembered that I had asked a Mrs Randle to phone me here at about this time, to let me know how her husband was. I had called there earlier in the day. He had been diagnosed by Alec Duncan many months before as having cancer of the bladder and had been deteriorating for weeks. I took the receiver off Marjorie and, as I turned away, I saw the lines round her eyes and the corners of her mouth twitch as she listened to the distant, drunken shouts of Moira Lowe.

"Mrs Randle?"

"Oh, hello, doctor." The voice was quiet and apologetic. "I wouldn't have rung you late like this, but you said you wanted to —"

"Yes, that's all right, Mrs Randle. Has there been any change?"

"Oh yes. He's passed away, I think. Difficult to tell, really, the way he's been these last few days. Will you be calling, doctor?"

"I'm leaving straight away," I said.

The back door burst open and Simon Crawley raced past me with startled eyes and with no shirt on. Mrs Randle said something which I didn't quite catch, for as I pulled the receiver away from my ear Moira charged through the back door whooping and yelling and carrying something under her arm wrapped in the shirt that Simon had been wearing.

"Viola! she piped, throwing the bundle down the hall in the stiff-arm way in which very young children throw heavy rocks into water. A large, terrified hen dropped to the floor,

184

defaecated twice, then ran into the kitchen. Marjorie followed, putting her hands to her face and gasping, "Christ!" Peter Lowe walked after her flapping his arms up and down, presumably in an attempt to establish empathy with the hen. It was a stunning climax to a bizarre evening which at the outset had showed so little promise. Much as I was keen to see how this shambles resolved itself, I caught Tanya's eye and we collected our coats, briefly explaining to Gerald why we had to go. The poor man was hollow-eyed as a result of a situation that was quite beyond his experience.

"I'm so sorry that we weren't able somehow to get round to talking about, er . . ." he mumbled lamely, ". . . it was awfully nice meeting you both, anyway. I'm sure we'll be able to get together another time, when perhaps we can . . ."

"Oh, hell, yes. Look forward to that, Gerald," I said brightly. My heart sank at the prospect and I took a firm grip of the door handle, opening the door before he had time to go into details about what we might discuss. "Thanks for inviting us round. We've both enjoyed it immensely, believe me."

Gerald smiled a martyr's smile, as if he was trying to make the best of a mortal injury.

"Oh good . . . glad you enjoyed it. It has seemed . . . I mean, it . . . it has been rather, er, different . . . hasn't it?"

We got into the car and drove down the lane to the main road without saying a word. Tanya squeezed my arm and I looked across. Her eyes were closed and she was smiling.

"Steven, have I been dreaming or did all that really happen?" she said softly. I began to laugh so much I had to grip the steering wheel tightly in order to keep from sliding off my seat.

"No. You weren't dreaming. It really did happen," I said. "I thought we had some weird colleagues in Overton, but this place is something else. I'd love to be a fly on the wall at Gerald's place tomorrow."

I drove into a narrow, badly-lit little street where the Randle house stood. I switched off the ignition and leaned across, kissing Tanya and breathing in the fragrant warmth of her skin.

"I really fancied you from across the table tonight," I breathed. We both burst out laughing. "You know what I

185

mean. Looking at you across the table." I reached for the door. "Mind you, had we made love across the table I'm not sure it would have created too much consternation, the way things had been going."

"No," Tanya giggled, "Marjorie would have moved the cut glass out of harm's way and Gerald would have probably engaged his trainee in a discussion about one of his research projects."

She sighed and rested her head on the back of the seat.

"See you later."

"OK. I won't be long."

The front door of the house was open and I went through into a dark, narrow hallway. Mrs Randle appeared from the lounge doorway, a thick cardigan slung over her stained, faded housecoat.

"I'm sorry you've had to come out to him, doctor. I wasn't sure what to do next."

She led the way back into the lounge where they had put the bed some weeks before. The banked-up coal fire was the only source of light, and the flickering yellow flames caused the shadows to jump and shift, giving the hollow eyes, sunken cheeks and dark, open mouth of the corpse a grotesque illusion of movement. I flicked the light-switch but there was no response.

"Bulb's gone," sighed Mrs Randle. "It's been gone a few days now. I haven't got round to changing it yet. Harold used to see to all that sort of thing, but the way he's been recently the house has gone to pot. I suppose I'll have to get to get used to the idea of doing these jobs from now on. Has he gone, doctor?"

It didn't need a lengthy examination to confirm death. I nodded.

"I thought he had. A blessing, really," she said without emotion, very matter-of-fact. I guessed that all the emotion and anguish had been drained out of her during the last few months of helplessly watching over Harold Randle's increasing emaciation.

"He's been ill a long time," I said. It was neither an observation nor a question. Only an invitation to Mrs Randle to say something else if she felt like it.

"It must be above nine months since he had his operation,"

she said. "Open and shut, what Doctor Duncan told me. Then he had some radium treatment which didn't seem to suit him. I never thought he'd outlive Doctor Duncan, though. He were always very kind when you got to know him."

"Have you looked after him by yourself?"

"Oh yes. The nurse comes in regularly and she's been very nice . . . but other than that it's been down to me, really. I've got a son in Shropshire who comes up when he can, which isn't very often. I'll have to ring him up and tell him, I expect. Of course, he's got his job to see to, and then they've got their own family now, their own lives, like."

It sounded as if she was apologising for her son. When she turned to look into the fire, I could see by her eyes that she was thinking about her own bleak future.

"Have you any good neighbours who can help you?" I asked. "You'll need to contact the funeral director now that I've been."

"Oh, yes," she said. "Mrs Jackson will come right away if I knock on the wall. We have a little code, you see. What about . . . shall I need some papers from you, doctor?"

"The death certificate, you mean? Yes, I'll do that in the morning, so someone can collect it from the surgery when it's convenient."

"Right. Shall I destroy his tablets and things, or will someone else be able to use them, d'you think?"

She pointed to a small bedside table on top of which were a large number of plastic containers.

"It's best to destroy them," I said, "But you needn't do that now."

"I might as well, while I think about it," she said. She picked up an armful of containers, each one holding scores of tablets and capsules of all colours and sizes, throwing them all on the fire. The effect was startling. The fire suddenly blazed and crackled with blue-green flames which made the whole room move with dancing shadows. From the doorway another figure suddenly stepped into the eerie light and made me jump out of my skin.

"It's only me, love," said a woman's voice. "I thought someone was talking, so I came round. Has he gone?"

"Yes he has, Miriam. Come in, love."

They both looked at me and Mrs Randle smiled.

187

"My next door neighbour – Mrs Jackson. I'll be all right now."

She said it in such a way that I was in no doubt that she was in good hands, and I knew that my presence was no longer required. She came with me to the front door.

"Thanks for coming round, doctor," she said quietly. "Miriam will ring the undertaker and that. I'm best on my own. Grief's a very private thing, really. I expect it'll be later on, when I'm trying to face what's left, is when I'll be seeing you. They say it's usually like that. Good night, doctor."

She closed the door. I stood for a moment on the front path and stared at the rusting letter-box. I heard a faint whirring sound coming from the car as Tanya switched on the heater fan and I turned and got inside, starting the engine and wiping the newly-formed condensation from the inside of the windscreen.

"You weren't long. How did it go?" said Tanya. I shivered and put the car into gear.

"No. There wasn't a lot for me to do," I said as we drove down the gloomy street. "I confirmed death. Then a neighbour came. That was it, really."

I said nothing more. When we got back on the main road and were a few hundred yards away from home, Tanya twisted round and stared at me.

"I sometimes wonder about you, Steven," she said.

"How?"

"Sometimes I have no idea what you're thinking. At the Crawleys' you were as impassive as a sphinx practically the whole time that pantomime was taking place . . ."

"I was holding my breath for fear of splintering the veneer of calm Gerald and Marjorie were pasting over everything," I said. "Now *that's* what I call detachment. They've elevated detachment into an art form."

"And just now?" she said.

"What d'you mean?"

"You've just been to a death in someone's house and your only response was a couple of muttered sentences when you got back in the car. I hope you were more communicative with the poor soul in that house."

"I was thinking, that's all," I said, turning the car into the courtyard. I pulled up the handbrake and switched off the engine.

"Tell me," she said. I looked at her and smiled.

"I think I'm learning when to shut up. When saying nothing is the right thing to do."

"I'm not with you."

"In there, I mean. I hardly know Mrs Randle, of course, but . . . a couple of years ago I would have felt slighted, I think, if my attempts at comforting were rejected so comprehensively. It's a natural response for a doctor to go crapping on when someone is bereaved, under the mistaken impression that in some way it's supportive to do so, but she made it very plain that she wanted to be left alone. Grief is very private, she said."

"What did she want you for?"

"I don't know – apart from confirming death. So she could get on with the mechanics of the funeral arrangements and so forth, I suppose. She seemed to hold all the cards . . . as if that bit was something she had to do and any comment from me would have been an intrusion. But she seemed to realise that she might not be able to manage later on – as if she was herself defining what she might want from me, rather than me being asked what she needed. Christ, I'm starting to sound like Gerald Crawley. D'you know what I mean?"

"I think so," said Tanya. "But that's not surprising, is it, really? I mean – she knows herself and her problems better than you do, and obviously knows more about bereavement than you do. So why should you intrude unless she wants you to?"

"That's what I was trying to say. She holds all the cards. So all I can do now is listen, not advise. Which is the hardest thing to do when you consider that it goes against the grain of all the patterns of medical teaching."

"In what way?"

"Well . . . doctors are on the whole happy when they're dishing out advice, without it ever having occurred to them that it may not be what the patient has asked for or even wants, but they do it because it puts them firmly in control of the situation – maintains their authority, if you like. On the other hand, shutting up and listening and letting the patient decide what he needs puts the patient in the driving seat. Which makes the doctor feel uneasy because he's never sure in what direction the patient is going to take him."

"Do you get uneasy about it?" Tanya said, putting up her collar and shivering with the cold air.

189

"No – not now," I said. "The penny finally dropped at Mrs Randle's house, just now. No amount of research and analysis from Gerald Crawley could have shown me that. It actually came from one of our great sources of learning – the patient."

"What an evening of surprises," murmured Tanya. "Come on – we'd better get indoors and relieve Mafeking."

Kathleen and Ron Leaford met us at the door. Both of them had their coats on.

"My God – fleeing the battle area?" I said. "Has everything been all right?"

"No problems at all," smiled Kathleen. "We heard the car so we got ready to leave. Ron's got an early start in the morning. We've just made some tea if you want some."

"Thanks. And thanks for looking after the children for us."

"A pleasure," Ron said, rummaging around in his overcoat pocket for his keys. "Any time. How did it go at the Crawleys'? Good do?"

Tanya and I looked at each other and laughed.

"Quite different from what we anticipated," said Tanya. "Steven will no doubt tell you about it some time."

"Hm. Did he twist your arm into helping him with one of his research projects, Steven?"

"He did start to," I said, "but mercifully we got side-tracked."

Ron chuckled. "Think yourself bloody lucky. He's always had a bee in his bonnet about research, has Gerald. Can never make my mind up whether it's because his wife's a bit, you know, put out that he never became a full-time academic, or whether it's because he's better doing that than talking to his patients."

They walked to the car door. The lock was frozen and he took out his lighter, playing the flame gently over the key before inserting it and opening the doors. He leaned on the open door as Kathleen got inside and his large frame began to shake with laughter.

"I must tell you about one of Gerald's pieces of research. He eventually wrote it up for the BMJ. I cut the article out and I've got it in a drawer somewhere at the surgery. Every now and again I pull it out because it reminds me of this incident."

He closed the passenger door and methodically began

190

scraping the frost from the windows, laughing quietly to himself as he did so.

"Some years ago I was up at Jessop's visiting one of my patients on the orthopaedic ward, and who should I see but Gerald, armed with a clip-board, note books and what have you. So, to be polite, I asked him what he was up to, and it turns out he was researching into patients' attitudes to illness. That's what he said. Anyway, I went to have a chat with this patient of mine and Gerald eventually sits down by the next bed where some poor bugger had driven his Mini at a hundred and ten miles an hour down the M6 and hit a bridge, head on. As you can imagine, he's bandaged from head to foot and got all sorts of pulleys and traction devices attached to every appendage, and he's lying there feeling pretty sorry for himself. I couldn't help overhearing Gerald talking to him because the whole ward had gone quiet by this time. So Gerald looks over his half-moon glasses and says: 'When you hit this obstacle, what exactly passed through your mind?' And the patient thought for a moment, then turned to Gerald and said, 'I'm not exactly sure, doctor – but whatever it was it was big and heavy. I think it must have been the bleedin' back axle.' The whole ward erupted into laughter, but Gerald was the only one who couldn't see the joke."

He roared with laughter and got in the car. They disappeared down the lane and I could still hear him laughing as I shut the door on the brittle, freezing night.

17

By the end of February I had been consulted by most of the people in the practice who were in the habit of coming to the surgery, and I had seen nearly all those whose needs were greatest. The patients' apprehension and curiosity had settled into a tacit acceptance that I was now there to see to their problems, and their references to Alec Duncan became less frequent. I had visited the most remote farms in this harsh, beautiful landscape, and got to know each street in the sturdy, insular town. Even though I soon became immersed in the individual problems presented by people whom I did not know, it became obvious that the move from Overton to Stonebridge made no difference in one respect: that the reason why the majority of patients came to see me – apart from the usual range of medical conditions I would have expected anyway – was as a result of unhappiness, frustration and isolation. The isolation that I saw was not a physical or geographical one – it was an isolation of the thoughts and emotions. On so many occasions I would be presented with a mangled relationship between husband and wife which need never have reached me had they attempted to talk to each other about it – but there I sat, asking: "What have you said to your husband?" only to get the reply, "Oh, he said go to the doctor – he'll sort it out." It was as if feelings and ideas needed to be made respectable by the application of medical terminology: the crude pasting over with diagnostic labels which obscured the real nature of the problem and which led inexorably to irrelevant treatment. It was a dismal platform on which the patient and the doctor together had to launch a choice of solutions.

It was about this time that I was beginning to see some of the results of my first consultations, not only in terms of whether or not I had done any good, but also in terms of how the patients and their families responded to their illness or adverse circumstances. What I was seeing confirmed a fundamental observation I had made years ago in Overton: that, in most cases, the degree of discomfort experienced in illness had very little at all to do with the number of bacteria seen on a microscope slide or the number of joints ravaged and distorted by degeneration. The concept of disease as a process, as taught in medical schools, now seemed to me to be woefully inadequate as a basis on which to understand its effect on people. The Buddhist interpretation of the word disease as 'dis-ease' or 'ill at ease' seemed to provide a clue as to what was actually going on. How often had I seen a dose of mild influenza put someone on his back for a fortnight with minimal symptoms, whereas another would ignore its unpleasantness and be back at work in a couple of days? How often had I seen a patient whose arthritic disfigurement had gone almost unnoticed by me because of her radiant cheerfulness, in contrast with others whose apparent pain and misery was the only over-riding manifestation? Doctors talked about patients having different thresholds for discomfort, without realising that this only raised other questions concerning the way individuals came to terms with the lives they had: the illness might be an excuse to withdraw temporarily from an unpleasant relationship with the boss, the spouse or whatever, and was an acceptable way of avoiding a greater problem for which there might be no solution. Where there was an atmosphere of love and care within a family or a community there was less dis-ease, no matter what the degree of disease.

At the end of the month, when I had pretty well forgotten all about her, Mrs Vivian Horrocks turned up to morning surgery, looking as immaculate and well-groomed as when I had first seen her. We exchanged greetings politely and she made some comment about the waiting room not being very full. Maybe that was a signal that she was going to have a lot to say.

"You asked me to come in and see you," she said, adding quietly, "when you came to the house, if you remember."

"That's right," I said.

"That's almost a month ago, isn't it? I think you had just started here in the practice. Time flies . . ."

She smiled briefly, but I could see by her eyes that she was trying to gauge whether or not I thought less of her for having broken down and wept at that first meeting. She was an intelligent and sensitive woman who would easily detect in me any display of acceptance or rejection, approval or disapproval, and I had the feeling that she would use my response in order to rationalise her own behaviour, with the result that we would learn nothing. It occurred to me that the way I responded would therefore completely change the outcome of the consultation. I held my breath as I stealthily waded out into these uncharted waters, outwardly trying to give an air of relaxed neutrality.

"You're not saying very much, doctor," she said.

"No. What should I say?"

"I don't know," she said, shrugging her shoulders. "I'm not really sure why I came. I thought, perhaps, after the last time . . . I made such a fool of myself, that's all."

"Is that how you see it?" I said.

"Mm. Don't you see it that way as well?"

"I only saw that you were upset."

"Oh. I see." She sounded faintly surprised. "That makes a change. What I mean . . . I expected you to make some sort of judgement about it, I suppose. People do, don't they?"

I shrugged. "They may do," I said, "but I can't judge what I don't know, Mrs Horrocks."

She was silent for a few seconds. She stared down at her hands and slid her wedding ring up and down her finger.

"There's not much to know, really," she said in a low voice. "I've thought about it, of course, since I last saw you. When you came to see Stephanie."

"And what have you thought?"

"Oh . . . about her illnesses. When you didn't dash off a prescription for her and walk out I knew it wasn't *her* – it was *me*. D'you know what I mean?"

"Not yet. Go on."

"I'm a fussy mother hen, I suppose – what you people call an over-protective mother. It's quite straightforward and under-standable, in a way. You'll see from my records that I was in my mid-thirties when Stephanie was born. Ken and I had been married for ten years, but with his career it never seemed the right time . . . When Stephanie arrived I knew she would be our first and last, so I suppose this is what makes me fuss so much about her health. That seems to be a perfectly rational explanation, don't you think?"

She looked up and flashed a tense smile, straightening her skirt as if signalling that that was as far as she was prepared to go. She was approaching an uncomfortable truth and had decided to avoid it, which meant that I had to let her arrive at it by a different route.

"Rational, yes," I said. "But you seem very tensed up about it, all the same."

She laughed, but the tears came into her eyes and her jaw wobbled, making the laugh an empty sound of self-mockery.

"Oh, I'm a tense sort of person, that's why. Probably because I seem to be totally lacking in self-confidence. I've never had any, come to think about it. It would be nice if there was a tonic for that sort of thing."

"How does this affect you?" I said. I was certain that this would lead us further but I was not sure where. She relaxed a little, as if she thought that she might now be on safer ground.

"What – the lack of confidence?"

I nodded. She pulled out a freshly laundered lace handkerchief from her expensive handbag, and wiped her nose.

"I've always been like that," she said in a stronger voice, "which is ridiculous in a way. I've had a good education – I mean I still feel capable of doing something with my life, even at my age. A lot more than I am doing, anyway – which, when you boil it down, is basically looking after the family and the house. Ken . . . you won't know my husband because he's registered with Doctor Crawley . . . I can't remember why, except that he couldn't get on with Doctor Duncan. He's a company accountant who doesn't suffer fools lightly – spends a lot of time winding up ailing companies and the like. And as if that isn't enough, he's got himself involved in local politics with one of the Tory candidates. Ken wanted me to get involved with that but I haven't the slightest interest in that sort of thing and all those people I'd have to meet . . . anyway, I wanted to do something for myself – not play second fiddle to what he's doing. I suppose that must sound a bit self-centred."

She folded the handkerchief back into a small neat square, waiting for me to comment. I remained silent.

"Ken was a bit fed up because I didn't want to help with his political thing. He couldn't understand it. He said, why the hell didn't I get a job if I wasn't happy with what I was doing." She smiled and shook her head. "That's just the trouble, though, you see. Every time an opportunity crops up I . . . seem to find an excuse not to take it on, because I simply haven't got any confidence in myself. It's like taking refuge behind things."

"Or behind people, too?" I said.

"People . . . ?"

"I'm thinking of Stephanie and her illnesses," I said. She looked at me sharply.

"I don't quite see what this has got to do with what we've just been discussing," she said.

"Don't you?"

"No I don't, doctor," she said, shifting uncomfortably in the chair. "I said it all, a moment ago. I'm over-protective about her. I explained why."

"Yes. But whom are you protecting?"

She looked nonplussed for a moment.

"Stephanie, of course. Who else . . . ?"

I watched her face carefully, and saw from her eyes that in asking the question she had suddenly made the connection, and because she had made it herself, without me telling her, the effect was infinitely more potent. A flash of surprise turned quickly into anger and I felt like a juggler with grease on his hands.

"That's a hell of an assumption, if you don't mind me saying so, doctor. What you are suggesting is that, all this time, I've been using my child's ill-health as an excuse for . . . for my own inadequacies!"

"I didn't say that, Mrs Horrocks," I said evenly. I was dry-mouthed at the thought that this whole consultation suddenly threatened to come apart at the seams. "I was trying to find out what you thought. It does happen, you know. Sometimes anxiety about a child's health reflects the anxiety that lies within the parent about herself or himself."

Just as suddenly as she had become angry, she burst into tears. I didn't know whether this was a good sign or a bad sign, but I let her carry on without interruption until, after about a minute, she blew her nose, took a deep breath and sighed, her shoulders slumping forwards. She dropped her hands into her lap, winding the handkerchief round her fingers.

"I'm sorry, doctor," she said quietly. "About getting angry just now. I had this horrendous flash of guilt when you . . . when I realised what was going on. Although I think I've

196

known about it but simply hadn't admitted it to myself." She looked up and gave a wry smile. "The question is – where do I go from here? I can't change the way I am."

"Maybe not completely," I said, groping in vain for inspiration. "But, er, being able to look at yourself honestly may enable you to make one or two small changes. After all, you've already done something important, I think."

She frowned. "What – apart from losing my temper and weeping like a child?"

"Apart from that," I said, "you came here of your own choice, Mrs Horrocks."

"Which means . . . ?"

"Which may mean that you wanted to air these thoughts. Otherwise you wouldn't have come, would you?"

She smiled again, but this time the smile was warm and relaxed.

"Yes, yes, I suppose you're right," she said. "Although, to tell you the truth, doctor, I also came half-expecting to ask for – and get – some sort of tonic to bolster me up. Ken said that's what I needed. A nice tidy solution."

"It . . . hasn't turned out quite like that, has it?" I said. She was about to reply when the extension phone buzzed on my desk. I lifted up the receiver and heard Mrs Addy's voice speaking from the reception desk.

"I'm awfully sorry to interrupt you, doctor," I heard her say. "Nellie Winston just rang, very distressed and agitated."

"Nellie Winston . . . is that the old lady down by the station, er . . . ?"

"Station Crescent. Number seventeen."

"That's right. Severe rheumatoid arthritis. I've referred her to Jessop's for —"

"That's what she rang for. The sitting ambulance should have picked her up this morning at nine but hasn't turned up. It takes her so long to get going in the morning she had to get up at six to be ready for the transport. D'you want me to try and get an ambulance, or should I arrange another appointment."

I groaned. "Hell, no – another appointment could take weeks." I looked across at Mrs Horrocks and got an idea. "Mrs Addy – don't do anything for the moment. Leave it with me."

"Right you are, doctor. She wants me to ring back. What shall I tell her?"

"Tell her we'll take care of it. I'll speak to you in a minute."

I put the phone down and swivelled my chair round to face Mrs Horrocks. She stood up and snapped her handbag shut.

"Sorry about that," I said, nodding towards the telephone.

"That's all right, doctor," she replied. "I really have taken up enough of your time. You seem to have quite a few other problems to see to. It has helped, anyway. Being able to talk about it, I mean. I've got a lot of things to think about, haven't I?"

"Hm. Let me know how things are going," I said as I got up. I got to the door before her and placed my hand on the handle.

"There is, er, one thing I'd like to ask you to do, if you will," I said.

She looked puzzled.

"To do with . . . ?"

"In a way, yes. Have you got your car nearby?"

"Yes. Why?"

"One of my patients is in a bit of difficulty. That's what I was on the telephone about, just then." I told her what the problem was. She swallowed and fingered her collar nervously.

"You mean you want me to take her there instead of the ambulance? Oh, I don't think I could do that," she said. "Besides, I've some things to pick up later, and —"

"Mrs Horrocks – I know that you're terrified at the thought of meeting strange people, but you're not half as terrified as this old lady is of hospitals. And she's going to have to go on her own."

"But what if she . . . ?

"She can walk with a stick. She just needs your arm. Once she's in the car, it'll only take five minutes to the hospital and then it's done with. It would be a great help to her if you could manage it."

She bit her lip and hesitated, but I kept a firm grip on the door handle and looked her straight in the eye. She stared back.

"I'm not sure who I am doing this for – you, the patient or me," she said.

"Does it matter?" I replied. "All three of us, maybe. You'll only know later."

"It sounds to me as if you've prescribed a bit of occupational therapy, doctor," she said.

"Maybe. It's not just that. It's a small step in the right

direction, if you like. But it's better than taking refuge, isn't it?"

She took a deep breath. "All right. I'll try it. I'll go."

"Great. Number seventeen, Station Crescent. Mrs Winston."

She repeated the name and address as if she didn't quite believe what she was doing, not as if she was committing it to memory.

"She's going to Rheumatology Out-patients at Jessop's. She'll have a letter with her with the address on it." I smiled encouragingly and opened the door for her. "You never know, Mrs Horrocks – you may actually get to like doing this sort of thing."

She smiled uncertainly and went out.

I heard nothing for about a week. The telephone rang as I was signing a pile of repeat prescriptions on the reception desk. Mrs Addy picked it up, said a few words, then held out the receiver.

"It's for you, doctor. It's Mrs Horrocks."

I took the receiver from her and put it slowly to my ear, crossing my fingers that our last consultation had not done more harm than good.

"Yes, Mrs Horrocks. What are you going to tell me?"

"Quite a bit as a matter of fact," she said. My heart sank. I wondered whether she had retreated back over all the ground which I had hoped we had already covered. "For one thing – your occupational therapy . . ."

"Let me explain . . ." I began defensively. "I only thought that —"

"Let me finish, doctor," she said. She had an assertiveness which was surprising and troubling at the same time. "For one thing, I thought that your little ploy was a trifle . . ."

"Crude?"

"Yes. Crude. But, on the other hand, I'm sure if you'd not put me on the spot I would never have done it off my own bat, so to speak. But I did it, and we managed remarkably well, even if I say so myself."

"Well, I'm very . . . er . . ." I glanced at the earpiece of the telephone with disbelief, for she sounded so different.

"But I wonder if you realise just how often this happens – difficulties about transporting patients to hospital and so forth. Or even difficulties encountered by visiting relatives, for that matter?"

"Well no, I hadn't thought . . ."

"No. Of course not," she said. "Naturally, I realise that you have other things to think about, so I did a little research – a little digging, so to speak."

"And what did you dig up?"

"You may well ask. You've absolutely no *conception* of the difficulties patients and their relatives are having getting to that place. The hospital say it's happening all the time – patients not turning up for their appointments because of this, I mean. Between the local public transport on the one hand and the ambulance service on the other, it's a whole hiatus filled with mischief, which leaves the local population at sixes and sevens and is, I believe, disadvantageous to the running of the hospital – to say nothing of the health of the patients."

"I see."

"Do you? I doubt it, doctor. It seems to me that when it comes to getting patients and their relatives to and from hospital, this area is bereft of facilities."

"Bereft," I said, stunned into wooden repetition by this unexpected outpouring.

"That's right," she said enthusiastically, "devoid of any discernible organisations through which the difficulties could be examined, and no infrastructure to effect a solution."

"No infrastructure . . ."

It sounded to me as if she had been attending a crash course in business management, or perhaps her accountant husband had given her a few quick tutorials. Either way, I was startled by the profound change in her attitude.

"You've been doing some homework, Mrs Horrocks, by the sound of things. What are you going to do now?"

"*Going* to do, doctor?" she cried, her voice swooping triumphantly. "I've started already. I've gathered a few friends and we're studying the size of the problem in the first place, so that we can define exactly what we need to do. And that's not all. We're in contact with the hospital administration and one or two voluntary groups, and we think we can organise a transport rota using our own vehicles. I anticipate that there may be a few wrinkles to iron out, but I'm pretty sure we can get something off the ground, judging by the response we've had so far. What do you think?"

200

"I'm, er . . . very impressed, Mrs Horrocks," I said with genuine admiration. "I can't believe . . ."

"That it's the same woman who was there a couple of weeks ago?" she said, laughing uproariously. "To tell you the truth, I don't think it is the same woman – if you see what I mean. And I am grateful, believe me. I can see a lot of things more clearly now, although Ken thinks I have gone slightly mad. Thanks again, doctor."

"No thanks are needed," I said. "I really haven't done anything. You seem to have done all the work."

"Well, I *did* think that your approach was a little odd at first," she said, "but I realise it was a way of giving me space and time to work it out for myself. Many thanks, doctor. 'Bye!"

I put the receiver back on its cradle and stared at it in amazement for a few seconds.

"Bloody hell," I muttered. Beatrice Addy glanced up from her chair and give a tight little smile.

"Does that comment indicate triumph or disaster, doctor?" she asked. I grinned and walked back towards my consulting room.

"I'm not sure yet," I called over my shoulder. "When someone unleashes energy they've been sitting on for years, who knows which way they'll spring?"

"If you say so, doctor," she replied softly, almost as if she was talking to herself. I looked back along the corridor as I went into my consulting room and saw that she was bent over a small pile of medical records, totally pre-occupied, as if she had never spoken. That's what I liked about Beatrice Addy: she had integrity and loyalty, she was calm and efficient and she was kind yet firm. But most of all, she knew when to keep quiet and say nothing.

18

The satisfaction I had gained over the dramatic transformation of Mrs Horrocks did not last long. At the end of a particularly busy evening surgery two weeks later, the telephone buzzed on my desk. The last patient had just gone through the door and I had slumped into my chair like an exhausted swimmer resting on dry land.

"There's a call for you doctor," I heard Mrs Addy say over the extension. I yawned into the earpiece.

"Who is it?" I grunted.

"A Mr Horrocks wishes to speak to you. He wouldn't say what it was about. If you don't take the call now he'll probably only ring you again later when you're in the middle of your tea, I should think," she said. Her voice was a mixture of sympathy and firm resolution. She sounded like a nurse about to perform an enema. "I'll put him through, shall I? I've cleared everything away, so I'm off home. Good night, doctor. See you in the morning."

"Thanks, Mrs Addy. Good night."

The telephone clicked, and then I heard someone at the other end clearing his throat.

"Hello?"

"Doctor Rushton? Ah. Ken Horrocks speaking."

His voice had a strangely familiar sound: even over the phone I could tell that his mouth snapped shut abruptly at the last syllable of each phrase, which gave his words a thin, clipped quality, as if his lower jaw was attached to his skull by means of a powerful spring.

"You won't remember me, I don't suppose," he said.

"No . . . should I?" I replied uneasily.

"Probably not. It was in the mid-sixties. Edinburgh. You were a medical student and I was a mature student doing pol-econ."

"Pol-econ? Sounds like an industrial adhesive," I said.

"Politics and economics, old boy." He laughed humour-lessly. "As I recall, the last time I saw you was when I was President of the Conservative Students Association. At our annual ball. You were there performing with that bloody awful jazz group . . ."

"Ah yes," I said. "We got thrown out, didn't we?"

I suddenly remembered, and my skin prickled round my collar. He was a tall, officious individual whose finger-stabbing authoritarianism got everybody's back up. He had double-booked us with an accordion band from Kirkcaldy who wore funny hats, and he had refused to pay us after we had played. In the row that followed, our alto-saxophonist, a ticket collector for British Rail who was also a confirmed marxist and drunkard, had punched him before snatching the microphone and making the Assembly Rooms on George Street reverberate with his screams of "Fascist bastards!"

"You most certainly did get thrown out – and rightly so, as I recall," he said. "However, that's best forgotten, I think. It's the present I'm more concerned with. About my wife, to be precise."

"Oh yes," I said warily. "What seems to be the trouble?"

"What seems to be the trouble? That's precisely why I'm ringing, old man. I thought you should be telling me."

"Telling you what?"

"For one thing, telling me what sort of consultations you've been having with her."

"I don't follow you," I said.

"I should have thought it was obvious, doctor," he said irritably. "Ever since she came to see you a couple of weeks ago she's been different – very different. And from what I can gather, it stems from what went on when you saw her. Now I should be grateful if you could . . ."

"Has she asked you to speak to me?"

"Well . . . no. I've hardly seen her for the last two weeks. What's that got to do with it?"

"Quite a lot," I said, trying to keep my voice as casual and conversational as I could, in an attempt to buffer the rising exasperation in his own voice. "I'm afraid I can't relate our conversation to you unless your wife specifically asked me to do so."

"Oh, come now," he snorted. "What's that supposed to mean? Sounds as if you're hiding behind your responsibility by trotting out the party line about medical ethics and confidentiality. Good God, man – I *am* married to the woman, when all's said and done."

"I'd like to help," I said. "I wonder . . . perhaps if she's there she could —"

"No she *isn't* bloody well here," he said angrily. "That's part of the problem. She's taken Stephanie round to one of her friends for tea while she's out holding a meeting with some women's guild or other, and I've come home to find a note telling me there's a Bird's Eye frozen turkey pie on top of the microwave. Christ Almighty . . . and it's been like this a number of times in the last two weeks. She's been dashing about organising this and that, full of what she intends doing to the point that I began to wonder whether she's . . . well . . . whether she's all right."

"Whether she's . . . all right," I said, dropping my voice at the end of my response so that it did not sound like a question, which would have irritated him, but making it sound like a confirmation that I understood what he had just said, hoping that this might encourage him to enlarge on it. It seemed to work. I caught him wrong-footed on the base line and he struggled to return the half-volley.

"Yes . . . well, I mean . . . it's the sort of thing one does wonder when one sees a complete change of behaviour," he said. "I mean – in the sense that Vivian . . . er, has previously been, er, for want of a better term, a retiring type of . . . What I'm trying to say is that she's never previously wanted to rush about away from the home – although, God knows, I've made an effort to interest her in what I'm doing. That's what gets my goat, you see – I've been trying for ages to get her to help me in some political work I've got into, but she wouldn't have any of it. On the other hand, I depend on her to see to things around here, if only because I have to dash off at short notice with these things I've got on, so I suppose that in that sense you can see that the status quo fits in. I mean, you're a professional man, you know how important the home support is. *Now* look what's happened – she has one consultation with you and God knows what went on, apart from the fact that the next thing I know she's into all sorts of bloody things —"

204

"Does she seem happy?" I asked.

"Does she . . .? What sort of bloody question is *that*?" he replied, his voice taking on a higher pitch. "I don't think you've been listening to what I've been saying."

"Have you asked her?"

"Asked her? Look – I'm *married* to Vivian, aren't I? She's my wife – not a patient. Or a social services client. It's a case of give and take in these matters. So I can do without all that philosophical claptrap, thanks very much."

"It's an important question, though, isn't it?" I said. "Because, unless you know the answer, it becomes difficult to handle the —"

"I would suggest, doctor," he said heavily, "that if *that* is your level of understanding of personal relationships, you should steer clear of it. All this female self-fulfilment stuff is far too involved when you don't seem to understand the effect that this has on the rest of the family, hm?"

"Now I am no longer sure who has the problem," I said.

"What?"

"You have described your wife's change of behaviour, as you put it," I said patiently, "but only in terms in which it directly affects *you*. If this is what she wants to do, then the problem is *yours*. I can't influence or even comment on the matter. How you come to terms with it depends on —"

"Oh, Christ!" he exclaimed angrily. "I might have known it would be a waste of time talking to you about this. Anyway – rest assured that it won't carry on like this if I have anything to do with it. I don't know what ideas you've been discussing between you, but they won't wash in *this* house. I think you're venturing into areas which are far outside your professional competence. May I suggest that in future you confine yourself to sore throats and nappy rashes, where any blundering by yourself will at least be confined to the unfortunate individual you are treating. Goodnight!"

The phone clicked abruptly. I put the receiver down slowly on its cradle, picturing Ken Horrocks staring resentfully across at his Bird's Eye frozen turkey pie on top of the microwave. I sat for a moment and wondered what I should do next. It didn't take long to reach a decision. There was nothing whatsoever I could do about the dust being kicked up at the Horrocks' house, so I decided to lock up the surgery, wander up the garden and join the family for the evening meal.

The next day I did my best to put it out of my mind. I felt sad that Ken Horrocks had shown such insensitivity, and in some odd way I felt guilty, insofar as I had probably over-estimated the family's capacity for dealing with the changes which now appeared to be taking place. I wondered how Stephanie Horrocks would react to relinquishing her role as the apparent patient. The whole thing would probably sort itself out in time, I thought hopefully.

The last patient that evening wiped out further thoughts which still lingered on the Horrocks family, for it was Jack Norton. For a second or two I was nonplussed, until Mrs Addy bustled in and handed me a temporary resident form.

"Mr Norton," she said, glancing coldly at the patient. "He says he knows you from when you used to be his doctor. I fitted him in only because you'd had a last-minute cancellation."

She pressed her mouth into a thin line and collected up the notes from my desk with a flourish, which was a clear statement that he had only got past the reception desk by virtue of her tightly controlled generosity and not for any other reason. She clutched the notes to her crackling white coat and went out, closing the door behind her.

I looked across at Jack Norton as he stood awkwardly in the middle of the room, clutching his cloth cap in his hands and breathing heavily, with his chin on his barrel chest.

"Hello, Jack. This is a surprise. Seems a long time since I last saw you," I said. I didn't know why I was so pleased to see him, but I was. It was like seeing a few frames of an old film I had enjoyed in the past.

"Aye, you're right there," he said. He cleared his throat. "Never thought I'd get to see you tonight with the lady outside, like." He jerked his head in the direction of the door and grinned. "She seems to have everyone weighed up. Very civil, mind you. And, anyway, it's a good thing having somebody like that around when you're like bloody King Canute keeping 'em all at bay."

I smiled and invited him to sit down.

"You're a bit off the beaten track, aren't you? I take it you must be visiting your family," I said. I knew that Peter Norton must have moved here a couple of weeks ago because I had signed their medical cards which they had dropped in at the surgery.

"Aye. Me and the missus are staying over at the lad's house for a couple of days, looking after the youngsters, while they're going round buying furniture and stuff to put in the house. They seem to have enough there already, but you know how it is . . ." he coughed and looked round the room, nodding approvingly. "Bit different from t'other place you had, doctor," he said. "This one looks something like a doctor's surgery should look. Last one were more like a broom cupboard, when you weighed it up."

"Yes, it's a distinct improvement. There are a few things I'm thinking of changing," I said, waving my arms about airily, "but on the whole I'm very pleased with things as they are."

"And how do you like it in these parts? Bet there aren't as many funny buggers as there was in Overton."

"I haven't been here long enough to tell. But it's not that different, really. Well now . . . what brings you in while you're over here?"

"Well . . . I'm not rightly sure, doctor," he said, putting his cap in his pocket and spreading his huge hands on his knees. "I thought . . . can you give me a check-up, like?"

"What makes you think you need a check-up?"

"Dunno. I feel out of sorts, some road." He screwed his face up and shook his head slowly, as if he was trying unsuccessfully to remember something from the dim past. "Can't put me finger on it. Just don't feel right, you might say. I mean – I've no aches or pains or owt like that, you know."

"Eating OK?"

"Oh aye, owt you put in front of me."

"Sleeping?"

"Mm. Spark out soon as I put me head down."

"Bowels?"

"Never had any trouble that road, never."

"Not still troubled about being out of work and all the . . ."

"Oh no, no," he growled. He was silent for a moment. "I mean, when I say *no*, I mean . . . it still bothers me at odd times. Bound to, isn't it? But this is different. It's . . . something *bodily*, I think. Inside, like."

And so it went on. I pursued all lines of enquiry but got no lead at all, except that his gestures were subdued, almost apathetic. It bothered me, but I had no idea why. He stripped off and I gave him a thorough examination, but I could find nothing. He dressed himself slowly as I scribbled a few notes down. "Well – what d'you think, doctor?" he asked. I looked up at him, watching him struggle with the knot on his tie which he carefully but inaccurately pushed up under one flap of his shirt collar.

"At the moment, Jack, all I can say is that you seem to be in reasonable order – apart from your weight. And of course your bronchitis, which doesn't seem any worse than it normally is," I replied.

"That's a funny how d'you do," he grunted. "I can't weigh it up at all."

"Neither can I," I said. "Anyway, I can't find anything that need give you any cause for concern."

"Well, that's something, any road, doctor. I feel better now I've heard you say that," he said gratefully. It sounded like doctor and patient reassuring each other over something that eluded both of them. I sat back and chewed the end of my pen, thinking that, of the two of us, he was more reassured than I was.

"Tell you what," I said, "come in tomorrow morning first thing and I'll take a blood sample from you and have it checked over at the hospital."

I was scraping the barrel here, but I thought that at least it would be a good excuse to have another look at him in case I had missed something.

"Oh aye? What for, doctor?"

"Just to . . . see whether you're anaemic or not."

"Righto. If you think that's best, doctor. Best be on the safe side, and it can't do any harm, I don't suppose."

"That's right. If we do it tomorrow we can maybe help sort things out while you're up here. How long are you staying?"

"Only a few days. Making the most of things while my mam and dad are having a fortnight's respite in Wishton."

"They're both in, are they?"

"Aye. Geriatric specialist came and arranged to take them in to give us a break, like. I don't think they were keen on the idea, mind you."

"I don't suppose they were," I said. "How are they both?"

"Not much different from usual," he chuckled. "Struggling on like the rest of us."

He glanced at the wall clock and hurriedly pulled his cap out of his pocket.

"I'd best be going, doctor. Have you seen the time? I'm sorry to have kept you late . . ."

"That's OK. I haven't far to go once I've finished here."

"I'll see you tomorrow, doctor. About nine o'clock be all right?" I nodded and he went out.

It was shortly after the next morning's surgery had started that Mrs Addy put a call through on the extension.

"I normally wouldn't have interrupted you, doctor," she said, "but it's a councillor Horace Pavey. I asked him what he wanted, but he sounds rather agitated. I think you should speak to him."

I felt my whole body sag a little. The last thing I wanted to do right then was speak to Horace Pavey. I knew that he lived in the district, but I had not seen him since the interview in Derby a few months ago. Mrs Addy's voice made it clear that it was not going to be a social call.

"Hello . . . ?"

"Is that Dr Rushton?" I heard the familiar grating voice. "Pavey here. I think you'd better come round to thirty-two, Barns Road right away. It's Jack Norton. I'm a friend of the family, you know."

"No I didn't know," I said, irritated by this last irrelevant piece of information. "What seems to be the trouble?"

Pavey coughed. "I think he has just passed away."

"I beg your pardon?"

I turned to stone and didn't hear his next few words.

". . . at the bottom of the stairs. He was just putting on his coat and he collapsed. Will you come right away?"

There was a click and the line went dead. The last sentence Pavey uttered was not a request – it was more like a chilling summons. My hands shook as I quickly pushed my stethoscope into a spare compartment of my case, cursing the fact that at times like this the inanimate coils of rubber seemed always to uncoil themselves like a snake, preventing me from closing the catches of the lid. The case sprang open again as I picked it up, threatening to spill out the contents all over the floor. I tucked it angrily underneath my arm and went out to the reception desk. Beatrice Addy looked up, raising an eyebrow in surprise.

"Everything all right, doctor?" she asked quietly. I became instinctively aware of the patients within earshot in the waiting room. I leaned over the desk towards her, smelling her starched neutrality which I found strangely reassuring.

"Sudden death," I muttered. "I'm not sure how long I'll be . . ."

"Right, doctor," she breathed. Then, more audibly, in a voice that was more formal for general distribution, she said: "I'll let everyone know. I'm sure they'll understand. See you when you get back, then."

After a quick glance at the map, I drove as quickly as I could to Barns Road. It took me ten minutes or so to leave the outskirts of Stonebridge, winding upwards into Dilshaw whose streets spread into the surrounding hills like the fingers of a hand pushed into dry sand: you imagined that if all the occupants were to leave suddenly, the streets and houses would eventually disappear without trace as they became engulfed by the hunched, rounded slopes, leaving only the sound of the wind whispering through dry grass.

Behind Barns Road, a vast quarry had cut vertical curtains of rock into the hills, the materials from which most of this village had been built. Number thirty-two was a large, detached house built of clean, sharp stone which stood shoulder to shoulder with the weathered gable-ends of miners' cottages on either side. As I opened the car door, my stomach turned over. I could see the tall, thin figure of Horace Pavey standing in the doorway with his arms folded. His bony face stood out like a death's head against the background of the darkened hallway.

He stepped to one side, allowing me through the door. Between the foot of the stairs and an antique umbrella stand lay the supine figure of Jack Norton, whose normally plethoric features were now in death the colour of slate. As I stepped forward towards the body Pavey grabbed my arm.

"Before you do anything, doctor," he said in a low voice, "I think I should tell you that Alice Norton is in the living room. Peter and his wife had already left when this happened. Dropped the eldest off to school before going into Manchester to do some shopping, from what I gather. So there's no way we can contact them. I'm telling you this because, apart from a couple of neighbours, there's only me to see to things until they get back. You appreciate that my responsibilities here are quite considerable. I hope you bear this in mind, doctor."

I stared at him briefly, wondering what the hell he was talking about. His responsibilities were the last thing I was bearing in mind under the circumstances.

"I'll be in the living room when you've finished," he said. "You'll be wanting to come through to have a word afterwards, I expect."

I said nothing, but turned away to examine Jack Norton. Pavey made his way into the sitting room which was at the far end of the hallway. I knelt down by the lifeless body, feeling physically sick at seeing him lie there. After a brief examination to confirm his death I made a major production out of putting my stethoscope back in my case and closing the locks, half-listening to the low murmur of voices in the living room and the sound of tea-cups being washed and put out on the sink to dry. The wretched memory of yesterday's reassurances was going through my mind, and the fact that Horace Pavey was here didn't improve things. There was something in his manner which promised to make an already unpleasant situation even more difficult. I had the feeling that he was going to be a comfort to nobody and could sour my previous good relationship with this family for years to come.

I stood up, braced myself and walked into the living room. Mrs Norton was sitting on the edge of a chair by the fire, clutching a box of Kleenex and staring at the flames with moist, red eyes. A youngish woman stood by her side, looking gravely at the floor. On the other side of the fireplace, next to Horace Pavey, was a stocky man in his thirties who was scratching his wrists as if he wasn't sure what he was supposed to do.

Mrs Norton looked up and gave a weak smile.

"Hello, doctor," she said. "I never expected to see you this way. You'll have to excuse the way I am . . . it's taken me all a bit sudden. I haven't grasped it yet."

"I'm sorry about Jack, Mrs Norton," I said, "Very sorry. I don't think there was anything any of us could have done to prevent this from happening, you know."

"How can you be so sure, doctor?" said Pavey. He was standing like a barrister addressing a jury, his thumbs hooked inside his waistcoat pocket and his body reclining slightly

211

backwards. "I mean, according to Mrs Norton here . . . when you examined him last night you said there was nothing wrong with him." He glanced quickly at the others in turn to see whether they were savouring his penetrating question as much as he was himself. "I find that very difficult to understand, doctor," he continued. "Very perplexing. Perhaps you'd care to enlighten us a little."

His voice had a patronising tone which made me grip the handle of my case so hard that it hurt. I was determined not to over-react to his intimidation which seemed to be so grotesquely out of place.

"I didn't say that there was nothing wrong with the patient, Mr Pavey," I said, quietly and calmly. "What I actually said was that I couldn't find anything wrong. Which I think you will agree is rather a different thing."

"Hm," he snorted. "Can't see it myself. Boils down to the same thing, to my way of thinking."

He turned to look questioningly at the man alongside him, who averted his eyes and began to scratch his neck. For a moment the ugly scraping noise he was making was the only sound in the room until an older woman entered, wiping her hands on a small towel. She glared at him. He coughed and stuck his hands in his pockets.

"I can't weigh it up," said Mrs Norton in a hoarse voice. "He never was one for doctoring in the ordinary way. Never complained about his heart or anything else. He got up this morning just before the paper came and pottered about in the garden putting bread out for the birds, just like he does every day at home. Peter pulled his leg a bit, but when he's at home and he opens that back door into the yard of a morning, they come hopping and flying in from all over the place. So he just did what he always does – out of habit, I suppose. Peter and the family had their breakfast and they fussed about, dropping Sarah off to school on their way down to Manchester. When they'd gone we had us breakfast."

I nodded and said nothing, knowing that she needed to talk – that going over the events, the minutiae from getting up that morning to the moment of his death, was important to her. I let her carry on because it would help her to come to terms with something that was incomprehensible.

"When we were having us breakfast he made some comment

about the two rashers of bacon I'd put out for him," she continued. "He normally only has one these days, with the price of it and us only drawing the dole, and, anyway, he doesn't eat so much now he's not working. Then he read the paper for a bit before putting his coat on to come and see you, doctor, only I wouldn't let him go until I'd sewn one of the buttons on. I says to him, 'Jack, you can't go and see the doctor with a button missing on your coat,' and he laughed a bit and took it off . . . then he put his hand on his chest and made this funny noise in his throat – you know, as if he'd swallowed something and it had gone down the wrong way. Then he went down . . . just like that. You don't think it were that extra bacon I gave him, do you, doctor?"

I shook my head.

"No, Mrs Norton," I said. "From what you say, he must have had a coronary . . . a severe and sudden heart attack. That's the only —"

"And to think that he was on the way to see you," she said, shaking her head. "He thought a lot about you, doctor. He came back to the house last night feeling proper bucked up after what you'd said to him." Her voice dropped. "We . . . we both used to have such a lot of faith in you, you know."

Her use of the past tense made me wince. Pavey looked on impatiently but said nothing. The man next to him spoke for the first time.

"What happens now? Don't you have to sign a form or something?" he said.

I cleared my throat unnecessarily. "Normally – yes. But . . . under the circumstances . . ." I said slowly, "I can't really issue a death certificate because there isn't enough firm evidence as to the cause of death. I simply don't know why he . . . I don't have any choice, I'm afraid."

"Will that mean a post mortem, doctor?" Mrs Norton asked quietly, without looking up.

"Yes," I said. She shook her head slowly and the others looked aghast. Pavey pulled down the corners of his mouth into a drooping line of contempt, then he turned and looked away. I felt wretched. I would have done anything to avoid a post mortem, but I knew that whatever I wrote on the death certificate would have been a guess based on very scanty evidence.

"I see," said Mrs Norton. "Best go ahead, then, if you can learn anything from it that'll help someone else."

I couldn't detect any bitterness or anger in her voice, but I knew that that would come later when the shock and numbness began to wear off. Pavey cleared his throat and moved forward a few inches as if he was going to say something, but he changed his mind. I turned to the woman who was holding the towel and asked her to show me where the telephone was. She took me into the dining room, her stony silence enveloping me like a funeral shroud.

I spoke briefly with the coroner who agreed that a post mortem must be done, then went back into the lounge to explain that someone would be around in a very short time to take care of things. Mrs Norton seemed more concerned with how her son and his wife would react when they arrived home, and I could only suggest that they contact me later if they wished to do so.

"Will you call again, doctor?" she asked. I couldn't tell whether she was wondering if that's what I normally did, or whether that was what she really wanted.

"If you like. Tomorrow?"

"Yes, if you've time," she said. "It'll have hit me by then. Jack's death and that. Thanks for coming, anyway."

I went out of the door and down the path, followed by Pavey who in turn was followed by the man who had been standing next to him. Pavey stepped down the path as I opened the car door.

"You may think I am speaking out of turn," he said in his council chamber voice, "but I'm bound to say that it's a sad reflection on the present-day medical profession, if you ask me." He pursed his lips and jangled a bunch of keys in his pocket. I turned and looked him in the eye, feeling ice-cold.

"What is?"

"Well for one thing, I mean to say . . . a post mortem! Your predecessor would never have allowed a thing like that. He would have been able to ascertain the cause of death as soon as he walked through the door."

"Mr Pavey," I said as softly as I could, for I was afraid that speaking even in a normal voice would reveal the tremor of anger rushing up under my diaphragm. "I knew Doctor Duncan for very many years and had the greatest respect for his skill and humanity. However, he would have been the first to refute those qualities of faultless judgement and extra-sensory perception which you are now ascribing to him. Very few of us are endowed that way, including myself. I can only do the best I can under the circumstances as I see them, not as others might have seen them."

I knew that I had already said too much, but I couldn't stop myself. Pavey grunted and jangled his keys.

"That's as may be," he said. "Either way you look at it, you'll be chalking this one up to experience, I expect, doctor. Not that it will help the family, of course – or your reputation, for that matter."

"Look, Mr Pavey," I said, opening the car door and throwing my bag across the front seat where the catches burst open, scattering the contents all over the floor, "if Mr Norton suffered a coronary thrombosis – and I think he did – then no doctor on earth could have prevented it. Not even Alec Duncan. Nothing is predictable when it comes to human beings. It's not like having a car serviced every so often to guarantee trouble-free motoring. We're dealing with people, not machines."

I jumped into the driving seat without giving him time to answer, turning the ignition key. There was a brief click but nothing else: the starter motor had jammed. It was the last twist of the knife.

Without looking at the two men on the front path, I got out and began to push the car up the road, not really knowing where I was going. I glanced ahead and saw that there was a side road about twenty yards away which turned gently downhill. It took a couple of minutes of collar-bursting effort to get to the corner where I was able to steer the car down the slope. By the time I had jumped in and put it into gear, my lungs were heaving and my throat was burning. The engine started the moment I let the clutch out and I sank back into the driving seat with relief. As I drove off, I glanced back quickly at the house, to see Pavey standing at the gate, staring back at me while the other man scratched his wrists again. I cursed both the car and Pavey about equally.

Later that day Peter Norton rang. He was quiet, calm and sensible and seemed to understand the reason for the post mortem. Whatever damage Pavey had managed to do did not seem to have affected his own judgement of the situation, which should have made me less uneasy. But it didn't, and I wasn't sure why.

The next day I called to see the family as I had promised. Jean Norton let me in but excused herself almost immediately to see to their youngest child. Peter came through from the living room and we shook hands.

"Nice of you to come, doctor," he said. "I don't think there's much more we can talk about just now, after speaking to you yesterday on the telephone. Mum's in there and I think she would like a word with you. I've got a couple of things to attend to, so I'll leave you to it for a bit. I'll see you before you go."

He picked up some papers from a small table in the hallway, and it was not difficult to see that this was all part of a carefully engineered set-piece, so that I could be alone with Alice Norton. I went through into the living room and found her sitting in the same chair, exactly as she had been yesterday. She looked up and smiled. I sat opposite her and watched her face as she began to talk about Jack. She appeared calm and matter-of-fact as she spoke about their good and bad times together, starting from a long time ago, before I knew them, up to when I had most recently been involved in his medical treatment. She examined each event like pieces of a jigsaw which had been scattered around her, trying to fit them together until she had built up a picture which made sense to her.

"Oh I know he had a lot of trouble this last year," she said, "but it were understandable, when you think about it. He were never the same after they saw him down the road at Johnson's, you know. He went there from another skilled job, thinking it were a bigger organisation where he'd never go short of work. And he'd always put in a proper day's work, wherever he was, always been that way. Them as did the dirty jobs should do it best road they could and them as manage should go ahead and manage – they'll always look after a grafter, he used to say. But they bloody didn't, did they? That changed him, really, though he never admitted it. I know a lot found themselves in the same boat, but if you've always believed what he believed it's hard to take. He never said much – not to me, any road – but I know how he felt. He might have been rough and ready but he wasn't stupid. All his life, all that stuff about a person's worth . . . it all went up the chimney when it came to profit and loss. All that

216

grafting counted for nowt when it came to all them shareholders' meetings with all them . . . them . . ."

"Accountants?"

"Aye. Money jugglers. Never see *them* dropping their books, though. Not bloody likely. They just drop *people* when it suits."

She pushed her hands down the sides of the chair cushion and hunched her shoulders up angrily.

"I cleaned the offices at Johnson's for a short spell, you know," she said. "Used to make me sick, the way they carried on. Teak panelling everywhere, Swedish carpets, air conditioning – you name it. We had to keep it spotless, I'll tell you. Managers could *hear* cigarette ash being dropped on the floor, they were that particular. And yet Jack used to come home every day with dust up his nose and grindings in his eyes because they reckoned it would cost too much to fit extractor fans and the like in the workshop."

She dropped her shoulders and clasped her hands on her lap, looking into the fire.

"I don't think he were treated right," she said quietly. "That's how it all ended up like this. They treated him no different than the dirt he used to bring home with him. That's what brought all this on, doctor. That's what I think. That's what I *know*."

She looked up and shook her head slowly.

"So all them fancy words on the post mortem report won't mean a lot to me, doctor. You'll understand all them medical terms, being that's what you've studied. But I understand what's *really* caused Jack's death, no matter what that report says."

"I'm sorry about having to . . ."

"Oh give over, doctor," she said, reaching out and touching my sleeve. "You haven't been listening, have you? I'm not angry at you, love. I understand why you had to do that. Peter explained. He's been very good. No, I'm not angry about that at all . . . In a way I'm glad you were honest and said you didn't know why he died like that, all of a sudden. Even if it did put you in a funny light."

"I'm not sure what you mean, Mrs Norton," I said, sensing that she still had doubts about me asking for a post mortem. To her it probably seemed like a declaration of ignorance on my

217

part which, rightly or wrongly, she did not expect. But, more importantly, it meant that the guilt which surrounded the relatives of someone who had died suddenly and unexpectedly, was suspended rather than discharged.

"I think you know very well what I mean, doctor," she said softly, smiling with watery eyes. "I know I was in a bit of a state yesterday when you came and it had just happened, but I could still tell that some of the things Horace Pavey said – his insinuations, I suppose you'd call them – they upset you. I could tell that."

I shrugged. "It wasn't very helpful. Least of all to you," I said.

"You're right, doctor. It wasn't. All the same, I sensed . . . you don't care for him, do you?"

"No," I said. "It goes back a few years . . ."

"I know. He told me. I'm afraid he doesn't seem to like you too much, either. Not that that should bother you in your position. We've known him for years, but we haven't seen him for a long while. Funny, really – it turns out he only lives up the road here."

She blew her nose on a small handkerchief and was silent for a moment, as if she was reluctant to go on. I stared at her, thinking uncomfortably that she was about to raise the question that so far I had avoided asking myself.

"He's always been a bit bombastic," she said quietly. "Yesterday . . . he just seemed to be casting doubt where none existed – not to my way of thinking, any road. I just wondered whether, if he hadn't have been here, you would have said there'd have to be a post mortem. He told me what you'd said when you got outside. When you were going in your car."

I blushed. The exchange between myself and Pavey must have sounded crude and irrelevant to her ears at the time, especially the way he would tell it. What an insensitive sod he was.

"He told you that, did he?" I said.

"He did. But I go along with what you said to him," she murmured.

"In what way, Mrs Norton?"

"Well, he only sees things in black and white. Always has done. And things aren't as simple as that in this life, are they, doctor? I'm sorry . . . I don't know why I brought this up after

218

all you've done for us in the past. And it won't bring him back to me, will it? You did what you thought was right and proper, and that's an end of it. Will it delay the funeral much, d'you think?"

I shook my head. "The post mortem? No. I shouldn't think so. Not more than a day or so."

She nodded. For a moment the only sound was the soft ticking of the antique wall-clock at the other end of the room. I could not be sure, but I thought that she had now resolved the question of the post mortem. I was not keen to pursue the question any further. She pushed her handkerchief into the pocket of her cardigan and adjusted the ends of her sleeves neatly round the wrists, as if signalling that as far as she was concerned, the matter was now closed.

"What will you do now, Mrs Norton?"

She sighed and sat back in the chair, resting her head on the cushion before turning away to look at the fire.

"Peter and Jean wanted me to stay for a day or two until things have been settled, but I'd rather get home. There'll be things I'll have to see to. I'll no sooner have got through this than Jack's mam and dad'll be back home from the hospital, and I'll have all that to see to again." Then, in a very soft, private voice, she said, "I've a good family, though. They'll see me right."

"That's right," I said. "Just make sure you look after yourself." I held out my hand. "I'm going to have to get moving now, Mrs Norton. When you're up here again . . ."

She turned and smiled at me. "Thanks for coming today, love. I know we're not the most sparkling buggers on earth and we've given you a fair amount to do between us, but you've always treated us proper. Goodbye, doctor."

She squeezed my hand and her eyes became moist again, but she said nothing more.

As I went through the hallway Peter and Jean Norton appeared as if from nowhere and walked out with me to my car, all three of us grimacing as an icy, buffeting wind stung our faces. They were anxious to know how I thought Alice Norton was, and seemed grateful for whatever reassurances I was able to offer. We parted company in a warm, friendly manner which was a pleasant contrast to yesterday's departure from the house.

I did a couple of home visits, then called at the surgery to drop off the record cards. Mrs Addy had gone home for lunch and had switched the telephone through to the house. I wandered distractedly round my consulting room, half-heartedly contemplating some of the minor changes which I planned to make in the next few weeks, to make the place exactly as I wanted it. After a few minutes I found myself sitting by the sink, fiddling with the microscope. I picked up a slide from the box on the work-top and gently placed it on the stage, securing it with the metal clips on either end. Twisting the triple turrets of the objective lenses, I felt a peculiar satisfaction as the medium power clicked quietly into position, a marvel of optical perfection and superb engineering. I gently wiped the eyepiece and looked down into the disc of light, ratcheting the fine focus up and down until the blurred pink visual field leaped into sharp detail. It took me a few seconds to recognise that it was a cross-section of a clotted-up coronary artery. The intima of the vessel had peeled away and was packed with the dark-staining army of polymorphonuclear cells: the inflammatory response to the presence of an amorphous pink mass which obstructed the whole of the lumen of the vessel. Of all the slides to pick at random, I thought, what a weird coincidence that I had picked this one. I gazed down the eyepiece, the whole image filling my brain, but I was thinking about Jack Norton again. There was little doubt, from his wife's description, that he had had a coronary thrombosis . . . I moved the slide a couple of millimetres, which sent miles of myocardium flashing across my view. A few more vessels, all normal . . . I *could* have written a death certificate. I had written out a few in the past on flimsier evidence, based on educated guesswork and probability, in order to save a distraught wife or husband from the further anguish of a post mortem or an inquest, or both.

I took the slide off the stage and ran my fingers round the edges, staring at the small label with its neat caption in faded grey ink.

"Coming in for lunch?"

I looked up and saw Tanya standing at the door; she was holding a piece of notepaper.

"I didn't hear you . . ." I mumbled. She cocked her head to one side and smiled.

"You were miles away. Got something on your mind?" She

220

nodded her head down at my hands. I had been turning the small piece of glass over and over without being aware of it. "You're fiddling about with that glass slide like Captain Queeg."

I smiled grimly and put it back in the box.

"I've got a message from a Doctor Gleason," she said, holding up the piece of paper. "He rang the house a few minutes ago. Shall I read it?"

I nodded. Gleason was the pathologist at Jessop's. This would be about Jack Norton's post mortem.

"'Post mortem on Mr Norton performed this morning. Cause of death due to massive coronary occlusion. All three main coronary vessels affected by severe atheromata.' I hope I've got that right."

"Yes," I said, "that's about right."

"Have you learned anything?" she said.

"Not really," I replied. "Not from that, anyway. There wasn't much doubt about it, apart from the fact that he didn't have any symptoms . . . I'm not sure it needed a post mortem, really."

I told her what had happened, including the bit about Horace Pavey. As I did so, I became certain of the fact that, even if I could have diagnosed his condition when he first came to see me, it would not have altered the outcome. But at the same time I realised that I had allowed myself to be rattled by someone who had nothing to do with the case: Horace Pavey. The doubts that I had mentioned were not mine, but *his*. He clearly believed that I could have prevented Jack's death, so that my response in asking for a post mortem was a way of proving that he was wrong. In retrospect, it seemed more like an act of self-justification than anything else.

"Technically, I'm sure it was the right thing to do," I said, as if still trying to convince myself, "but thinking about it now, I'm not so sure . . ."

"Don't you think, Steven," said Tanya, "that you are getting all this out of proportion?"

"In what way?"

"All that anguished self-examination," she said. "You're beginning to sound like Gerald Crawley. And what good will it do? I'm not trying to sound . . . but the poor man is dead, whatever you do or say now. You did what you could and you

221

did your best to comfort his wife. They're the only people who matter in this. You seem to be more upset at allowing yourself to be intimidated by what's-his-name —"

"Pavey."

"Pavey – you seem more upset by him than by the fact that you lost your patient."

"Christ, that's a thought," I said. "Is that what it sounds like?"

"A bit," she said. "And, anyway, you can't win."

"Win? Win what?"

"Look – you were the only person there who could honestly decide whether or not a post mortem was necessary with all the additional grief it might cause, and you were the only person who knows what brought you to that decision. You can't win, because the way you are looking at it, you either made the wrong decision for the right reason, or the right decision for the wrong reason."

"Maybe you're right," I muttered. "I didn't quite see it that way at the time . . ."

"I know you didn't," she said, "but chewing yourself up isn't going to make any difference now. It's past history. What else is there to say? Just don't go looking for the sackcloth and ashes – your lunch is on the table and Conrad is probably throwing it all round the kitchen by now. Come on – let's go and eat. Who said, 'It is better to fill the stomach and starve the ego than feed upon one's remorse and starve the soul'?"

"Adam Bede?" I said, laughing, "or maybe it was Attila the Hun. OK, I take your point. Let's go."

Tanya turned and went out. I locked the main door of the surgery and followed her along the path leading to the long, sloping lawns at the front of the house. I watched her stride to the door. When she opened it, a warm, delicious smell floated down on the hostile wind and I increased my pace. I was feeling hungry again.

19

"That's your last patient this morning, doctor," Mrs Addy said breezily as she swept up the record cards from the corner of my desk. "There are just two people waiting to have some stitches removed. Mrs Windsor rang up from the district somewhere, to say that she would be in a bit late . . . having a job with one of your patients, apparently."

I got up and went to the sink to wash my hands, glancing out of the window to see the slender branches of a group of silver birch bend in the March wind.

"Did she say how long she would be?" I asked.

"No. Do you want to see to them?"

"Yes, OK. I might as well get them out of the way. Are there many visits?"

"Two. I've set up a tray with all you'll need. I'll send them through when you're ready."

I went into the small treatment room and saw the stainless steel trolley standing next to the couch and free-standing adjustable light. It was neatly and obsessionally laid out, with instruments and dressing-packs ready for the district nurse's daily visit. Mrs Addy kept the room as spotless and as serviceable as an operating room. It was her pride and joy, and I had learned very early on that although she tutted and clucked each time I used it and left things all over the place, she actually relished cleaning up and reinstating it to its normal pristine condition.

The first patient to come in was accompanied by his wife who brandished a little pink card to tell me that her husband had received a tetanus jab at Jessop's.

"I brought this to show you, doctor, because they said you would give Arthur the rest of the course," she said earnestly, "which I'll be glad of, really, because he's always forking pig-muck on the garden at this time of year, and you never know where that stuff's been, do you?"

223

After making a few reassuring noises I inspected Arthur's injuries. His face and bald head had at least a dozen small, healed lacerations. The black silk stitches resembled small flies settling on his skin. There were a few cuts on his hands and a larger wound on his thumb which looked like a dog bite. As I proceeded to remove the stitches, I asked him how he had injured himself in this way. He grinned sheepishly and shot an embarrassed glance at his wife.

"You might well look at me like that," she said to him. "Go on – tell the doctor how you did it."

He shifted his feet uncomfortably. "Well, it were like this, doctor," he said. "Me and the wife had been out celebrating us ruby wedding and I'd had a skinful of ale, I'll admit. Anyway, the taxi had dropped us off at the front door. We've just had a new door put on – one of them fancy glass ones, you know. So I'm standing there in front of the door, struggling to get my keys out of my pocket, and I kind of lost my balance and fell forward straight through the glass."

"I see," I said, trying to keep my face straight. "And the dog bite on your thumb?"

"Aye, well . . . we've this here Alsatian. Good house dog, he is. When I goes crashing through the door he comes bounding down the bloody hallway thinking there's an intruder. Wrapped his teeth round my thumb before we could call him off, the barmy sod."

I could hardly take the last few stitches out for laughing. They both joined in, perhaps relieved that I thought the whole thing was funny rather than reprehensible. The fact that he had been extremely fortunate in not fatally severing a major blood vessel in his neck or wrists had clearly never entered their minds.

The other patient requiring surgical attention was a massively built young man whose broad shoulders and barrel chest made him look as if he was wearing an inflated life-jacket underneath his anorak. His blue shirt, black tie and heavy shoes indicated that he was either in the police force or the fire brigade.

"Brian Ottley, doctor," he said, rolling up his trouser leg to reveal a calf the size of an average man's thigh. He began to unravel a crêpe bandage from the limb. "Had a few stitches put in last week following a dog bite. They're due out today, I believe."

I peeled off a non-adhesive dressing and saw a series of tears and lacerations of the skin. From the size of the wound, it must have been a large, powerful animal. I nodded and began to remove the redundant stitches one by one.

"How did this happen?" I asked. He blushed and turned his head away.

"I'd rather you were spared the details, if you don't mind, doctor," he said ruefully. "I'm the dog-handler down at the station. I think you know my boss, Mr Early."

"Ah yes," I said. "How is he?"

"Same as he always is. Pulled my bloody leg over this, though. How long will it be before I'll be able to do duties, d'you think?"

I inspected the wound. It looked pretty sound.

"A few days – just to let it toughen up a bit more. If you happen to knock it before then it might open up again."

I wrapped it up with a fresh bandage. He thanked me and lumbered out. I tossed all the used instruments into the sink, and the sound of metal on metal brought Beatrice Addy rushing in like a mother hen.

"Leave those, doctor," she piped briskly. "I'll clear up. You get on your way. With a bit of luck you should get an early lunch for a change."

She rolled up her sleeves and I left her scrubbing the instruments as if she was attempting not only to remove any dried blood or debris attached to them, but a layer of nickel plating as well.

I drove across the town, experiencing a sense of satisfaction I always felt after doing something mechanically simple. Removing stitches and occasionally syringing ears had the virtue of being immediately beneficial to the patient while making almost no intellectual demands on the doctor, and in the face of so many problems which required unflinching attention but where there were no short-term solutions – even if there were any at all – the observable effect of successfully performing a simple act such as stopping a heavy nose-bleed was as therapeutic to the doctor as it was to the patient.

By now I was beginning to get on top of the running of the practice and to see more clearly the areas which needed improving. I had decided first of all to tackle the problem of the medical record cards. Alec Duncan had meticulously recorded all his consultations so that, over the years, a lot of information had gathered in the notes about his patients. The problem seemed to be that the more information there was, the more difficult it became to glean out of it what was important: at a glance, it was impossible to summarize what had happened to a particular patient, what he had suffered from in the past and what current medication he or she was on, and therefore it made it all the more difficult to assess the problem that the patient presented on a particular day in relation to what had happened to him in the past. As a result, I had begun the laborious task of putting the notes in order and devising a simple but effective system of summarising and itemising the problems both past and present. Tanya, whenever she could, came in to help, which made the mind-boggling task much easier. Mrs Addy showed not the slightest resentment at her being there – in fact she went out of her way to be helpful, knowing full well that she had more than enough to do anyway, without getting involved in a scheme as long-winded as this was going to prove.

I began to develop a genuine enthusiasm for drawing up plans to shape and improve the organisation of the practice, but I realised that I would have to take my time – that any innovation, no matter how simple, would have to be introduced gradually, in an evolutionary manner, rather than being thrown in without regard to the consequences. Without realising it, I had begun to examine what I was doing and the way that I was doing it, in order to make better use of my time and energy in the future. The years I had spent with Ian McDonald were beginning to pay off: his solid aphorisms, arising from years of experience, I was now beginning to translate into practical application. Single-handed practice brought sharply into focus the fact that my work-load was related not only to the amount of illness in the community, but also to my effectiveness in dealing with it. I could no longer leave problems only half dealt with, because I no longer had partners willing to pick up the pieces. Being alone concentrated the mind. It was introspection spawned by necessity.

Ron Leaford had been a great help in these early weeks. We had worked closely together in our off-duties and he had never once pulled out or cribbed over the sharing between his or my own patients' demands. The more I came into contact with him, the less I was fooled by his brusque manner, for he was even more generous and accommodating than was my first impression. Whenever we got together over a pint and I voiced my ideas about making better use of my time, he smiled patiently, calling them the basic principles of single-handed practice – the survival of the doctor in the endless sea of demand by the patients.

When I had done my two calls, I drove back into the town along the banks of the river Dill, whose clear shallow water chattered along its bed of rounded cobbles. In the distance it wound round the outskirts of the town, where the untidy stone sprawl met the rising slopes of the other side of the valley, flowing south-west between the hills into the reservoirs which served the industrial conurbations beyond.

My brain must have been out to lunch because I only noticed the collection of vehicles in front of me when I was almost on top of them. Two police cars and an ambulance. I stopped the car and looked again. The ambulance had gone over the bank of the road and was resting axle-deep in the river. Three police officers were standing at the water's edge; one of them was Inspector Early and one of the others I recognised as the officer who had stopped me going down a restricted street a few weeks before, when I had been up to the ears in Leonard Garlick's home-made wine.

"Anything I can do?" I called as I approached them. One of them turned away from the wind and muttered into his two-way radio, while the other two stood grinning at me. Early banged his gloved hands together.

"Good morning, doctor," he said. "How fortuitous. Help is nigh. I can't get over how you keep turning up like the proverbial bad penny."

I laughed. "Is that the same as the proverbial bent copper?"

"Ho ho. Very droll, doctor, I'm sure," said Early. He turned to the other officer. "Ted, have you met Doctor Rushton? He's the medical profession's latest answer to plague and pestilence in these quarters. Ted Savage, doctor. Sergeant, traffic."

Savage nodded. "I think we have met, haven't we? Read any good road signs recently, doctor?"

I ignored his remark, looking over his shoulder into the cab of the ambulance. The driver was slumped over the wheel, groaning and rubbing his head with a bare forearm.

"D'you want me to take a look at him?" I asked. "He looks a bit groggy from where I'm standing."

Without waiting for them to reply, I took off my shoes and socks, rolled up my trousers and waded through the freezing water to the cab. I opened the door and climbed in. The driver moaned and cursed quietly to himself, paying no attention to me while I did my best to look him over. He was about thirty years of age, dressed in jeans and a blood-stained tee shirt. His skinny arms were heavily tattooed and, apart from a fresh bruise on his forehead, he had a number of carefully stitched cuts on his face.

"How did this happen?" I asked. I seemed to have been asking that question all morning.

"Sod off," he grunted. He wiped his nose on his sleeve. I didn't need any persuading – I had cramp in my thigh and my feet were aching with the cold. I backed out of the cab and waded back to the bank.

"He seems all right," I said, struggling to put my socks back on. "What's the score?"

"How d'you mean, doctor?" Early said.

"He doesn't look like an ambulance driver to me, that's what I mean."

Early leaned back and laughed.

"Full marks, professor. Nice to see all those years as police surgeon have honed your powers of observation to a keen edge. No, you're right, of course. He isn't an ambulance driver. He's a patient."

"A patient?"

"Correct, doctor. One of the suffering breed on the other side of the desk, so to speak. Here's the man who can shed light . . ."

He looked over my shoulder and I turned round to see Ron Leaford's mud-caked Land Rover clatter to a halt on the soft bank next to the other vehicles. He got out, put on a pair of wellington boots and strode down the sloping turf to join us.

"Morning," he growled. "Hello, Steven. All under control, are we?"

"Yes, doctor," said Early. "Doctor Rushton here has just this minute waded out and checked his vital signs, as you people call them. He's in no immediate danger of snuffing it, I understand."

228

Ron watched me putting on my shoes, chuckling to himself.

"One piece of essential equipment round here, Steven," he said, "is a good pair of wellies. Anyway, I'm glad you've done the necessary because I'm getting too old for this sort of game." He turned to Early. "Terry, is it?"

"The very same, doctor," Early said, lighting up his pipe with cupped hands against the wind. "Our little crown of thorns."

Ron nodded. "Terry Steel, Steven. One of my patients. A well-known psychopath. In a state of perpetual pubescence, that lad. Been arsing about all his life doing silly things to himself. Seen his father into an early grave – now his mother's on the slippery slope coping with all his nonsense. He lives with her, you see. I don't think a week goes by without either me or these lads here being involved in some daft business or other. D'you remember a fortnight ago, Inspector?"

Early clenched his teeth on his pipe hard enough to break the stem.

"Mm – not half," he said, shooting a sideways glance at me. "We get three nines at six o'clock one morning from a call box, and it's Terry. Says he's going to end it all by drowning himself in the Dill – not very far from here, as a matter of fact. So we make our way down to where he said we'd find his body and find him lying on his back in three inches of water, looking up at the sky and singing his bloody head off. Soon as he sees us charge down the bank flashing our torches he shouts, 'Hurry up – I'm drowning,' whereupon one of my lads shouts back, 'No danger there, Terry – not unless you start breathing through your arse!' Then he wades in, picks Terry up and throws him on the bank looking a right sorry sight. Hey up – here's the other ambulance."

Early and Savage went over to speak to the crew. Ron turned to me and shook his head.

"Pathetic, really," he grunted. "He once cut his throat and made a right mess. Managed to miss all the important bits, mind you. His mother brought him to the surgery with his neck wrapped in an old shirt, wanting me to stitch him up, but Terry wouldn't let me touch him because I wasn't going to give him an anaesthetic first."

"How did you get involved today?"

"Oh . . . he was breaking into some offices in the early hours

229

and fell through a sky-light. They took him to Jessop's to get him stitched up before putting him behind bars, or whatever they do these days, only he nipped out of casualty and pinched an ambulance."

"What were you hoping to do?" I asked. Ron shrugged.

"God knows. They rang me up at the surgery and I thought, well . . . I suppose I felt sorry for the old lady. I've known the family for donkey's years. The psychiatrists have given up on Terry, so there's nobody else, really. I can tell his mother he's all right, anyway. She'll be worried sick. As a matter of fact, I was going to come up this way for a quick bite at the Hare and Hounds on Quarry Hill. Want to join me?"

"No thanks, Ron. I'm on my way home."

He nodded and we clambered up the slope to the cars, leaving the others to haul Terry Steel out of one ambulance and into the other. Ron leaned on the door of his vehicle, breathing heavily.

"You all right?" I asked anxiously.

"Aye. These March winds seems to make you catch your breath more each year you get older. See you soon, Steven."

He drove off and I went over to my own car. Early caught up with me as I was opening the door.

"Just a quickie before you go, doctor," he said. "Won't keep you a moment. Did one of my lads come in to see you today about his leg?"

"Brian Ottley?"

"Mm. How's he doing?"

"Mending nicely. Should be OK in a few days."

"That's good. He's a very useful lad, is PC Ottley. Did he tell you how he did it?"

"No. As a matter of fact he seemed a bit embarrassed when I asked him."

Early scraped the bowl of his pipe with a pen-knife and laughed quietly.

"I'm not surprised," he said. "You know Frankie and Johnny's fish and chip shop in the square, opposite the Ram's Head?"

"I've seen it, yes."

"Run by a right fragile pair of fruitcakes – harmless, mind you. There's a fight in there every Saturday night after closing time. You can set your clocks by it. Funny thing is – whenever either of this pair gets on the blower he'll always ask us to send Ottley. 'Send PC Ottley,' one of them'll squeak down the telephone, 'he's so big and strong.' It's always the same. That poor lad has been down to Frankie and Johnny's so many times he's known as the Gayfriar's Bobby back at the station. Mind you, his dog loves going down there – have you seen his dog, by the way?"

I shook my head and buttoned up my coat against the wind. Early tapped his pipe on the heel of his shoe.

"Big black Alsatian. Like something out of Bram Stoker. It can bite the tyres off an eight-ton truck. Well, this dog loves going down there, you see, because, apart from getting the chance to wrap his jaws round a few legs, he gets a few meat pies from the proprietors on the way out. Anyway, last weekend was running par for the course, about six lads causing a bit of a fracas in the shop. Ottley sends the dog in as usual – only this time the dog runs right through the shop and disappears into the back. Ottley sorts out the commotion in his own inimitable way by knocking all the customers down and sitting on them, before going into the back room where he finds the dog standing on its hind legs with its paws on the table, wolfing a big pile of meat pies as fast as it can. Ottley tries to pull him off and the ungrateful bloody animal turns round and nearly bites his leg off below the knee. Now, aren't you glad you know how he came by his injury? Adds a little piquancy to the dreary business of taking out the poor lad's stitches." His eyebrows danced up and down as he laughed quietly to himself. "I'm glad he's healing up, though," he said, "because Frankie and Johnny sent us a bill for those meat pies yesterday, so Ottley's going to have to square up with them when he gets back."

"They sent you a bill?" I said. I burst out laughing.

"That's right," he cackled. "There's some buggers in this town who if they snagged their jacket going through the pearly gates would send in a repair bill, plus VAT."

He scratched his head with the stem of his pipe and waved to the driver of one of the police cars as he took off down the road. The driver of the other vehicle leaned on the open door and looked at his watch.

"Right, doctor," Early said, stuffing his pipe into his raincoat pocket, "I'll be off. I'm sure you've got a lot to do. Keep smiling. My old boss used to say that if you look down into the pool of human misery and it makes you want to throw up, remember that it's your own silly mug you're looking at."

"What the hell is that supposed to mean?" I said.

"Buggered if I know, really," Early replied with a puzzled frown. "I suppose I was thinking of that no-hoper, Terry Steel. I mean – he hasn't got a single thing going for him, as I see it. When they heard he'd dumped himself into the river, most of the lads at the station were hoping that he'd get washed down to the sea, probably because somebody like Terry reminds some of them how close to misfortune they tread half the time – like they're forever picking up the fag-ends of people's misdemeanours and so forth. Very stressful. That's why I have a lot of time for your colleague."

"Ron Leaford?"

"Yes. He seems to huff and puff a lot, very cynical like, but as soon as he heard Terry was in the river he came out of his way, just to see if he was all right, so he could have a quick word with his old lady. He knows better than anybody what a dead loss someone like Terry is, but he still came. What I like about him is that he manages to show an interest in people who – for one reason or another – have lost interest in themselves. And yet, in spite of all life's ridiculousness and futility, he can still smile over it. D'you know what I mean?"

"I think so," I said.

"A very uncommon quality, that," Early continued, ignoring Savage who was rattling his keys and coughing theatrically a few yards away. "You only have to go into your average town hall department, your average social security office or, for that matter, your average police station, to know that there's bugger-all commitment – I mean, nobody really cares a shit about people like Terry Steel. He radiates despair like a bloody beacon and everybody switches off, hoping that if they're indifferent long enough he'll go away." He looked at me and laughed. "Go on – tell me I sound more like a social worker than a policeman. I can see it in your face."

"Not at all," I said. "You seem to be getting more introspective in your old age, that's all."

"Not so much of your old age, you cheeky bugger," he said, grinning. "Nice to see you again, doctor. And remember what Confucius said."

"What was that?"

"When you are pissing against the wind it is always best to wear a waterproof garment."

He slapped my arm and trudged over to the police vehicle, buttoning up his coat and laughing to himself. Savage jabbed his black-gloved hand in the air and jumped into the driving seat. The doors slammed shut and the car juddered away from the grass verge with violent acceleration, disappearing down towards the town.

20

"Is that Doctor Rushton? I'm so sorry to trouble you on a Saturday evening, but I wonder if you would come to see my husband?"

I gripped the earpiece of the telephone tightly to my ear and glanced across at Tanya. She was talking to Bet Duncan who had come over for the evening. It was the first time she had been since we had moved in, and from the time she had arrived the children had dominated the proceedings in response to her questions about their new school and the new friends they had made. Conrad, not to be left out of things, had wandered in and out, showing off his various broken toys, finally trapping his finger in the door, which resulted in a tearful half-hour while warm water, TCP and sticky plasters were produced. A distracting ritual was enacted which, besides soothing his aching finger, satisfied his need to share in the attention previously afforded his elder brothers. It was only after the three of them had gone to bed that we got the chance to hold a proper conversation, so that I now resented the fact that our limited time together was being further eroded by this call.

"I'm sorry, Mrs er . . ."

"Allerdyce. Sally Allerdyce. It's my husband. He's been taken ill – and I'm very worried about him. The point is . . ."

"Mrs Allerdyce, I'm not on call this weekend. Doctor Leaford is the doctor taking emergency calls."

"Oh I see. But they – the people we're staying with – advised me to ring you. They only wanted you to come. My husband isn't registered with an NHS doctor, you see –"

"Not registered? You mean he's not my patient?"

"No, but the people we are staying with are. Will you come, doctor? They did ask specifically . . ."

"Look – I'll tell you what I'll do. I'll ring Doctor Leaford. Can you give me some details?"

There was a brief silence. In the background there was a lot of braying laughter and slamming of doors. It sounded as if they were having a party. When she replied she sounded agitated and evasive.

"Sam's got a TV recording to do tomorrow. It's a political thing, you know," she said quickly, tumbling over the words as if she was distracted by something going on in the background. "He's taken some tablets he has for his nerves and I'm afraid he's got some reaction or other. We can hardly rouse him. He's in a terrible state. I simply don't know what to do, that's why I —"

"What's the address?"

"Number eight, Poplar Close."

I wrote it down and my heart sank. It was the Horrocks's address. I wondered what the hell was going on.

"I'll ring Doctor Leaford," I said firmly.

"They specifically asked me to ring your number . . ."

"Yes. So you said," I muttered. "Either way, I'll sort something out. Leave it with me, Mrs Allerdyce."

I put the phone down and groaned. Tanya looked across and her shoulders slumped a little.

"You've not got to go out, surely?" she said. "I thought that . . ."

"It's OK," I replied soothingly. "Ron's taking calls. I'm just going to ring him now."

Bet sighed and smiled sympathetically at Tanya, but said nothing. I dialled Ron Leaford's number and waited. When he answered, he spoke softly. His voice was tired and apologetic.

"Hello, Steven. I was just going to ring you, as a matter of fact."

"Uh-huh. I've just had this call which sounds as if it needs doing. We've, er, asked Bet Duncan round so I wonder if I could pass it on to you since you're the lucky man this weekend."

"That's what I was going to ring you about," he said. "I'm sorry, Steven . . . I wouldn't normally ask this, but I feel a bit rough. Kathleen's nipped down the road to see a friend for an hour . . . I'm just going to put the car away, then I'm going to bed. Can you see to this one? I'm sure I'll be all right in the morning, so you needn't worry about the rest of the weekend."

"Are you sure?"

"Oh yes. It's some 'flu bug or other I've picked up. Arms feel like lead – you know the kind of thing. Taloia."

"Taloia?"

"T.A.L.O.I.A. There's a lot of it about."

"That's what we all say. D'you want me to call round?"

"Oh hell, no," he replied gruffly. "An early night in bed and I'll be as right as rain. But I'd be grateful if you could sort this call out – and any others that come through tonight, God forbid that they do."

"Don't worry about that," I said. "Give me a ring if you're no different tomorrow."

"Thanks, Steven. I owe you one. Give my love to Bet and Tanya." He rang off. I put the receiver down slowly and turned to the others.

"Ron's not too good. He wants me to cover for him until tomorrow, so I'm going to have to do this call, I'm afraid."

"That's a pity," said Bet Duncan. "It's very unusual for Ron to be ill. In all the years he and Alec worked together I can hardly remember . . . Is he all right, d'you think?"

I shrugged. "I don't know. He's got some sort of 'flu bug. Says he'll have shaken it off by morning."

"I'm sure he will have. Oh well, it can't be helped. You get off and we girls will enjoy a natter while you're away."

"Right," I said, searching my pockets for my car keys. "I shouldn't be too long. See you both later."

It only took me ten minutes to get to Poplar Close – not enough time to figure out, in view of my last conversation with Ken Horrocks, why they had asked for me. It didn't add up.

All the lights were on in the house and, as I walked up the gravelled path, weaving my way past a dozen parked cars, I heard the sound of breaking glass from round the back, followed by a high-pitched squeal of laughter. Ken Horrocks opened the door, holding a glass in his hand. By the look of his lop-sided grin and flushed, sweating face, he had obviously been drinking heavily for some hours.

"Ah, the man himself," he said affably. "We weren't sure whether you'd be coming, so we . . . come in, anyway. You'll have to fight your way through here, I'm afraid. We've a bit of a shindig going on."

"So I see," I said. I stepped into the hall. The loud conversation and laughter from the handful of well-dressed men leaning against the wallpaper dried up into a subdued murmur and they exchanged uneasy glances. I sniffed. Apart from the smell of sweat and cigarettes, there was a sweetish odour which I had smelt before somewhere, but which I couldn't identify. Horrocks saw me hesitate and grabbed my arm.

"There's, er, something I ought to . . ." he began.

"Patient upstairs?"

"Yes, but there's —"

"Tell me up there," I said. "There are too many people around down here."

I reached for the polished oak stair-rail and strode up the stairs two at a time. He followed so closely behind that when I stopped on the landing he nearly knocked me over.

"Hang on, for God's sake," he said hoarsely, putting down his glass next to a vase of artificial flowers on a small window ledge. He wiped his face with a large handkerchief.

"Look, doctor," he continued in a low voice, "we've got a pretty embarrassing situation on our hands here, one way and another, so I'm banking on your professional integrity and absolute confidentiality. Fact is, Sam Allerdyce is supposed to be doing a video recording for the BBC tomorrow evening, for local transmission later in the week – a sort of forum-type of thing; but well, I mean, the state he's in . . . he's taken some pills for a nervous situation or something. In retrospect, I don't suppose that was such a good idea, in view of the fact that we've been celebrating a windfall . . ."

"You mean he's had a few drinks as well?"

"A few? Hell, no – it's more than a few, I'm afraid. He's consumed practically a whole bottle of scotch since late this afternoon, I should think."

"You'd better let me have a look at him in that case," I said grimly. As I stepped across the landing, a woman appeared at one of the bedroom doors carrying a bucket of water. She looked tearful and distraught. She dashed into the bathroom and emptied it into the bath, reappearing a moment later, brushing hair from her face. From the bedroom came the sound of running water and someone gagging.

"Ken – I asked you to keep everyone downstairs," she said. She saw my case and looked questioningly at Horrocks.

"Oh dear. Is this . . . ?"

"Sally – this is Doctor Rushton," Horrocks said. She looked surprised.

"But I thought you said . . ."

"Hold on a minute, old girl," said Horrocks quietly, holding up his hands and turning to me. "I was going to explain. We weren't sure whether you were coming, so we managed to contact Sam's private physician and he dashed round here straight away. He's in there now sorting things out. Raj Mukherjee. Very switched on sort of chap, actually. D'you know him?"

"No. In that case you don't really need me at all, do you?" I said.

"Oh no, no – I mean, yes, of course," said Mrs Allerdyce uncertainly. "I would like you to, er . . . I don't suppose it makes any . . . I'm sorry about this."

She fumbled with a string of pearls round her neck. The high collar of her dress did not completely hide the loose, coarse skin beneath her chin which betrayed her middle age, in contrast with her smooth face which was a credit to the many hours of attention by a beautician.

"All right," I said without enthusiasm, "I'll take a look at him."

The bedroom stank of vomit and stale tobacco smoke. The patient lay half-conscious on the bed, having his stomach pumped out by a tall Indian who glanced at us briefly as we went in. He poured a jugful of water into a large plastic funnel attached to a length of rubber tubing leading down the patient's throat, holding it up for a moment to allow the water to swill round the stomach before plunging the funnel down below the level of the bed, allowing the gastric contents to siphon into one of the several plastic buckets on the floor around his feet. He removed the tube and flung it into the marble basin in the corner of the room.

"You won't be needing any more water, I take it?" said Mrs Allerdyce faintly. She looked as though she was going to pass out. Mukherjee shook his head.

"I've used about twenty litres. That should have done the trick." He stuck out his hand towards me. "Raj Mukherjee," he said in clipped, perfect diction. "You will be Doctor Rushton, isn't it? and now you will excuse me, please, while I take another look at Sam."

He snatched up his stethoscope, flashing his eyes and teeth at Horrocks and Sally Allerdyce, and proceeded to examine the restless, groaning patient at lightning speed. His jumpy, bird-like movements and his curious habit of rattling off the clinical finding every so often, as if he was speaking into an imaginary dictating machine, I found disconcerting at first – until it dawned on me that it was his way of demonstrating effective, purposeful activity. It had more to do with impressing the holder of the purse than with assessing the clinical state of the patient.

While he was doing this I wandered round the room, partly in an attempt to look as if I was doing something useful, but mainly to shake off a growing sense of unreality. I quickly examined a bowlful of vomit and saw that it contained bile but no fragments of tablets or capsules. Whatever Sam Allerdyce had taken had long since been absorbed from his stomach and was now pushing its way round his circulation. In which case all these twenty litres of water had been a waste of time and effort. I picked up a small bottle from the dressing-table and looked at the label. Barbiturates. I looked at Mrs Allerdyce.

"They're Sam's," she said quietly. "He's been taking them on and off for years."

"How many has he taken today?"

"I – I'm not sure," she replied. "I know he took some this afternoon, but I mean, I don't keep count."

"That's a bad combination," I said grimly, putting the bottle down. "Alcohol and barbiturates. Which hospital will he be going to?"

The three of them looked at each other as if I had broken wind. Ken Horrocks cleared his throat.

"I, er . . . we hadn't actually envisaged doing that," he said. "I'm sure Sally won't mind me saying this, but we couldn't . . . the fewer people who know about this, the better it will be. If the word gets around it could be disastrous for his political future. Sam is our prospective Conservative candidate, so Central Office naturally would . . ."

"Perhaps we should talk together, you and I," said Mukherjee, straightening up. "On medical grounds. That would be a good thing to do, isn't it?"

He smiled at me as if he didn't give a damn what I thought.

"That might be an idea," agreed Horrocks. He signalled to

Sally Allerdyce and they both went out of the room. I sat down on a small chair in the far corner of the window and looked at Mukherjee. He put his stethoscope back in his case and proceeded to unravel an intravenous drip set.

"It's really nothing to do with me, but would you mind telling me what the hell's going on here?" I said wearily. He stopped what he was doing for a moment and stared at me with dark, watery eyes.

"It is like Ken says. To go to hospital would probably bring to an end a most promising political career after much hard work by a lot of people," he said earnestly. "I have known him for some time and it would be truly a travesty for this to happen, I do assure you. He is a very influential man in these parts . . ."

"So I gather," I said dully. "Have you examined his vomit, by the way? All that gastric lavage won't have done much good, apart from making him alkalaemic."

"That is not of much consequence. I am going to set up a rapid intravenous infusion to flush out the circulatory system, and give diuretics to eliminate the toxic products. I'm sure you will agree —?"

"All that without hospitalisation?"

"I told you why we cannot consider hospital," he said patiently. "You must understand that there are many other factors here. When you have a private patient you have to take into consideration the wishes of the people —"

"Who pay the piper?"

He smiled and shrugged his narrow shoulders.

"If you wish to say these things, I am not going to argue with you. When I have set up this infusion I shall not move from here until the patient recovers – no matter how long it takes."

"You mean that after flushing him out with twenty litres of water, you're going to run several litres of IV fluids through his veins, without being able to check his electrolytes?" I said, amazed.

"Precisely so," he replied. Without hesitation, he swiftly and expertly stuck the canula in a forearm vein and connected it up to the sterile sachet of saline. I watched in dazed fascination as he erected a telescopic stand and suspended the sachet from it. The patient lay still and snored noisily, each exhaled breath sending small flecks of frothy saliva from between his bloated lips onto the pillow. Mukherjee took a strip of adhesive plaster and placed it over the forearm at the point where the canula pierced the skin, anchoring it firmly into place. He turned and smiled again.

"There, it is all done now," he said. "All we have to do is wait until he comes round."

"I stood up and shook my head. "When you say *we* I hope you're not including me in this. This man should be in hospital."

"So you said, doctor," he murmured. "And of course the responsibility is entirely mine. That is what I am being paid for."

"Where there's Mukherjee there's brass," I muttered in disgust.

"I beg your pardon, Doctor Rushton?"

"Nothing. Just an old Lancashire saying. It means, I hope to God you're up to date with your Medical Defence Union fees."

He held up his hand. "I think we have discussed the matter quite enough, doctor," he said coldly. "And you have made your position very clear. Goodnight."

I went out without replying. On the landing, Ken Horrocks and Sally Allerdyce were engaged in whispered conversation. They looked up.

"Going so soon, doctor?" Horrocks said, genuinely surprised.

"The patient is entirely – and I stress the word entirely – in the hands of his private physician," I snapped.

"Good. Then you agree that we are doing the right thing?"

"I didn't say that. I have expressed my medical opinion to Doctor Mukherjee. You must ask him. Now, if you'll excuse me . . ."

"I'm awfully sorry about this, doctor," Mrs Allerdyce said. "But you do see how awkward it would be if he were to go into hospital. And with no disrespect, Raj has our full confidence from our past dealings with him."

"Come and have a quick drink before you go," Horrocks said. He took my arm and nodded to Sally Allerdyce. "I'll go down with the doctor. I won't be many minutes. Join you later."

The hi-fi thudded like a pile driver through my head when we got downstairs. More dazed, perspiring figures were spilling out of the lounge into the hallway, pulling in their stomachs and holding their drinks close to their throats as we pushed our way into the kitchen. The peculiar, sweet odour that I had detected earlier was now quite strong. When I saw the two fair-haired teenage lads standing by the refrigerator giggling and passing a ragged-looking cigarette backwards and forwards, I realised what it was.

"Everything all right up there?" shouted someone from the hallway.

"Yes," Horrocks called back, helping himself to a large gin from a central table which was a wasteland of broken crisps and half-empty bottles. "He just needs rest, that's all. He's exhausted. Turn that bloody record-player down, will you, Philip? What would you like, doctor? Large scotch is it?"

I shook my head, feeling my tongue sticking to the roof of my mouth.

"No thanks. A glass of water will do."

"Oh, come on . . ."

I ignored him, taking a glass and filling it from the tap. The two lads by the refrigerator mumbled and sniggered incoherently. Horrocks glared at them and they staggered out through the back door into the garden. He watched them go, then closed the kitchen door.

"Sam Allerdyce's two lads," he said. "Very bright but a bit wild."

I smiled. "I must admit I didn't expect to witness pot-smoking at a gathering of the party faithful."

Horrocks sniffed and looked aghast.

"Christ Almighty – is *that* what it is?" He swallowed half the gin and wiped his mouth. "As if I didn't have enough trouble. I hope to God you don't breathe a word about this to anyone." He stared through the window, but in the darkness could only see his own reflection. "That's something else I'm going to have to sort out . . . Jesus. D'you think Sam will be all right up there?"

He turned and searched my face for signs of doubt. I shrugged.

"I'm not the person to ask. Doctor Mukherjee is in sole charge of that," I said flatly.

"Yes, I suppose you're right," he replied thoughtfully. "Look . . . er, I hope there aren't any hard feelings, old man . . ."

"About tonight, you mean?"

"Not exactly. I was thinking about the other week when I phoned you. About the wife."

He said 'the wife' like 'the car' or 'the central heating'.

"That seems a long time ago now," I said. "I gather she's not here, tonight?"

He shook his head. "Down at her mother's with Stephanie. Recharging her batteries, I think she said. D'you really think . . . ?"

"I don't think this is the time or the place to talk about it," I said. "Quite apart from the fact that you seem to have enough problems to deal with tonight, as you have already said."

He leaned against the table and laughed nervously.

"Fair enough, doctor. I take your point." He finished the rest of the gin in the glass and poured himself another. "All this shambles started quite simply as a gentle celebration this afternoon. We had a bloody good lunch at the Open Door first of all – Sam's been accepted as parliamentary candidate for this area, you know."

"Yes. You said so."

"Did I? You're not . . . interested in politics, I take it?"

"Not particularly," I said. "From what I've seen, one lot's got mince where its brain should be and the other lot's got a stainless steel abacus where its heart should be."

He smiled. "That's a pretty intolerant analysis, old boy, if I may say so. Sounds almost as despotic as the folk you're putting down. Live and let live, I always say."

"Live and let live . . . that sounds as if you're advocating tolerance from where you stand on the pile. Which is tantamount to dispensing tolerance. Another form of despotism, isn't it?"

"Look, old son," he said, grinning expansively from the effects of alcohol, "you can be as cynical as you like about power and politics, but the fact is, we live in the real world, you and I. Let me tell you about the other reason we were celebrating – you'll appreciate this, having a social conscience and all that sort of thing. First of all – apart from the odd pocket of intractable poverty – what's the biggest socio-medical problem in a civilised country like ours?"

"Old age?"

"Right first time, doctor. Ten out of ten," Horrocks said, leaning over the table and jabbing me in the ribs with his finger.

"Old age brings infirmity, disabilities and God knows what else, which needs human helpers – not bushels of useless medication. Which is no doubt the reason why you people must feel frustration and impotence, why you must feel it's an overwhelming problem which just gets bigger. Now then – the thing is, that this all takes money to pay for. Where will it come from in a crumbling economy? It's all paid for out of direct taxation – right?"

"I don't see . . ."

"Hang on. Now – we've got a declining standard of living, people going out of work right, left and centre, which means we've got a shrinking tax base to pay for all the so-called caring services. Which makes your job even more impossible when it comes to the old folk. You medical people can influence nothing, and that's where power and politics come in."

"I don't see what this has got to do with —"

"I'm coming to it now," he said, smiling triumphantly and waving his gin about. "We're part of a business consortium – Sam's at the helm, so to speak. A holding company with a lot of capital tied up in heavy engineering which has been dying the death. We've been winding down a big place in Overton over the last year or so – that's where you come from, isn't it? Right. Well, now we've finally shut this place down and sold the land and building to a property company, releasing a lot of capital – two million to be precise. A bit hard on the employees, I grant you, but there's a lot of it about. Know what we're doing with the money?"

"Food parcels for the elderly?" I said. He smiled.

"Not quite – but close. We've earmarked twenty substantial properties, with a likelihood of ten more, for conversion into private rest houses for the elderly."

"That's quite a step – from heavy engineering to social engineering. My God."

"Old age, doctor, is the growth industry of the foreseeable future!" he exclaimed, swaying slightly at the other side of the table. I looked at his heavy-lidded eyes, expecting to see dollar-signs spinning across the cornea like a Warner Brothers cartoon character. "D'you realise that in less than twenty years, a quarter of the population will be over seventy-five years of age? And a hell of a lot of them will need constant care and attention, which you people and the health service haven't a hope in hell of coping with. We'll be helping to satisfy that need."

"Sounds to me more like a licence to print money," I said grimly.

"All right – if you say so," he snorted. "Let's see – twenty old ladies in thirty homes at, say, a hundred and fifty a week, that's an annual gross of over four million. You say that's a licence to print money. I say that's enlightened self-interest – and I'll tell you something, old man . . ."

"What's that?" I said. He was sounding more like a second-hand car dealer every minute and I began to shake with anger.

"There's never any quibble over planning permission for these establishments. Not likely. The local authorities and the social services never give us any high-handed comments like the one you've just made – they're only too bloody glad to get this problem out of their hair. They're falling over back-wards —"

"Yes I'll bet they are," I muttered, I turned to go, feeling that I was in danger of throwing up. "There's just one thing. The place you closed down in Overton . . . it wouldn't have been Johnson's, would it?"

He finished off his gin and slapped the glass on the table.

"That's the one. Big outfit. Why?"

"Nothing, really. I had a patient who used to work there, that's all. He became a casualty of your scheme one day. They were nice people."

I pictured Jack Norton at Wishton General, swinging his giant feet over the edge of his bed offering me his grapes – his golden handshake.

"Oh, we're *all* nice people, old man," Horrocks said, laughing humourlessly, "but you have to swim with the tide. That's the way it is, these days. What it boils down to . . ."

He waved his arms about as he spoke but I had stopped listening. There was a commotion at the front door which seemed to travel up the hallway. The kitchen door opened. In the frame of the doorway stood the tall, sombre figure of Jim Early. Horrocks barked a harsh, tense laugh.

"Well, well, well. Evening all. If it isn't the local con-stabulary," he said with heavy sarcasm. Early eyed him coldly for a few seconds, then looked at me. Behind him, in the orange light of the hall, a dozen sweating faces bobbed about, trying to see into the kitchen.

"It's the doctor I wanted to see," he said. He turned to me. "Sorry to interrupt you, sir."

His voice had a grave formality which chilled my blood.

"How did you know I was here?" I asked.

His nostrils twitched and his eyes pivoted round the room, fixing themselves for a moment on the top of the refrigerator.

"I didn't," he replied quietly. His face remained grim. "We just happened to be in the vicinity and I noticed this car parked almost in the middle of the road; I realised it was yours, sir."

He maintained his stiff, measured tone which I realised was not simply for the benefit of the rest of the people in the house.

"We had a message over the radio. It's your colleague – Doctor Leaford. He was found in his car about half an hour ago. I'm afraid he'd dead, sir."

I opened my mouth to speak but couldn't. Early put his gloved hands in his raincoat pockets and I knew by his face that I had heard it right.

"He was putting his car in the garage," he said. "It wasn't . . . the engine was switched off. Ambulance people said it was a coronary."

"Ron Leaford, eh?" I heard Horrocks say, a million miles away. "Dear, oh dear. The medical profession seem to be keeling over like flies in this town – you'll have the whole town to yourself pretty soon at this rate, Rushton. Exit another pillar of mediaeval medicine, eh?"

I swung round quickly and, in the same movement, without thinking, I lunged forward over the table and hit him as hard as I could. He collapsed like a sack of carrots. The forward momentum of my own weight tipped over the table on top of him, sending the bottles and glasses crashing all over the kitchen floor. I looked at him as he picked himself up slowly, vaguely aware of the noisy reaction in the hallway as a dozen bodies surged forward into the doorway. I moved forward to help him up but Early grabbed my arm, probably thinking that I was going to hit him again. Horrocks looked pale and dazed. He dabbed his bleeding lip, looking down with disbelief at the blood on the white linen handkerchief he had dragged slowly out of his pocket.

"You shouldn't have said that," I said quietly, shaking with anger. He looked up.

"Maybe not," he replied, looking at me steadily. "But that was a pretty bloody stupid reaction . . ."

"Bloody right, Ken – that's common assault, plain as hell," growled a pop-eyed, sweating hulk at the door, "and there's no shortage of witnesses – including the officer here." He waved his glass around as he stepped forward into the kitchen, spilling the contents down his lapels. "What are you going to do about it, seeing as you saw it all, like the rest of us?"

Early gave him a dismissive glance, took off his gloves and sniffed. He stepped to the refrigerator, picked up a short, flat cigarette end and held it under his nose. He sniffed again, looking at Ken Horrocks.

"As I saw it, sir," he said slowly, "you fell forward and the doctor here accidentally caught you in his attempt to save you from doing yourself a mischief. Unless my nose deceives me, of course."

He stared coldly at Horrocks, holding up the cigarette between finger and thumb.

"What the bloody hell is that supposed to mean?" said the indignant figure next to Early. "Everybody here saw what happened. Are you seriously trying to say . . ."

Horrocks tore his glassy-eyed stare away from Early's hands and looked towards the kitchen door.

"It's all right, Phil," he muttered, shaking his head. "Go back into the lounge, please. I'll take care of this."

"But you can't —"

"Go back into the lounge, Phil, for Christ's sake!" snapped Horrocks. "And take everyone else with you. I'll explain later. Now go on!"

"OK, OK . . ."

I watched them file slowly out into the lounge where their bewildered murmuring was drowned by the throb of the hi-fi. My body felt as if it had been encased in cement.

"Now then, sir . . ." said Early grimly, taking a small buff envelope from his inside pocket. He placed the burnt-out cigarette end inside the envelope, sealed it and put it back in his pocket. Horrocks held the handkerchief to his mouth, but his eyes watched Early's methodical movements as if he had been hypnotised.

"I, er, I shan't be pressing any charges," said Horrocks. His hands shook as he picked up a half-emptied bottle of gin and an intact glass. He poured himself a stiff drink. "Under the circumstances that would be, er . . ."

"Very wise, if I may say, sir," murmured Early, putting his hand lightly over his pocket. "Under the circumstances, as you so rightly put it. I'm sure you're making the right decision. I'll keep this piece of . . . debris, shall we say, until a suitable time arrives for me to dispose of it. There's very little else to say." He stepped toward the door, paused, then turned round, adding icily: "I think you understand, sir."

I looked at Horrocks, but he turned away and stared out of the window at his ashen reflection in the glass. As I walked down the hallway I was only half-aware of the bewildered, accusing protests from all around. It sounded like the rumble of distant traffic. It was not until I felt the cold street air and the icy metal of the car against my hands that I realised what had taken place.

"You all right, doctor?" I heard Early say. I took a deep breath and straightened up.

"Yes," I replied. I looked down at my hand. "Thanks. In there, I mean. I don't know what made me . . . it was a combination of things, I think."

"I gathered that, doctor," said Early. "I'm sorry you've had your evening spoilt by a piece of news like that."

"It wasn't a social call," I said. "It was medical. Not that it makes any difference and I don't want to talk about it, anyway."

"Fair enough, doctor."

"I was speaking to Ron Leaford only an hour ago. Jesus – I can't believe it."

I opened the car door and threw my case into the back seat, slumping into the driving seat. I shoved the ignition key into its slot and started the engine, glancing up through the half-open door at Early who stood looking at his shoes.

"I'll see you again, sometime," I said. "Thanks again for . . . straightening things out back there."

"Forget it, doctor," he said. "If you hadn't hit him I would have done it myself, which would have been a damn sight more awkward. Now why don't you get home and put a poultice on your hand. Take care of yourself."

I closed the door and drove off down the street, looking back only once in my driving mirror to see him strolling towards the parked police vehicle – a stooping, desolate figure in gloomy monochrome under the harsh, orange glare of the street lights.

I drove back home with my eyes, hands and feet functioning in a simple reflex fashion, for in my head I could only think of poor old Ron Leaford slumped over the wheel of his car – a thought that was superimposed on the bizarre image of Mukherjee stooping over the semi-conscious figure of Sam Allerdyce. It was a montage which made no sense but which would not go away.

When Tanya opened the door, I saw by her face that she had heard the news. For a few seconds neither of us spoke.

"How did you know?" I said eventually.

"Kathleen rang. God, I must have sounded like an idiot. I just didn't know what to say to her." Her eyes filled with tears and I put my arm round her as we went into the lounge. I poured out a large scotch.

"Feel like one?" I asked. She shook her head.

"I got a message from the police while I was doing this call," I said. "That's how I know. Where's Bet?"

"She left right away, as soon as I had put the phone down. She was very shocked – I didn't want her to drive but she wouldn't listen. She's over there now, with Kathleen."

I went over to the telephone and tried to get through to the house, but the number was engaged.

"Probably taken the thing off the hook," I muttered. I turned to look at her again. "Bet was in a state, was she? I can imagine. First Alec, and then Ron. They'd been close friends for years. You know, it's a strange thing – I never really knew, years ago, why Alec got on so well with him, but recently I think I began to see the reason. He'll be missed around here, that's for sure."

Tanya said nothing. A silent tear rolled down her cheek which she brushed away with her hand.

"Come on. Get your coat on," I said.

"What?"

"Get your coat on. Let's go outside for a breath of fresh air."

She sighed, then went into the hall, reappearing a moment later at the doorway.

"My God you look awful," she murmured. She watched me

button my coat. "What on earth have you done to your hand?"

I looked down and saw the typical swollen deformity over the knuckle which meant that I had fractured the third metacarpal bone. It was as if it belonged to someone else, for I felt no pain, nothing.

"I, er, hit someone."

"You did what?"

"I hit someone. Oh don't worry – it wasn't the patient."

"I see. That makes it all right, then, does it?"

"No, of course it doesn't. It made me feel better, though."

I took her arm and we walked in silence across the courtyard. The wind had dropped and the full moon turned the sandstone walls into a pitted grey mosaic. We strolled down by the side of the house, past the crab-apple trees to where the silver lawn sloped down to the hunched, dark shapes of the bushes hiding the surgery.

"You are going to tell me, aren't you?" Tanya said.

"Oh, well . . . I'd just heard about Ron. Someone said something about him. I didn't like it. It wasn't just that . . . there were other things."

I told her what had happened and she made no comment until I had finished.

"It sounds as if you were surrounded by all your favourite types," she said eventually.

"Unscrupulous wheeler-dealers, you mean?"

"If you like."

"That's a charitable description for a bunch who carry on like that," I said, feeling the anger rise again as I spoke. "When you get a tame physician to prance about in order to do something that defies all common sense, then glibly talk about the old folk as if they're a blue-chip investment, all in the name of —"

"So it's not what was said, but what he represented, that made you —"

"If you mean . . . OK, yes, I suppose you're right. I really thought I'd seen the last of that kind of crap when I left Overton."

She sighed. "Oh, Steven, you're so naive. Those kind of people are all over the place – in town halls, the health service, big business. Your own profession, for that matter. But you can't go round hitting people who hold a different set of beliefs, run their lives by a different set of ethics from those you do yourself. Don't you see that? You didn't come to Stonebridge to dump that sort of thing somewhere else, did you?"

"Hell, no. Of course I didn't."

"I hope you didn't. Because you'll never escape from that. No more than you can escape from yourself."

I took her hand. It felt cold and soothing against the swelling which was beginning to throb painfully over the knuckle.

"Hells bells," I said, smiling grimly. "You make me sound like a pain-in-the-backside idealist. I thought I was more realistic than that."

"I'm not sure," she said, frowning. "Maybe you don't know yourself as well as you think you do."

"Perhaps. The fact is, I can hardly think at all at the moment. There are so many other things . . . Ron's death, above all else."

"I know," she said. I put my arm round her and she leaned against me, her breath warm and moist down the front of my neck. "What will happen now?"

"Oh, well . . . it'll be pretty rough for a few months, I expect. Ron's patients will be spread around the various practices, but I'll probably end up doing most of it. Seeing that there was a previous long-standing arrangement for cover."

"Just when you were beginning to get on top of things," she said wearily. "It'll be like going right back to the beginning again. How long will it take to get a replacement for Ron? I know it sounds . . . I was just thinking of how much you're going to have to do."

"Months, I should think," I said. "They may get a locum in for a bit, but they won't get a replacement until well into the summer. If they get someone reasonable, we'll soon get back to normal – then maybe we can all start spending a bit more time together. The first thing after that is going to be a holiday. God knows, we'll need it by then."

Tanya shivered. "Come on, Steven. Let's go back. I'm cold. And you should see to your hand."

As soon as we stepped indoors the telephone rang. With a sinking sensation in the pit of my stomach, I answered it, thinking it would be from the Leafords' house. It was the district midwife. One of Ron's patients, who should have been delivered in hospital, had waited too long and had delivered abruptly at home. She required a few stitches. The midwife had got no reply from the Leaford House. I didn't tell her why she hadn't but simply said that I would come right away.

"Have you got to go?" asked Tanya softly when I had put down the receiver. She looked pale and tired. I nodded.

"Afraid so. One of Ron's confinements needs a few stitches. I've no idea how long I'll be, so don't wait up."

"How on earth are you going to stitch anybody with your hand in that state?" she asked. "At least let me —"

"It's OK," I said. "I'll have it X-rayed in the morning. It won't come to any harm. If I can't handle the scissors I'll use my teeth."

She turned and walked towards the stairs.

"Have it your way. I think you're mad, but I'm too tired to argue. Try not to be too long – I can't bear the thought of being on my own. Not tonight."

I set off once more into the night, trying not to think of anything apart from what I had to do in the next hour, but I found myself thinking what the next few months would bring and what the practice would be like without Ron Leaford trundling around the place in his rattling Land Rover, dispensing his bantering but shrewd advice to his patients.

I did what was necessary at the house, stitching up the patient with only marginally more difficulty than usual, while the midwife kept up a constant stream of breezy encouragement to both the patient and myself. The father was so pleased with the whole thing he gave me a shoulder of pork and a large polythene bag of frozen chips from the family freezer – a gesture which gave me a great deal of pleasure. Besides being unexpected, it was far more practical than cigars and was the Stonebridge equivalent of beaver-pelts and salted moose from the Canadian backwoods.

As I walked across the courtyard to the door, an icy breeze blew up around the walls, disturbing from underneath the holly tree last year's crisp, dead leaves which scuttled across the stones, making a sound like rats' feet over dry cinders. Inside the house it was silent and warm and felt as if we had always lived there. I stepped quietly up the stairs until I heard a small sound at the top. I looked up and saw Carl on the top step, faintly silhouetted in the dim light from his half-open bedroom door. He was sitting on his haunches, hugging his knees which were flexed up to his chin.

"Hello. What are you doing sitting there?" I asked. He yawned and blinked slowly. His pupils were hardly visible, being partially hidden by his long dark lashes and the sleep-disturbed puffiness of the lids.

"I've been for a wee," he said. "I heard you go out. Mum made a cup of tea after that and it made me go to the toilet. And then I heard you come in so I waited. Mum was crying, but only a bit."

"Was she?"

"Mm. Because of Uncle Ron. He wasn't a real uncle, was he?"

"No. Like one, though. A very good friend who helps."

"Yes. He came once and told me a story about a big giant who kept falling over. I laughed because he was very funny. I like him."

"So . . . did I. Mum did, too. I expect that's why she was crying."

"Mm." He yawned again. "Dad . . . if I grow up to be a doctor, can I come in late like you do? You're always coming in late. I can hear you because I'm awake sometimes. Not like the other two. They're asleep because they're babies, really. Can I?"

I sat down on the stair and looked at his round, innocent face.

"Yes, I suppose you can come in late like me. But after a while, it isn't very exciting. It makes you very tired, you know. Aren't you tired?"

He yawned again and scratched his cheek. "Yes. A bit . . . Dad . . . Jeremy Cartwright at school says doctors make everybody better. Is that why you come in late? So that you make sure the poorly people have those special needles?"

"Sometimes," I said, smiling. "But other times they don't get better. And sometimes we don't even know when they're ill."

He frowned. "How don't you know? I thought you got spots when you're ill."

"Not always."

"Did Uncle Ron get spots?" he asked. His voice was soft and serious, radiating so much innocence and vulnerability that I could feel my throat tightening. He looked at me and reached up, gently poking the corner of my eye with his fingers as if he were touching a drop of rain from a leaf.

"Are you crying, too – just a bit?"

I smiled and took his hand. "No. There's a cold wind outside that's made my eyes smart. That's all."

He was silent for a moment, then he waggled his shoulders and drew his knees up even closer to his chin.

"I'm cold now as well."

"Then let's get you back to your bed. Come on."

I led him to his bedroom, where he climbed into his bed, rubbing his eyes and yawning before pulling the covers up to his chin. He blinked and looked up at me as I sat on the edge of the mattress.

"Dad . . . ?"

"Mm?"

"Won't we be able to go on holiday at Easter like we did before?"

"Probably not this time. Not at Easter."

"Because of all the poorly people?"

"Mm. I'll be looking after Uncle Ron's poorly patients as well for a while, until another doctor comes to help."

"Can we go on holiday after that? I like holidays."

"When summer's here. That's when we'll go."

He rubbed his nose on the sheet and nodded. "All right," he whispered. He closed his eyes and I stood up, turning off the light. As I crept towards the door I heard his sleepy voice again.

"Dad . . . will summer be a long time?"

"No," I said softly. "Summer will be here very soon. You'll see."

I held my breath in the darkness and waited, but I could only hear his gentle, regular breathing as he fell asleep.